A 20-MINUTE WAR
A COLD WAR NOVEL

IRV HAMILTON, JR.

iUniverse, Inc.
New York   Bloomington

A 20-Minute War
A Cold War Novel

iUniverse books may be ordered through booksellers or by contacting:

iUniverse
1663 Liberty Drive
Bloomington, IN 47403
www.iuniverse.com
1-800-Authors (1-800-288-4677)

ISBN: 978-1-4502-1808-5 (sc)
ISBN: 978-1-4502-1810-8 (dj)
ISBN: 978-1-4502-1809-2 (ebook)

Library of Congress Control Number: 2010907568

Printed in the United States of America

iUniverse rev. date: 07/28/2010

ACKNOWLEDGEMENTS

This book is dedicated to Clarence, Jesse, Jim, Nelson, Ron, Sid and a long list of other 2d Cavalry troopers who served their country with honor and dedication during the Cold War.

Also recognized are the troopers of the 11th ACR and the 14th ACR who were responsible for adjacent border sectors.

Special thanks to John Roberts who took part in many of the episodes, and over the years has shared his friendship and recollections.

Thanks to my wife, Patricia, whose encouragement and perspectives were invaluable.

Finally, exceptional credit is given to Eric Kizziar-Lee and Gregory Canales of Jiva Creative in Alameda, CA. Their support, talent and assistance literally made this book possible.

INTRODUCTION

I was ten years old when the Second World War ended on August 14, 1945. But even after all these years, I remember it as one of the most exciting days of my life.

I can still imagine myself on my bike, pedaling hard to deliver newspapers—with bold, black headlines carrying the good news—to the subscribers on my route. Even though I was playing a very minor role on that day, I felt I was participating in history, and it was a wonderful sensation.

I was also extraordinarily happy. Soon, my father—away in the navy— would be home, along with my uncles and the neighbors and friends who also had been gone for so long.

Some, I sadly realized, would never come home—the ones whose pictures were on the front page of the small-town daily paper I carried.

They were all clean cut, handsome, and sharp in their dress uniforms. Except they were dead, killed in places I'd never heard of before.

Some I knew slightly. But I can't say I had really hung around with them, because I was just a little kid, and most of them had been in high school.

After that wonderful day, it didn't take long for things to begin getting back to normal. The vets, including my father, came home. The car dealers began getting new models that we'd admire through the showroom windows.

Everyone was talking about the future and how good things were going to be, now that the war was over.

The war had definitely changed our lives. My father had been drafted into the navy, and we had moved from Chicago, away from my friends, to a small town where my grandparents lived.

The newspapers, magazines, and movie newsreels were full of the war. The toys we played with were model tanks and planes and soldiers. Outside, we attacked each other with wooden guns or our index fingers extended, thumbs in the air, making a noise that we thought sounded like gunfire.

Rationing meant we couldn't have many of the things we wanted. But there were a few bonuses. By getting an unneeded pot or pan from my mother and taking it to the scrap-metal drive at the movie theater on Saturday, my friends and I got into a matinee free.

Then, all of a sudden, it began to change. We had led the victory against the Japs and the Nazis and were the strongest country in the world. Stores that had posted signs saying "Closed for the Duration" on their doors were open again.

The anxious days that had gone on for so long were over. For people such as my parents, it was a wonderful new beginning.

As the 1940s ended and the next decade began, the dreams of owning a home, making a good salary, and sending their children to college were being fulfilled for millions of Americans.

But overlaid on all the good things that were happening was an ominous cloud. In the years immediately after the war, much of the world had been divided into two camps. We headed the group that had democratic government as its goal for the good of the world's people.

The Soviet Union, our very recent ally, led another group—the Communists—who, we were told, were out to dominate the world and spread their anti-democratic doctrine. The subjugation of Poland, Czechoslovakia, Hungary, and East Germany by the Soviets in the late 1940s was cited as evidence.

On June 25, 1950, even those who were skeptical of that threatening scenario had to think again, as Communist North Korean forces crossed the 38th parallel and took over much of neighboring South Korea. For those who were already worried about Communist aggression, there could be no more obvious proof that their fears were well founded.

The resulting three-year conflict cost nearly 34,000 American lives.

At the conclusion of the Korean War—and that's what it was, regardless of the label—U.S. forces were positioned on the 38th parallel as a deterrent against future aggression by the Communist North Koreans. Fifty years later, as this book is being written, combat-ready U.S. troops are still there.

In Europe, the forces of the West and Communist troops were also positioned—eyeball-to-eyeball—ready to fight, along a north-south political line that was dubbed "the iron curtain." On one side were the Czechs, Poles, Hungarians, East Germans, and others, serving as an involuntary buffer between the West and the Soviet Union. On the other side were the forces of the North Atlantic Treaty Organization, NATO, formed to keep the Soviets from further western expansion into Europe.

In other parts of the world, the collapse of colonial empires created additional political uncertainty, with the potential for serious strife. The French, for example, were being beaten by Communists in Indochina—a place that would later split into three countries: Laos, Cambodia, and Vietnam, which in turn was broken into Communist North Vietnam and South Vietnam.

The happiness of being out of a world war was coupled with the anxious prospect of new wars in places around the world. Small wars that could become large ones. And large ones that could use the weapons that ended the Second World War, nuclear bombs, and their more modern counterparts, nuclear missile warheads.

We'd seen what they did to two cities in Japan: Hiroshima and Nagasaki. Now the Soviets and we had massive stockpiles of the stuff, capable of wiping out other cities and probably, civilization itself.

We'd gone from dealing with the trauma of a war that was happening to the worry of a different kind of war that could happen at any time. In our cities, air raid shelters in the bowels of office buildings were identified with yellow-and-black signs. We listened to air raid sirens each week that blared to make certain they worked, and we learned to know what the signals meant.

Our cities were ringed with Nike missile sites, their blue-and-white rockets positioned to shoot down Soviet bombers that made it past our then limited air defense systems, ideally before they could drop their payloads on places such as Chicago or New York or San Francisco.

A new industry was spawned as companies built "fallout" shelters in our backyards. Children were drilled in the technique of "duck and cover" should a nuclear attack occur while they were at school, when parents weren't there to protect them. Even so, there was little confidence that covering our eyes and crawling under a desk would fend off the nuclear blast.

The situation was called the cold war. It reflected the fact that another world war hadn't started, but ignored the reality that people in places around the world were dying as democracy and Communism vied for power.

This is a book about that time. Nearly everything happened—to me, to friends, or under circumstances about which I learned. The details have been changed and events have been amalgamated to make a story out of it. But this book is based almost entirely on things that actually happened.

It isn't, however, intended to be autobiographical. None of the characters are meant to represent real people. Like the events, most are composites of people with whom I served in the army, or heard about.

This book is about a young man named Joseph Novotny. Born of Czech parents in Chicago, he, his brother, and his mother moved to Michigan to be near his grandparents when his father went into the service in 1943.

In June 1950, North Korea invaded South Korea.

Three years later, in June 1953, Novotny graduated from high school. The same month, there was a display of opposition to the Soviet-run government of the Democratic Republic of Germany, or East Germany, as it was more commonly called. The Soviets quickly put it down, and in the process, many demonstrating East Germans were killed.

The Korean armistice was signed on July 27, 1953, and a few weeks later, just after his eighteenth birthday, Novotny registered for the draft. He entered college in September and took a deferment exam, which allowed him to finish school before being eligible for the draft.

In 1956 the Hungarians went to the streets to express their resentment toward the autocratic puppet government under which they were forced to live. As with other uprisings, the Soviets used tanks and troops to quell the demonstrations.

While in his senior year in college, in March 1957, Joseph Novotny volunteered for the draft, asking to be inducted as soon after graduation as possible. He got his diploma in June and was ordered to report for induction in July.

That's where the story begins.

PART I

BECOMING A SOLDIER

"Thanks for the ride," he said, shaking hands with the old man behind the wheel.

"Don't mention it. And good luck." The Ford pulled away, turned right, and disappeared in a wake of tan dust.

Joe Novotny pushed his horn-rimmed glasses back up the bridge of his nose and looked back in the direction from which he'd come. There were no cars, just a black ribbon of asphalt heading toward the horizon and bisecting neat apple orchards.

He glanced at his watch. Nine fifteen. That gave him about an hour and a half to go five or six miles. Should be easy, as long as someone came along fairly soon.

He walked up the road a short distance and set his gym bag on the gravel at the asphalt's edge. Funny how some hitchhiking places seemed comfortable, whereas others didn't. Satisfied this would do, he ran his hand through his sandy hair, smoothing it into place. He tucked his plaid shirt tightly under his belt and dusted the tops of his loafers against the back of his slacks.

"The way you look is the most important thing there is in getting a ride," Tony DeLapp had told him one night at the Sigma Nu house. And Tony would know. He'd hitchhiked from Evanston to California and back last summer.

One afternoon, he and a few of the brothers had sat on the sunporch at the frat house, listening to Tony rattle off a string of adventures for his envious fraternity brothers.

He talked about having to sleep in a grove of trees by the side of the road one night for lack of a ride. About an older couple that gave him a ride, bought him dinner, and had him stay overnight in their spare bedroom.

And, of most interest to the young men, he described in some detail how a forty-year-old woman in a nearly new Cadillac had picked him up, taken him home, and seduced him. "You'd be surprised at how older women will stop and pick you up," he'd said. "They can be pretty wild."

"Oh, sure, Tony. Of course we believe you," Bill Bartlett had kidded. "You probably got picked up by some queer and just don't want to admit it." The others sitting on the porch agreed, chuckling and laughing. Novotny knew DeLapp well and suspected it was all true. Tony wasn't the sort to exaggerate or make up a story like that. If anything, he was more likely to understate it.

He had only a few miles left to go, but he hoped Tony's formula for getting rides would work. Stand straight. Look sharp. And get your thumb out in plenty of time for the drivers to see it.

Novotny listened to the locusts and the birds and focused his attention on the details of the farm across the road. Directly in front of him was a silver-painted mailbox, perched on a metal pole. With its rounded top, little red flag, and a door that opened downward, it was like just about every other rural mailbox he'd ever seen. Behind it was a tree with an old tire hanging by a thick rope. Probably some kids live there, he thought, though no one was in sight.

Up a dirt driveway was the house: white clapboard and architecturally nondescript. He imagined the people from *American Gothic* standing in front of it. The long-faced farmer with his bib overalls and pitchfork. And his equally long-faced, apron-clad wife with her hair tied in a bun.

He looked to his left, estimating he could see two or three miles up the road. Still no cars. Patting his shirt pocket and feeling nothing, he bent down to his gym bag, unzipped it, and poked around. In it was a pair of shorts. He felt a T-shirt. A shaving kit his father had given him a couple of weeks before. Clean socks. A sweater. And finally, at the bottom, two packages of cigarettes.

Opening one, he carefully put the cellophane and foil into his pants pocket. Taking a cigarette from the pack, he tapped it against his thumbnail and lighted it.

Wish I was there already, he thought, taking a deep drag and pulling the smoke into his lungs. Maybe I should've let Jerry drive me over. No. I'm glad I did it this way. We had a few beers last night, I said goodbye, and that was it. He formed a circle with his lips and pushed the smoke out in perfectly formed rings that stayed intact for several feet until they dissipated in the gentle June breeze.

The sound of an engine in the distance made him look quickly to the left. It was a yellow sedan, about a mile up the road. He dropped the cigarette and ground it out in the gravel with the sole of his shoe. He stood straight and put up his thumb.

Waaaaaaaaaaaahooooouuuuuuu. He kept his eye on the car as it raced by him. What makes the sound of a car change pitch? We studied it in freshman physics. Somebody's principle. He frowned, trying to dredge up the name, and then shook his head. Guess that's why I wasn't a physics major, he decided.

The car was a '57 Oldsmobile Rocket 88, brand new, and it must have been doing seventy at least. The woman behind the wheel, blonde, pretty, and probably in her thirties, acted as if she hadn't even known he was there. Right, Tony, older women like to pick up younger guys, he said to himself. Sure, Tony.

He watched the Olds disappear around a bend in the road and then imagined that the car had screeched to a stop on the highway, its taillights glowing bright red. As it slowly backed up on the shoulder, Novotny pictured himself jogging toward it.

"Hop in," the blonde said. As he closed the door, she took off, kicking up gravel from the shoulder as she gunned the 88 back onto the road. "I'll take you anywhere you're going, on one condition."

"What's that?" he asked.

"We're going to stop at my place first. I've got some ideas for things we can do. Things I think you'll like a lot," she said, turning to him and winking.

"I appreciate the offer. But I can't. I'm going in the army. I've got to be at the draft board to sign up in about an hour."

The blonde lifted her skirt slowly, showing more of her smooth white thigh. "You sure I can't change your mind?"

"Wish you could."

"No strings. No charge. I'll even buy the beer."

Novotny shook his head. "Nope. Sorry."

She stopped the car in front of the draft board.

Taking a piece of paper out of her purse, she wrote on it and handed it to him.

"My name is Annie. Here's my phone number. When you get back, give me a call. You can tell me war stories."

Novotny laughed at the games his mind played on him. If nothing else, you lead a rich fantasy life, he told himself. Maybe that's really what happened to DeLapp and his story about the forty-year old. Maybe it's some kind psychological syndrome that affects hitchhikers on lonely, empty country roads when rides are scarce.

Taking a deep breath, he kicked some gravel with his toe and looked at his watch again. Twenty to ten. "Come on, cars," he shouted at the empty road.

A few more minutes passed and then he heard another vehicle coming from the left. He recognized it as a faded green Dodge pickup, and it slowed just as he got his thumb in the air, easing to a stop in front of him.

"Where you headed?" the driver asked through the open window.

"I'm going to Bradley," he answered.

"Jump in."

The truck slowly gained speed, and Novotny positioned his gym bag on the seat between them, careful not to let it get in the way.

"Thanks for stopping," he said.

"Not much traffic out here," the driver said. He was wearing almost exactly the same clothes as the old man in the Ford. Gray trousers, a gray shirt, and scuffed black work shoes.

"Where you headed?" the man asked.

"I'm going into the army today."

"You got drafted?"

"Not exactly. I volunteered. I just graduated from Northwestern, and I didn't want to sit around and wait to get drafted. Figured I'd get it over with."

"I don't blame you," the driver said. "You know Ed Larson, over at the draft board?"

"I've never met him. But he's the one who sent me my papers."

"He's a fine man." The driver took a pack of Camels from the top of the dashboard. "Want one?"

"Thanks," Novotny replied, reaching for his Zippo and lighting both cigarettes.

"He's been there ever since the board opened, back in—when was it?—

'39 or '40." The driver put his left elbow on the ledge of the open window, keeping the truck at a steady fifty miles an hour. "He's got a tough job."

"How so?"

"Well, it's not so bad now, with Korea over. But he's put up with a lot. Tryin' to do his job in a way that was . . . well, that was fair."

The man paused a moment, as if he was retrieving thoughts from the deep recesses of his brain. "He drafted me. Rather, the board did. He just processed the papers. In '43. I was just a kid. Like you."

"Did you go into the army?"

"Yup. I was thinkin' about joinin' the navy, but before I made up my mind, I got drafted. Don't suppose it made much difference, though, one way or another."

For a moment, Novotny thought it might be rude to keep asking questions. Then he decided it didn't matter. The guy seemed decent enough. "Where'd you take your basic training?"

"Down at Fort Knox, Kentucky. Where all the gold is."

"Did you go overseas?"

"Yup. I went to Europe with the 2nd Armored Division. 'Hell on Wheels' is what they call it. And it really was a hell of an outfit. Still on active duty, as far as I know."

Novotny sat quietly for a moment, not wanting to sound too inquisitive. "Were you in tanks?"

"No. I was in mechanized infantry. We were still dogfaces. But we rode part of the time."

Again Novotny paused. Even though he had a long string of questions he wanted to ask, he was fearful of overdoing it. "How long were you in?"

"Well, I got banged up. Came back in November of '44."

The truck continued its droning progress down the country road. The two men looked straight ahead, saying nothing. One was reflecting on events that had happened thirteen years before. The other wondered about unknown things that were about to happen.

"My family's from Europe," Novotny said. "I'd like to go there."

The driver crushed his cigarette out in the ashtray, already nearly full of cigarette remains. "Well, you never know. They'll just send you where they need you. Today that could be anywhere. Korea. Europe. Someplace here in the States. You just don't know."

The open farmland had given way to more buildings. A propane gas distributor. A John Deere dealer. A Marathon gas station and some houses. Even though he'd never spent much time in Bradley, it was beginning to look familiar.

Everything of much consequence was on Center Street, in a three-block stretch of plain, two-story, brick buildings. The geographic center of town seemed to be the Rexall drugstore, and that's where the truck stopped. The driver pointed to the door just to the left of the pharmacy. "The draft board's up there. On the second floor. Say hello to Ed Larson for me. My name's Earl Breen."

The man put out his hand, and the two men exchanged a firm shake.

"Thanks for the lift, Mr. Breen."

"Glad to do it. And good luck to you."

Novotny lifted his bag from the seat, closed the door, and watched the truck pull away. Nice guy, he thought. Really a nice guy.

Neatly lettered in gold on the glass door were the words "Selective Service Commission—Local Board 44." Novotny stopped, hesitated for a moment, and then opened the door. He looked up the long flight of stairs, swallowed hard, and began the climb. Each step made the quiet creaking sound of old wood.

At the top was a wooden railing, through which he could see a few gray metal filing cabinets and an old wooden desk. Seated at it was a slightly built, gray-haired man in a gray suit and gray tie, looking toward the steps.

"Good morning," the man said. "You must be Mr. Novotny."

"Yes. That's me." Novotny was aware that how he'd said those few words had given away the fact that he was a little nervous.

"Come on in," he said warmly, standing to shake hands with the young man approaching him. "My name is Ed Larson. Please sit down," he said, pointing to the chair next to his desk. Moving his own chair closer to the desk, he reached for a file folder and opened it. "This won't take but a few minutes."

He began a routine that he'd obviously done hundreds, maybe thousands of times before. Instructions about this and that. Forms to be filled out. A rigid sequence of steps that must have become boring after all these years.

At certain points in the process, he would take a form, insert it in the aging Underwood on a stand next to his desk, ask questions, and then peck information onto a line here and a line there.

Finally, he took all the forms, placed them in a neat stack, and leafed through them one at a time.

"That just about does it," he said. "Now let me just go over these with you. They'll ask for them in Detroit, and you'll want to know what they're all about."

Novotny listened to each of the instructions, signing each time he was told to do so.

"Here's your bus ticket. It comes through at 12:10, and this time of year, it'll probably be right on time. You don't want to miss it."

He handed the documents to the young man. "All your papers are here, along with a meal ticket."

Carefully putting the documents in the envelope, Novotny slipped the meal and bus tickets into his shirt pocket and got up to leave. "I almost forgot," he said quickly. "Someone said to say hello to you." He tried to remember the name. "Oh, jeez. Earl. Earl something."

"Breen?"

"That's it. Earl Breen. He said to say hello." Novotny leaned against the wooden railing. "He gave me a ride this morning."

"Earl's well known around here," Mr. Larson said, turning in his chair to face Novotny. "People still talk about the parade we had when he came back."

"You had a parade?"

"Oh, yes. As I recall it was in the spring of '45." He squinted, as if it would help him remember the details. "Seems to me that Earl came back before that, but the mayor wanted to wait until the weather got a little better. It was just before the end of the war. Seems like a long time ago. But it was only back twelve years."

"What was the parade for? There must have been a lot of guys coming home."

Mr. Larson paused for a moment, getting the facts in order. "Well, now, Earl was drafted during the war. In '43, I'd guess. He sat in that very chair, where you were just sitting. Place hasn't changed much since then. That is, this office hasn't." He quickly added, "The world, of course, is a very different place."

Pausing again, he seemed to be pondering thoughts that may or may not have had anything to do with Novotny's question. "He was sent to Europe. And in '44—I don't remember which month—he was wounded. Fell on a grenade to save some buddies." Again the man paused.

As eager as he was to hear more, Novotny said nothing, letting the older man go through the recollection process. "They gave him the Distinguished Service Cross. Only the Medal of Honor's higher than that."

He got up from the desk, walked to a window, and looked down on the street. "There was a big controversy about it. One of the men he saved tried to have them give him the Medal of Honor. But the army wouldn't do it for some reason." He turned and looked at the young man listening to his story. Novotny wondered what he must be thinking, having sent so many men to whatever turned out to be their fate in the service.

"People around here think that if he'd been killed, he would've gotten the medal he deserved. But because he lived, they didn't give it to him."

He walked back to his desk and sat down. His voice changed from reflection to fact. "At least that's the way people around here think. When he got out of the hospital and came home, a group of people decided to give him a parade. Just to let him know the folks in his hometown hadn't forgotten what he'd done."

"I never would've guessed all that," Novotny said. "He just seemed like a . . . like a regular person."

"He never talks about it. Just works his dad's farm. His dad died about six years ago."

"Does he live by himself?"

"No. Married a local girl. Marilyn Best. They don't have any children. Maybe they can't have. But he seems to get along pretty well, considering how badly wounded he was."

There were a dozen questions he wanted to ask the man in the gray suit and gray tie, this cordial, warm-spirited, and efficient processor of papers and people. What was it like twelve or thirteen years ago, to have such power? To be able to say to one person, "You're essential here in the war effort. You don't have to go. And I don't need to remind you that in telling you that, I may be saving your life."

And to say to another, "Here's your bus ticket, your meal ticket, and your manila envelope. If they make you a replacement rifleman, no one here may ever see you alive again. But if you're lucky, you'll spend a couple of years in Hawaii or England and come back a hero, just because you wore a uniform."

I wonder what he thinks these days, Novotny thought. His head must be full of ghosts. Guys who sat in that chair, went to the bus, and came back in a box, if they came back at all.

And guys who came back like Earl Breen, in whatever shape his body is in. Not just twelve years ago. But four and five years ago too, when we were fighting in Korea. What a job, he thought. What a hell of a job to have. Quietly filling out papers and sending guys to who knew where.

He suddenly realized how long he had been standing there, saying nothing. "I guess I'd better get something to eat so I can catch that bus." He extended his hand to the older man. "Thanks very much, Mr. Larson."

"You're welcome," he replied. "Good luck to you. And when you get back this way, stop by any time. Let us know how you're doing."

He headed quickly down the stairs toward the door. As they had on the way up, the steps creaked under his feet.

13

Davidson's Coffee Shop was nearly empty when he walked in. It was just after eleven o'clock, a little early for lunch. But the bus would be here soon.

"Sit anywhere you like," the waitress said as she put a cup of coffee on the counter in front of a man reading a paper. She was plain, middle-aged, and had a friendly smile. He took the second booth, sitting so he could see the door and watch for the bus.

The waitress filled a glass with water, walked to him, and put that and a menu on the table. "How are you today?" she asked, taking an order pad and pencil from her apron pocket.

"Pretty good," Novotny replied, looking at the menu.

"If you don't mind a suggestion, I'd order the meat-loaf sandwich," she said, her pencil poised to write. "We make it fresh every day. I guarantee you won't get meat loaf like this in the service. All the fellas like it."

He looked up, startled, and was about to ask her how she knew, when he remembered the gym bag and the large manila envelope on the seat next to him. "I guess it's pretty obvious why I'm here."

She nodded with her pleasant smile. "It's that time of the month. The fellas always go through here about now. You want to try the meat loaf?"

"That sounds fine."

"It has gravy and comes with peas and carrots. And there's coffee with it too."

"Fine."

A few minutes later she returned with a steaming plate of food. He took a bite. She was right. It was good meat loaf. Simple, honest-to-god, real American food.

"Don't hurry," she advised, refilling his water glass. "It'll just knot up in your stomach." He nodded agreement and deliberately slowed his bites. His stomach was knotted even so.

As soon as his plate was empty, she came to refill his coffee cup. "How about some dessert? We have fresh pie today. Cherry and apple."

"Is that part of this, this . . . ?" he asked, pushing his meal voucher toward her.

"It's not supposed to be. But we always throw it in for the fellas. Figure when they come back, they'll come see us again."

"That's very kind. I'll take the cherry pie."

The bright red cherries were topped with a crisscross of flaky pastry, and on top of that was a scoop of vanilla ice cream.

Enjoying the sweetness, he took the last bite of pie, washed it down with a sip of black coffee, and reached for his cigarettes.

The bus wasn't due for fifteen minutes, so he sat back to relish his cigarette. The bell at the top of the door rang as it was opened and another customer came in.

"Good morning, Earl," the waitress said. "How are you?"

"Fine, Elsie. Just fine." The man turned to take a seat and saw Novotny in the booth. "Did Ed get you all squared away?"

"Yeah. I'm all set. Just waiting for the bus. You want to sit down?"

"Sure." He turned to the waitress. "Elsie, I'm just gonna have a cup of coffee and a piece of that apple pie."

Novotny crushed out his cigarette in the ashtray as the man slid into the booth across from him. He had assumed he'd never see him again. But he was here, and there was a question. An important question.

"I don't want to pry into anything personal . . ." Novotny paused, wishing he had made a better attempt to say what he meant. "Well, I just wondered if I could ask you a couple of things about the service."

The man in the work clothes waited for a moment as his coffee and pie were placed on the table. "Thanks, Elsie. Sure, go ahead. I'll answer if I can."

"Mr. Larson told me what you did. And I just wondered what you thought when you did it." He added quickly, "That is, if you want to say anything about it." He took a sip of coffee. "I guess I just wonder what I'd do in that kind of situation."

"You mean you wonder if you'd be scared?" he said, taking a bite of the pie.

"Yeah. I guess that's it."

He looked at his coffee and then at the young man across from him.

"Well, that was a while back. And I don't particularly talk about it. But since you're goin' into the service today, I'd be glad to tell you."

The man sat quietly for a moment and then gently drummed his fingers on the table. "People around here still think I'm some kind of hero." He stopped to take a drink of the rich, black brew. "But it was actually pretty simple. I was in a big shell hole with five other guys. It was raining and the hole was full of mud. We were pinned down by some German infantry. We just wanted to stay out of sight until we figured out what our platoon was gonna do."

He took a bite of the pie and continued matter-of-factly. "A German grenade came flyin' into the hole. It landed about three feet from me."

He stopped, not for dramatic effect, but as if he were trying to get the details clear in his mind. "I was between the grenade and the other guys, and I just fell on it. The mud absorbed most of the impact. Otherwise, I'd be dead."

"But when you saw it, did you think, I'm gonna get killed in a couple of seconds?"

The man stopped to think about what had happened that rainy night.

"No. It was like slamming your foot on the brake when a dog runs in front of your car. Someone could hit your rear end. But you don't think about that. You just do it. That's all I did."

Taking another sip of coffee, he again seemed to be thinking about that. "I'm not a hero," he said. "It was just something that happened. I don't doubt that any of the other guys would have done what I did, if they'd been in the spot I was."

For Novotny, that wasn't enough. "But when you went into combat, did you think about how you'd act?"

"Sure. We all did." He looked directly at Novotny. "But there's something you'll see when you get in the service."

"What's that?" Novotny asked.

"Well, when we were in England—before we went into France—I knew guys who'd sit around and sharpen their bayonets and talk about how much they wanted to kill some krauts. When we got there, some of them did just that. They'd do things like volunteer for patrols to get krauts. And a lot of those guys were killed."

He held up his cup for the waitress to see.

"But some of those guys who sat around talking about how many krauts they were going to kill ended up crouched in their foxholes shaking and crying and afraid to move."

He took a sip from his freshly filled cup. "You just don't know until you do it."

He looked at Novotny. "But there's something else you'll learn in the service. Most guys will do just about anything so as not to let their buddies down. You do it even if you're really scared. You do it because you know they'll do it for you."

The waitress came to Novotny and said, "That bus will be along in a couple of minutes."

He got up, put some change on top of the meal ticket, and picked up his gym bag and the manila envelope. "Thanks," he said, shaking the man's hand. "I really appreciate your talking about it."

"Glad to do it. And good luck. If you get back this way, stop by and let us know how you're doing."

"I sure will. Thanks again."

Standing under the blue-and-white Greyhound sign, Novotny looked for the bus. A couple of minutes later, it pulled up and stopped. He handed the driver the ticket without saying anything and put his gym bag and manila envelope on the rack overhead. Settling in next to the window, he listened as the driver made his way through the gears and picked up speed. In a few minutes they were in the country.

Novotny tilted the seat back and turned his head so he could look out the window. Orchards, fields, and an occasional farmhouse passed by. His eyes tried to close, but he wouldn't let them. Right now he wanted to think, not sleep. He had no idea where he'd be in a week, and in a way the uncertainty appealed to him. He'd probably see parts of the country he'd never seen before. Maybe even parts of the world.

And a lot had happened in just the past couple of hours. He had officially received his first certificate, making him the leader of a group of one.

"I'm the leader of this group," he said under his breath. "And I don't want any screwing around between here and Detroit. Understand?" He smiled at how ridiculous this self-conversation was, but answered nonetheless. "Yes, sir. I understand. No screwing around, sir."

He thought about his father, three uncles, and several friends of his family who had been in the Second World War and must have done just what he was doing, taking a bus or a train to a place where their futures would be determined.

He'd known a lot of people who had gone into the service. High school friends had gone to Korea. No, he abruptly said to himself, shaking his head. He didn't want to think about Korea just now. He wanted to focus his attention on today.

He'd already met a hero. A friendly, gentle-speaking hero. A hero who still didn't accept the idea that he was one, even though the people in town had given him a parade and the government had given him a medal. A hero who must be carrying around all sorts of metal, plastic, and whatever else they use to put soldiers back together when a grenade tears them apart.

He had tried not to stare at the scars on the man's cheek and forearm. And there was obviously a lot more he couldn't see. Maybe that's why he and his wife don't have children, Novotny thought. Maybe he lost the equipment down there between his legs.

Or maybe he just doesn't want to have children. Maybe he doesn't want to risk the possibility of having a son who will fall on a grenade somewhere and won't be so lucky.

It's easier to give rides to guys you'll probably never see again and wish them luck than to worry about what might happen to a son if the Russians make good on their threats.

You don't have to worry whether the North Koreans and the Chinese are going to decide to cross the border again. Or whether we'll end up fighting in someone's colony, like with the French, who seem to be losing their wars in Indochina and Algeria.

Whatever happens and wherever I end up, Novotny thought, one thing is for sure: I'll do what I'm told because I believe we have to protect the system we have. We have to keep the Communists from taking over more than they already have.

But I'm going to keep a little distance. I'll give them my body for two years, but not my mind. And when I'm done, I'll be able to say I did my share. They didn't have to call me up. I went in on my own. But that's it.

And what if there is a war? What if I end up missing some parts? Or what if I end up in pieces somewhere I'd never even heard of before? Well, that's the chance you take.

Right now. I'm on a bus to Detroit. What's next? I'll just have to wait and see.

The red-haired kid sitting next to Novotny stared out the window as the train rattled through the rolling woods and farmland. "Jeez, I wish we'd get there," he said without looking at Novotny. "We've been on this train forever."

The time in Detroit had gone by quickly. Novotny and a few hundred other inductees had arrived from an assortment of midwestern cities and towns. They'd been sworn in and told about their responsibilities as soldiers. They were then handed another envelope—this time with a train ticket in it—and taken to a nearby hotel to spend the night.

Some of the recruits who were old enough found bars and sat around drinking beer. Novotny had one beer and went to bed early. Wake-up was at 5 AM. and he wanted to be alert for the long train ride to Missouri.

At the railroad station the next morning, the men were lined up and counted off into the five old passenger cars that made up the entire train. The cars were like so many he'd seen over the years, painted olive green with square windows and faded gold lettering on the side. Inside, the seats were covered with worn cloth upholstery in a nondescript pattern.

Every seat in the train was occupied by restless inductees. A little more than a day ago they'd all been civilians. Now they were in the army, even though all they had to show for it was another manila envelope and a serial number they'd been told to memorize. Novotny closed his eyes and recited the number. USA55625067.

Most of them looked as though they had just gotten out of high school, fuzzy chinned and with that innocent look that comes from having had almost everything in your life decided for you. At twenty-two, Novotny felt strangely old.

For the first few hours, there'd been a lot of roughhousing. But boredom and fatigue had set in, and now the trainload of soldiers-to-be was mainly sleeping, reading, or, like the red-haired kid next to him, just staring out the window and watching the farmland pass by.

There wasn't a dining car, but at appropriate times, a porter in a traditional railroad uniform and round, brimmed hat would come through with a boxed meal. A second porter followed with paper cups of lukewarm, tasteless coffee. Half an hour or so later, the porters retraced their steps with a trash bag, collecting the boxes and garbage.

The men slept sitting up, as best they could, during the long dark night. For some, it seemed easy. But Novotny found that the bouncing of the car and having to sleep upright made it nearly impossible to doze off. He was glad he hadn't stayed up last night.

Unable to sleep, he let his mind re-create thoughts and pictures. Amazing how your brain can conjure up this stuff, he marveled.

He recalled the day that Eddie Wozack had told him what he had done. It was June 1952, almost exactly five years ago and just after Eddie had graduated from high school. They were sitting on a bench by the Phoenix Street Market, having a Coke.

"I signed up," Wozack had said, as routinely as if he were talking about baseball scores or the weather.

"What'd you do?" Novotny asked, surprised.

"I enlisted in the army."

Wozack and Novotny had been on the track team together. They'd often double-dated and been good friends since grade school, even though Wozack was a year ahead of him.

"I decided to sign up, do my tour, and then go to Ann Arbor on the GI Bill. I couldn't do it otherwise. I've always wanted to go to the U of M."

"You know the odds are pretty good you'll go to Korea."

"Yeah, I know. That's the chance you take. But the peace talks have been going on for quite a while. It'll probably be over before I finish basic training." He tipped the green bottle up and gulped the few ounces of sparkling liquid that remained. "Have you talked to Denny?"

"Haven't seen him. Why?"

"He signed up too. We're going in together."

Denny Hubbel was also on the track team. And like Wozack, he was a year older than Novotny. The three boys got along well and made a point of sitting together on the bus when the team had "away" meets.

They were also the first to congratulate each other when they ran well. And when they ran poorly, they encouraged one another and talked about doing better in the next race.

After basic training, Hubbell was sent to truck-driving school and Wozack was assigned to artillery. By the time Novotny was back in school, starting his senior year in September '52, both had written him to say they were being sent to Korea.

Wozack took some leave before heading overseas. On the first night, he and Novotny had gone to Tom's Place on the outskirts of town to have a "Big Tom" bacon burger, some fries, and a malt.

"What are you going to do over there? What kind of job do you have?" Novotny asked, shaking ketchup onto his fries.

"They made me an FO. A forward observer."

"What's that?"

"I just look where the enemy is and radio their position to the artillery so they know where to fire." He chuckled, and said, "It's all math and geography, my favorite subjects."

"But you'll be right up on the front lines. Right?"

"Yeah," he acknowledged hesitantly.

"And if those guys you're shooting at know where you are, they'll probably want to get rid of you. Right?"

"Probably," he said haltingly.

"I think Denny got a better job, driving a truck." Novotny didn't ask any more questions or say anything about the army after that. Instead they talked about the track team and girls.

About ten o'clock they paid, and they joked with Tom as he took their money. As they walked to their cars, Wozack asked, "What are you going to wear to the prom?"

"That's months from now. I haven't even thought about it. Why?"

"Well, I've got a favor to ask of you."

"Sure. Go ahead."

Wozack opened his car and took out a garment from the backseat. "It's my suit. I'd like you to take care of it for me while I'm gone." He straightened the coat on the hanger and held it up against Novotny's back. "We're about the same size. It'll fit. If you want to, you can wear it to the prom."

"Sure, Eddie. I'll take care of it." Novotny was too surprised at the request to say anything else.

"And if somethin' happens to me, it's yours. OK?"

"Thanks, Eddie. It's a great-looking suit. I'll take care of it. Have it cleaned and all that."

That night, just before he fell asleep, he said in a quiet whisper, "Please don't let Eddie get killed." He didn't feel religious enough to ask God. So he just said it straight out, hoping that someone who could help would hear.

He said exactly those words every night until May 11, 1953. That was the day that Eddie called from Fort Lewis, Washington, to say he was back. He'd been wounded, but it wasn't anything serious. He'd have a scar on his leg, but it would heal just fine.

On June 20, just over a month later, Novotny, Eddie, and four other friends were pallbearers at Denny Hubbell's funeral. At the cemetery, the minister talked about patriotism, duty, and sacrifice, explaining that Denny's truck had run over a mine and that several men were killed along with him.

Seven soldiers fired a salute from their rifles and an army bugler blew taps. Just before the casket was lowered, two of the soldiers took the American flag off the casket and folded it into a tight triangle, the way Novotny, Denny, and Eddie had learned to do in Boy Scouts.

They gave it to a smartly dressed, be-medaled officer who took the flag to Denny's mother and presented it to her. She just looked at the flag and then at the officer. She didn't cry or say anything. She just stood there.

"This is for you, ma'am," the officer said.

She shook her head ever so slightly. "No," she said in a whisper.

The officer waited for a moment, in case she changed her mind, and then put the flag under his left arm. Saluting her, he turned and walked over to where the honor guard was standing, looking straight ahead as the casket was lowered into the ground.

After the ceremony, Novotny and Eddie stood looking at the rectangular hole where their friend had just been deposited.

"It stinks," Eddie said bitterly. "They're still arguing over at Panmunjam like they've been doing for almost two years. And meanwhile, guys are getting killed." He stared at the grave. "It stinks."

He patted Novotny on the shoulder and walked slowly toward his car.

Novotny hadn't cried at the funeral. But when nearly everyone had left the cemetery, he walked over to a small pond, sat on the ground leaning up against a tree, and sobbed, tears steaming down his cheeks and leaving moist patches on his white dress shirt.

Just four weeks after Denny's funeral, the armistice was finally signed at Panmunjam and the hostilities ended.

Novotny listened to the train making its way to Missouri. He looked into the dark of the night and thought about Korea. Maybe that's where he would end up. As far as Novotny could tell, no one had won, even though a lot of guys had been killed, including Denny. Police action, he thought angrily. What was the point?

A real war. That's what the Communists want. A war that would show that their system was best. But we have troops all over the world to hold them back and prove them wrong.

He looked out the window and tried to make out buildings in the dark. Maybe he'd see a sign or get a clue about where they were.

Slowly the sky turned gray and then into a bright and beautiful morning. Fishing around in his gym bag, Novotny pulled out his dopp kit and went to the ancient bathroom at the end of the railcar. His face shaved, his teeth brushed, his hair combed, and cool water splashed on his face, he felt better as he settled back into his seat.

"I never even heard of Fort Leonard Wood," the red-haired kid said, still looking out the window. "I sure don't know where it is. Except that it's in Missouri."

Gradually there were more houses in the countryside. And more railroad crossings. Then a town started to develop, with gas stations, a Dairy Queen, and then a tavern, Dave's Place, sitting by itself at an intersection. The train slowed and most of those asleep woke up, sensing that something was about to happen.

"It looks like we're pulling off to the side," the kid by the window said.

Novotny leaned to the window and looked ahead as far as he could see. "I think we're here."

An NCO, a non-commissioned officer, stood on a platform and tapped the PA microphone to be sure it was working. "Form five rows," he announced. And when I tell you, I want the first row to load into the first bus. But only when I tell you."

No one spoke, and no one moved. "OK, the first group into the first bus."

When the first group had boarded the bus, he stood looking at the rest of the young men waiting for the next order.

In all, it had taken him about four minutes to obtain total submission.

"Now, gentlemen," he said, "the second group will board."

Novotny sat on the wooden steps in front the barracks with four other listless inductees. They were dressed in the green fatigue uniforms and visored caps they'd been issued that morning. The boots they wore were black, with the shine and smell of new leather.

It was hot, close to 100 degrees, he guessed, and sweat was starting to form dark patches on their uniforms. Aside from being in the 7095th Reception Station, they knew very little about where they were or what was in store for them over the next days or weeks. All they could do was wait until they were told what to do next.

The red-haired kid who had sat next to Novotny on the train walked quickly toward them and sat down. "I just talked to some guys in that other barracks," he said excitedly, pointing to a building a couple of hundred feet away.

"What'd they say?" one of the men asked.

"We get shots and stuff, and then they send us to basic training somewhere. About twenty guys went to Fort Polk, Louisiana, this morning." He seemed pleased at being able to bring the news.

"I hope we get outta here soon," another said.

"They said the worst is to stay here," the redhead reported. "One guy said that Fort Leonard Wood is the only place you can be gaggin' from dust and knee-deep in mud at the same time."

Novotny just listened, drinking from the Coke he'd bought from a vending machine and relishing the tingle of the bubbles each time he swallowed. He thought about how anonymous they all were. At least until tomorrow. That's when they got the white cloth nametags that would be sewn on their fatigues. Then everyone would know everyone else's last name. Novotny preferred the anonymity.

The conversation had stopped and the men just sat there in sun, smoking and looking at the rows of old barracks or at nothing in particular. They turned to watch as an overweight Negro in a soiled white cook's uniform and fatigue cap walked toward them. As the soldier got closer, it was obvious his uniform was greasy and smudged with what appeared to be soot.

"How you boys doin' today?" the cook asked, standing in front of the young men.

"OK," someone said a little suspiciously.

"How you like the food you been gettin'?" he asked no one in particular.

"It's not bad," another one of the men answered.

"It's better than I thought it'd be," another volunteered.

"I'm glad," the cook said. "We want to make this place nice for you boys while you here. So we take a collection. We go to town and buy stuff we don' get issued. Cost you twenty-five cents."

No one volunteered to pay. They just sat there.

"Do we have to pay?" someone asked.

"No. It ain't required. But if you make a donation, we take you off the KP list for the weekend."

One of the men reached into his fatigues, pulled out a quarter, and handed it to the cook. "That sounds good to me."

The cook fished a pad and pencil from his uniform. "What's your name?"

"Poulos."

"How you spell it?"

"P. O. U. L. O. S," he recited slowly, making certain the cook had time to write each letter.

Five of the six men on the steps, including Novotny, made a contribution, and each name was carefully logged onto the pad. Only a lanky recruit on Novonty's left held out. The cook smiled at the men and walked toward the next barracks.

"How come you didn't do it? You think you're gonna like KP?" the red-haired kid asked.

"I'll take my chances," he replied coolly, adding, "I can't believe they'd do that."

"Do what?" asked the red-haired kid.

"Take guys off KP. If everybody pays, who's left to do the work?"

"That's just the point," the redhead said. "Not everybody pays. It makes sense to me. They get some extra money for the mess hall and give some of us a break. So I'm gonna be at the PX drinkin' beer, while you're cleanin' pots and pans." He paused and smiled, as if he'd made a major discovery. "You just gotta learn the system."

Novotny listened to the conversation, finished his Coke, and walked over to a stack of wooden Coke cases set against the wall of the barracks. He turned the bottom over to look at where it was from. Noting that "St. Louis" was molded into the green glass, he placed the empty bottle in a slot.

He thought about going for a walk, but decided instead to sit on the steps and just kill time until someone told him otherwise. Taking off his cap, he leaned back, resting on his elbows, and relished the warmth of the sun on his face.

So far it wasn't too bad. A little boring. But relaxing at the same time. Just hanging around waiting for someone to tell him what to do next.

Novotny spent the day getting shots, filling out forms, picking up his nametags, and taking them to a civilian tailor, who sewed them on his fatigues in about four minutes flat for a buck. Wonder how much he has to kick back for that job, he thought. The guy'll be able to retire in a couple of years at the rate he's going.

But most of the day was spent sitting on the steps in front of the barracks, smoking, drinking Cokes, and talking with a handful of fellow inductees. The day was clear and hot, and Novotny felt relaxed, even though he knew very little about what the next months would bring.

About three o'clock, a sergeant they hadn't seen before tacked the weekend duty roster on the bulletin board just inside the barracks door.

There was a latrine cleanup detail, which wasn't all that pleasant but had the benefit of being brief. For about an hour and a half you took a brush and scrubbed toilets and urinals and then mopped the floor. After that you were finished, leaving plenty of free time to sit around, smoke, drink Cokes, and speculate on what would happen next.

At the bottom of the duty list were the names of the KPs, listed in alphabetical order. Novotny saw his name at the middle of the Saturday list. Poulos and Selig, the red-haired kid, were on the Sunday list. The names of the other two men who had given the cook money were missing from the document.

Jesus, I'm dumb, he said to himself, shaking his head. It wasn't the quarter. It was the principle of the thing. The fact that the cook was taking advantage of raw recruits made him mad.

But more than that, he hated admitting that he'd fallen for such an obvious trick. I'm going to have to smarten up fast, he thought. This isn't going to be a Sunday school picnic.

The sergeant walked down the line of bunks in the darkened barracks, pointing the beam from his flashlight from side to side in front of him. On his left, he saw a white towel tied to the metal bunk frame. He leaned over and shook the curled figure under the olive drab blanket. "Wake up," he said. "KP. You awake?"

"Yeah," Novotny replied groggily.

"Hustle it up," the anonymous figure said. "Report to the mess hall in twenty minutes."

Novotny dressed quickly, shaved, and brushed his teeth, and walked out into the cool, predawn air. Stopping under a streetlight, he looked at his watch. It was 4 AM. Even in the darkness, he could make out other figures walking toward the mess hall. One headed his way and walked next to him.

"Helluva time to get up," the stranger said.

"Yeah," Novotny replied, not particularly wanting to talk.

"One of the guys in our barracks said I should try to be the outside man," the recruit said. "That's the easiest. You just wipe off tables, fill salt and pepper shakers, and make sure there's enough silverware."

"That doesn't sound bad," Novotny said, still not interested in talking but not wanting to be rude.

They walked into the mess hall and stood with about ten other recruits, all quite awake from the walk in the cool air. A sergeant called the roll and made the assignments. "Walker."

"Here."

"You'll be washing dishes."

"Novotny."

"Here."

"You'll be outside man." The recruit he'd walked over with looked at him and winked. Novotny gave him the thumbs-up sign in return.

All things considered, breakfast went well. Novotny stacked glasses, wiped off tables, and filled salt and pepper shakers. He placed knives, forks, and spoons in plastic bins and generally kept himself busy as the recruits came through for breakfast starting about 6 AM.

By 9, breakfast was over and everything was in order, so he just puttered around waiting for the lunch rush. He estimated it was already about 80 degrees in the mess hall. In the kitchen it must have been 90 and getting hotter all the time.

With the lull between meals, the cooks came out into the mess hall to drink coffee, smoke, and talk. Their white uniforms were spotted and grimy. And all of their bellies hung over the brass buckles of their belts.

With any luck, he'd be away from this place before long. He hoped he'd go somewhere else, unlike the guys who'd been assigned Leonard Wood for basic a couple of days ago.

After three of the cooks had gotten settled at a table, Novotny watched as a fourth walked out of the kitchen, got a cup of coffee, and sat down with the others. He looked again. There wasn't any doubt about it. It was the cook who'd taken his money. Cautiously staring at the cook, he wondered if he should say something to him. What could he say? What good would it do?

But watching the fat cook get up from the table and walk to the drinking fountain, his anger took control and replaced any rational feelings he had about the incident.

Novotny slowly walked to the water cooler. "Excuse me," he said carefully.

The cook looked up from the stream of icy water. "Yeah."

"I was one of the guys who gave you some money so I wouldn't get KP on the weekend. I was on the list for today."

The cook squinted at Novotny. "Well, I guess there was some mistake." He reached into his pocket, pulled out a handful of change, and gave Novotny a quarter. "Here," he said, turning to walk away.

"There were two other men who gave you money when I did. Poulos and Selig. They've got KP tomorrow."

The cook turned and stood just inches away from Novotny. Glaring at the young recruit, he said, "I don' like whatchu sayin', soldier. You tellin' me ah cheated you?"

Novotny made no attempt to back away from the cook. "All I'm saying is it's a little strange that five guys gave you money and three of us have KP after you told us we wouldn't have it. Seems kind of funny to me."

The cook stared meanly at Novotny. "You got your money back. But if you want to do something about it, you can complain to the commanding officer." He let the message sink in. "That's gonna keep you here three, maybe four weeks. Nothin' but details and hassle. But that's up to you."

"Well, I'll think about it," Novotny said, deciding this was no time to pursue the point.

The cook looked at his bright new nametag.

"Novotny. Gonna remember that." The cook stared at him with squinty, bloodshot eyes. Then he walked back into the kitchen without saying another word.

Novotny had spent another twenty minutes or so, filling, wiping, and straightening things when one of the KPs walked over to him from the kitchen.

"You Novotny?"

"Yeah."

"One of the cooks wants you."

The kitchen smelled of old grease and acrid coal smoke. It looked as though it had been there for fifty years, and it probably had. The cook motioned to him. "I want you to relieve that man. He looks like he's having trouble with the heat."

It took Novotny only a couple of minutes to explain the duties of the outside man, and when he was finished, the recruit thanked him. Apologetically, he explained, "I don't know what the big deal is. I feel fine."

Novotny shrugged and walked into the kitchen.

"You're going to work the stoves," the cook said. "Keep coal in them. Keep them hot." He handed Novotny a worn-down metal brush. "You get a spill on the top, you scrub it down with this. You start feeling the heat, you take a salt pill. You understand?"

"Yeah, I understand."

By now it was at least 100 degrees in the kitchen and still climbing. Near the stoves it must have been 120. Novotny started out doing exactly as he was told, but it didn't take long to figure out what was happening. The cook made certain he stayed close to the stove without a break. As soon as Novotny scraped the black steel top clean, the cook would spill soup or gravy on it and tell him to clean it again.

Every few minutes, he told Novotny to clean ashes from the grate and put in new coal, even if there were almost no ashes to clean and there was plenty of fuel. Each time Novotny opened the door to the stove, a blast of superheated air would hit him in the face and burn his lungs. So he carefully took a deep breath and turned his head away from the door each time he opened it.

Despite the heat, Novotny thought he was doing pretty well, even though he'd been at it for four hours. He took salt pills every so often, and he was careful to take small, frequent sips of water instead of big gulps. When he was given a short break to get some food, he ate lightly and stood in the doorway, taking in the outside air, which was hot but still cooler than in the kitchen.

But about three thirty, he started to feel a little odd, kind of dizzy and lightheaded. And by three forty-five, with the heat in the kitchen at its peak, he was beginning to get worried. The other cooks gave the KPs a cigarette break on the back stair landing. But when that happened, the cook made sure there was something for Novotny to do around the big, black stoves.

It was clear the cook wasn't about to offer Novotny a break. And he wasn't going to ask for one. Somehow there seemed to be some sort of vague principle involved.

Novotny was starting to feel noticeably weak and unsteady—enough that he was beginning to worry about what would happen. He thought about asking the cook for a break. To hell with him, he thought. I'll make it.

Bending over to scrape the stovetop, he suddenly felt his head spinning. He stood up and took a deep breath of the hot kitchen air, trying to regain his balance, but it was too late. His legs buckled under him and he fell, ending up sprawled out on the worn tile floor.

"Damn," he said softly as he sat up and shook his head to clear it. He felt a throbbing soreness on his left forearm and saw a red area about an inch wide and two inches long. He lifted his arm to look at the damage and smelled the acrid scent of singed hair.

He slowly put everything together. He'd sort of blacked out, lost his balance, and run his arm along the searingly hot edge of the stove as he fell. The mess sergeant rushed in from the dining room and knelt next to him.

"This man's got to pay more attention to what he's doing," the cook said.

"You all right?" the sergeant asked.

Novotny nodded. "I'm OK. I guess I lost my balance."

The sergeant took Novotny aside, opened a first-aid kit hanging on the wall, rubbed ointment on the red area, and covered it with a bandage. It hurt where he was burned, but Novotny decided it wasn't anything serious.

"Go out on the landing and have a cigarette," the sergeant said. "Then see how you feel. If the heat's really gotten to you, I'll release you."

He wondered how 90-degree air could feel so good. Tapping the white filter on the railing to compact the tobacco, he lit the Kent and drew the smoke deeply into his lungs. He could get off for the rest of the day if he complained to the mess sergeant. How much time was left? It was hard to know. It was four thirty, and who knew how many hours they had to be there after dinner was over.

He thought about the cook. He didn't even know his name because he'd never noticed his nametag. He was a con artist and a lying bastard. A sadistic, lying bastard. Guys like him are jerks, he thought.

He flashed back to the scene in *From Here to Eternity* where they stayed on Frank Sinatra's back. It could be done under this system, he decided. It could easily be done. Get a few people who want to get you, and it was definitely possible. He crushed the cigarette out with the heel of his combat boot and went back in.

The mess sergeant stopped him. "You sure you're all right?"

"Yeah, I'm all right."

"Go help the outside man. You've had enough heat for today."

"Thanks, Sergeant."

Although he was in the dining hall, he could still see the cook in the kitchen through the open serving line. When the cook would bring something to the steam tables, Novotny made a point of standing and watching him. The cook looked the other way to avoid any contact. But every so often, their eyes would meet, and Novotny just stared at him.

When dinner was over, the mess sergeant left, and with little to do in the dining hall, Novotny and the other outside man were ordered to help finish up in the kitchen.

As jobs were finished, one by one the other cooks released the men working in the kitchen. But Novotny was kept there doing real and made-up tasks by this one cook. Nothing very demanding, just time consuming. Rewashing this and repolishing that.

It was getting noticeably cooler in the kitchen, and Novotny knew he could make it for as long as the cook wanted to play this game. He seemed to have settled into a state where his body was working without him having to tell it what to do. His arms and hands scrubbed and rubbed and wiped and did all the dumb-ass things the cook told him to do, without even thinking about it. All he had to do was slowly and carefully keep at it until the cook got tired of this whole exercise.

Finally, after everyone else had left, the cook looked around the kitchen. "Well, that's it."

Novotny stood a couple of feet from the cook, saying nothing. Just staring at him.

"You want to talk to the CO about that money, let me know. I'll arrange an appointment."

Novotny looked straight at him. "No. I know where his office is."

"Don't forget," the cook said with a hint of concern, "I gave you your money back."

"Right. But what about the other guys?"

"Oh, yeah." He paused. "I'll make sure they get their money back too." The cook was getting increasingly anxious.

Novotny stood there, his hands in his pockets. "You know, I'd be really interested in hearing about all the things you buy for the mess hall with that money. Over a few weeks, it must add up to quite a bit of cash.

The cook looked around. "Well, time to close this place up."

Looking at the cook's nametag, he said aloud, "Leason." He reached in his pocket and pulled out a ballpoint pen and a scrap of paper. Writing slowly, he said, "Leason. I just want to make sure I have it right. What's your first name?"

"My first name?" Novotny could see that the cook was almost in a state of near panic. Taking quick, short little breaths, he said, "Why do you want my first name?"

"Don't worry. I can get it from the mess sergeant tomorrow if you don't want to give it to me."

"No. No. That's all right. James," he said quickly. His eyes had widened, showing more than the usual amount of white and making him look like a pudgy-faced Amos or Andy.

Novotny wrote it neatly in front of the name *Leason*.

"Let me ask you something. Now, you wouldn't want to hang around here for a long time, would you?"

Novotny shrugged. "Wouldn't matter to me one way or the other. I've got two years to kill." Novotny tried hard to say that as convincingly as possible, even though he couldn't wait to leave this place and get on with his tour of duty.

"I'm sorry about the misunderstanding," the cook said, obviously
concerned

"Well, to be honest with you, I'm still not sure that's what it was,"
Novotny said coolly. "We'll just have to see what happens," Novotny said
coolly. "Am I done?"

"Yeah. Yeah. You're done."

He left the cook standing in the kitchen, put on his fatigue cap, and
walked out of the mess hall. Vengeance, he thought as he walked down the
steps. Sweet vengeance. Even if all he did was make the cook sweat a little, he
was glad he had done it. Maybe the cook would decide there was a little too
much risk in this con. Maybe he'd quit doing it.

The guy was a thief, plain and simple, taking advantage of green recruits
who didn't have a clue what was happening. All they wanted to do was get
out of here. Actually, it was a pretty smart idea, he thought. The odds of getting
caught were probably pretty slim, unless someone asked a lot of questions.

Stopping under a streetlight, he sat on a rock, lit a cigarette, and reached
into his pocket for the small piece of paper. He studied it for a minute—James
Leason—and then wadded it into a little ball and threw it out onto the
gravel road.

He looked at his watch. Nine twenty. He had been in the mess hall
for more than seventeen hours. He took a deep breath of the night air,
now reasonably cool again. It felt almost liquid. And it seemed as if it were
replenishing something that had been drained from his body.

There hadn't been many people in his life he had truly disliked. As far as
he could remember, there hadn't been anyone that he'd really hated. Until
now. He hated Leason.

But Leason wasn't even worth hating. He was an ignorant, amoral, fat, greedy guy. He'd had friends in school of all races. Classmates. Guys he ran track with. Guys he'd sat next to in class.

Even a girl from school that he'd gone to concerts with. And with whom he'd sat around after class and talked for hours about exciting ideas that were just becoming known to them as they listened to their teachers lecture and read books about subjects they had never considered before.

He couldn't really say they'd dated. But if his skin had been brown or hers white, he had no doubt that it would have happened.

No, Leason was different. His skin color didn't matter. But what really troubled Novotny was the possibility that something was happening to him. Maybe after only six days in the army, he was already changing. All he could say for certain, as he got close to the barracks, was that he was exhausted and needed sleep.

His body was tired, no doubt about that. But it was his brain that concerned him. It seemed as though he was thinking differently from the way he before he had become a soldier. If he was going to sort this out, it would have to happen some other time. A time when he was rested enough to think it through.

He lifted the green duffel bag to test its weight, estimating it at somewhere around sixty pounds. In it was everything he owned as a soldier. His green combat fatigues. Summer and winter Class A dress uniforms. T-shirts, shorts, socks, handkerchiefs, his shaving kit, and combat boots.

Crammed farther into the bottom of the bag were civilian slacks, a sport shirt, socks, a sweater, and loafers. That was it. Everything in one heavy, green canvas bag.

The skinny, redheaded kid, whom he had met on the train coming over from Detroit, sat on a bunk and watched Novotny close the top of the duffel bag and secure it with a padlock he'd bought at the PX.

"I really wish I was goin' with you," he said.

Novotny tightened the knot in his tie against the collar of his new khaki shirt. "I wish you were coming along too. But don't worry. You'll get out of here in a few days."

Looking at his watch, he realized he had just ten minutes to get to the formation area. He picked up the bag, slung it over his shoulder, and shook the redhead's hand. "Take care of yourself."

It was sad, leaving the kid behind. Even in these few days, he'd gotten to like him. But that was part of the process, he decided. You get thrown together with guys, and then you get split up. That's just the way it works.

In all, twenty-two men had gathered at the assembly area. Novotny had seen some of them during processing, but none of the few he'd really gotten to know in his barracks were in the group. So he just stood by himself, smoking a cigarette and waiting to be told what to do next.

At precisely eight o'clock, two sergeants walked into the area. One was wearing fatigues, and Novotny recognized him as the NCO who had greeted his group at the train when they'd arrived here. How long ago was that? Nine days, Novotny calculated. The other was in a perfectly pressed khaki Class A uniform with rows of decorations over his left pocket. Novotny had never seen him before.

"Good morning, gentlemen." Everyone turned to hear what the fatigue-clad NCO had to say. "As you know, you're going to Fort Meade, Maryland, for your basic training. You'll proceed by bus from here to the airport and then to

Baltimore. Sergeant Coburn here will be traveling with you."

The sergeant looked over the group. "You look much different from when I first saw you at the railhead. You're not soldiers yet. But you're starting to show some promise. I wish all of you good luck in your basic training. Work hard and learn everything you can."

He turned, shook hands with the other sergeant, and walked back toward the office from which he had organized all of this.

"Seems like a decent guy after all," a GI standing next to Novotny said quietly to him.

Once at the airport and aboard the plane, Novotny settled himself into a window seat, cinched his seat belt tight, and turned to watch the engines start. He'd flown many times before, but he never ceased to be fascinated by the process, both on the ground and in the air.

First one engine coughed, puffing clouds of blue-white smoke and clattering as the propeller began to turn uncertainly. A minute or so later the process was repeated with the inboard engine.

When all four were running, they settled into a noisy, rattling idle. With a brief roar the propellers broke the inertia and the old chartered DC-4 began to pull slowly away from the terminal and taxi toward the end of the runway. The pilot set the brakes and revved the engines until the transport began to vibrate and creak as it struggled against the locked wheels, trying vainly, like a tethered hawk, to fly.

Suddenly, engines roaring, it lurched forward and raced along the concrete, streaked with ribbons of black where tires had screeched in hundreds of landings. Novotny watched the runway speed by and then drop away slightly. The plane hesitated, as if deciding whether or not to actually leave the ground, then steadily lifted away from the pavement, confidently gaining altitude.

Bits of frothy white clouds raced over the wing and past his window, obscuring the Missouri hills as the plane left them for the sky above. Bumping through a blanket of gray overcast that left rivulets of water on the window, the plane finally broke into open blue sky with brilliant white puffs of cloud covering the earth below.

His seatmate didn't seem interested in talking, and Novotny didn't mind at all. He was just as glad to look at the sky, the clouds, the aluminum wing that was holding the craft up here, and the engines that were pulling them east.

He was excited about finally getting on with the process. Until now all they'd done was fill out forms, get shots, draw gear, and pull details. Now, at last, he would soon get to the place where he would start basic training.

How long would he be at Fort Meade? Where was it? All he knew was that it must be somewhere near Baltimore. Where would he go after that? What was he going to do for the next two years? What kind of assignment would he get? Would he be sent back to Fort Leonard Wood to spend two years issuing uniforms to shaved-head recruits? He hoped not.

Another couple of days and he should have a pretty good idea about all this. But right now he was detached from the planet and he liked it. He felt free, just being up here at however many thousand feet they were flying, looking down at clouds and at the land below whenever the overcast opened up to let him look.

The voice of a stewardess woke him. "Fasten your seat belt and bring your seat-back up," she said. He tightened the web fabric around his waist and looked out the window. The clouds were gone and he could see everything. Cars. Houses. Streets. Stores. As the ground came steadily closer, the buildings below formed neighborhoods, and he could make out people going about their business.

"Looks like we're here," he said to his seatmate.

"Seems that way," he replied, leaning over Novotny to look out the window.

The plane lurched and the wheels screeched as they left their own black marks on the concrete, just like the ones he'd seen as they took off. He heard the engines rev and felt himself straining against the seat belt as the pilot reversed the propellers and used the engines to slow the plane. Once down to a reasonable speed, the pilot turned off the runway and headed back toward the terminal.

"Welcome to Baltimore's Friendship International Airport," a stewardess said over the PA system. "Please remain seated until the plane has come to a complete stop."

Friendship Airport. Nice name, he thought. But kind of a strange name for an airport. I wonder if there's Happiness Airport somewhere. Or a Kinship. Or an Esprit International Airport.

Probably is, he decided. They're more interesting names than airports named after people no one had ever heard of, like Jones or Smith or Murphy.

But maybe this was named after some guy called Bill Friendship. Or Ernest Friendship. That's it. No, wait. The airport was named after a guy called Earnest Friendship. He smiled at the play on words. Have to remember that. Pretty clever. Earnest Friendship International Airport, in honor of a state senator who kissed babies, shook a lot of people's hands, got rich taking money under the table, and was ultimately thrown out of office. He had a great name for an airport. Obviously, that's the story.

The plane taxied to a virtually abandoned part of the airport where almost nothing seemed to be happening. The engines sputtered as they stopped, and the troops lined up in the aisle, waiting to get off.

By the time Novotny walked down the portable steps to the pavement, baggage handlers had already begun stacking the identical and obviously brand-new duffel bags in rows on carts pulled by a small truck. The only distinguishing marks were the names and serial numbers neatly stenciled in black at exactly the same place on each one.

Sergeant Coburn led the line of khaki-clad troops down the steps from the plane and toward the terminal. Novotny suspected this was pretty much what being in the army would be like. Do what you're told and then wait to be told what to do after that.

Earnest Friendship International Airport. He laughed softly, but loudly enough for two men standing next to him to turn and give him a strange look. Embarrassed, he patted his shirt pockets and found his cigarettes.

Inside joke, he reassured himself as he lit up. Pretty funny. But they'd never understand. There was no point in trying to explain.

The two buses parked in front of the terminal looked exactly like the ones they'd left in Missouri—olive drab with white numbers stenciled on the side. The new GIs stowed their duffel bags in the back of the vehicles and settled into the seats.

There was little conversation—partly because they were tired, but largely because they hardly knew each other. They appeared to have been selected at random and had spent very little time together at Fort Leonard Wood. Not one of the group had even been in Novotny's barracks. It was about six thirty when the bus stopped at a guarded gate identified with a large sign saying "United States Army, Fort George G. Meade." A military policeman (MP) with a polished helmet and white holster smartly waved them through.

Novotny had taken a window seat and watched every detail as they slowly made their way down the tree-lined thoroughfares. He estimated that the stately brick buildings they passed must be more than 100 years old, looking more like the buildings of a small midwestern college than a military installation.

At one intersection, several olive drab artillery pieces were displayed on neatly trimmed lawns.

The recruit sitting next to him said, "Can you believe this place? It looks like it's out of a movie."

"It really does," Novotny replied, still looking out the window.

The buses continued slowly through the military post. Novotny pointed out the window. "Look over there. We shouldn't have gotten our hopes up."

The old brick buildings were behind them now. In their place were exact duplicates of the wooden barracks they'd left in Missouri. Row after row of them. All the same two-story design. All the same tan color with green roofs.

Scattered among them was an occasional mess hall, just like the one where Novotny had spent those hot, exhausting hours. They even had the same brick chimneys, suggesting to him they had hot, smoky coal stoves like the one he had scrubbed and rescrubbed that long day.

Disappointed at the sight of the old, wooden barracks, Novotny slumped into his seat. At least, he thought, the weather seems better here.

Leaving the rows of barracks, the bus passed open grassy areas that Novotny assumed must be used for parades or other kind of drills, and slowly the buses stopped. Sitting up abruptly he saw they had parked on a street lined with what seemed to be brand-new concrete buildings.

The bus stopped and the driver opened the door.

A sergeant boarded the bus and everyone immediately stopped talking.

"Gentlemen, let me have your attention. My name is Sergeant Morrell, and I'd like to welcome you to Fort Meade. I'm sure you want to get settled, so I'll be brief. Take your gear to the second floor of this building," he said, gesturing with his thumb.

"Claim a bunk without linen, and then go to the supply room and get your bedding. The mess hall is over there," he explained, pointing toward another structure. "It'll be open late so you can get dinner. Reveille is at oh five hundred. Morning formation is at oh five thirty. And breakfast is at oh six hundred. I want all of you to be in the classroom in the basement, in fatigues, at oh seven hundred. Are there any questions?"

There were obviously hundreds. But no one asked. They were either too tired or too confused. They were also stunned, grateful, or both, at being assigned to these modern buildings instead of the old barracks they'd driven past. All of them were eager to get a bunk, get something to eat, and square away their gear.

Novotny found his duffel bag and headed up the stairs in the center of the building. A sergeant with a clipboard stood at the top of the stairs. "Name?" he asked.

"Novotny."

The sergeant looked at the clipboard and said, "In there."

Novotny walked tentatively into the long room lined with double bunks. Dividers separated the bunks into groups of four. Some were already occupied, but most were empty, with a bare mattress folded over on the metal springs. For each bunk there was an olive drab footlocker and a wall locker of the same color.

Novotny slowly walked down the aisle, looking for what seemed to be the right place to live for however long they'd be here. He felt like a dog, looking for a particular spot to curl up.

At Fort Leonard Wood, he'd had a lower bunk. Even though his bunkmate was reasonably considerate, he swore he would live only on an upper after being jostled awake time and again as his bunkmate climbed up and down from his bed.

He hadn't complained. But he decided to take the top whenever he could.

He passed a couple of uppers that just didn't seem right. Funny how things that are exactly the same can convey different feelings. There wasn't any explanation for it. It was like DeLapp's theory about finding just the right place along the roadside to catch a ride. It was hard to define, but a strong enough feeling for him to keep walking.

Ahead he saw a recruit lying on a lower bunk reading a copy of *The New Yorker* magazine. It wasn't that he was an avid reader of the publication. But he liked the cartoons and the strange little items scattered through the magazine. The ads were fun to read as well. Given that, he took the magazine as a sign of potential compatibility.

"Is that bunk free?" he asked, pointing to the bunk above the reader.

"Sure," the GI answered, putting down his magazine. "Go ahead and take it."

Novotny unfolded the mattress and dumped his duffel bag on the bunk. "My name's Joe Novotny."

The GI on the lower bunk stood and shook hands. "I'm Bob Johnson. Glad to meet you." He was medium in height, had sandy hair and, like Novotny, wore glasses. A few moments later, another resident of the cubicle arrived. Lanky and standing about six feet, he smiled as he saw Novotny standing there.

"Jesse Stein, this is Joe," Johnson said.

"How're you doing, Jesse?" Novotny asked, shaking hands.

"Good. You just get in?"

"Yeah."

"We got in this morning," Jesse said.

Novotny started to say he was going to get his bedding, when another recruit came into the cubicle. He was shorter than the others and seemed a little tentative about coming into the area that was, in fact, his home.

Again Johnson handled the introductions. "Turner. This is our new bunkmate. Joe." He paused, trying to remember the last name.

"Novotny," he said to Turner. "Joe Novotny. It's a little hard to remember."

"Hi," he said softly. "My name's Harold Turner. But everybody here just calls me Turner." He appeared to be apologizing, even though everyone seemed to call everyone else by their last name.

Introductions done, everything else went smoothly. Novotny got his bedding, had a roast-beef dinner that actually was pretty good, and unloaded his duffel bag full of uniforms and gear into the lockers next to his bunk. He was tired and glad to be here.

Although he hadn't had much time to talk to them, his cubicle mates seemed to be decent guys. And when the lights went out at ten o'clock, he curled up in his bunk feeling a comfortable sense of well-being, even though he knew very little about his situation or what would happen tomorrow.

Whatever is going to happen, at least it's about to begin, he thought. He closed his eyes and immediately fell asleep.

Irv Hamilton, Jr.

By 6:55 am, all of the men were seated in the classroom talking quietly. Although he'd fallen asleep quickly, Novotny had slept fitfully, unused to the surroundings and anxious to know what would happen next. Waiting for the meeting to start, Johnson, Stein, Turner, and Novotny all sat together. Just being from the same cubicle gave them a bond in this otherwise uncertain situation. On the wall at the front of the classroom was a round yellow-and-green crest with the motto Toujours Prêt. At precisely 7 am, an officer walked to the rostrum at the front of the room. A few men stood, self-consciously, but most just sat and watched him enter the room, not sure what to do. Walking behind him was Sergeant Morrell. "Ten-hut," the sergeant said loudly. With a scraping of chairs, those who weren't already standing got up. Some stood casually, and others were stiffly and uncomfortably at attention.

"Good morning, gentlemen. Please be seated," the officer said, looking over the roomful of recruits. "Welcome to H Company of the 2d Armored Cavalry Regiment. My name is Lieutenant Wilson. I'm your commanding officer. And for those who haven't met him, this is Sergeant Davis, the company first sergeant."

He paused for a moment and again looked around the room. The lieutenant was about five ten and stood straight, but without any military affectation. Novotny stared at the officer's fatigues. The shirt was trim and fitted. His field trousers had a sharp, starched crease, even though they were nothing more than green cotton designed to be worn in combat.

And his black combat boots glistened, with a radiant shine that seemed to come from deep within the leather.

On the pocket of his shirt was an embroidered patch with a green-and-yellow coat of arms. Tucked under his open collar was a neatly pressed yellow scarf.

He wasn't speaking loudly and there was no microphone, but his voice carried throughout the room. He explained that they were part of a special training program. Usually, he pointed out, recruits would take basic training and then go on to advanced schooling in what was to be their military specialty. That done, they would be assigned to a unit that needed them.

But training for these new soldiers would be done very differently. "The regiment has been staffed with a full complement of officers and non-commissioned officers—NCOs," he explained. "But all of the slots for the lower ranks are open."

He smiled slightly. "You're in the 2d Cav and you'll stay with it. You'll take eight weeks of basic training with this company. From there you'll go for additional training in a specialty, and then come back here to H Company— or as we call it in the cavalry, H Troop."

He paused again and seemed to be reviewing in his mind what he was going to say next. "When that training is complete, the entire regiment will be deployed to Germany for border patrol duty."

He paused again.

"I know for some of you that'll come as good news. And others won't be so happy about it. But because of the nature of the training and our assignment over there, no one will be released from the regiment except cases of severe hardship."

Novotny looked at Johnson and smiled. What great news. Two years in Europe paid for by the U.S. Army.

"Our assignment will be to patrol the border between West Germany and two Communist countries—East Germany and Czechoslovakia."

Novotny couldn't believe what he'd just heard. Being assigned to the Czech border. It wasn't possible. He didn't even know American soldiers were stationed on the border.

"It's a very important assignment," the lieutenant continued. "That border and the 38th parallel in Korea are the two places in the world where we're face-to-face with the Communists. If the Russians decide to make a move against Europe, we'll be the first troops engaged in combat. Our mission will be to slow Ivan down until NATO can counterattack."

He paused to let that message sink in, and then continued. "For that reason, I encourage you to learn everything you possibly can during the next few months. You'll be taking on one of the most important assignments in the United States Army today."

Again he looked around the room as if evaluating these men he hadn't even met yet. Novotny instinctively sat up straighter in his chair, making no effort to hide the smile on his face.

"This regiment is the longest continuously serving unit in the army. Historically, it's a very special outfit. It's distinguished itself in combat since 1836. I suggest you visit the regimental museum in the headquarters building to learn of that history. Now, are there any questions?"

One or two of the men took the lieutenant up on his offer. But Novotny was too excited to pay attention to what was said.

As soon as the meeting was over, he rushed to the PX and found an empty phone booth. He put in a dime and placed a collect call with the operator. Soon his mother was on the other end of the line.

"Hello."

"Mom. This is Joe."

"Joe. Where are you?" Even though she'd lived in America for thirty years or more, there was still a slight accent in her speech. Before he could answer, she said, "Wait a minute. I will get your father.

It was still hard to believe. He was going to the Czech border. His mother had left Czechoslovakia as a little girl in the 1920s. Until the end of the First World War, the area had been part of the Austro-Hungarian Empire. But in 1919, the Czechs, in Bohemia and Moravia, and the Slovaks who populated Slovakia were fused into Czechoslovakia, linked by a common Slavic heritage, but with slightly different languages and cultures.

Under the new flag, Czechs and Slovaks were free again, after centuries of being ruled by others. They practiced a democracy modeled after the United States. The Czechoslovak constitution had even been drafted in the United States. Then, in 1938, the British had turned their backs on the Czechs to appease Hitler, and soon afterward, the Nazis took over Czechoslovakia.

His father had been born in Chicago of parents who had come through Ellis Island in the late 1800s. They were also Czechs, with German as their official language and their Czech heritage suppressed. Novotny wasn't sure how they'd been able to do it, but his grandparents had managed to get to Vienna, then Berlin, and finally Chicago.

When the war ended in 1945, the Czechoslovak republic had once again been established, and his grandfather proudly spoke of their independence. But in 1948, the Russians were able to install a puppet Communist government, and once more the Czechs had lost their freedom.

His grandfather had talked longingly about going back one day to see the town he had left as a young man, before their new country even existed. But the Depression, then the Germans, and finally the Russians made that impossible. His grandfather died in 1950, never having had an opportunity to go back to the country he loved.

Novotny thought about the subtle but clearly present sadness in his grandfather's voice whenever he spoke about Prague, his childhood, and the oppressor-plagued history of his birth country.

Proud of their Czechness, his grandparents had spoken the language the Habsburgs had sought to permanently replace with German. Novotny had never studied Czech. But hearing it at home, he'd absorbed the rich sounds of the Slavic language into his young brain.

Over the years, his grandparents had written to relatives, but wars and death and relocation had broken the linkages between the family in "the old country" and the relatives who had settled in the Czech neighborhoods of Chicago.

Novotny's grandfather had verbally walked him through the streets of Prague, across the Charles Bridge spanning the Vltava River and up the hill to Hradcany, the historic seat of the Czech monarchy. In his mind, he imagined what it would be like to go to Kolin, the town of his grandfather's birth, and stand in the church where he had been an altar boy—to look at the altar and the stained-glass windows that had been described to him in such detail.

And now he was actually going there. Not exactly to Czechoslovakia, but right next to it. Right on the border between Germany and Bohemia.

"Joe?"

"Hi, Dad," he said excitedly.

"Where are you?"

"I'm at Fort Meade, Maryland. It's not far from Baltimore."

They finished the conversation in Czech. Yes, he was fine. The food was good, if the one breakfast and dinner he'd had so far were any indication of what they would be fed.

And there was wonderful news. He was going to be stationed in Europe. On the Czech border. Wasn't it incredible? He wasn't sure how much leave he would have before he went overseas. Or when he would actually be going. He'd let them know as soon as they were given more information.

His bunkmates seemed like very nice guys. No, he didn't need any money. It didn't look as though he would have a need, or even opportunity, to buy anything.

No, they shouldn't worry. The Russians wouldn't invade Europe as long as we had NATO there, regardless of what Khrushchev threatened. He said that confidently, though he wasn't completely sure it was so. But there was no point in bringing that up. There was also no point in telling them what the lieutenant had said about the 2d Cavalry being the first troops to be in combat if the Russians decided to cross the border.

"Don't worry, Mom," he said. "There won't be a war."

Yes, he'd write as soon as he could. But from what he could tell, they were going to be kept busy day and night. So they shouldn't be concerned if he didn't write a lot. Yes, he would send his address. It was too long to give them over the phone.

His father knew what it was like to be in the service. He had been drafted into the navy during the Second World War. "Just pay attention to what they teach you, Joe," he said. "And don't let them wear you down. You'll do just fine."

Three recruits were now lined up, impatiently waiting to use the phone. "I'd better let some of these other guys use the phone," he said. "I'll call next week."

The men sitting around each table in the PX had a distinctively common appearance, despite the differences in size, shape, and skin color. Their green combat fatigues still had the sheen of being new. Their hair was cropped to an even quarter of an inch. And they all exhibited a visible uncertainty and discomfort in their new role as rookie soldiers.

Novotny looked around the PX and saw his cubicle mates sitting together. Stein and Johnson were drinking beer. Turner had a Coke. They waved him over.

"Have a seat, Novotny," Stein said. Tipping the can to empty the last drops into his mouth, he got up. "You want one?"

"Sure. Sounds good."

They were a classic sampling of American youth. Novotny: Czech parents. Just graduated from Northwestern. Bob Johnson: from upstate New York, with a degree in English from Hamilton College. Jesse Stein: stocky but agile. Finished high school in Detroit, took a job in production planning with Chrysler, worked there for a couple of years, and got drafted. "Didn't think they'd get me," Stein told Novotny. "I was wrong." And Harold Turner. About five seven. Slender and tentative in his speech and actions. He was working in a gas station in Youngstown, Ohio, when he got his notice.

Novotny opened a new pack of cigarettes and offered them to his cubicle mates. Johnson and Stein accepted. Turner shook his head, declining.

"Did you get hold of your parents?" Turner asked.

"Yeah. Got right through."

"What'd they think about your going to the Czech border?"

"They were surprised," he said, smiling as he lit his cigarette. "Shocked is more like it, I'd guess. My mother's pretty worried about the situation over there. But I told her there wasn't any problem."

Johnson laughed. "That probably put her completely at ease."

Novotny shrugged. "What else could I say? And I don't think the Russians are going to do anything."

Stein returned with three beers and a Coke. "Thanks," Novotny said.

Stein settled into his seat. "You know, Novotny. You're gonna have to get another name."

"Why's that?"

"Too long," Stein said. "Your name's too long."

"Joe?"

"No, that's too common. Too many Joes. I mean Novotny. It's too long. Too hard to remember." Stein took a drink from the can. "You've got to have a workable name. What'd they call you in college?"

"In the fraternity they called me Novo."

"Well, that's what we'll call you," Stein said. "Novo. That's easier."

They sat, mostly talking about what was likely to happen. A black recruit walked in and looked around the PX. Pointing to an empty seat, he asked, "OK if I sit here?"

"You in H Troop?" Stein asked, as if it mattered.

"Yeah."

"Then have a seat."

They went through the introductions and learned that his name was Charles Morris, though he preferred to be called Chas. He was from St. Louis and had spent a year or so looking for work after he graduated from high school. "Man, I tried everything. Didn't do any good. There just weren't no jobs there. At least no jobs you'd want. So I signed up. I sure didn't believe I'd go to Germany."

"What platoon are you in?" Johnson asked.

"Second."

"So are we," Turner said, seemingly pleased at the coincidence.

"What do you think of Sergeant Duff?" Johnson asked no one in particular. Their platoon sergeant, William Duff, was about five ten and probably weighed 180. He had a face that reminded Novotny of a cowboy-movie hero. Coarse features, tanned, and in a way, handsome. Novotny guessed he was in his late thirties, and on his sleeve he wore three chevrons up and two down—the mark of a sergeant first class.

"I only talked to him for a little while," Novotny said. "But he seems like a pretty good guy." He added, "I saw him in Class A's, and he's got rows of medals. I don't know a lot of them. But I recognized the European Theatre ribbon. And he's got the blue-and-white ones from Korea. I had some friends over there."

Novotny took a drink from the can. "He's also got a Purple Heart, so he's been wounded."

"I wouldn't exactly say he was friendly," Stein said. "He reminds me of a baseball coach I had in high school. You could talk to him, all right. But you didn't ever feel that you knew the guy real well."

"Jesse, I have a feeling we're going to know Sergeant Duff pretty well before we're done here," Johnson said, leaning back in his chair and stretching.

No one disagreed.

For two days, very little happened. Equipment was issued and the recruits pulled miscellaneous details, including KP. But it was very different from Fort Leonard Wood. The officers and NCOs seemed to have a keen interest in the men they were about to train.

In his soft-spoken way, Sergeant Duff made a point of talking to each of the men in his platoon, asking where they'd come from and what they'd done before coming into the army. He, in turn, seemed willing to answer questions, though everyone was careful about what they asked, not wanting to seem dumb or anxious.

"How we gonna be able to talk to the Germans? I don't know German," a recruit named Perreti asked.

"You'll get by," the sergeant said. "Girls on the street and the people who run bars will know enough English to take your money," he said without a smile.

"Were you ever stationed in Germany?" Novotny asked one afternoon.

"I was with the 4th Armored Division in '44 and '45."

During a break from barracks cleaning, Novotny heard someone ask, "Do you think the Russians would ever cross the border or try to take over West Berlin?"

"I can't answer that. But if they do, we'll be there," he answered matter-of-factly.

Straight. To the point. No BS. Novotny liked that about the sergeant.

On their third day at Fort Meade, basic training officially began and the demanding routine was quickly set. The lights in the barracks went on at five in the morning, and virtually every minute of the day was full until the lights went out at ten o'clock at night.

It was apparent to everyone what basic training was meant to do. It would get them into shape physically. They would learn all the things that were required to be soldiers, such as firing weapons, marching, and reading a map. And there was an obvious effort to instill pride in their unit, the 2d Armored Cavalry Regiment.

They knew little about their company CO, First Lieutenant Wilson, except that he was in his late twenties and had come into the army as a private during the Korean War. He'd worked his way up through the enlisted ranks and earned a commission.

Like Sergeant Duff, he spoke with a quiet voice. He also radiated pride at being part of this regiment.

The lieutenant fascinated Novotny because he said things that could be viewed as propagandistic pap with such understated conviction that Novotny could do nothing but believe him. Like Sergeant Duff, he appeared to see the world in very clear, uncomplicated terms. Here's the way it is, and that's that. Novotny decided that, if they were ever in combat, that trait would be important.

"When you're finished with basic and advanced training, this troop will be the best company of the best regiment in the United States Army," Lieutenant Wilson had said at formation one morning. Most of the trainees took it as the kind of thing every coach says to the team before the first game. But Novotny had no doubt the lieutenant believed it.

He also did things the trainees found a little unusual, given the silver bars on his collar. Novotny had assumed the NCOs and officers wouldn't do physical training, PT, with the recruits. But both Lieutenant Wilson and

Sergeant Duff did everything along with their men.

When they were in the field, lined up to get a hot lunch from the field kitchen set up in the back of a truck, Lieutenant Wilson always ate last, filling his mess kit only after every man had been fed.

"Rank has its privilege," Novotny once said to Johnson as they stood in a chow line. "But Lieutenant Wilson sure doesn't flaunt it."

"Probably because he was a private once himself," Johnson observed.

Sunday was a perfect Maryland August day: warm and sunny. Johnson and Novotny relished having a few hours with nothing to do. They walked to the parade ground and stretched out on the grass, enjoying the warmth of the sun, smoking and talking about the week that had just passed.

Johnson snuffed his cigarette out on the heel of his combat boot and broke open the butt, as they'd been trained to do. He scattered the remaining tobacco on the ground next to him, wadded the white paper into a tiny ball, and flicked it a few feet away. "What do you really think about going to Germany, Novo?"

"I think it's great. I've always wanted to go to Europe," he answered, and then added, "What do you mean—really think?"

"Well, your family's Czech. And we'll be on the Czech border." He rolled over onto his back and put his hands behind his head. "Could you shoot a Czech, if the Russians and Czechs come across?"

Novotny thought for a minute. "To start with, I don't know if I could shoot anybody. Right now that's a bigger question than who it might be."

Johnson laughed. "By the time we're done with basic, we'll be trained killers. We'll probably look forward to an invasion so we can use what we've learned."

"I'm serious," Novotny said, stretching out on the grass like Johnson and looking up at the cloudless blue sky. "And the idea of the Czechs being on the other side makes it even more complicated. My grandmother was from a town called Domazlice. It's only about five miles from the border. For all I know, I have relatives in the Czech border patrol."

"Shades of the Civil War."

"Yeah." Novotny enjoyed this quiet time, lying in the grass talking to this guy whom he already liked, even though he'd known him only a few days.

He looked up at the endless blue over his head. "The other thing that complicates it is that the Germans are on our side," he added. "That seems really strange to me. Twelve years ago—which isn't all that long ago, when you think about it—the Germans were sending Czechs to the gas chambers. That's not much time to forget."

Novotny remembered the pictures he'd seen as a boy. The swastikas. The goose-stepping *Wehrmacht,* Germany's army. And the corpses at Buchenwald and Auschwitz. It surprised him at how clearly these strange-sounding names had been imbedded in his brain, even though he'd heard them as a little kid and never really thought about them after the war had ended. Bergen-Belsen. Mauthausen. Dachau. The names were as familiar to him as Memphis or Portland or Tucson.

He would never know, but some of those skeletons in those photos covered with nothing but skin could easily have been a relative. He wasn't Jewish, but the Nazis used those places to get rid of resistors and dissidents as well.

Now he was being sent to Europe to protect the Germans from the Russians and the Czechs. It didn't make much sense.

Given what the Second World War was about, he thought, the Czechs should be free, along with the Poles, the Hungarians, the Lithuanians, the

Latvians, the Estonians, and a long list of others—including the East Germans.

The Russians should be happy that German isn't their official language today, and go about the business of modernizing their country. With appropriate guilt, the Germans should be helping the people they did terrible things to.

It was that simple. And why not? The cold war wouldn't be happening. The draft would be abolished, because it wouldn't be needed anymore. And he would be looking for a job, instead of starting basic training in Maryland.

But that isn't the way it is, he reminded himself. So now he was here and he had no choice but to learn what they were going to teach him and hope he never had to fire a shot in anger at a Czech. Or at anyone else, for that matter.

"Hey, Novo. I've got an idea," Johnson said.

"What's that?"

"Let's go over the regimental museum and see what's there."

Novotny first thought he'd rather just lie there on the grass, look at the sky, and relax. But on second thought, taking a look at whatever they had on display might be interesting. "Sounds good," he said, getting up, giving his friend a hand, and pulling him upright. "Let's check it out."

The blocky, brick architecture of the headquarters building was similar to the barracks. In front was a large sign boldly displaying the regimental crest. *Toujours Prêt*, it said. Always Ready.

Just inside the door, a sergeant sat at a desk reading the Sunday *Baltimore Sun*. "Can I help you men?" he said, putting down the paper.

"We're from Company H," Johnson answered. "Can we see the museum?"

"Sure," the sergeant replied, pushing a form and a pencil across the desk. "Sign in here."

They wrote their names and added their long serial numbers by memory.

"Just go down the hall on your left," the sergeant instructed.

The tile floors of the headquarters building glistened, and the sound of their boots echoed through the empty hall. The museum was in one large room, its walls lined with glass cases. In the center were more glass-enclosed displays, all filled with military memorabilia.

One shelf contained small, olive-drab models of tanks used at various times by the 2d Cavalry. There were also a number of foreign types, including gunmetal gray Panzers from the Second World War.

There were photos of the horse-mounted regiment on parade at Fort Riley, Kansas, not long after they had battled the Indians all over the West and fought in the First World War.

The two men walked from display to display, quietly absorbing the artifacts and thinking back to decades long ago when other young men like them had been part of the 2d Cavalry, and before that, the 2d Dragoons.

In one glass case, Novotny saw an open thick, leather-bound book filled with ruled pages. Each line contained essential information about cavalrymen who had served with the unit in the late 1800s. Their names. Their height. Their weight. Their state or country of origin. Novotny was surprised at how many were from other countries. Ireland. Germany. Scotland.

The records showed the date they joined the unit, the date they left the regiment, and the circumstances of their departure. "Separated." "Transferred to 4th Infantry Regm't." "Deserted." "Honorably discharged." "Wounded. Sent to Fort Abraham Lincoln for treatment." "Killed." "Missing. Assumed dead." "Died of wounds."

Johnson, standing by another glass case on the wall, quietly called to Novotny. "Hey, Novo. Look at this."

He pointed to a regimental flag. Part of it had been torn off, and there were rips and tears in what was left. The green and yellow of the regimental crest had faded to a point where the color was barely visible on the silky cloth. Blotchy brown stains covered a good third of the it.

A typewritten card displayed next to the flag told the story of a Civil War battle. "On that morning in 1863, the 2d U.S. Cavalry led an attack against Confederate forces. Trooper Owen W. Shea, Headquarters Troop, carried these regimental colors into battle until a Confederate bullet felled him. Immediately Trooper William McKenzie took the colors and rode with them at the head of the regiment as it charged the enemy forces. Then he too was killed by Confederate rifle fire. Seeing McKenzie fall, Corporal Thomas Fenton retrieved the colors and carried them for the remainder of the battle against the Confederates, despite a serious gunshot wound in the left shoulder."

Johnson looked at the brown stains on the flag. "That's blood."

"Yeah," Novotny said. "Carrying the colors made those guys great targets.

"You wonder why someone would do it. It's like committing suicide."

Novotny shook his head. "I met a man the day I came into the army. He fell on a grenade in Germany in the war." Novotny re-created the conversation in his mind. "He said he didn't even think about it. He just did it instinctively."

They stood, looking at the flag, not saying anything, when they were startled by a voice from behind them.

"Good afternoon, gentlemen."

They turned quickly and saw a man standing in the entrance to the room. He was tall, stocky—but trim—and about forty-five years old. They snapped to attention.

"Good afternoon, sir," they said, nearly in unison.

"At ease, gentlemen." His voice was strong but had a distinctively gentle quality. His fatigues, like Lieutenant Wilson's and Sergeant Duff's, were tailored and perfectly pressed. Like the lieutenant, on one collar he wore the crossed sabers and tank that identified him as an armored cavalry officer. On his other collar was an eagle with spread wings.

"What company are you men with?"

"We're with H Company, sir," Novotny answered.

"I'm glad to see your interest in the regiment's history. As you can see, this is quite a unit. I hope other men will visit here as well."

The two young men stood there, not knowing what to say next.

"So you're from H Troop."

"Yes, sir," Johnson acknowledged.

"Well, I'd like you to take a message back to your company for me," the colonel said. "Ask Sergeant Duff to stop by my office. It's nothing urgent," he added. "I'd just like to see him. We were in Korea together."

"Yes, sir," they both answered, again nearly in unison.

"Glad to have you with us in the 2d Cavalry." With that, he turned and left the museum.

Novotny took a deep breath. "I guess we just met the regimental CO."

"He seems like a nice guy," Johnson remarked.

Novotny walked back over to the glass case displaying the battered flag. Why would someone do that? he thought. Carry that piece of cloth, knowing that the odds were very good you'd soon be dead for doing so? Maybe the guy who fell on the grenade was right. Maybe you don't think about it. Maybe something other than your brain takes over. In fact, that's probably what they will try to teach us.

He imagined an instructor standing in front of the trainees. "Gentlemen, today we're going to learn about how to behave in combat," the instructor would say. "First, remember to repress your natural survival instincts by setting aside the reasoning portion of your brain. It'll just get in the way. This is particularly true if you have to do something that will very likely cause you to die in a violent and unpleasant manner, early in your life, in some muddy or dusty place that no one you know has ever heard of."

OK. No problem, Novotny said to himself, looking at the bloodstained flag. I've got that down pat. Now what's next?

Novotny slowly became aware of his surroundings. He liked waking slowly. Relishing the transition from sleep to consciousness. Rolling over onto his back, he stretched and yawned, staring up at the ceiling of the barracks through the gray-black light of the early morning.

Looking at his watch, he tried to see what time it was, but there wasn't enough light. Four thirty, he guessed. Since getting here, his brain and his body had developed an automatic wake-up system that took him through this gentle entry into the new day.

From wake-up at five to lights out at ten, this was the only time he had to think about what was going on and to be by himself. Every other minute of the day was filled with classes, drills, chow, and PT, all done with a hundred or more other trainees.

It was amazing to him how much training had been crammed into the few weeks he had been a soldier. And when he crawled into his bunk at the end of each day, he was so tired that it was almost impossible to stay awake for more than a couple of minutes.

One of the disappointments he had experienced since his first day as a soldier was reveille. H Company had no bugler. Instead, the upbeat notes of the morning call were played on a phonograph in the first sergeant's office, using a scratchy old 45 that should have been replaced a long time ago. The sound was blasted through the barracks on large, olive-drab loudspeakers that would test out at something well below low fidelity.

Novotny had imagined that, like in the movies, every company in the army had a bugler to play reveille and taps.

"You've got a great lip," Novotny would say to him after hearing the bugler practice all by himself on the parade ground. "You ought to be playing for Ray Anthony or one of the other big bands," he imagined saying.

"Nah. I'd rather be a bugler," the soldier would say.

Novotny closed his eyes and heard the sound of the bugle in his mind, clear and perfectly played. A moment after he conjured up the last note of the morning call, the raspy amplified sound reverberated through the barracks, and he quickly rose.

The line of dull green trucks moved slowly down the gravel road, kicking up a trail of orange-brown dust. Each had a canvas cover protecting trainees sitting on two wooden benches that ran the length of the truck bed. The GIs sat facing each other, all dressed exactly alike in green fatigues and combat boots. All wore a steel helmet and a cartridge belt to which a canteen, first-aid packet, and ammunition pouches were attached with metal hooks.

Each held an M1 rifle between his legs, butt down and barrel pointing up. Usually when they went from one training assignment to another, there was joking and talking. But today the troops were quieter than usual.

The men from cubicle four, Second Platoon, H Company—Johnson, Novotny, Stein, and Turner—sat side by side in the third truck of the convoy.

Their M1s, along with their combat boots, which they shined constantly, had become a major focus of their attention. They had learned how the rifle worked, how to disassemble it blindfolded, and how to hit a target at 100 yards and more.

They had learned that you never, ever called a rifle a gun, no matter what you might have done as a kid. It was a weapon or a rifle, and that was it.

On the rifle range they had also learned how to avoid "M1 thumb," the painful result of getting one's thumb caught in the breech as the bolt sprang forward when loading a full clip of ammunition.

And day after day, they had cleaned their M1s, inside and out. "A clean rifle could save your life someday," Sergeant Duff had said as he made them re-clean what had appeared to be an already spotless weapon. "A dirty rifle can cost you your life."

The helmets all moved up and down in unison as the vehicles bounced along the dirt road. Turner frowned, stared straight ahead, and said nothing as the truck droned on.

"What's wrong?" Novotny asked.

"I don't think I'm gonna like this," he said softly.

"Don't worry about it," Novotny said. "It'll be done before you know it. It might even be fun."

"You're crazy, Novo," Chas Morris said. "This ain't gonna be no fun. I talked to a guy who said a trainee saw a snake. Stood up and got cut in half by da machine guns."

"That's bullshit," someone said.

"You jus' wait and see," Morris said, unconvinced. Turner seemed even more anxious than before.

The trucks finally pulled to a stop and the men jumped to the ground and formed up by platoon. They had arrived at what was called the "confidence" course, designed to do away with fears they might have about attacking under fire.

At the far end of the course was a long trench slightly more than 6 feet deep and 100 feet long. In front of the trench was the actual course, made up of barbed wire and assorted other obstacles on otherwise flat terrain. About 300 feet from the first trench was a second trench, much like the first.

The object was to form up by platoon in the far trench, climb onto the course, and make your way across the course to the second trench, with your M1 carefully cradled in your elbows as you crawled on your belly. The intent was to get from the first trench to the second one with your weapon clean and ready to use.

There were a few hitches to this otherwise relatively easy exercise. One was that ahead of the trainees, as they crawled across the course, were a number of machine guns, set to fire over the men at a height of about four feet. The .30-caliber weapons were using live ammunition.

Another disconcerting aspect of the exercise was that scattered around the course were deep pits, surrounded by sandbags, each loaded with dynamite charges. Detonated at random during the exercise, they simulated the impact of incoming artillery.

Compounding this further were barbed wire, logs, and other obstacles that had to be dealt with in order to make it to the other side.

Johnson, Novotny, Turner, and Stein stood in the far trench with their platoon, crouching slightly. A voice over a PA system shouted, "Next group. Go! Go! Go!"

Novotny slung his M1 over his shoulder and climbed up the two-by-fours that formed steps on the side of the trench. He could feel his heart beating faster as his head came up over the lip. At the top, he rolled over, placed his rifle across his arms, and looked ahead to the machines firing over his head.

Papapapapapapapapa. Papapapapapapapapapapapa. Papapapapa.

Johnson crawled over to his left. Stein climbed out of the trench to his right. They waited for Turner, and finally saw his head peeking over the top of the trench.

"Come on, Turner. Let's go," Novotny hollered to him. Slowly he crawled between Novotny and Stein.

At the top of his voice, Johnson shouted, "The unstoppable men of cubicle four are on the attack," and the four men began to edge forward.

Stein added as he crawled, "The men of cubicle four are tough and never afraid." Saying so seemed to help him believe it was true.

Novotny knew the bullets flying overhead were harmless as long as you stayed down. But even so, the idea of having invisible copper missiles streaking overhead was more than a little unnerving.

The foursome moved slowly, careful not to get snagged in the strings of wire with their razor-sharp barbs.

Papapapa. Papapapapapapap. The guns kept firing almost nonstop.

About thirty feet ahead of him, Novotny saw a pile of sandbags. "Head to the right," he shouted, and the four men angled away from the pit as they crawled. Just as they were even with it, a thundering explosion shook the ground and sent dirt flying into the air. As the clods fell on them and the dust choked their breathing, there was nothing they could do but lie there with their hands covering their heads until the air had cleared.

"Jesus," Novotny said under his breath.

"Everybody OK?" Johnson shouted. Since no one seemed to be hurt, he said, "Let's go. Let's get this over with."

Novotny crawled close to Johnson. "You know, Bob, this is abnormal human behavior."

"You can say that again."

They continued crawling side by side. "There's something else I just realized."

"What's that, Novo?" Johnson asked, breathing in short gasps.

"Did you ever play war"—he took a deep breath—"play war when you were a kid?"

"Sure, everybody did," Johnson said. "There was a war goin' on. We all pretended we were soldiers."

"Do you remember the sound you used to make for a gun?"

"Yeah."

"It was like saying *too* with your teeth closed. Right? Too. Too," Novotny demonstrated.

"Yeah. That's what we did."

"Well, we were wrong. Listen." They stopped crawling. "The sound starts with a *p*. Like *'pa.'* We should have been going *'Papapapapapa.'* Not *'tootootootoo.'*"

"Novo, you're crazy. Thinkin' about that now. Come on. Let's go."

About two-thirds of the way through the course there was a break in the barbed wire. In its place was a more frightening obstacle: a line of logs. The logs themselves were harmless enough. But it meant their bodies had to leave the relative security of the ground by a dimension equal to the diameter of the log. That put them a foot or so closer to the bullets whizzing overhead.

The men of cubicle four got to the logs at about the same time. Stein laid his rifle on the coarse bark and gingerly started to climb over the obstacle.

Johnson did the same thing a few feet away.

Novotny saw Turner crawl to the log and press his body against it, the way someone might squeeze into a narrow doorway trying to find protection from a blowing storm. Novotny crawled to him.

"You OK?" he asked.

"I'm not goin' over that log," he said. His body was shaking visibly.

"You have to, Turner."

"I don't want to get shot. I'm gonna wait 'til they stop."

"You can't. You gotta go. Johnson just did it. He's got a bigger butt than you do. So did Stein. Come on."

"I'm not goin'," he said, nearly in tears.

Papapapapapapa. Papapapapapapapa.

"Look," Novotny said forcefully. "I'm goin' over the log. Then you hand me your rifle and climb over. You've got plenty of room to spare. You're not gonna get shot."

Novotny climbed over the log and carefully put down his M1. "OK, Turner, lay your rifle on the log." Nothing happened for about a minute. "Come on, Turner," he said impatiently. "We gotta get with this thing over with."

A rifle slowly materialized from the other side of the log. Novotny laid it next to his. Cautiously, Turner pulled himself onto the top of the log and rolled down onto the dirt on the other side. Novotny handed him his M1.

"The worst part's over. Now just keep moving. We'll be done in a few minutes." Ahead were Johnson and Stein, waiting for their cubicle mates. Together the four men crawled the last fifty feet or so and carefully lowered themselves into the trench.

The sound of the machine guns coming from just above their heads was louder and more persistent than it was on the course. *Papapapapa.*

Papapapapapa. Papapapapa.

But it didn't matter. They were done. They'd made it. All four of them had made it. They walked the length of the trench to the gathering area safely off to the side, their M1s slung over their shoulders and their fatigues covered with dirt and blackened with sweat.

Johnson gave Novotny a gentle punch on the shoulder. "The Russians better think twice about comin' across the border when we get there."

"Yeah. We're tough all right, and we made it," Novotny said, grinning. He turned and looked at Turner walking just behind him. "That goes for you too, Turner. You made it."

Turner smiled slightly and said, "Yeah. I made it."

Gradually, the collection of trainees was beginning to behave like soldiers. Things that were foreign and unnatural to them when they were civilians were becoming a normal way of life.

They managed to get by on less sleep. And even though the days were long and strenuous, most seemed to be responding positively to the process. There was a strong sense of purpose as they moved through one week after another of the training regimen.

They all were looking toward that day when they could really call themselves soldiers.

Wearing green fatigues and combat boots had become a comfortable way of dressing, Saluting and saying, "yes, sergeant," and "yes, sir" happened automatically, without thought.

PT had caused almost all of them to shed pounds and tone their bodies. Soon, most of them were able do calisthenics or march or run for as long as the sergeants told them to do it. And they did so without question or complaint.

In the evenings, if they weren't doing some kind of night training, there was almost always something that had to be done. They disassembled, cleaned, and reassembled their M1 rifles over and over, presenting them to Sergeant Duff until he said they were acceptable, which was generally about fifteen minutes before lights out.

They waxed and buffed the floor of the barracks and wiped every ledge and corner of the long room so that when Lieutenant Wilson ran his finger over any surface within reach, there was no trace of dust.

They spit-shined their black combat boots to a gloss in which they could nearly see themselves, and the next night, they would do it again.

One night, Sergeant Duff passed out ballpoint pens, with special indelible ink. In small groups they sat on the floor, joking, talking, and smoking as they waited their turn to use the pens. The instructions were simple. They were to carefully and legibly write their full name and serial number on the inside of both boots.

One trainee, intent on making the letters readable, said to no one in particular as he wrote, "I can see why we have to do this. They all look alike."

"That's not why," another trainee said.

The trainee with the pen looked up. "How do you know so much?"

"Sergeant Duff told me. Sometimes that's all they find."

"What's that supposed to mean?" the young man with a pen asked.

"Well, if you get killed, sometimes all they find are parts. Like a foot or a leg. That way they know who it belonged to. They can figure out who you were."

The joking and talking stopped, until someone brought up the baseball season and the conversation began again.

Novotny sat quietly by himself, waiting for the pen. When I came in, I said I'd give them my body and do what I was told, he thought. But I wasn't going to buy into this thing completely. My mind is going to keep just a little distance from it all, he reminded himself.

On Saturday morning, their battalion, dressed in their green fatigues, was formed on the parade ground to see just how well they had perfected their marching skills. One by one, the companies went through a series of commands while moving as a single, multibodied, living entity as the battalion officers watched.

G Company was performing while H, I, Tank, and Howitzer companies stood in perfect ranks at parade rest and watched. Novotny was at the far right end of the second rank, keeping his head straight ahead, but moving his eyes from left to right to see how G Company looked.

The company was staying in nearly perfect step, and their changes of direction were neatly executed. Not bad, he thought. But we can do better, he decided.

For no particular reason, he took a quick look down at the ground. He noticed that the flagpole to his right was casting a shadow that formed a black line about six inches in front of his shiny black boots.

Looking up, he heard G Company's CO command, "To the rear . . . march." The men made a 180-degree turn and had barely taken two steps when the lieutenant repeated the command. Again the entire company changed direction, smoothly and without the confusion that these maneuvers often produced. Those guys are really good, he thought.

Out of curiosity, he again looked down at the ground, tipping his head downward ever so slightly. The shadow had moved and was now about an inch from the toes of his boots. He tried to concentrate on watching G Company leave the field, but his mind was on the shadow and its encroachment on the territory he had claimed by standing on this particular piece of ground.

Again he looked down and saw that the shadow was now a fraction of an inch from the black leather of his boots. Looking straight ahead, he edged first his left boot and then his right back about a quarter of an inch.

He couldn't imagine why he was doing this. It was completely dumb— moving his feet so the shadow of the flagpole wouldn't touch his boot. What's more, it was dangerous. If he wasn't careful, he'd gradually edge back from the rank in which he stood, which would make him obviously out of place.

Sooner or later, he'd have to let the shadow cross his boot. It was either that or end up completely out of rank. Just one more minute, he said to himself. I'll keep it off for just one more minute. Again he moved his boots an eighth of an inch or so, one at time, continuing to look straight ahead.

"Novotny," the voice to his right said quietly. He recognized it as belonging to Sergeant Duff.

"Yes, Sergeant," he said, nearly whispering.

"Get back where you belong."

"Yes, Sergeant," he said, moving forward an inch and a half or so.

"And when we're dismissed, I want to see you in my quarters."

"Yes, Sergeant," he said. Seeing the sergeant walk to a position ahead of him, he looked down and saw that his boot tips were in shadow. Damn, he said to himself, partly because of what he saw, but mostly because he realized what a stupid thing he had just done.

Sergeant Duff's room was in the center of the barracks, at the top of the stairs. Novotny walked up the steps slowly and knocked on the door.

"Come in."

"You wanted to see me, Sergeant," he said. The tone of his voice was like that of an errant child approaching an angry father. He stood in front of the desk, not quite at attention, but definitely not at ease.

The sergeant sat at a desk, reading a report. He finished reading a page, closed the folder, and looked at the young soldier.

"Novotny. What in the hell were you trying to do out there?"

"I don't know, Sergeant."

"Do you think this is a good company?"

"Yes, Sergeant."

"Did you want us to win today?"

"Yeah. I really did," Novotny answered.

"Did it occur to you that what you were doing could have cost us points? And that even if we had beaten G Troop on the parade ground, we might not be first because some donkey of a recruit couldn't manage to stay in his rank?"

The sergeant paused momentarily to let the thought sink in. "Did that thought cross your mind?"

"No, Sergeant," he said, shaking his head. "I didn't think about that." Novotny couldn't remember when he had felt more ashamed than he did right now.

"Well, I want you to remember one thing. A company or a squad or a regiment succeeds or fails on the basis of what every person in that unit does. One or two guys screwing off can affect a whole unit. In peacetime, it can mean a unit doesn't win an award it might otherwise have gotten."

The sergeant's voice took on a hard edge and he looked directly at Novotny. "In combat, you're talking about guys' lives. Do you understand?"

"Yes, Sergeant. I won't do anything dumb like that again."

Novotny stood tensely, waiting to be excused and hoping it

would happen soon.

"I'm sure you won't." The sergeant pointed to a chair next to his desk. "Now sit down. There's something else I want to tell you." He pulled a cigarette from a package on the desk, lit it, and pushed the package and the matches toward Novotny. "Help yourself." Novotny did.

"I think you'll make a good soldier, Novotny."

Novotny wasn't sure where this was leading but was pleased that the tone of the conversation had changed. "Thanks, Sergeant."

"But there's one thing you've got to learn." He took a drag on the cigarette and slowly exhaled. "That shadow crossed your boot the day you got here." He looked directly at Novotny, who couldn't look away from the sergeant's eyes. "And you'll never get rid of it. No matter what you do, either in the army or out of here, you'll never be the same. For better or worse—and it can go either way—you've been marked. Moving your boot won't do you a damn bit of good."

Novotny couldn't believe what he was hearing. Two hours ago he was behaving like a kid without knowing why. Now this sergeant, whom he barely knew, was telling him exactly what had gone on in his mind, even though he himself hadn't been aware of it.

"I think you've got me pretty well figured out, Sergeant," he said.

"It's healthy for guys like you not to give in 100 percent to the system. There's nothing wrong with that. But do it in your head. Don't fight it out in the open, unless you really have to. Because you'll almost never win. The system doesn't like to be challenged."

The sergeant smiled slightly. "But the thing that makes the system strong is when guys don't buy every part of it. Because gradually that's what helps make the system change. So keep your independence. But don't waste it on things that don't matter. Save it for those times that make a difference."

The sergeant put out his cigarette, and Novotny did likewise.

"One more thing."

"What's that, Sergeant?"

"You know why G Troop beat us?"

"No."

"Because we've got a handful of trainees who have a hard time knowing left from right. And no matter how well the rest of you perform, these people will cost us points."

Novotny wasn't sure how to respond, so he said nothing.

"One of those low performers is in your cubicle. Do you know who I mean?"

"I think so, Sergeant. You mean Turner?"

"Yes, Turner. I want you to work with him during your free time on Sunday."

Novotny wasn't thrilled with the idea. Sunday was the only day of the week that they had any time off. His silence said what was going on in his mind.

"I know it's an imposition, but I want you to do it. See if you can help him. Otherwise he won't make it. We're about ready to send him home as unfit for service. But if he can learn close order drill, it'll help."

"OK, Sergeant."

"That's all, Novotny."

"Thanks, Sergeant."

Without replying, Duff opened the file folder on his desk and picked up reading where he'd left off a few minutes before.

The convoy of trucks had hauled them down an unpaved road to the far end of the military reservation. Each soldier carried a full field pack and his M1 rifle. All they knew was that they were going to do a "forced march."

"As you know, in armor we generally ride," Sergeant Duff told his assembled platoon. "But there are times when you can't ride. When we've got to act like infantry. That's what we're doing today."

After that brief introduction, the sergeant formed up his platoon into ranks, waited as other platoons passed by, and then ordered his men to march. The road was dusty and brown, and in a matter of minutes, Novotny's shiny black boots were covered with fine, tan powder.

For a while, they'd march in step, as they'd learned to do on the parade ground. Then Sergeant Duff would call "route step," and they could walk to their own stride and pace, as long as the ranks stayed in place.

Ahead were the other platoons from H Company and in front of them, the trainees of G Company. Once on the road, Novotny turned to look behind and saw that the line of troops extended back to a point where the road turned. He guessed that they were I Company, Tank Company, and Howitzer Company. The entire battalion appeared to be on the road.

"OK men, let's cover some ground," the sergeant said, starting to jog. There was a synchronized clanking as the men's canteens, bayonets, gas masks, and other gear flapped against their bodies with each step. The pace they were maintaining wasn't grueling, but there was no doubt it would begin to take its toll on their bodies.

"Slow it down," the sergeant said. "Let's march." The platoon eased to a walk. Once they were stepping in unison, the sergeant began to chant.

"You had a good home but you left," he said, timing it so that the last word was said as their left feet hit the dirt road.

"You're right," the platoon responded as their right feet struck the loose gravel of the road.

"Sound off," the sergeant called.

"One. Two."

"Sound off," he called again.

"Three. Four."

"Cadence count," he intoned.

"One, two, three, four, one, two. Three four!"

Sergeant Duff recited a litany of rhymes, all done with a precise rhythm to which the men marched. His repertoire included tales of women who'd led GIs astray. About long nights with too much whiskey and too little sleep. About living a hard army life with never enough money. About women who would have made good wives but for the fact the men were called away to fight, leaving other men behind to take over their love and enjoy the pleasures of their womanhood.

It's a form of folk poetry, Novotny thought. Someone ought to get this stuff down on paper and publish it.

Mainly, the melancholy rhymes made the time and the miles pass more easily. Sergeant Duff then began what would become Novotny's favorite marching chant, even though it seemed outrageously childish when he really thought about it.

"What's my name?" the sergeant said in time to their steps.

"Your name is Duff," the platoon replied.

"And what are we?"

"We're mighty tough."

"Sound off."

"One. Two."

"Sound off."

"Three. Four."

"Cadence count."

One, two, three, four, one, two. Three four!"

For Novotny, the chanting made him forget about each step and the many steps that were yet to be taken. The rhythm seemed to give the entire group a special kind of energy. All the pieces of this marching machine were moving like the gears and pistons. They apparently still had a long way to go. But there was no question in Novotny's mind that they would make it.

The sergeant then began the part Novotny really liked.

"Where we goin'?" the sergeant shouted to the platoon.

"Around the hill," the men replied in unison.

"Like hell we are. Now where we goin'?" he asked again.

"Over the hill."

"Let 'em hear you," the sergeant shouted. "Where we goin'?"

"Through the hill!" they all shouted together.

With the last response, the platoon let out a cheer that caused men in the platoons ahead of them to turn and look at what had happened.

Sergeant Duff worked his way around the platoon, covering more ground than any of the men. First he'd be in the lead, then at each flank, then at the rear, watching them march. Even though he was probably twice as old as most of the men in the unit, it was obvious that no one was in better shape or had more stamina.

Every hour, right to the minute, he would call the platoon to a halt.

"Take five. Smoke if you got 'em. Conserve your water," he'd say each time.

An ambulance that had been 100 yards or so behind them all morning stopped when they did, seeming more vulture-like than benevolent.

Five minutes later they field-stripped their cigarettes, scattered the remaining tobacco to the wind, and wadded up the paper in a little ball, which was flicked into the weeds. Taking a small drink from his canteen, Novotny took his place in the platoon, and a minute or so later they were on the move again.

The bright summer sun was high now, and the pace had decidedly slowed. They still alternated jogging and walking, but they walked more and jogged less.

Novotny wasn't sure how many miles they had gone, or how many were left. He had also decided not to look at his watch. Seeing how long they'd been at it would make it worse, he decided. He guessed, however, that it had been forty minutes since the last break. Probably fifteen minutes until they'd be able to stretch out again.

He made a mental check of the state of his body. His legs were holding up pretty well, and he didn't seem to be getting any blisters on his feet. That was good news. Other than being incredibly tired, the only thing he could find that was causing him any problem was his heavy M1 rifle. The web sling was cutting into his shoulder, and he could feel the area getting raw and sore. But that was minor compared with other things that could be going wrong.

They passed a platoon that had stopped along the side of the road even though it wasn't time for a break. He wasn't able to see why they'd stopped, but no one from either group spoke. No sense rubbing in whatever might have caused them to pull out.

He looked to his left and smiled at Johnson. "You hangin' in there, Bob?"

"Yup," his friend replied. "No problem."

Turner was just ahead of him, and he was about to ask him how things were going when he noticed that Turner's head was moving slightly from side to side. Not a lot. But enough for Novotny to see it.

Hang in there, Turner, he thought. The idea had just passed through his brain when Turner's right leg crossed in front of his left and he fell in a pile on the gravel road.

"Platoon, halt," Sergeant Duff commanded as he jogged over to Turner, lying unconscious on the dirt. He felt Turner's forehead and lifted open his eyelids. "Split up his gear," the sergeant ordered.

Novotny took Turner's rifle and slung it over his other shoulder. Turner's web belt was unhooked and taken by Stein. Johnson undid Turner's pack and started handing gear to other men who had gathered around. One man picked up Turner's steel helmet, which had rolled off to the side of the road.

"Splash some water on that man," Sergeant Duff ordered, and in an instant someone was rubbing a handful of water on Turner's face. A minute or two later, Turner came to, groggy and disoriented. One of the medics in the ambulance—which had stopped just behind them—started walking toward them, but Sergeant Duff shook his head and the medic turned around and went back to his vehicle.

The sergeant looked at the ambulance for a moment and then pointed to two men from the platoon. "Pass out some of your gear to others and carry this man," he said. "I'll have you spelled off in fifteen minutes. Let's go."

The two men handed their packs and weapons to men standing nearby and lifted the semiconscious Turner to his feet. Each taking an arm around their necks, they began half carrying, half dragging him slowly down the road, surrounded by the rest of the platoon.

When platoons behind them bunched up because of their slow pace, Sergeant Duff waved them past. After stretching out for a few minutes during the next break, Turner was able to walk more and more on his own. Even though their pace was slow, he moved pretty much under his own power.

Finally, as they came around a bend in the road, they saw a cluster of trucks parked a half mile ahead of them. They had just about made it. Nearly all the rest of the troops had already headed back to the barracks when Sergeant Duff's platoon finally arrived at the crossroads where they had begun, followed by the ever-present ambulance.

Once there, the platoon let out a cheer nearly in unison. Some whistled and shouted, and several men came over to Turner, patting him on the back and shaking his hand.

Sergeant Duff went to Turner and walked him over to the ambulance. The two medics helped him into the back and closed the door marked with a large red cross on a white square.

Parked at the intersection were trucks that would take the weary, sweat soaked, and sore soldiers back to their barracks. Behind the trucks a jeep was parked with Lieutenant Wilson sitting in the right front seat. As the men boarded the trucks, Sergeant Duff walked to the jeep and saluted the officer. Novotny watched the two men talk. They saluted again, and Sergeant Duff came back to the trucks and climbed in the front seat of the lead vehicle.

Lieutenant Wilson's jeep led the convoy of trucks back to the barracks. Although he couldn't see it, Novotny thought about the fact that somewhere ahead of them on the gravel road was the ambulance with Turner inside. He seemed to be all right at the end of the march. He hoped there wasn't anything really wrong.

At least he had made it, and that was important.

The door was simply labeled "platoon sergeant," and normally, as the men had learned, entering it meant trouble. The only time Novotny had ever been here was after the dumb shadow episode.

This time, Novotny, Johnson, and Morris were there on their own. Even so, they were all a little anxious. Johnson knocked, and they heard a voice from inside say, "Come in."

The three entered the small, neatly kept room and stood in front of Sergeant Duff's desk. He was sitting on an olive-drab chair, reading a tan-covered army training manual open on the desk.

"Yes, men. What is it?" he said, closing the book.

"We just wanted to tell you we're sorry about what happened, Sergeant," Novotny said awkwardly.

"Yeah," Johnson added. "We respect Lieutenant Wilson and all that. But we didn't think he needed to do what he did."

The sergeant sat there, his hands folded on top of the manual, looking at the men and saying nothing.

"We jus' wanted to know if we could do somethin'," Morris said.

The sergeant looked at the men and nodded. "I appreciate your coming to say that," he said, obviously touched by the presence of the three young soldiers.

He sat straight, and said in a cool, detached voice, "The lieutenant did what he had to do. Don't ever think anything else. I made a decision about Turner and it turned out OK." He added emphatically, "But if I had made a mistake about his condition, it could have been a real problem. I violated a regulation and it cost me a stripe. It's as simple as that. In time, I'll earn it back."

From the sound of his voice, he was ready for that to be the end of the conversation. But the three men had more on their minds.

"I'm not trying to be rude or anything, Sergeant, but why did you do it?" Novotny asked tentatively. "How come you didn't have the medics take Turner in? The ambulance was right there."

The sergeant looked directly at the trainees, his brow furrowing and his eyes turning hard. "When I was in Korea, coming down from the Chosin reservoir, we left a lot of guys behind. Guys I knew. Buddies of mine. They're all dead."

"You mean they were intentionally left behind?" Johnson asked, a touch of anger in his voice.

"Sometimes. Sometimes officers and NCOs would order men to leave the wounded and sick behind because they knew it would slow them down. We were runnin' like hell when the Chinese came across the Yalu."

"You made it OK, though. Right, Sergeant?" Morris said, sounding a little like a kid talking about his favorite comic-book character.

"I got hit pretty good in the leg. Small-arms fire."

"What happened?" Johnson asked.

"My battalion commander saw me fall. He didn't know me. I was just another GI in one of his companies. But he came back and got me. The gooks were coming fast, and it was about ten below, but he came back anyway. Carried me about a mile. He saved my life."

"Oh, man," Novotny said half under his breath. It was probably only five or six years ago.

"I decided I'd never leave a man behind if it was in my power to avoid it," the sergeant said matter-of-factly. "I want to teach everyone I can to do the same thing."

The sergeant nodded. "But this time, with Turner, I didn't use good judgment. The lieutenant was right in taking a stripe."

Novotny swallowed hard. Seeing the sergeant as a vulnerable human being rather than an invincible, cool, and detached warrior touched him. "Would you talk to Turner, though?" he asked. "He feels pretty rotten about it. He thinks it's his fault. And he takes that kind of thing pretty seriously."

"Sure, I'll talk to him. Is he all right now?"

"He's taking it easy. But he's fine," Johnson said.

"Tell him to come in and see me tomorrow. And tell him not to worry. It wasn't his fault." A thought obviously flashed across his mind and he looked at Novotny. "Are you working with him on drill?"

"Yeah. I do on Sunday afternoons."

"Good. I'd like to see him make it. He's a decent kid, and at least he's trying."

The men were walking toward the door when Novotny turned and said, "Sounds like that officer in Korea was quite a guy."

"He is that," the sergeant said. "He's our CO. He was a major back then. Got a bronze star for it. He's a hell of a soldier."

They left the room and Morris said, "He's a hell of a guy himself."

"Sure is," Novotny replied, but his mind was elsewhere, trying to sort out the complex rights and wrongs of being in the army.

The parade ground looked like a football field with no line markers or goalposts. At one end were rows of bleachers where spectators could watch the units drill and parade. Near the bleachers was the flagpole that had cast the

Ierv Hamilton, Jr.

shadow Novotny had tried so childishly to avoid.

Two lone figures wearing fatigues stood at the center of the field, strangely out of scale in this area designed to accommodate hundreds of marching troops. It was about two in the afternoon on Sunday, and no one else was in sight.

Turner was standing at parade rest, his feet slightly apart and his hands interlocked behind his back. Novotny walked around, checking the position of every part of Turner's slender body.

"You're looking good," he said. "Now let's get back to drill." He took a position beside the young GI and stood at attention. "Ten . . . hut." Turner brought his boots together and put his hands to his sides, awkwardly looking straight ahead.

"Forward . . . march." Turner hesitated for a moment and then began to walk.

"Hut . . . hut . . . hut . . . hut," Novotny said quietly, marching in step next to Turner. "By the left flank . . . march." Turner turned to the left and continued marching.

Every so often, Novotny would call a halt and have him review his execution of a particular movement and then begin marching again. About three o'clock, Novotny called Turner to attention.

"Good work, Private Turner," he said with an exaggerated voice of authority. "Dis . . . missed."

The two men walked to the nearby bleachers and sat down.

"I appreciate you workin' with me," Turner said softly. He looked down at the worn wood of the bleachers. "Are you doin' it because you were ordered to?"

"I'm doing this because I want to." It would have been more truthful to

90

say that Sergeant Duff had also asked him to help Turner. But Novotny didn't feel it was dishonest to acknowledge just the first part of the question. The fact was that he felt sorry for this kid and the way he was struggling to make it through training. And he really did want to help him.

Novotny wasn't sure where to take the conversation from there. On one hand, he felt as though he should drop the whole subject. But at the same time, he felt an obligation to say something.

"Do you really want to be a soldier?" he asked.

"I don't have any choice," Turner said. "I got drafted."

"You could probably get out if you really want to," Novotny said, making an effort to introduce the idea casually and with minimal drama.

"What do you mean? Go AWOL?"

"No. You could ask for a discharge by saying you're just not cut out to be a soldier."

Turner continued looking down at the splits and cracks in the wood of the bleachers. "Is that a dishonorable discharge?"

"The way I understand it, it's just some kind of special discharge. A guy in Company G got out a couple of days ago. Some guys just aren't natural GIs. The army realizes that."

Turner looked at Novotny and said almost inaudibly, "Do you think I'm one of those guys?"

"No. You're doing a lot better at drill. You're hanging in there with PT. Seems like you're following the classes all right."

"So why did you bring up getting out?"

"I just thought you ought to know it's a possibility." Novotny now wished he had never raised the subject. "Let's head over to the PX. We still have some time to goof off."

As they approached the PX, Turner stopped, looked down, and said, "If I got out on some kind of unfit discharge, my father'd think it was the funniest thing in the world."

"You mean he'd be glad you beat the draft?"

Turner shook his head. "Uh uh. When I went in, he told me I wouldn't make it. He'd laugh his head off if I walked in the house and said I'd been kicked out of the army." As he spoke, he was practically in tears.

Novotny couldn't imagine what was going through Turner's head right now. He had no idea what kinds of anger or fear or whatever was occupying his brain. All he knew was that he'd opened up something very intense and personal in this kid's mind. And because he had done so, he had to do something to set it right.

"Well, as far as I can see, then, you'll just have to make it." Novotny patted Turner's slender shoulder and they started walking into the PX. "You can do it. We're just about done with basic. You'll get some advanced training, and then we'll be off for Germany. You'll do fine."

The group of about a dozen men sat drinking beer at the same cramped PX tables they'd favored during the past eight weeks. They took these particular tables partly by habit, and partly by territorial imperative. It was the place they'd staked out almost from their first day at Fort Meade, just as other men had taken other corners of the room.

They'd had little time to think about what, in addition to just being a soldier, they'd be doing for the next two or three years. But today they had gotten confirmation of their assignments.

Most of their platoon would train to be cavalry scouts. They were the ones who would actually be patrolling the Czech–German border. A few were being sent to Fort Knox to become drivers of tanks and armored personnel carriers. And some would be leaving H Company.

"How 'bout you, Johnson?" someone asked from the end of the table.

"They've got me going to intelligence school. I'll be assigned to regimental S-2." He looked around the table and smiled. "I'll be putting together reports about what you guys see on the border to try and make some sense out of all that BS you'll be radioing in."

"I'm goin' to regiment too," Morris volunteered. "They're sending me to weapons school and I'm gonna be in the security platoon." He beamed and took a drink of his beer.

Johnson added, "The colonel's not dumb. He wants good men in that platoon. Men like Morris here." He laughed as he ruffled Morris's short, kinky black hair.

"Damn right," Morris agreed. "How 'bout you, Novo?"

"I already speak Czech, and they've got me going to a crash course in German. I'm going to be in operations, and be an interpreter for the headquarters sections."

Johnson looked across the table at Turner. "What about you, what's your assignment?"

"I'm gonna be with you and Novo and Morris," he said in his soft, gentle voice. "I'm goin' to mechanic's school. Guess it's because I pumped gas back home. But I'm glad about it. Then I'm going to the regimental motor pool." He smiled slightly and looked at Novotny. "I'm glad I'm going with you guys."

"I'm glad you'll be with us," Novotny replied. Then looking at the rest of the men, he added, "I'm sorry we're not all gonna be together. But you won't be far from Nurnberg, where we'll be. We'll be seeing you."

They didn't say much after that. Mainly they sat, talked, drank beer, and relished the excitement of what was ahead.

The company was broken into two-man teams to take on the "assault course." At first, Johnson and Novotny had paired up, but Novotny swapped so he could do it with Turner. It was a clear afternoon, a good day to be outside instead of sitting in a classroom. The men stood around the staging area, waiting their turn and watching as each team went through the drill.

"Next team," the training sergeant shouted.

Novotny swatted Turner gently on the butt. "Let's go."

"You men understand the course?"

"Yes, Sergeant," Novotny said for both of them.

The sergeant reached into a box and pulled out two clips of .30-caliber ammunition. "This is a live ammo drill, so be careful." Handing a clip to each of the men, he ordered, "Lock and load."

The men clicked the safety lever on their M1s to prevent accidental firing and inserted the ammunition into the heavy, walnut-stocked rifles.

"Keep the butt tight against your shoulder when you fire," Novotny half whispered to Turner. "And stay to my left."

"You men ready?"

"Yes, Sergeant," Novotny said, looking over at Turner and winking.

"Prepare to assault." He paused for just a moment, and the men tensed, waiting for the next command. "Assault!"

Novotny carried his rifle at the ready, jumped over the log that marked the start of the course, and jogged straight ahead, scanning the scrubby, weed-covered field as he ran. He looked over his shoulder and saw that Turner was lagging behind. "Come on," Novotny shouted. "Keep up with me."

To his right, a life-sized figure popped up, kneeling and aiming a rifle at the two men. "Hit the dirt!" Novotny shouted as he fell forward, breaking the momentum with the butt of his rifle. Turner did the same.

He clicked off the safety, sighted on the figure, and squeezed off two rounds, feeling the M1 stock punch him in the shoulder as it recoiled. The figure fell backward.

"Let's go," he hollered. "And next time, fire."

Weapons ready, they half jogged and half ran across the nearly knee-high grass and scrub brush of the field. To Novotny's left another figure popped up without notice. "On the dirt," Novotny shouted, falling and getting his rifle ready to fire. "You get this one."

Nothing happened. "Get it, Turner." Still nothing.

Novotny fired three rounds and the figure tipped backward and out of sight. Again the men quickly got up and rushed forward.

Angrily, Novotny, now gasping for breath, shouted, "We've got a deal, remember? You have to at least try, damn it."

Dead ahead of them, a third figure rose as if taking aim at the two men. Both fell onto the ground. Novotny felt a rock, hidden in the grass, smack into his ribs, sending a sharp pain through his left side.

He couldn't see Turner in the weeds twenty or so feet away from him. But before he could position himself more comfortably, he heard the sound of two rounds from Turner's rifle. He sighted on the figure and emptied his clip, which ejected from the chamber with a metallic clang. The figure disappeared into the tall grass.

The third figure was the last, and Turner still had ammo in his weapon. Novotny didn't want him to fire accidentally. "Set your safety," Novotny shouted as he rubbed the left side of his body to see if he'd really hurt himself.

No big deal, he decided. Just a bruise.

"Let's finish it," he shouted, and the two men, now winded and tired, got up and ran across the open field toward a fallen tree. Tucked against the trunk, they rested for a few seconds. "You got him, Turner. You got the last one. Good shooting."

Just ahead of them was a crude structure. You wouldn't really call it a house. It was more like a beat-up shack with weathered wood siding, a window with no glass, and an entry with no door.

"Fix bayonets," an amplified voice boomed across the field. Novotny pulled the long, knife-like attachment for his rifle from the sheath on his hip and looked at the mean gray steel and the sharp point. Sliding the handle over the end of the barrel, he made certain the latch had securely locked and then looked over at Turner.

"Got it?"

"Yeah," Turner said.

"You do it first."

Turner reached into an olive-drab case slung over his shoulder and pulled out a practice fragmentation grenade. It looked exactly like the real thing, except it was painted blue instead of olive drab. Novotny got his out at the same time.

"Pull the pin and throw it," he said.

Turner put his finger in the metal ring, pulled the pin, and lobbed the projectile toward the shack. It hit the wall to the right of the window, dropped to the ground, and detonated, sounding like a loud Fourth of July firecracker.

"Close," Novotny said, throwing his grenade in the stiff-armed way they had been taught. It went through the window and a few seconds later exploded.

"Let's go, Turner." Novotny stood, climbed over the tree trunk, and charged for the open door of the structure, weapon at the ready; the bright metal of the bayonet gleaming in the sunlight. Turner was a few steps behind him. Novotny was glad he'd told him to put the safety on his rifle. With ammo in the chamber, he would have worried about Turner falling or stumbling and sending a round his way.

"Yaaaaaaaaah!" he shouted as he ran into the building. Jabbing his bayonet into invisible defenders, he hollered, "Take that, you commie scum. Death to the reds."

Turner stood silently in a corner of the dark room, watching and showing no interest in either participating or leaving. He just stood there, almost as if nothing was happening.

Taking a deep breath, Novotny said, "That's it. Nothing left but a bunch of Russian corpses. Let's get out of here."

The loudspeaker blared once again, echoing off the wooded areas that lined the course. "Good job, men," the anonymous voice said. "Now clear the course, please. Next team, move up."

A path had been cut through the trees heading back to the staging area. It was far enough from the line of fire for the course to be safe, unless someone really screwed up and fired toward the trees.

Stopping for a moment, Novotny pushed the latch on the handle of his bayonet and slid it off the rifle barrel, holding it up to study its lethal shape. "Nasty-looking thing, isn't it?"

After watching Novotny slide it carefully into the sheath secured to his web cartridge belt, Turner replaced his own bayonet into its sheath.

As they walked back, Novotny patted Turner on the back. "You did just fine."

Turner said nothing for a minute or so. Then, with the quiet hesitation that seemed to characterize almost everything he said, he murmured, "If we ever get in combat, I could never do that."

Novotny didn't say anything in reply as they walked slowly along the tree-lined path. Then, sounding more like Turner than himself, he said, "I'm not sure I could either."

Novotny and about twenty other men were herded into an area defined by barbed wire, next to a large olive-drab tent. They wore full combat gear and carried their M1 rifles. It seemed a strange way to conduct training, having a bunch of guys just milling around instead of the usual regimentation. But everything so far had been done with such careful organization that Novotny had no doubt there was a point to it, even though it made little sense.

The subject of the last class just before lunch was the Geneva Conventions and the Military Code of Conduct.

From the first day at Fort Leonard Wood, Novotny had seen posters illustrating the Code of Conduct displayed on the walls of barracks and classrooms. In one picture, a soldier without a weapon or a helmet was hiding beside a log, watching a couple of enemy soldiers walk by.

One poster said, "If I am captured, I will continue to resist by all means possible."

In the morning class, the instructor said it had become part of training a couple of years ago, after the Korean War. There were a lot of stories about guys who were captured by the North Koreans and Communist Chinese, tortured, and psychologically "brainwashed," as the press liked to call it.

Novotny remembered one newspaper article that said some guys were so depressed by the process that they totally gave up. There were cases, it said, where GIs just sat in a corner of their cell and died—not from the mistreatment, but because they just couldn't handle it anymore and packed it in.

The message of the class this morning had been clear: Don't give up. Resist in every way you can.

He was glad that his high school friends Eddie and Denny hadn't been captured and put through that. But then, he let himself think sadly, he'd rather Denny had been mistreated as a prisoner and returned home alive than blown apart by a mine.

The rest of the morning's class dealt with the third Geneva Convention, an international meeting where countries met to discuss the treatment of POWs. You can't abuse them, the diplomats had agreed. They then signed a document to formalize their position.

He looked at the men around him, all standing there wondering what was going to happen. Unlike the training they'd had thus far, they were from different companies throughout the regiment. He looked around and realized he didn't know any of them and that there were only a few that he even recalled seeing before. He had no idea where the rest of his platoon was.

They'd been told to stand, not sit. And they weren't allowed to talk or smoke. For about half an hour they stood there, hot and increasingly frustrated.

"Damn waste of time," one soldier whispered to Novotny.

"Yeah," he answered softly without turning to see who was talking.

Finally, a soldier in combat fatigues came into the compound. He had no nametag, and the three stripes on his sleeve were sewn on upside down, the way the British do it. He walked through the group of standing men, looking them over as if he were searching for someone in particular.

"You," he said to one soldier, pointing to the tent. "Over there." The GI started walking toward it. After selecting four others, he walked right past Novotny, then turned around abruptly and pointed at him. "You. There," he ordered, gesturing toward the tent.

This is really strange, Novotny thought, realizing that instead of feeling bored and frustrated, he was now anxious. That, obviously, was what they wanted to happen. His rifle slung over his shoulder, he stepped into the dark confines of the tent, permeated by the heavy, acrid smell of oiled canvas. Looking around, he tried to get used to the dim light and figure out what was going on. Before he could see anything, a hand grabbed him by the arm and shoved him into an area defined by heavy pieces of olive drab (OD) canvas hanging from wooden frames and serving as walls.

A man sat at a folding desk under a small lamp hanging from the roof of the tent. He wore two silver triangles on each collar. It was not an insignia the U.S. Army used, but it had the look of an officers' rank. There was no other identification. Novotny estimated he was in his late thirties.

"Stand at attention," the officer—or whatever rank he was—said without looking up from the file folder open in front of him. Novotny did so, his M1 held smartly to his right, the butt on the dirt floor.

"Hold your rifle over your head."

"I'm sorry," Novotny said, thinking he had misunderstood.

"I ordered you to hold your rifle over your head," he said.

Don't say anything else, Novotny reminded himself. Just do as you're told. He lifted the nine-pound rifle and held it over his head with both hands. In the few words that had been spoken, he had heard an accent in the man's voice, but he wasn't sure what it was.

The man said nothing and didn't look at him. Jesus, he thought, let's get this over with. He didn't know how many minutes it took for the blood to drain from his arms, but it wasn't many. He could actually feel it happening, and at the same time, the rifle began to get heavier and heavier. Worst of all, he could sense himself having trouble keeping his balance with his feet so close together. He did his best to keep his body rigidly and properly at attention.

"Your name?" the man asked, without looking at him.

"Joseph Novotny, sir." He decided to play it safe even though he didn't know if this guy was an NCO or an officer, or for that matter, whether he was even in the army.

The interrogator wrote something on a yellow pad. "Your rank?"

"Private. United States Army."

Again, the interrogator made a note. "Your serial number?"

"USA55625067."

Novotny could see that he was writing down the number. "Your unit?

He swallowed hard, his mouth sticky and dry. It seemed particularly dry as he stood there, not answering the last question.

In accented English, he repeated, "I asked you what unit you belong to, soldier."

"Sir, under the terms of the Geneva Convention, I'm required to tell you only my name, rank, and serial number."

He was really uncomfortable now. His arms ached, he was thirsty, and he was really starting to feel increasingly unsteady.

"Let me ask you again, Novotny. What unit are you with?" He was certain now. The accent was Slavic. Maybe Czech or Slovak. But possibly Polish or Ukrainian.

"My name is Joseph Novotny. I'm a private in the U.S. Army. My serial number is USA55625067." He added. "Sir."

For what seemed like an hour, but was only a few minutes, the man at the desk said nothing and continued to rummage through papers on his desk. Novotny's arms really ached now. In the class this morning the instructor had said that the best way to deal with torture was to focus your mind completely on something else. This wasn't what you could really call torture, but he decided to try the technique while he waited for this stupid exercise to end.

In his mind, he started at the end of the block where his parents lived and thought about each house in turn, trying to conjure up as many details as possible. The sunporch on the house next door. The flowers in the yard of their neighbors on the other side. The wonderful old elm tree in front of the house three doors down.

"Put down your rifle," the man ordered without warning. Novotny was glad to remove what now seemed to be a 100-pound weight from over his head. "Stand at ease."

Novotny relaxed, took a deep breath, and spread his legs to get a more stable stance, hoping this was the end of it.

"You handled that very well," the man said with a slight smile. "Some of your fellow recruits apparently paid little attention to the class about the Geneva Convention this morning."

"Thank you, sir.

"You are of a Czech family?"

"Yes, sir. I was born here. But my mother was born there. My father's parents were from Prague."

The man nodded. "You probably know from my accent that I am a Slav."

"Yes, sir. I thought so." He wanted to ask where he was from, but decided not to.

"I will say you handled the questions very well." He opened the file folder, leafed through the papers, and pulled out a form. "This is a report for your personnel file, and I will comment about your performance under these—how would you say it—ah, anxious circumstances. It may help you get a better assignment when you finish basic training."

He took a pen from his pocket and began filling in the lines.

"Novotny," he said, writing. "You said Joseph?"

"Yes, sir."

"Private. U.S. Army. Serial number again, please."

"USA55625067"

"Which company?"

"H Troop, sir."

"H Troop," the man said as he wrote. "That's Captain Melton's troop, isn't it? Jim Melton?"

"No, sir. The CO is Lieutenant Wilson."

Neatly and carefully, the man wrote on one of the blank lines. Then, without warning, he wadded the paper up and threw it angrily into a black metal wastebasket in the corner of the tent.

The man stood up abruptly, nearly causing his chair to fall over, and glared at Novotny. "Soldier, what have you been trained to say?"

In an instant, Novotny understood very clearly what had just happened. He was mad at himself for not being more careful. At the same time, he was angry at having been tricked.

"My name, rank, and serial number, sir," he answered, his anger putting a hard edge to his voice.

"Then why did give me not only your unit, but the name of your CO and information about your family?"

"From what you said, I thought we were finished," he shot back. He tried to keep from saying the next sentence but let it out anyway. "I didn't know you were going to trick me into saying something I shouldn't tell you."

"So, Private Novotny, you are angry because you feel I tricked you." He sat back in his chair, still glaring at the trainee standing in front of him. "Let me tell you something, soldier. Trickery is the essence of interrogation. And every small piece of information is useful. Even if it seems obvious that they know this information, they will use that information against you, against your friends, and against other prisoners."

The man stood up, slowly this time, and walked around the small enclosure. He spoke softly, but with an alarmingly hard edge to his voice. "They will try to get these facts from you every way possible. By treating you kindly. By appealing to your fears. By threatening to harm you."

He paused and looked straight at Novotny. "They may, in fact, cause you harm, regardless of what the Geneva Convention says. They may starve you. They may beat you. They may even cause you pain in the most sensitive and personal parts of your body."

He paused and looked directly at Novotny. "It is also possible they will kill you. Or kill a close friend, saying you will be next if you don't answer their questions."

Novotny listened and, in his mind, illustrated the words with pictures he'd seen as a boy in *Life* magazine and the newsreels. He imagined the photos of the Malmedy massacre. The bodies of GIs, their hands tied behind their backs, half buried in the snow. He wondered if the Nazis had asked these men about their units.

"Remember this. Tell them one small fact and they will want more. Once you begin, you will never be able to give them enough. Now, what information are you required to provide under the terms of the Geneva Convention?"

"My name, rank, and serial number, sir."

"Dismissed." Novotny turned and left the enclosure.

The trucks that would take them back to the barracks were lined up about a quarter of a mile from the compound. Novotny walked slowly toward them, his M1 slung over his shoulder, wondering if all the men going through this exercise would have the same experience. How many, he asked himself, would be dumb enough to fall for the trap the way he had?

There had been a curious quality in the way the man spoke. There was almost no emotion, except for the real or dramatized anger. But the man spoke about interrogation with such conviction that Novotny wondered if maybe he had experienced the terrible things he had described.

He estimated that the man must have been twenty-five or so during the war. Maybe the Nazis had interrogated him. But maybe, on the other hand, he had asked the questions. Maybe he was in the brutally efficient Russian NKVD. Either way, he'd know firsthand how the process worked.

He could imagine an SS officer in the war doing such things. And he could see some North Korean or Communist Chinese interrogator using brutality to get a couple of facts. But would an East German do that today, if the Communists invaded? Probably. There were bound to be some SS guys in the East German army. Would a Russian do them? Maybe.

Would a Czech officer or soldier do those things? That was hard to imagine, though he wasn't sure why he thought so. Somehow the Czechs seemed immune to that kind of behavior.

The big question was, would an American soldier do that? You've got two Russian privates standing there, tired, dry-throated like he was, and scared as hell. You know they can tell you things that can save the lives of guys in your unit. They give you only their name, rank, and serial number. Nothing else. You tell them that you're going to kill them if they don't tell you what you need to know.

One says, anxiously, that the Geneva Convention prohibits such treatment of a prisoner. One of your guys nods in agreement, then pulls a .45 and puts a round through the head of one of the Russian soldiers. The other guy is scared as hell and tells you what you want to know. Then, given the fact that you've violated the Geneva Convention by killing his buddy, one of your guys shoots the second one. Who would know?

You do it to save the lives of your guys. In the process, it probably means it'll also cost the other guys more lives, which is an added bonus, given the fact that this is a game of numbers.

It costs two of theirs to save how many of your guys. Twenty? Thirty? More? Not a bad deal, Novotny thought.

Besides, if these two Russian GIs hadn't been shot standing in front of your guys, they could just as easily have been shot running across a field or shredded into little pieces by an artillery shell, with nothing but the names on the inside of their boots to let anyone know who they were. If the Russians do that, the way we do.

So what the hell difference would it make? It's a matter of luck. The result is exactly the same. Except that twenty or thirty of our guys—maybe including me—might not get killed.

Novotny stopped and looked down the slope at the large tent and the barbed-wire compound still full of recruits standing outside, all of them puzzled, frustrated, and wondering what was going on.

"What's happening to my brain?" he asked himself. "How can I be thinking this stuff? Two days ago, I wasn't sure whether or not I could shoot an enemy in an assault or run a bayonet into his gut. Today, I'm thinking that it may not be totally wrong to murder a couple of guys in order to get some facts."

He shook his head and continued on toward the trucks. I have to sort this out, he told himself. Somehow, I have to step back and figure out what the hell I really believe about this stuff.

This is drill. Practice. But the iron curtain is real. I could end up as a POW. Or I could have a couple of their guys as prisoners. I have to know what to do in either case.

The men of the second platoon sat on the dirt, their M1s cradled in their laps. They wore full combat gear, their web belts laden with a canteen, a first-aid packet, a bayonet, and ammo pouches. Strapped over their shoulders was an awkward and uncomfortable olive-drab case containing a gas mask. It was hot and sunny, and most had taken off their steel helmets.

"Last week, we did a two-man assault drill," Sergeant Duff said. "Today, we'll do it company strength, so you can practice the movements in a larger group."

The exercise was pretty simple. They'd be issued blank ammunition, and when ordered to assault, they would run across a field about fifty yards long. At the far side of the field was a line of logs, where they'd wait for the next command.

The logs were at the base of a hill that Novotny estimated to be about 30 degrees in slope and maybe 100 yards to the top. Dug in at the crest was G Company, which would provide simulated defensive fire.

When the command was given, they'd leave the shelter of the logs and attack toward the top of the hill. In each platoon, two of the squads would provide covering fire for the third squad, which would move up. The process would be repeated over and over until the entire company made its way up the hill.

In actual combat, they would have fixed their bayonets and fought the defenders hand to hand. Today, it was just a matter of getting to the crest of the hill. Looking at the hill, Novotny was glad that they'd had such intense PT. Charging up that steep slope, with all the gear they carried, would take a lot out of them.

"There's only one way to win a fight," the sergeant said. "And that's offense. Good defense will keep you from getting beaten. But in the end, you have to take ground to win."

The men were given four clips of ammo, which they slipped into the pouches attached to their waists. They adjusted their gear to make sure everything was properly secured, and then lined up, kneeling and waiting for the command.

"Commence assault," the booming voice said over the PA system.

Novotny looked at Johnson a few feet to his left and gave him a thumbs-up. "Guess we might as well start this thing." The two men ran, rifles at the ready, moving at a quick but comfortable pace. Their gas masks and the other appendages attached to their bodies flopped with each step.

At the logs, the men lay down on the grass, breathing hard and waiting for the next command. Novotny looked up the hill and spotted the round shapes of helmets, barely visible at the ridgeline.

They waited anxiously for the next command.

"I wonder what's happening," Johnson said.

Novotny shrugged. "Beats me. But we should've been out of here by now."

The sound of an aircraft engine caught his attention, and he turned to see where it was coming from. Just over the trees to their right was an olive-drab, single-engine airplane. It was flying perpendicular to their route up the hill, and as it got closer, Novotny saw that a door on the left side of the fuselage was open.

Small, dark objects were falling from the plane as it passed in front of them. As the objects hit the ground, clouds of white smoke formed and were blown toward H Company by a downhill breeze.

"Gas! Gas! Gas!" someone shouted. Novotny repeated the cry as he struggled to unfasten the snap on his gas-mask pack. Once it was open, he knocked off his steel helmet and slid the mask over his face. As they'd been trained to do, he blew hard once it was on and then adjusted the rubber mask to make a seal around his face.

Although he'd responded quickly, the air inside the mask burned his eyes and his lungs. He knew it was a lot better than breathing the smoky air around him. But it was still uncomfortable.

The plane circled and made a second pass, dropping more gas canisters. There was nothing to do but wait until the air was breathable, so Novotny closed his eyes tightly, trying to get rid of the stinging, then opened them to see what was happening.

He watched the plane pass in front of him and tried to place an experience in time. His father hadn't been drafted yet, so it must have been 1943. He would have been eight. They still lived in Chicago, and his teacher had said that the Civil Defense people needed runners to carry messages. If anyone was interested, she had forms that could be taken home for parents to sign.

Novotny remembered raising his hand and taking the form home to his mother and father. His mother nodded approvingly as she wrote her name, saying she thought it was good that children could help in the war effort.

About two weeks later, his teacher gave him a slip of paper telling him to report to a nearby apartment building at two o'clock on Saturday. He showed it to his mother, who again nodded approval.

"Don't forget now, Joseph," she said.

"I won't, Mom."

He was reading a sign on the entrance to the apartment building when a man wearing a Civil Defense helmet approached.

"Need help?" the man asked.

"I'm a runner and I'm supposed to be here today," Novotny replied.

"Good. Come with me, son," the kindly man replied.

On the rooftop was a group of people with white helmets and binoculars. Not very much was happening, except that the people kept looking up into the sky. He was instructed to stand by until he was needed. He sat on a metal chair and looked up in the direction the binoculars were pointed.

"Here they come," one of the men said excitedly, pointing toward the northwest. They all trained their binoculars upward, and Novotny could clearly see the planes with his naked eye. There must have been about ten of them, single-engine and painted olive drab. As they flew over, he saw that objects were falling slowly from the planes.

Several landed on the rooftop where they stood, and he ran over and picked one up. It was a small piece of ordinary cork with a red crepe-paper streamer about a foot long attached to it. He walked over to the men and handed it to one who was holding a clipboard and hastily making notes.

"Thanks, young man. We'll need you in a few minutes."

Novotny watched the planes grow smaller and smaller, leaving a trail of crepe paper and cork behind them.

"OK," the man who had met him downstairs said to Novotny, handing him an envelope. "We need you to take this report to the Kenwood School gymnasium right away. You know where that is, right?"

"Uh huh," Novotny replied. "That's where I go." He was just about to head down the stairs when he asked, "What's this all about?"

"Oh, I should have told you," the man said apologetically. "This is an air raid drill. See this?" he asked, holding up a red-tagged cork like the one Novotny had picked up. "It's a pretend incendiary bomb. We're working out how we'd put out the fires and take care of the people who were hurt if there was a real air raid." He patted Novotny gently on the shoulder. "Now, you'd better get going, because they need this report at the school as soon as possible."

"OK," Novotny said. "I'll run all the way."

Stopping to look both ways before crossing the streets, he ran the three blocks to the school as fast as he could. Another man in a white Civil Defense helmet took the envelope from him and began writing on a clipboard. "Thanks, son. You've been a big help," he said without looking up.

"You're welcome," he said politely, and then added, "Do you think the enemy could actually bomb us?"

The man stopped writing his report and looked at the boy standing in front of him. "We hope not," he said. "But if they do, we want to be ready. Thanks again, son."

Novotny nodded in reply and quickly walked home.

"Are you finished?" his mother asked.

"Uh huh," he said.

"How was it?"

"It was OK. I carried a message from the apartment building to school. The people were really nice and thanked me." He stood quietly for a moment and then asked, "Is it OK if I go to my room and read for a few minutes?"

"Of course," his mother said, motioning him over to her, giving him a hug, and kissing the top of his head.

In his room, he climbed onto his bed and curled up into as tight a ball as he could make his little body. He saw in his mind's eye the corks with their colored tails falling from the planes. He thought about what would have happened if they had been real.

He brought up the pictures of burning apartment buildings, like the ones on his block but somewhere in Europe. Buildings in some place he'd never heard of before. He saw the pictures of firemen shooting streams of water into the structures, hopelessly trying to put out the blazes. And he saw the photos of dead people lying on the street in front of piles of brick and broken wood.

He opened his eyes wide to get rid of the pictures. But even with his eyes open, they didn't go away. He started sobbing. Not crying—there weren't any tears. Just sobbing. Hoping his mother wouldn't hear him, he put his pillow over his head, even though that made everything dark and the pictures more vivid.

The acrid smoke had been blown away. Novotny saw other men tentatively taking off their gas masks, so he did the same. There was a lingering sting in the air. But it wasn't bad.

Minutes later, a voice roared over the PA system, "Lock and load." Novotny set the safety on his M1 and carefully inserted a clip into his rifle.

Sergeant Duff shouted, "Second squad will move out first. First and third squads cover."

Novotny turned to Johnson and smiled.

"Shades of San Juan Hill," his friend quipped.

"Where's Teddy?" Novotny answered. Before Johnson could say anything, the anonymous voice over the PA system ordered, "Commence assault."

Novotny stood up, jumped over the log, and began running up the hill. From his left and right came the sharp sound of close-in gunfire from the other two squads in his platoon. As he ran, he began hearing the muffled sounds of fire aimed toward him by the G Company troops at the top of the hill. Even though it seemed a little silly—given the fact that everyone was shooting blanks—he zigzagged as he ran, pretending to make himself a more difficult target for whoever was sighting on him from the crest of the hill.

His legs were tired as they pumped up the slope, his breath was coming fast and hard, and he felt his heart pounding from the heat and the exertion. As soon as he'd run the specified distance, he fell to the ground and assumed the prone firing position: legs at an angle from his torso, the butt of his rifle hard against his right shoulder. Taking the safety off his trigger, he sighted on the shape of a helmet on the ridgeline and fired three rounds.

He fired two more shots at another G Company trooper and then emptied the clip at a third silhouette to the right. Before reloading, he wiped the stinging sweat out of his eyes and tried to get his breathing to slow down by taking deep breaths. But it didn't work. It kept coming in gasps so pronounced and intense that they sounded almost like sobs.

God, I hope I don't ever have to do this for real, he said to himself. Unsnapping an ammo pouch on his web belt, he pulled out a clip and loaded his rifle with another eight rounds of .30-caliber ammunition. Tipping back his helmet so he could see better, he spotted another G Company soldier aiming a rifle in his direction.

Firing three rounds, he was almost surprised when the man in his gun sight failed to collapse and die.

From behind him, Sergeant Duff shouted, "Second squad, move out!" Novotny rose quickly and once again began running toward the top of the hill, exhausted, winded, and wondering how anyone in their right mind could actually do this in combat. At the same time, he realized that it actually could happen.

The 3rd Battalion's six companies—G, H, I, Tank, Howitzer, and Headquarters—stood at attention, neatly lined up along the west side of the parade ground. The regimental band was formed next to the reviewing stand, where the battalion officers were taking their places.

On the pole beside the reviewing stand, an American flag was waving, its colors brilliant in the morning sun. In bleachers next to the flagpole, a small group of relatives and friends were seated.

Novotny looked at the reviewing stand and saw the regimental CO. There was definitely something special about him, an impression he and Johnson had shared long before they'd talked to him in the museum and learned about the incident in Korea.

The morning was warm and Novotny felt very soldier-like in his summer dress Class A's. Aside from differences in height and skin color, the young men had been shaped into a trim group of soldiers, all looking very much alike.

Their khaki uniforms were perfectly starched and pressed. Their belt buckles and the insignia at their collars glistened as if it were made of the finest gold rather than simple brass. Their black combat boots and green helmet liners glistened from the wax that had been applied and then rubbed into a rich sheen the night before. The walnut stocks of their M1s shined as well, oiled and polished as if they were pieces of fine furniture rather than devices designed to take people's lives.

Novotny was especially proud of the yellow scarf he wore under his open collar. It too was pressed perfectly, with a crease running vertically on its visible length. Yellow was the color used by all troops who served in armored units. But its origins were in the cavalry. "Around her neck she wore a yellow ribbon," he sang in his brain, recalling an old John Wayne movie about the Cav.

The men of the battalion stood without moving as the officers on the reviewing stand settled into their places. A lieutenant approached the microphone, tapped it to be sure it was on, and stepped back

This is it, Novotny thought. I'm almost a soldier. Almost a cavalryman.

The battalion CO stepped to the mike and addressed the men standing at attention.

"Battalion . . . parade rest," he said, his voice strong and resonant. Almost in unison, the troops moved to the more relaxed position, their feet apart and their left hands held in the small of their backs. Their rifle butts were placed next to their boots, barrels pointing to the sky.

"First let me congratulate you on completing your basic training with the 3rd Battalion of the 2d Armored Cavalry Regiment," he began. "I want to commend you, the officers and the NCOs of the battalion, for the effort all of you have put in over the past eight weeks."

He paused for a moment and looked at the assembled troops. "I now want to introduce the commanding officer of the 2d Armored Cavalry Regiment."

The colonel took his place behind the microphone. Novotny liked the idea that he had met this man. Even though the encounter had been brief, he'd had a personal glimpse of the officer, and it had already made a strong impression.

"Thank you," he said, pausing to look over the precise ranks of troops formed in front of the reviewing stand. "Men, I too would like to compliment you on the way you've handled yourselves for the past two months. Your performance is a tribute to you and to the 2d Cavalry."

He again paused, obviously thinking about what he was going to say. "We will be going to Germany soon, and I want to impress on you the importance of our assignment there. No troops will be closer to the Soviet Army and the Warsaw Pact forces than we will. We'll be on the border watching them every day, reporting on everything we see. Our reports will be important for the planning and decision-making done by NATO commanders."

Even though he was saying things that were obviously important, his voice was calm, without a hint of melodrama. "We don't know what will happen. But if the Russians make a move against Western Europe, we'll be among the first troops to engage them. It'll be our assignment to slow their advance while NATO prepares its response to counter their movement."

He nodded ever so slightly, as if to reinforce what he would say next. "Should that happen, I know that every man in this regiment will perform his duties in a way that will be a credit to himself and to this unit."

There wasn't really time to think it through now, but Novotny wondered if that would be so. The colonel must know that some would perform better than others.

Still, the comment didn't seem like a pep talk from a coach or a canned speech by a politician. The colonel seemed to believe that statement and everything else he was saying. Maybe he's right. Maybe that's the way it works. Maybe no one ends up cowering behind a tree while other guys shoot and get shot. Maybe that's the way it is. Maybe we are now so different from when we came in that every one of us will do exactly what needs to be done, even if it puts us at terrible risk.

Novotny's mind came back to what the colonel was saying. "But our primary job there won't be to engage in war. We'll be there to help prevent it. To keep reminding the Russians that we're prepared for whatever they may think about doing. By being there, well trained and well equipped, it's our hope that the Soviet government will realize that any further intrusion into Europe simply won't be tolerated."

Again he paused, to gather his thoughts. "You are members of one of the most decorated and honored units in the entire United States Army. Men wearing the insignia of this regiment have fought in campaigns going back to 1836. In the Indian Wars, the Civil War, the Spanish-American War, World War I, and World War II. Be proud that you're part of the 2d Cavalry."

Again the colonel looked at the young men standing in neat ranks and listening intently to what he was saying. "I want you to know that I'm proud to be serving with you."

Novotny felt the skin on his arms tingle. This man somehow seemed to be able to set himself apart as an officer and the commander of this regiment while at the same time letting everyone know that he was just a soldier like they were. A guy in a uniform who was ready to do his job, whatever it might be, and whatever dangers it might place him in. How could you not respect and admire this man?

Maybe this is the speech everyone gets. You get gas-mask drill, first-aid training, the POW test that he had blown so completely, and the speech from the CO. It's all in the script.

No. He doubted that. It couldn't be so. The colonel would have to be a heck of an actor to pull off something like that. But he'd soon have a chance to learn for himself. After all, he would be in the same headquarters as the colonel.

"Thank you," said the battalion CO. "Gentlemen, you will now pass the reviewing stand. Leading will be H Troop, which achieved the highest overall rating in the eight weeks of training we've just completed. Congratulations to Lieutenant Wilson and the men of his company."

At a college or high school event, the participants would have let out a cheer and jumped up and down. But the men stood silently at parade rest. Even without any show of emotion, Novotny knew that everyone—the officers, the NCOs, and the rest of the company—was beaming. He knew he couldn't repress his own smile, so he didn't bother trying.

"Pass . . . in review," the battalion CO said loudly, his words echoing around the parade ground.

Immediately, the regimental band began playing the regimental song "Hit the Leather and Ride."

Lieutenant Wilson commanded, "Companeeeee. Ten-hut." The men snapped to attention. "Right shoulder, arms." In the three precise movements they had practiced over and over, the men lifted their M1s from beside their right legs to their right shoulders.

"Forrrrrward . . . march." In perfect unison, the men stepped off and moved out of the line of companies formed on the parade ground's turf. "Column right, march," the lieutenant commanded. Without missing a step, the company turned to the right, the men on the right side taking shorter steps while the men on the left extended their strides to make the turn. There was a slight breeze, and the company guidon, carried by a man in the front rank, was fluttering, making it easy to see the crossed sabres and tank silhouette with a numeral *2* above it and an *H* below.

Novotny watched the arms ahead of him swinging in precise time to the rhythm of the old military tune. After hours and hours of close-order drill, marching now came naturally to them. A few ranks ahead of him, Novotny saw Turner, marching in near perfect time with the rest of the company.

For the young troopers there was no more struggling to keep in step. No more awkward execution of commands. In eight weeks, the officers and NCOs had done what they had set out to do. They'd taken a bunch of guys off the street, away from jobs and out of school, and made soldiers out of them.

"Column left . . . march," Lieutenant Wilson ordered, and the men neatly executed the maneuver.

The company was now headed toward the reviewing stand, where the officers stood at attention. The visitors stood in the bleachers and watched the company march toward them.

When H Troop was nearly in front of the reviewers, the company guidon was dipped and Lieutenant Wilson saluted smartly. The officers on the stand saluted in return.

Novotny noticed that the morning sun was causing the shadow of the flagpole to form a narrow line ahead of them. It took just a few seconds for the first row of men to pass under the shadow. For an instant the sun's light was blocked from their glistening helmet liners, creating a momentary, man-made eclipse.

The shadow crossed the second rank, then the third, and then Novotny's rank. In an instant it was gone, crossing the ranks behind him. We're now officially marked, he thought. We are all indelibly, irrevocably marked. We are different people than when we came here. We are soldiers. Cavalry soldiers.

Part II

The Thin Line Between East and West

Novotny looked out the window, watching the unfamiliar landscape roll by. Johnson sat across from him, reading a book about the history of World War II. Sitting in the middle was Stein, writing a letter on a notepad. To his left was Morris, sound asleep.

Turner was directly across from Morris, his hands folded in his lap, looking at the passing countryside. Twenty-four hours ago, they were leaning on the railing of the USNS *Rose,* watching a tug nudge the troopship against a dock in the German port of Bremerhaven. And twenty-four hours before that, they'd leaned on the same railing, peering through a North Sea fog and wondering when they'd get their first glimpse of the German coastline.

Novotny looked around the compartment. He was fascinated by the spotless maroon upholstery and the beautifully finished wood trim of the car. He thought about the difference between this and the ratty, old rolling stock that had taken him from Detroit to Fort Leonard Wood. But, he realized, by 1945 there probably weren't many functioning railcars left here. No wonder it's so new and clean.

The seats were comfortable, even though people tended to bump knees with the people sitting across from them. Might be an interesting possibility, if the person were some great-looking German girl, he decided. Above Stein's head was a neatly framed, black-and-white photograph of a castle that seemed to be growing organically out of a wooded hilltop.

He turned to look at the photo on the wall behind him. It was a large church, identified in German, French, and Italian as the cathedral at Ulm, a city he had never heard of before.

Watching the countryside glide by, he focused on a village a mile or so from the rail line. "Hey, Bob. Look at that."

The village must have been the prototype from which all German villages were created. Thirty or so gray stone houses were clustered around a church steeple that rose to a cross-covered point. All of the houses had brownish-orange tile roofs and deeply set windows. Some had exposed timbers, forming precise triangles and squares.

All around the village were bare fields, marked with brown lines of frigid soil showing through the snow. Smoke snaked up from chimneys on this cold, gray, and windless February day.

Taking in the scene, Johnson observed, "That's postcard stuff. Do you know where we are?"

Novotny rummaged through his AWOL bag on the rack over his head. He pulled out a map and unfolded it on the empty seat next to him. We haven't come to Kassel yet. My guess is that we're about here," he said, pointing to the map.

Morris opened his eyes to see what was happening. "Where we at, Novo?"

"Right about here."

"Where we goin'?"

Novotny found Nurnberg, where the regimental headquarters would be stationed. "We're headed here." The patrols that would actually be on the border would operate from outposts just a few miles from the line separating the two countries.

For centuries, the line had been an imaginary one, plotted by surveyors and noted on maps. But now it was real. A line marked with barbed wire and minefields. The "unfriendly" side—which was the way the army referred to the Czech half of the line—was punctuated with watchtowers, which looked like the prison towers in the States.

The towers would serve little purpose if there were a movement of U.S. troops from west to east. Standing high on their spindly steel legs they'd be knocked out in a minute. No, that wasn't their purpose at all. They were there to discourage the movement of people from east to west. To prevent people from leaving Czechoslovakia.

Stein said, "I think it's going to be great being here." He added, "I'll be in Amberg, but I hope you guys come over and see me once in a while."

"We're expecting you to come to Nurnberg too," Johnson said. "We can always find a bunk for you."

The train kept up its steady pace to the south, through Kassel, Wurzburg, and finally, late in the day, to Nurnberg. The train would go on to Amberg, so Stein shook hands with his buddies as they gathered their gear and stepped off the train.

A line of buses, looking exactly like the ones they'd left in the States eleven days earlier, was waiting as the men walked out of the station into the cold of the early evening, their heavy duffel bags over their shoulders.

Johnson and Novotny had asked to be roommates and had gotten approval. Once at Merrell Barracks, they picked up their bedding, made their bunks, and were soon asleep, too tired to be much interested, for the moment, in where they were or what would happen next.

Novotny opened his eyes and tried to look around. The room was black, except for light leaking in through the window from the street. He sat up, trying to orient himself. For a moment, he couldn't tell where he was. Then he remembered. He was in Germany. For the first time in his life, he was waking up in Germany.

"You awake, Bob?" he whispered.

"Just about."

From the hall, reveille could be heard on the blaring PA system. "If you can name that tune," Novotny said, mimicking the popular radio show, "you'll win an all-expense-paid tour to Europe!"

"You're funny as hell, Novo. What time is it?"

Novotny walked over to the door of their room and turned on the lights. "Five thirty."

"When I get out of the army, I'm never going to get up earlier than eight," Johnson said, covering his head with his pillow.

"This is a pretty nice room," Novotny said, checking it out in the light.

By then, Johnson was up and sitting on the edge of his bunk. "Sure beats living with thirty guys in a typical army barracks."

Dressed in combat boots, fatigue pants, and white T-shirts, they walked down the hall to the latrine already filled with young man, all dressed alike. Some were brushing their teeth. Others shaved. Most were still half asleep. All seemed a little disoriented, uncertain about what was where, though they purposefully went about the routine of getting ready for morning formation.

The 100 or so men of Headquarters Company milled around in the cold morning air. It was still black, without a sign of dawn. Their breath formed steam, and almost all blew into their hands and rubbed them to keep warm. A few had had the good sense to wear their just-issued olive-drab wool gloves.

At 6:15 AM, Master Sergeant Dwight Olson, the company first sergeant, walked briskly out of the barracks and took a position near where the men stood.

"Fall in," he ordered. Quickly the milling stopped and the men formed six neat ranks. "At ease." The men relaxed and quietly listened to what he had to say.

"Welcome to Merrell Barracks," he began. "In case some of you are confused—and I wouldn't blame you if you were—today's Saturday. I've been here for a while with the advance party, so I'm pretty settled. But it'll take you a few days to get used to the new post."

He looked at the first rank of men, nodding to some as their eyes met. "I know most of you from Meade. But for those of you I haven't met, I want you to come over to my office when you have a break."

Novotny and Johnson had met Sergeant Olson soon after they had been transferred from H Company to the regimental headquarters. They both liked him. He seemed friendly, reasonable, and a decent sort of guy. Like Sergeant Duff, he had the aura of a good soldier. Someone who had seen combat and knew what he was doing.

Sergeant Olson passed out maps of the post, suggesting that everyone take a walk around the facility to become familiar with the various buildings.

"Bed check is at midnight, every night. Miss it and you're AWOL," he cautioned. "There's also a curfew. Even on passes or leave, you have to be off the streets between midnight and oh six hundred. If the MPs pick you up, you're in big trouble."

He thought for a minute, and then added, "Be careful of hookers. They like American dollars. But if you aren't careful, you're likely to have a souvenir between your legs." He smiled slightly. "If you don't know what I mean or what to do about it, go see the duty NCO at the Medical Section."

A few of the men laughed.

He paused again to organize his thoughts. "Oh, yeah. One other thing. The Russians are very interested in what we're doing here. They'd like to know how we run our patrols, what we're learning about them, and what we do with the information that gets reported to us from our scouts on the border. There's no doubt they've got plenty of supporters on this side of the curtain." His voice took on a very serious tone. "So keep what we're doing to yourselves."

When they were dismissed, some of the men headed back into the barracks. Johnson and Novotny looked at the map they'd been given and started walking toward the mess hall.

"He's all right," Johnson said. "He's a guy to be close to if there's any trouble."

They walked into the mess hall and stood in line. The ever-present line. Each took a stainless-steel tray and began filling it with the staples of an army breakfast. Scrambled eggs. Toast. Hash-brown potatoes. Bacon. And black coffee, ladled from a huge aluminum container into brown plastic cups.

The two men found seats at a table and began to eat. Johnson took a sip of coffee from his cup and held it up for Novotny to see. "I'll tell you one thing, Novo."

"What's that?"

"If I get hooked with some spy, there's no way I'll ever give away this secret."

"What secret?"

"How the army can brew up something that looks like coffee and smells like coffee, but tastes as awful as this stuff does."

The headquarters building was at the far corner of the post. Brick and two stories tall, it had the look of an efficient structure, designed to rigid, Nazi architectural standards. Probably from the mid-1930s, Novotny guessed. What he did know was that this post, with its large buildings, expansive parade ground, and extensive support areas, had been the home of an SS unit during the war.

S-2, intelligence, where Johnson worked, was on the second floor. Operations, S-3, his part of the headquarters, had been assigned the first floor, along with S-4, supply and logistics.

The S-3 section was headed by Captain Lawrence Nordholm. The ranking NCO in the section was Master Sergeant Edmund Rogers. Novotny had spent some time with them at Fort Meade, but he didn't feel he really knew them.

One thing was certain, however. Sergeant Rogers was a sour sort of man. And Novotny was very aware that the NCO had little use for outspoken, college-educated guys who were just in to complete their tour and then, in a couple of years, would be on to other things.

Novotny walked into the S-3 office. Sergeant Rogers was sitting at a desk decorated with a wooden plaque carrying his name.

"The captain's in there," the sergeant said as soon as Novotny entered the room, pointing toward an office to his left. "Report to him. And do it right."

Captain Nordholm was writing notes on a yellow pad when Novotny walked in. The young soldier stood at attention in front of the desk and saluted smartly.

"Pfc Novotny reporting for duty, sir."

The captain returned the salute. "Please sit down, Novotny." When he was settled in the chair facing the officer, the captain said, "You speak both Czech and German, is that right?"

"Yes, sir."

"Well, on the staffing chart, we have you as a public-information specialist. But we'll be relying more on your language abilities. We have the border communities to deal with, as well as the Czechs who make it across the border."

"I understand, sir."

"How was your trip?"

"The *Rose* is hardly the *Queen Mary*. But it wasn't bad."

"When did you fellows finally get in?"

"Last evening, sir."

"You probably have unpacking to do. So why don't you get your desk squared away, and then take off. There isn't much that'll get done today. And we close up at noon on Saturday anyway."

"Thank you, sir."

Sergeant Rogers watched Novotny as he came out of the office. "Your desk is in there," he instructed, pointing to an open door, "with Freeman."

The room was large enough to house two desks comfortably.

"Hey, Novo. Welcome to Merrell," said the GI, getting up from his desk.

"Hello, Sandy," he replied, shaking his hand. Sandy Freeman had taken basic in D Troop and then been sent for operations training. He'd gotten back just before the unit had shipped out from Meade.

He was stocky, about five ten, and starting to go bald. He always seemed to be smiling, as if he knew something funny and was about to tell it. Often he did, and it was always funny.

"This is it," Freeman said, gesturing around the office. "This is home. Notice anything special about it?"

Novotny looked around. The OD office furniture was just like the desks and chairs that they'd left at Fort Meade. The door handles were the lever type that he had noticed on the door to his room, rather than a round knob like the ones at home.

"The only thing I can see is that the walls are all tile, instead of being painted."

"You got it," Freeman said, laughing. "Look." He moved his chair aside and revealed four capped pipe fittings extending from the wall, and then two others positioned in other parts of the office. "It was a latrine. The SS guys would come in here to take a whiz. That's why it's all tiled."

Freeman came close to him and said softly, "I think it's going to be great. Except for Sergeant Rogers. He's a mean guy."

Johnson and Novotny unpacked their duffel bags, sorted out their uniforms, and hung them neatly in their wall lockers. Their civilian clothes and personal gear were in a container somewhere between Baltimore and Nurnberg. They had been told they wouldn't be issued combat gear until Monday, and were ordered to wear dress uniforms if they went off post.

There was a knock at the door to their room, and Morris walked in. "What's happenin'?" he said, smiling.

"We were just thinking about taking a look at the town," Johnson said.

"You want to go along?"

"Yeah. That'd be great. I'll get my Class A's and meet you by the Orderly Room."

Smartly dressed in dark green dress uniforms, the three men walked under the arched entry to Merrell Barracks, stopping to show the MP their passes.

"You guys know about the midnight curfew, right?" the MP asked.

"Yeah, thanks," Johnson acknowledged as the MP waved them through.

Once through the arch, they looked back at the front of the four-story building. At the center of the entry arch was the 2d Armored Cavalry's yellow-and-green regimental crest. Flanking it was the heraldry of support units stationed here.

Johnson motioned toward the wall at the right of the entry arch. Row after row of gouges had been chopped out of the brick-and-concrete facade. "Looks like this place took a beating."

"It must have been machine-gun fire," Novotny noted.

Morris frowned. "It got pretty shot up."

"That's right, Chas. We shot it up."

Johnson piped in, "After the war there was a trial for the Nazis here in Nurnberg. They convicted and hanged a bunch of them."

"Man," Morris said, shaking his head, so overwhelmed by the importance of it all that there was nothing else he could say.

It was cold and gray and looked as though it might snow. But the men were warm enough in their wool winter uniforms and dress topcoats. Their well-shined, plain black shoes crunched the thin layer of snow as they walked to the street.

Lined up in front of the barracks were three black Mercedes sedans. Each had a white stripe along the side identifying them as taxis. Their diesel engines clanked as they idled, waiting for GI fares. The driver of the first cab sat up straight and looked at the men as they approached.

Johnson turned to the others. "Let's walk downtown and ride back." No one disagreed and they turned left on *Allersbergerstrasse*, or Allersberg Street , following a sign that said *Stadtmitte*, city center.

The street was lined with bare trees and brick apartment buildings. They were all dark, old looking, and bleak in the dull light of the winter afternoon. At some intersections were a few stores—small butcher shops, bakeries, and grocery stores, with signs in the windows saying they closed at noon on Saturday.

As they walked, Johnson pointed to letters painted on a basement window across the street. "What do you think that means, Novo?"

"LSR. It obviously stands for something." He shrugged. "Beats me."

On every block, the letters were painted over one or more stone window frames, raising Novotny's curiosity. Ahead, at an intersection, a man about fifty years old was shoveling snow from a narrow sidewalk. The soldiers nodded as they walked by, and the man nodded in return.

"Wait a second," Novotny said, walking back toward the man. The two other men followed. "Good day," he said, speaking his best German. He saw this as an opportunity to get an answer to the question, as well as to test his German on a local citizen.

The man looked up from his shoveling, surprised. Perhaps because the three GIs had stopped. Or maybe because he was being addressed in German.

"Good day," he replied, leaning on his shovel.

"Please excuse me," Novotny said, pronouncing each word carefully. "There is a question we would like to ask you."

"Yes, we seek some information," Johnson added in equally careful in the

German he had learned in college. Morris stood quietly watching the process, with no idea what was being said.

"What do you wish to know?" the man asked, his eyes making it clear that he was cooperating only to avoid being completely rude. He had little interest in talking to these young men.

"We have seen the letters *LSR* on the buildings," Novotny said. "Can you tell us what they mean?"

The man's expression hardened even more. "Yes, I can tell you. It means *luftkrieg shutz raum.*"

Morris couldn't be quiet anymore. "What're you guys talkin' 'bout?"

"I asked him what *LSR* means," Novotny answered. "He said it stands for air-attack protection room."

"Air raid shelters," Johnson added.

"We got those at home. Yellow signs on buildings."

Novotny quickly pointed out, "The difference is we haven't had to use them. At least not yet."

The man was now glaring at the soldiers as he said, "There was much damage from the bombs. Many apartment buildings were knocked down."

The three soldiers stood silently, waiting for him to finish what he obviously wanted to say.

"My father and my mother were in one of the buildings that was knocked down. In March 1945. They were both killed."

Still the soldiers said nothing—Novotny and Johnson because they were not sure what to say, Morris because he had no idea what was being said.

"It was a raid during the day," the man explained. "They were your planes. You bombed us in the day. The British bombed us at night." He paused for a moment, and then added, "The LSR was of little protection when an entire building was knocked down. The people were trapped inside the LSR."

The man stood silently for a moment; his lips so tightly clenched that he could hardly speak. "So, does that answer your question?"

Johnson nodded. Novotny studied the bitter expression on the man's face for a moment. "It saddens us to hear about the death of your parents," he said. "Many people died in those years. Germans. And Americans. We must hope that there will not be another war such as that."

The man took a deep breath. "Yes," he said, nodding, his face looking less angry. "What you say is true."

"Until we see you again," Johnson said, using the phrase that ended most conversations.

"Until I see you again," the man replied, pushing the shovel blade into the snow.

As soon as the men were a short distance from the man, Morris asked, "What was that all about?" He listened carefully as his two friends related the conversation, almost verbatim. "Oh, man. That makes me feel so bad."

"Sure, it's sad," Johnson acknowledged. "But don't forget who started the war. It was a little guy with a funny mustache and a swastika on his arm."

The men continued to walk along Allersbergerstrasse toward the center of the city. They passed block after block of dreary old apartment buildings, and then, all of a sudden, the architecture changed. The buildings that lined the street were modern, colorful, and efficient looking. Many of the apartments had balconies and terraces. It looked like a different city.

They waited for a light at an intersection and Johnson pointed to a cross street to the left. "Let's see what some of the side streets look like." The buildings on the smaller street were a mixture of old and new. Then a block and a half from the main thoroughfare, there was another abrupt change.

They stopped and stood silently in front of one three-story apartment building. It looked as though a giant claw had ripped at the front of the building, tearing away the facade and exposing what was left of the rooms inside. You could easily tell what each room had been used for. Colorful wallpaper still covered living and dining rooms. A bathtub was in its place in one second-floor apartment, even though the front half of the bathroom was gone. There was no furniture to be seen. But in one room, a painting of a forest was hanging on a wall.

At the base of the torn building were piles of bricks, surrounded by a wire fence to keep people out. From the random way the heaps were deposited on the sidewalk, it looked as though they were lying where they had fallen when the bombs dislodged them from the neat rows set by some unknown bricklayer.

"I wonder if anyone was in those buildings when they were hit," Johnson said quietly.

Partly hidden by the rubble on the sidewalk was a basement window. The letters *LSR* were plainly visible. "Look at that," Novotny said. Not much protection there.

Morris looked and said what Johnson and Novotny had both thought but chose not to say. "Maybe that guy's parents were in there."

They started to walk down the street and saw that the next several blocks were lined with nothing but shells of apartment buildings, separated by an occasional vacant lot.

Without saying anything, the three young soldiers turned around and silently headed back toward Allersbergerstrasse and the center of the city.

A few blocks ahead, they could see the taller buildings that marked the center of town. They passed the railroad station where they had arrived and walked through an arch formed by a massive wall that surrounded the old part of town.

At its highest points, the wall was thirty or forty feet high, and probably twenty feet thick at the base. Parts of the wall faced a dry moat. Round turrets were strategically placed, offering the archers of centuries ago a clear field of fire to repel anyone who tried to assault this old city.

Novotny noticed that the stones were a mixture of dark and light colors. The lighter stones were obviously replacements for ancient ones that had been damaged during the war. As they walked the streets, taking everything in, they saw that virtually every old building had the same look. The pale-colored stones seemed out of place against the aging old brown of the original materials.

They found an appealing little restaurant and ordered plates of *Nurnberger* bratwurst—delicate sausages that originated in Nurnberg—with German-style cabbage, potato salad, and black bread, washed down with a stein of Tucher Brau, a local beer. The meal was graciously served by a waiter in a tuxedo, something Novotny had seen only in the most posh of Chicago restaurants.

It came to just over six marks per person. At the exchange rate of four marks to a dollar, it was about a dollar and a half.

"Pretty good deal," Johnson said. The others agreed.

It was dark when they left the restaurant, and they continued poking their way around the city center, with no particular destination in mind. Seeing a sign for music they decided to take a look.

Bars and nightclubs lined both sides of the street, and at the end of the second block, a colorful sign identified the Club Holiday. A flashing neon sign just above the door said *Tanz Musik.*

"We can't miss this," Novotny said, pointing to a poster in the window. "Look who's playing." The sign said, *"Heute Abend. Hans Altman und seine Kometen."*

"What's it say, Novo?" Morris asked, slightly frustrated.

"It says, 'This evening, Hans Altman and his Comets.'"

"You mean like Bill Haley," Morris asked.

"I guess so," Novotny replied. "You want to check it out?"

"We've got to do it," Johnson said, nodding.

Inside the dark club, the band clumsily blasted its way through a collection of rock-and-roll classics. For the three GIs, it was a strange combination of familiar and alien sensations.

Novotny ordered a stein of beer, and the other two men did the same. He took a big drink of the cold, foamy brew and relished the taste, the coolness and the tingle of the bubbles rolling down his throat. "I could really get addicted to this German beer," he announced.

About ten minutes after they'd arrived, a young woman, probably in her early twenties, walked in and looked around at the tables full of GIs and locals. Spotting an empty seat between Morris and Novotny, she asked, in English, "Is this place free?"

"Sure," Johnson said. "Why don't you join us?"

Johnson and Novotny stood as she sat down. "Thank you," she said smiling. "Are you just arriving here in Germany?" she asked, noticing that they were all in uniform.

"Yes," Johnson replied. "We have been here only a few days."

"I must tell you," she said, in accented but well-spoken English. "It is a custom in Germany to share places at a table such as this," she said, obviously uncomfortable with the fact that she felt the need to say this. "I tell you this so you understand my, ah, my position."

Realizing her discomfort, Novotny asked in German, "What is it that you want us to know?"

She smiled. "Good. You speak German. I am more comfortable explaining this in German." She paused for a moment, and then said, "I only want you and your friends to know that I am not a woman of the street. I was afraid you would think so, because I came to your table."

Johnson nodded. "I understand." He turned to Morris. "Our guest just wanted to be sure that we know she's not a hooker. People share tables here in Germany."

"I got it," Morris said.

"Thank you," she said, glad to have gotten the matter cleared up.

Novotny pulled out a package of cigarettes and offered one to her. She gladly accepted.

"You want something to drink?" Johnson asked.

"Yes, I would like beer."

He motioned to the waitress, who brought another stein to the table.

"Thank you. My name is Helga. What are your names?" she asked of the group.

"Novo. I am called Novo."

"Novo," she repeated

"My name is Bob Johnson."

"Bob," she said, nodding to him. "And vat is your name?

"My name is Chas."

"Jazz. You are named for jazz music?"

"Nah. It's for Charles. That's my real name. Charles. But they all call me Chas."

"You look like jazz music player. I will call you Jazz."

"OK. You can call me anything you want."

They sat listening to the ersatz Comets work their way through a few songs before taking a break. When they came back, Morris asked, "You wanna dance?"

"Yes, I like to dance."

Novotny and Johnson watched the GI and the young German girl on the floor. She danced reasonably well, but without the fluid movements of their friend.

Taking a sip of his beer, Novotny said, "I hate to say this. I know it's a cliché. But Chas sure has rhythm."

Johnson patted his buddy on the shoulder. "Yeah, I know. And he likes watermelon. Come on, Novo."

"No. I'm serious. I wish I could dance like that." He looked at the people on the dance floor. "What do you think of Helga? Do you believe she's really not a hooker?"

"I think I believe her," Johnson said. "She's not bad looking. Got a nice body, or so it seems, given what we've seen of it. Seems nice. I think she's all right."

The four talked and drank beer, and every few numbers, Helga and Morris would dance.

Novotny looked at his watch. It was eleven o'clock. "Guess we'd better get goin'." The three GIs stood.

The girl looked at Morris. "Jazz, you will come here again?"

"Yeah. I'll be back."

The black Mercedes cab headed down Allersbergerstrasse back to Merrell Barracks. The men looked out the windows, picking out places they'd seen on their walk to town. Novotny strained to look down the street where the ruined apartment buildings were. But it was dark and he couldn't see anything.

Johnson put his arm around Morris. "Chas, I think you're falling in love on your first full day in Nurnberg."

"Nah, man. But you gotta admit she ain't bad."

"I didn't say she was bad looking. Just be careful. She could end up being expensive."

Morris sat up abruptly and said angrily, "You tellin' me she's a hooker. After she told us she wasn't."

"I didn't say that," Johnson said, realizing the effect of his comment. "I'm just telling you to be careful. We don't know how they do things around here yet."

Novotny turned to Morris. "Come on, Chas. All Bob's saying is to be a little careful."

For the rest of the ride, the colored GI just sat, sulking and saying nothing.

His hands full, Novotny gently kicked the door to his room with the toe of his boot. "You there, Bob?"

"Yeah," Johnson said, walking to the door and opening it.

"I got us a present," Novotny announced proudly. In his hands was a large radio. He gently put it on the OD table between their bunks, took out his handkerchief, and wiped it off.

It was a truly magnificent radio, measuring about eighteen inches wide and about a foot high. The sides and top were dark wood, the grain glistening under who knew how many coats of varnish. The front panel was recessed with an assortment of knobs and fabric that protected the speakers behind it. The dial was marked with a number of bands, selected with push buttons.

"Wow," Johnson exclaimed. "Where'd you get it?"

"I was talking to a guy from the medical company. He's going back on some kind of hardship transfer. He didn't have time to pack it up, so I offered him what I could afford and he took it. I got a great deal. You know what it cost me?"

"Let's see. Two dollars and eighty cents."

"No. Come on. Look at this beauty. Thirty-five bucks. A third of a month's pay. But worth it. I'll bet it would cost a hundred or more. Easily."

Johnson nodded approval at the deal, got down on his hands and knees, and looked for an outlet. Plugging it in, he said, "Let's see how it works."

He turned the indicator to Armed Forces Network, Nurnberg. The familiar sounds of Buddy Holly singing "Peggy Sue" confirmed they had the right station.

"That's number six in this week's Hit Parade back in the States," the announcer said in the exaggerated casual style of disc jockeys. "Now I've got a song especially for the guys from the 2d Armored Cavalry. They just got here to keep the border safe for the rest of you garrison jockeys."

Johnson and Novotny smiled and nodded in approval. "The next tune is to remind you troopers about curfew. In your bunks by twelve. So listen carefully, troopers. Pay attention. Stay out of the ol' stockade."

"Here it is, troops, the Everly Brothers and 'Wake Up, Little Susie.'" They sang along, and when the song ended, the DJ said, "It's not your ma and pa you've got to worry about. It's your first sergeant."

Johnson said, "Let's check out some of those other bands."

Novotny studied them and noticed that one had the names of major European cities positioned along the dial. In the middle was Prag, the German spelling of the Czech capital. Pushing the band-selection button, he turned the tuning knob until the vertical marker lined up with the city name.

Dang, ding, dong. A gentle bell sounded a simple three-note melody. "'You are listening to Radio Prague,'" Novotny translated for his friend, beaming. "Isn't this great."

He sat on the floor next to the radio and his friend stretched out on his bunk. It was a little like when he was a kid and would take the same position next to the family Philco to listen to *Terry and the Pirates.*

The man on the radio spoke with little enthusiasm; obviously he was reading the material. Most of the words were familiar to Novotny, though some terms were completely unknown to him and he had to guess at their meaning or skip over them.

"What's he saying?" Johnson asked.

"The district office in Ostrava reports that . . . ah . . . steel . . . I guess *production* has increased by only two percent. This is . . . ah . . . this is less than the five-year plan. Ah . . . and the production committee has made . . . ah . . . . made changes in the . . . it must be . . . ah . . . *management* . . . to meet the plan requirements."

"Exciting stuff," Johnson observed. "Wonder what happens to the guys who get canned."

"Meanwhile," Novotny continued, "milk production for the western region . . . ah . . . has increased by more than six percent. The director of the region, Dr. Miroslav Placek, has been given a . . . I guess *award* . . . for this excellent record."

"Novo, let's try Switzerland or something. I think I get the picture about Radio Prague."

"Yeah," he agreed, thinking that he'd listen to this station on his own, when an opportunity came up. It was boring stuff. But interesting to him nonetheless, just because it was in Czech.

He was just about to change the station when the droning male announcer was replaced by a woman's voice. "Listen to that," Novotny said. "I'll bet she's gorgeous. I'd love to have her whisper sweet nothings in my ear."

"You mean like copper production statistics and railroad schedules."

Novotny sat up abruptly and looked at the radio as if focusing on it would somehow make translating easier. "Wait a second," he said urgently.

He hesitated, then translated, "Ah . . . we will now have a biography of the German general Ritter," he translated.

"A German general?" Johnson questioned.

"Yeah, that seems strange." He listened carefully. "General Ritter was born in Berlin in 1915. He . . . ah . . . joined the German Army in 1935 and went to officers' school."

The woman's voice was replaced by the sound of marching troops and German-style military music. Novotny reached into his pocket, pulled out a cigarette, and lit it, handing the pack to Johnson.

"We all know of the British . . . it must be *traitor*, Chamberlain . . . who turned his back on us in Munich. When the Nazis invaded our country in 1938, Captain Ritter was among the Wehrmacht military who . . . ah . . . made such terror for our people."

Novotny took a deep breath and then a drag off his cigarette. "This isn't easy to translate. But it's amazing."

"Yeah, keep going."

"In 1942, the Czech . . . I think it's *heroes* . . . killed the Nazi general Reinhardt Heydrich."

Novotny smashed his cigarette in the ashtray and took a deep breath. "This was followed by . . . ah . . . the. . destruction of the village of Lidice by the Nazis. At that time, all of the men and boys of the village were shot." The woman's voice was replaced for a few moments by the sound of automatic-weapons fire.

"The women were sent to concentration camps, where many of them also died."

He took another deep breath, his shoulders rising as he filled his lungs. "Jesus."

"Keep going," Johnson said somberly, now sitting on the edge of his bunk.

"Major Ritter was one of the officers who . . . I don't know the word . . . this . . . ah . . . terrible act."

Again German martial music replaced the voice for a few seconds.

The woman's voice, which had begun in such calm and appealing tones, turned hard and cold. Novotny continued to translate. "Today this General Ritter . . . the same man who did . . . ah . . . all of these things . . . is now the officer who is planning NATO . . . I think it's *strategy*. Who is NATO? It is these people, such as General Ritter, a Nazi well known to us.

Novotny took another deep breath. "NATO speaks of freedom. But we know what is true. We know who these criminals really are."

A blend of sounds replaced the woman's voice. Boot steps. Military music made obviously German by the chorus that now sang with it, and the sound of automatic-weapons fire. The sounds faded out slowly to silence.

Dang, ding, dong, the bells chimed. Another Czech male voice announced, "Good day. This is Radio Prague."

145

Novotny pushed the button that turned off the radio and just sat on the floor, saying nothing.

"Do you think all that's true?" Johnson asked quietly.

"The stuff about Chamberlain is. The British tried to appease Hitler by turning their backs on the Czechs."

"What about that general? General Ritter. You think that's true?"

"I don't know. I hope not. Maybe it's just propaganda," Novotny said, shrugging.

"Whatever it is, it's potent stuff."

Novotny nodded in sullen agreement. "Yeah. It's a lot different from Armed Forces Network."

Novotny looked at the polished wood of the radio and thought about what he had just heard. He thought about how his grandfather had hated the Nazis. And now, here he was, a soldier with the Germans as allies. It didn't make sense.

Novotny was concentrating on the translation of an article in the *Nurnberger Nachtrichten*, a local newspaper, when Sergeant Rogers, standing in the door to the office, interrupted him.

"Come here, Novotny. I want to see you," he said curtly, turning and walking back to his desk.

Novotny folded up the paper and looked at Freeman, who rolled his eyes and smiled.

He stood in front of the sergeant's desk, not quite at attention. "Yes, Sergeant."

"Take this report over to Sub-Area at Furth," he said, leafing through a small stack of forms and typed pages. "They need it this morning." Satisfied that everything was there, he put the papers into a manila envelope, sealed it, and wrote a name on the front. "Make sure it gets to Lieutenant Allen in the Finance Section there."

He handed the envelope to Novotny, along with another form. "Here's a requisition for a jeep from the motor pool. The duty NCO'll give you a map on how to get there." He folded his hands on the desk and looked squarely at Novotny. "Now, do you think you can handle that without getting lost?"

"Yes, Sergeant. I'm sure I can handle it." He tried not to be sarcastic in his reply, but as soon as he'd said it, he knew there was at least a touch of sarcasm in his voice.

He walked to the motor pool and checked in with the sergeant who issued vehicles. "It's over there," the NCO said, pointing to a row of Jeeps. "HQ-26. Here's your trip ticket and map to Furth. It's easy to find. Take you about twenty minutes."

"Thanks," Novotny replied, folding the papers and putting them into a pocket of his field jacket.

"Be sure you fill in every line on that trip ticket," the NCO cautioned. "They'll hang your ass if you don't. Trip tickets are a big deal in Seventh Army."

"Thanks again." Novotny walked down the line of Jeeps and got into the one with 2AC HQ-26 stenciled in white on the bumper. He carefully filled out the first line of the trip ticket. Fuel. Mileage. Time. Destination. Driver. Purpose of trip. The paperwork done, he headed toward the front gate, stopping to show his vehicle requisition to the MP, who then waved him out.

Making a left on Allersbergerstrasse, he looked at the buildings that he, Johnson, and Morris had walked by that first weekend. The light was red at the intersection where they had turned off the street and seen the bombed-out apartments. He looked at the hulks of buildings down the block and shook his head.

Turning just before the city center, he followed the signs to Furth. As he drove, he could see that bombing and street fighting had damaged virtually every block in the center of the city.

Some of the evidence was in the form of rubble and vacant lots. But equally poignant were the blocks in which every building was obviously no more than a few years old—blocky, modern, and colorful structures instead of being made of old stone with ornamental stone entries. Pulling over once en route to check the map, he found the Sub-Area Headquarters building with no problem. It was an old structure that looked as if it might have contained some government offices, and it appeared not to have been damaged. He parked his jeep and walked briskly through the main entrance.

On the right was a bronze plaque. The inscription was in three languages; German, French, and English. "In this building, between November 21, 1945, and October 1, 1946, were conducted the War Crimes Trials following the defeat of Nazi Germany."

He looked around at the impressive lobby. Ahead and to his left were three sets of massive double doors. He walked to a desk in the center of the lobby. A master sergeant watched Novotny as he approached.

"Can I help you?"

"Yeah, Sergeant. I'm supposed to give this report to Lieutenant Allen in the Finance Section."

The sergeant pointed to the elegant stairway leading to the second floor. "Up there, around to the right. Room 245."

"Thanks," he said. He started to walk away and then returned to the desk.

"Uh. Where did they actually have the trials?"

"Over there," he answered, gesturing toward the imposing doors. "The cells were in the back of the building. That's where Goering committed suicide." The sergeant shook his head. "I was kind of sorry he cheated the gallows. They hanged the others in an area at the south corner of the building. It's all blocked off. You can't go in there."

"Thanks, Sergeant."

"Don't mention it."

Novotny walked over to the huge doors and admired the beautiful craftsmanship, wondering what kind of wood they were made of. Imagine who had walked right here, where I'm standing, he thought. Goering. What was the admiral's name? Doenitz. The whole gang.

In his mind's eye, he could picture Goering at the trial, pudgy, with a thin-lipped smirk on his face and bulky earphones on his head so he could hear the testimony translated into German. Behind him stood a couple of GI guards, wearing Class A's and polished helmet liners.

His mind began to re-create a whole series of images. He was ten and eleven when the trials were held, but he could still see the pictures as clearly as if he held them in his hand. The pictures and newsreels that went along with the stories as the trials went on week after week. The bodies piled high, naked and nearly fleshless. The living skeletons, eyes sunken in their bony sockets. The baggy, striped uniforms that looked as if they were made of mattress-cover material.

For some reason, while the trial was going on he had a strange need to look at these terrible images. He did so, even though he knew they'd haunt him as he tried to go to sleep. And knowing that once he was asleep, he'd wake up terrified after dreaming that he was actually there with these dead and dying people.

He shook his head, which brought him back to today. Walking quickly up the stairs, he followed the sergeant's instructions and walked into the Finance Section offices. A Pfc sat at a desk in the entry.

"Help you?"

"Yeah," he said, pointing to the envelope. "This is for Lieutenant Allen. I'm from the 2d Cav."

"Sure. Hang on," he said, picking up a phone.

Novotny wondered what it would be like to work in the building where so much history had happened. Maybe you didn't pay any attention to it once you were here for a while. He was glad he was at Merrell Barracks and not here. Looking around at the GIs sitting at OD metal desks and pushing papers all day, he was equally glad he was in the Cav and not in a support section like this. I'd go nuts here, he decided.

Concentrating on what he saw, he didn't hear the fatigue-clad figure walk up to him from the left. "You've got a report from the 2d Cavalry?"

It was a woman's voice, which surprised him. Turning, he saw a WAC standing next to him.

"Yeah. It's for Lieutenant Allen," he replied, standing casually.

"I'm Lieutenant Allen."

"Oh, I'm sorry, sir. I mean, ma'am," he said awkwardly, quickly coming to attention and obviously flustered at seeing the silver bars on her collar. He wished he'd been paying more attention when she first walked up.

"At ease," she said. "I know you don't have any women in the 2d Cavalry. But, as you can see, not all officers are men." Her voice was more hurt than angry.

"Yes, ma'am. My mind was elsewhere and I wasn't paying attention. I'm sorry." He handed her the report. "Is there anything else, ma'am?"

"No. Thank you."

He came to attention and gave her a sharp, snappy Cavalry salute.

Now she was caught off guard. Self-consciously, she returned his salute. But unlike his, hers was an obviously uncomfortable gesture. As she did it, she began to blush in embarrassment, realizing how clumsy she looked in comparison to the tall, lean cavalryman standing at attention in front of her.

"That's all," she said self-consciously. "Ah. Thank you again."

"You're welcome, ma'am," he said gently. He was very aware of how embarrassing the exchange had been for her in front of the enlisted clerks sitting at their OD desks.

As he walked out of the building, he turned and again looked at the heavy wooden doors. In an instant, his mind went from the uncomfortable exchange he'd just had with the first WAC officer he'd ever met to the events that had happened here just over a decade ago. Events that had disgusted the world as it read about them and saw them in the movie theaters. Events that, as a small boy, had terrified him. Since then, he had pushed the images out of his mind. Until now, standing here at a place that was part of that awful time.

The sound was loud. But loudness wasn't what made it work. It was a blaring noise that seemed to make the marrow in their bones vibrate, waking them from the inside out.

Novotny folded a pillow over his ears. But the sound waves appeared to have been set at an auditory frequency able to penetrate it, and a voice shouted, "Let's go! Let's go! Combat gear, field packs, and weapons. Let's go!"

The shouter had come and gone so quickly that neither of them knew who it was.

The two young men leaped out of their bunks and threw open their wall locker doors. Responding properly, their adrenal glands pumped fluid into their blood. Their hearts were pounding and their minds were jarred into intense consciousness. Every movement was quick, precise, and nearly in unison.

First, long underwear: tops, then bottoms. A pair of olive-drab socks, and another pair on top of that. A combat fatigue jacket, then fatigue trousers, the brass buckle carefully centered out of habit, even in this rush. Thermal "Mickey Mouse" boots, so called because they were heavy, bulky, and black. An OD winter cap with earflaps. And finally, a heavy, puffy winter combat jacket.

All through the process—which took only a couple of minutes—the penetrating sound of the alarm continued. Johnson scowled and shouted at no one in particular, "Jesus, we're up already. Shut off the damn alarm."

Novotny took a quick look at his watch. Ten minutes after two. He glanced out the window at the blackness of the night, the occasional streetlights brilliant in contrast. Still nearly in unison, the two soldiers reached for the equipment stowed on the floor of their wall lockers. Around their waists, they latched on their web belts with a full canteen, ammo pouches, a sheathed bayonet, and a first-aid kit already in place.

From the top of their lockers, they each grabbed two packs: one with clothes, shaving gear, a toothbrush, and miscellaneous personal items; the other packed tightly with half a pup tent, a sleeping bag, an entrenching tool, and other essential hardware. Strapped to the outside was a dull green steel helmet.

They finished the process at just about the same time and stood for a moment, breathing hard. Novotny gently poked his friend's padded stomach. "You look like Charlie Brown in an OD snowsuit," he said, smiling.

"Thanks a lot," Johnson replied, chuckling.

Carrying their two heavy and awkwardly shaped packs, they jogged down the light green halls, past the empty gun racks that lined the walls. Novotny wondered how many times the SS troops that had been billeted here had done just this. He wondered when the last time was, and if the soldiers running down this hall had known when the final alarm had been sounded.

They rushed to the arms room where weapons were stored. Lined up at the door were thirty or so cavalrymen. "Call out your numbers. Let's go!" shouted a sergeant from behind a counter.

"Seventy-six," Johnson said, putting his weapons card on the counter. A Pfc took the card, turned to a rack behind him, and handed him an M1 rifle with "76" stenciled on the wooden stock.

"Forty-four," Novotny called out. Once again the GI grabbed the card, dropped it in a box, and returned with Novotny's weapon, a carbine. Novotny flashed back to a moment when he'd fallen in love with a hatcheck girl at the Blackhawk Restaurant in Chicago. Nothing serious. Just a twelve-and-a-half-second romance while he watched her take his ticket and retrieve his raincoat.

Slinging the carbine over his shoulder, he ran up the stairs behind Johnson.

Vehicles were already lining up on the parade ground, and the two men rushed over to the two-and-a-half-ton truck that would carry them east to the Czech border. It was 2:29 AM. Just nineteen minutes after they had first jumped out of bed.

Officers, NCOs, and men were rushing around, their breath steamy in the frigid night air. The tailgate of their truck was down, and the men placed the packs and weapons on the floor of the vehicle.

Just as they'd been drilled to do, they ran to an office and carried a heavy OD safe to the truck and slid it against the cab.

"Do you know what's in there, Bob?"

"Codes. I know that for sure. Piles of German marks. I don't know how many. But a lot. And a bunch of files. That's about it."

A sergeant walked quickly from one vehicle to another, checking the loading. Seeing Novotny and Johnson, he ordered, "That ambulance" and pointed down the line. "Get over there and give the medic a hand."

"Right, Sergeant," Novotny said, starting to run as he replied.

A medic they'd never met was struggling with a heavy cardboard box, trying to get it into the ambulance. Without a word, Novotny jumped into the vehicle while Johnson and the medic got under the box and lifted. Novotny moved it back from the tailgate and jumped back onto the gravel.

"Thanks for the hand," the medic said. "Those damn body bags weigh a ton."

Novotny frowned. "Body bags?"

"Oh, that's right. You guys are new. It's a rubberized bag that we use to bring bodies back from the field."

"Did you ever use one?" Novotny asked.

"Filled a lot of 'em in Korea," the medic replied. "Ain't much fun."

"I can imagine," Johnson said.

The medic nodded and pointed to the box in the ambulance. "If Ivan decides to come across the border, we'll use those up in a hurry." Then he added, "Even if he doesn't, we could still use a few out in the field."

"On alerts like this? And in training?" Novotny asked incredulously.

"Hell, yes. Guys do dumb things. Like sleep under tanks or trucks to keep warm and then get run over."

"That is pretty dumb," Johnson agreed.

"Sometimes it's not their fault, though. Last year, we were on a NATO maneuver and a faulty round misfired in an M-48. We took parts of three guys back in bags." He looked over his shoulder and saw that most of the convoy seemed to be loaded. "Gotta get goin'. Thanks for the hand."

Novotny and Johnson jogged back to their truck. An officer they didn't know was running along the line of vehicles. "Mount up, and turn 'em over. Get ready to move out."

The two men jumped onto the back of the deuce-and-a-half, folded the tailgate into the upright position, and latched it. Then carefully positioning their gear and their weapons, they took facing seats on the wooden benches that ran the length of the vehicle. They couldn't see ahead of them. But behind them was what appeared to be an endless line of trucks, jeeps, M–41 and M–48 tanks, APCs, as the armored personnel carriers were called, and a few ambulances.

Novotny listened to the sound of their engines starting, and it reminded him of an orchestra tuning for a performance. At the bottom of the scale were the M–48 tanks, with their 700-horsepower engines deep and resonant as they turned over. The smaller M–41s were somewhat higher, more like cellos than basses. At the top of the scale were the jeeps. Their four-cylinder engines had a distinctive rattle when started, a sound that wasn't terribly musical but seemed to smooth out after running for a while.

Soon, all of the engines were idling. A loud and urgent voice brought the line of vehicles to life. "Move out! Move out!" the voice shouted, and the convoy slowly began to snake its way through the open gate in the chain-link fence and onto Allersbergerstrasse, turning right, away from the center of town and toward the Czech border.

As the column gained momentum, the sound became even more musical to Novotny. Chords were formed as the diverse pitch of the various engines blended. Melodies were formed as the drivers took them through the gears.

The beat of the percussion section came from the tanks and APCs, their tracks hitting the pavement with a precise, staccato rhythm.

Novotny looked again at his watch. Two forty-seven. It had taken them thirty-seven minutes to get the regiment on the road. If the battalions were also on alert—and he assumed they were—that would mean that about 5,000 2d Cavalry troops were moving east. It was probably just a drill. But it could be much more than that.

Johnson reached into his jacket and pulled out a pack of cigarettes. Lighting one, he offered the pack and his Zippo to Novotny.

"Thanks, Bob." He took a deep drag on the cigarette and relished the smoke as he exhaled.

"Do you think Khrushchev would ever cross the border?" Bob asked, his nervousness apparent in his voice.

"I don't know. Dulles calls it brinksmanship, and we're part of the game. You've gotta have chips to play it. And if someone calls your hand, you might lose a few." He took a deep drag on his cigarette. "We're chips."

"You're right. We're chips."

Kilometer after kilometer, the convoy droned on. Novotny sat quietly, watching the dark landscape pass behind them. Occasionally they'd go through a village, the streets empty and the buildings dark except for an occasional lighted window, the occupants looking out anxiously as the convey passed. But mainly it was just forest—black, dark, dense forest.

Johnson had taken the softer of his two packs and put it on the seat, using it as a pillow. He tried to sleep, but the bouncing and the noise of the truck kept him awake.

"You know, Novo, I can think this through logically and feel pretty sure that Eisenhower and Khrushchev are too smart to start a war. They both know what it's like."

"I can go along with that."

"But," Johnson said, and then paused. "But I'm not so sure everyone's that smart. I'm not sure there aren't jerks out there—on our side and theirs—who'd like to start a war."

"Doesn't that kind of undermine your logic, Bob? That means somebody might set things moving in a way that would send us, or them, across the border on one of these rides."

"I think it could happen," Johnson said quietly.

"And if it did happen, like the medic said, we'd use up those body bags in a hurry, since we'd be the first to engage Ivan."

"Yup. You're right, Novo. We sure would."

Novotny thought for a minute. "You're talking about someone doing something deliberately. But there's another thing to worry about."

"What's that?"

"What if something happened accidentally. Something that wasn't intended to start anything. But something that just . . . just happened. And the other side reacted. And before anyone could do anything about it, it got completely out of hand."

"Like what?" Johnson asked.

"I don't know. I'm just thinking that in as tense a situation as we have now, something unplanned thing could happen and trigger something bigger."

"Well, odds are this is just an alert. We should know one way or the other pretty quick."

"Right," Novotny agreed.

"Let me ask you something, Novo. Even though it's probably an alert, are you a little nervous about this?"

Novotny nodded. "Yeah. I wouldn't admit that to everyone. But I'm a little nervous." As he spoke, he became aware that his heartbeat was faster and more noticeable than usual.

"So am I," Johnson admitted. "But if we do enough of these, I'm sure we'll get over it."

"No doubt about that," Novotny said, making certain that the sound of his voice was more confident than the thoughts rattling around in his head. "We're well trained, but we don't know how we would play in a real game. We need a small war to test our team."

At about nine o'clock—after several breaks along the way—they stopped in the forest to stretch, talk, eat cold C rations, and pee against a tree. With engines turned off, drivers performed the precise maintenance regimen spelled out in their training.

Within an hour, the vehicles were heading back to Nurnberg.

It was late afternoon when the convoy headed down Allersbergerstrasse and turned into the gate to Merrell Barracks. Novotny and Johnson knew little about the route they had taken, other than it had been essentially to the east and then back home.

Johnson rubbed his sleepy eyes and looked at the familiar brick buildings. "I guess Eisenhower and Khrushchev kept everyone in line."

Novotny nodded. They unloaded their gear and returned the heavy safe to its place in the office, waiting for the next alert. Then they walked to the nearby ambulance to help the medic unload the unopened box of body bags.

It was a gorgeous Sunday, and Novotny decided it was a perfect day to wander around the city. No agenda. No plan. Just some classic poking around.

As he pulled the crewneck sweater over his white shirt with a button-down collar and slipped on his charcoal Harris tweed jacket, he realized that in its own way this outfit, like the khakis and green fatigues he wore every day, was a uniform. He picked up his pass and walked down Allersbergerstrasse toward the center of the city.

He visited the city museum, sat in on the end of a service at St. Sebaldus Church, and had a delicious lunch at a small restaurant tucked away on a side street. It was about two o'clock when he made his way up the curved cobblestone entryway that led to the hilltop castle.

Most of the structures had been rebuilt, and Novotny wondered what treasures had been lost—in addition to lives—when the bombs fell on these beautiful buildings. In a courtyard at the top, there were benches along a stone wall, and Novotny sat to enjoy the view and imagine what might have happened here hundreds of years ago.

He had never heard of the German artist Albrecht Duerer until he arrived in Nurnberg. But he had recalled seeing Duerer's most famous work—the praying hands—somewhere before he even knew who had drawn them. Duerer was one of Nurnberg's most famous residents, and reprints of the praying hands were available in shops all over the city.

He looked at the church spires, most of them rebuilt after the war, and wondered how a people with such a history of piety and religious devotion could have allowed the Nazis to take over and do what they did.

It was very hard to understand.

As he looked at the rooftops and thought, he heard slow, halting footsteps. A man, probably in his forties, was walking toward his bench. He had a cane and wore a black suit with a white shirt open at the collar.

The man nodded at Novotny as he sat down with some difficulty at the other end of the bench.

"Good day," the man said in German.

"Good day," Novotny replied.

"You speak German," the man noted.

"Yes, some. But I understand better than I speak," Novotny said somewhat apologetically.

"You are American?" the man asked.

"Yes," Novotny acknowledged, nodding.

"Student?"

"No, I am a soldier." He added, "I am stationed at the South Barracks." He used the original SS designation, rather than the name given to it by the U.S. Army. "I am in the 2d Armored Cavalry."

The man smiled. "I was also in the armored forces. On the eastern front. I was fortunate to come back," he said.

"You were wounded?" Novotny asked.

The man tapped his right thigh, making a thumping sound. "I left this leg behind. But I get around even so."

"What happened, if you do not mind saying," Novotny asked.

"No. I can tell you. Our regiment was ordered to advance against the Russians. Our commander objected because we could move only in a long column. There was too much mud for the tanks to leave the road." The man used his hands to illustrate his point.

"But the Austrian corporal would not listen," the man said, shaking his head in disgust.

"Who is the Austrian corporal?" Novotny asked, thinking he may have misunderstood.

"Hitler. He was born in Austria. And he was a corporal in the First World War. That was his only military qualification."

Novotny repeated the last word. "Excuse me," he said, reaching into his pocket and pulling out a small, red-covered English-German dictionary. "Yes, *qualification*. I understand."

"The Russians destroyed the first tanks and the last tanks, so we could not move either way. Then they destroyed the entire column. It was a tragedy."

The man squinted as though he were trying to bring some image into focus, maybe a picture of that day in his brain. Then he wiped his face with both hands, smiled, and said, "We must forget that and think of this beautiful day. My name is Dieter Holtz."

"I am Joseph Novotny."

"It pleases me to meet you."

"And me also," Novotny replied. "What do you do?"

"I am a teacher at the Nurnberg Technical School."

"Do you have a family?"

"No. I am not married."

The tone of his answer caused Novotny to drop the subject. "How do you like Nurnberg?" the man asked.

"I like it very much. I am lucky to be stationed here."

"You like German beer?"

"Yes, it is very good. Much better, I think, than American beer."

"I prefer wine," the man said, nodding and smiling in a way that caused

Novotny to like him. "You have had German wine?"

"Some. But not good wine."

"Then, Joseph . . . May I call you Joseph?"

"Yes, of course. And what shall I call you?'

"Dieter. Please call me Dieter." The man's face once again took on a warm, gentle smile. "Joseph, if you would come with me, there is a wine bar just down this street, and I would enjoy having a glass of good German wine with you. Would you like to do that?"

"Yes, thank you, Dieter. I would like that."

Novotny took the man's arm to steady him as they walked down the cobblestone street. When they reached the bottom, the man pointed to a narrow alley on their right. A few doors down the block was a place called Weinstube Fidelio.

Inside, it was modern, yet cozy and warm. There was a small bar at the far end, and behind that were racks of wine and a cooler stocked with slender wine bottles.

A man, obviously the proprietor, dressed in black trousers, a white shirt, and a bow tie, beamed as he greeted them.

"Good day, Dieter," he said, taking the man's hand and holding it in both of his hands. "I am always happy to see you, my dear friend."

"Gerd, this is Joseph . . ."

"Joseph Novotny," Novotny said, bowing slightly.

"Joseph and I were talking up at the castle. He has not had good German wine. So I asked him to come here with me."

The owner ushered them to a table set apart from the others. A brass ornament was placed on the center with the word Stammtisch cast into it. The owner gestured for the men to sit.

"You know about the Stammtisch, Joseph?" Dieter asked.

"No."

"It is for the special guests. You must be asked by the owner to sit here. But now that you have been here, you may sit at this table the next time you come here."

Novotny liked the tradition and immediately liked this place.

"Listen," Dieter said.

Novotny turned his head and concentrated on the quiet sound of music coming from two speakers placed high on the wall.

"You know this music?"

"No," Novotny replied.

"It is the opera *Fidelio* by Beethoven. That is the only music Gerd has here. It is perfect for drinking wine," Dieter said, smiling again and obviously pleased to share this opinion with his new friend. "Gerd and I were in the army together. And this was our favorite music."

"Dieter, I think I know which wine you want," Gerd said.

Dieter nodded.

The proprietor returned with a silver tray that held a tall, slender green bottle of wine, two wineglasses, and a corkscrew.

"Will you join us?" Dieter asked.

"Only for a few minutes. We will soon have more people here," the owner said, walking to the bar for a third glass.

The man held the bottle for Novotny to see. "This type of bottle with green glass is from the Mosel district." Pointing to the label, he explained that *Bauendorfer* meant the wine was from the village of Bauendorf. *Kirchen* indicated that the grapes were grown in a vineyard next to a local church.

The owner carefully opened the bottle and poured the wine into the three glasses. Novotny lifted it and looked at the slight golden color of the cool liquid. He put the glass under his nose and breathed in the fragrant perfume.

Dieter held up his glass and the other two did the same. "To the comradeship of ordinary soldiers." They touched glasses and Novotny took a small sip of the wine. He had never tasted a wine like this before. It was fruity and slightly sweet, almost like a nectar. But it wasn't syrupy and overpowering.

"This is wonderful," he said, looking at the contents of his glass.

"This wine is special for us," the owner said. "Dieter and I took a trip to this town, Bauendorf"—he pointed to the name on the label—"the week before we went into the army in 1940. Dieter, what was the name of the hotel where we stayed?"

"It was . . . ah . . ." He paused to recall the name. "It was the Hotel Golden Eagle."

"Yes. Yes. That was it," Gerd agreed. "That was where we first had this wine. We were young. I was only twenty-one. And Dieter was two years older. We were about your age, I suppose," he said, putting his hand on Novotny's shoulder. "And we were looking ahead to becoming soldiers."

"We didn't know, of course, what it would be like," Dieter interjected. "But we quickly learned," he added slowly, taking another sip of his wine.

"Joseph," the proprietor said, "you know that Dieter was not an ordinary soldier."

Novotny wasn't sure how to respond, so he said nothing.

"Dieter, show him the photograph."

"No," he declined. "It was long ago."

"Show him. He is a soldier. He will be interested."

Reluctantly, Dieter reached into the pocket of his coat and pulled out a small leather folder. Opening it, he handed it to Novotny.

"What do you see?" the proprietor asked.

Novotny looked at the photo, took another sip of his wine, and relished it as he looked at the image. It was a picture of a younger Dieter Holtz in a Nazi Wehrmacht uniform. The slight smile seemed to be one instructed by the photographer, rather than the smile reflecting happiness that Novotny had seen in the short time he had known this man.

The eyes seemed pained, reflecting physical pain or a hurting of the mind. Or both.

Above the left pocket of the uniform were several decorations. And at the collar of the uniform jacket was a Maltese cross.

Novotny asked, "You got the Iron Cross?"

His new friend nodded slightly.

"You see, Dieter. I knew he would be interested." Gerd filled the glasses again. "He will not talk about it. But I will tell you. The Russians trapped our regiment. Dieter was in one of the front tanks, and I was in a tank at the back. All of the tanks were destroyed." He looked at his friend. "It is better if you tell about it, Dieter. He wants to know about your Iron Cross."

The man shook his head.

"Well, then I will tell it as I know it. And if I am wrong, you tell me." He sipped his wine and continued. "Dieter was a sergeant and a tank commander. His gunner and loader were killed. Dieter and his driver were wounded. Dieter got the driver from the tank, but a Russian patrol was attacking. He fought them off and then pulled his driver more than 100 meters—where we had made a safe position to help the wounded. For this courage, he got the Iron Cross."

"He must be grateful to you for taking him to the safe place," Novotny said, thinking about Sergeant Duff's experience in Korea.

The man shook his head almost imperceptibly. "When we got there, he was dead." He took the leather folder and reached in under his photo, pulling out a second image. Novotny looked at the young soldier's face, with his bright eyes and confident smile.

"His name was Hans Lessing," Dieter said. "He was eighteen years old." He pointed to the picture. "This photograph was taken in Dresden when we were on leave before going to the front. You can tell by his face that we had not seen war yet." He looked at the photo, and then explained. "He was going to mail it to his mother, but he never got to it while we were on leave. When we were at the front, it was not possible to send it."

Novotny looked again at the photo and saw that there were brown stains along the bottom. Maybe the photo had gotten wet. But looking more carefully, it was obvious the stains were blood.

"Hans was also from Nurnberg," Dieter explained. "When I was out of the hospital and came back here, I went to his mother to give her this picture. She looked at it, but would not take it. So I have kept it."

He put the photo back in its place, slipped the leather folder back in his pocket, and lifted his glass again. "I have another toast to make." The other two men again held up their glasses. "To the comradeship of soldiers, but also to the hope that we and the Russians will not go to war."

The three men drank again. A small bell at the front door rang as two German couples entered.

"I must now work," Gerd said. Taking Novotny's hand, he said, "Joseph, I hope you will come again."

"Thank you. I will come again," he replied.

The man held up his partially filled glass. "So, Joseph, how do you like this wine?"

"It is the best wine I have ever had," Novotny said, holding up the glass to admire the wine.

"I am happy to make such a new experience for you."

"Have you been to Zeppelin Field?" Dieter asked. "You Americans call it Soldiers' Field."

"No."

"Do you have time to visit this now? There is much history there."

"Yes. If you have time."

"Fine, we will go there." The men drained the last drops from their glasses and the man placed a twenty-mark note on the table.

As they left, the proprietor waved and said, "Until I see you again, Joseph."

Novotny waved back. "Until I see you again."

The cab headed south on Allersbergerstrasse, past landmarks that were now becoming familiar to Novotny.

It pulled up to the back of a huge stone building. Dieter paid the driver, and the two men slowly walked along a paved entry to the front of the structure. At ground level, it was hard to get a real idea of how big this place was, other than to see that the main structure was several hundred yards long.

The long structure wasn't really a building. It was more like the end of a stadium, with long rows of stone shelves that served as seating. The center of this place was a massive open area, surrounded by other, smaller structures with the same kind of stone-shelf seating.

Novotny and his new friend were the only people in the entire place. Its emptiness seemed strange and disconcerting as he looked at the scale of it all. Painted in black letters on one wall—in English—were the words *Soldiers' Field*.

"Come," Dieter said, pointing toward the stairs at the closest part of the main structure. Novotny took his arm and helped him as they walked about halfway up the rows of stone seats. Dieter selected a row and walked toward the center of the structure. At exactly the midpoint was a large stone podium that overlooked the open field.

As they approached it, Dieter stopped, took several long breaths, and shook his head. "I must sit for a moment." Novotny sat next to him on the cold stone and took in the size of this place. It was hard to guess the dimensions. But in three of the four corners of the grassy center were baseball diamonds, facing inward toward the center. In the fourth corner there was a soccer field. The sports fields, obviously built by the army, took up only a small portion of the total area.

"Do you know of this place, where the Nazis had their events?"

"Yes, I have seen this place in the news," Novotny replied, flashing back on newsreels and photos in *Life* magazine.

"Go stand there," the man said, pointing to the podium. The gentle tone of his voice made it obviously a suggestion, rather than an instruction. "I will wait here."

Novotny walked along the seats to a set of stone steps that led up to the podium. He looked back and smiled at his friend, who nodded and gave him a slight wave. From the podium, he had a perfect view of everything. The huge grassy area. The smaller seating areas that defined the perimeter of the place and the seating that went on for probably 150 yards to his left and to his right.

He turned and studied the columns behind him, looking like part of a Greek or Roman temple. In his mind's eye, he remembered from the newsreels that there had been a massive Nazi eagle and swastika at the top. He also remembered footage of the eagle being blown up when the war ended.

Looking again at the panorama, he suddenly realized that he was standing exactly where Hitler had stood during the massive Nazi rallies. He peered down at his feet, thinking of the strange connection he now had with the man who had done such terrible things to so many people.

To the right of his foot, someone had taken chalk and drawn a swastika. In the style of the European traffic signs, a circle had been drawn around it and a diagonal line through it. Nazis not permitted here, he said to himself. He stood for a few minutes more, marveling again at the fact that he was standing exactly where Hitler had been. Then he walked back to his friend and sat down.

"Do you come here often?"

"No. I have not been here for some years. It makes me feel too sad. But not today," he added quickly. "I am happy to bring you to this place so you can see it."

"Were you ever here when they had the . . ." He looked up the word *rally*. "The rallies? Did you ever see any of them?"

"Yes, I was here once. When I was in the hospital. There were many of us recovering from wounds. I was sitting not far from here," he said, pointing to the right.

"It must have been something to see."

Dieter gestured toward the field. "Out there, I don't know how many soldiers there were. Perhaps 200,000. Maybe even more. All in perfect lines." He looked at the acres of grass spread out in front of them, and Novotny assumed he was re-creating the picture in his mind.

"It is hard to believe," Novotny said.

"Yes. It is hard to believe. So many men. And within one or two years, so many of them were dead." He took a few more deep breaths. "We were so young, and we knew so little. We had no idea about war." He shook his head slightly.

A question crossed Novotny's mind. At first, he hesitated to ask it. Then, telling himself that it was this man's idea to come here, he decided to ask.

"When you were a soldier, did you know about the other things?"

"The other things?" the man said, puzzled by the question.

"About the Jews and about the concentration camps." His new friend turned and looked at him, and for an instant, Novotny was sorry he had asked.

"These are things we Germans are uncomfortable talking about," he said. "I think especially here in Nurnberg, because the trials were here." Dieter thought for a moment. "Before I went into the army, I knew the Jews were being treated badly by the government. That was no secret."

"What about the concentration camps?" Novotny asked. "Did the Germans know about this?"

"At first, I think not. But as the war went on, more and more people came to know about this situation."

Novotny nodded.

"Joseph, your next question is probably how we could let it happen."

"Yes," Novotny answered quietly.

"I was on the Eastern Front when I heard of the special SS troops who were murdering Russian and Polish Jews—I believe for most Germans it was something that brought us shame."

"But was there anything that could be done about it?"

Dieter paused for a moment, and then said, "We enjoyed the early victories of the Nazis. We felt that this man—the Austrian corporal—was making our country strong again. He was bringing back our German pride.

I was proud to serve in the army when I first was a soldier. We all looked the other way at those things that we felt were not right."

Novotny looked across the stone steps and said, "It is still difficult for me to understand how these things could happen. Germans have such a history of culture. And this was so terrible."

"When he knew what was happening it was too late."

"There was no way to change the situation?" Novotny asked.

Dieter thought for a moment. "I suppose there is always a way to change such a situation—if the people are willing to make the sacrifices that would be needed."

Novotny pulled out his dictionary and found the word he didn't understand. *Sacrifices.*

"The sacrifices," he repeated.

"Yes. Only a few were willing to do that, because the sacrifice could mean a terrible death. One such man was Colonel Klaus von Stauffenberg. Do you know of him?"

"No," Novotny replied, shaking his head.

"He was an excellent army officer. He was wounded in Africa." Dieter looked at the vacant seats as though he were seeking an image of the German colonel. "He and some other officers tried to kill Hitler in 1944."

"Is that so?" Novotny said, obviously surprised.

"Yes, but they were not successful. And when they failed, they were shot."

"I did not know about that," Novotny said.

"Hundreds of people suspected to be part of this plan were also killed." Again Dieter took several deep breaths.

"This is difficult to believe."

"I know. But it is true." Dieter nodded "You know of General Rommel."

"Oh, yes. The Africa Corps."

"He was a very famous German general. A very fine soldier. He was suspected of being part of this plot. But no one knows with certainty if that is true."

"And what happened to him?"

"The Gestapo told him that he would be taken to the court, which meant certain death and dishonor to him. Or, they said, he could take his own life."

Novotny reached for his dictionary and leafed quickly through the pages, finding the word he wanted. "You mean for him to . . . ah . . . make a suicide?"

"Yes. That is what happened."

"These are all things I did not know," Novotny said. "Thank you for helping me understand such things."

Looking at the young soldier standing next to him, Dieter said, "We Germans are a difficult people to understand."

Novotny wasn't sure what to say, so he stood saying nothing.

"Now it is time for me to go, Joseph. I teach tomorrow, and I must prepare."

"Of course."

They waved down a cab that took them to Merrell Barracks. Novotny shook hands warmly with Dieter. Even though he had known him for only a few hours, he felt a special kinship to him.

"I am very happy that we have met," Novotny said. "Thank you for the wine. And thank you also for answering all my questions."

"I am also happy that we have met. And I hope it will be possible to see you again at Fidelio. I am there every Sunday to see my friend Gerd." He smiled the pleasant smile that Novotny had come to like so much. "And, of course, to drink some Bauendorf Kirchen wine."

"Until I see you again," Novotny said.

"Until I see you again," Dieter replied, waving as Novotny closed the cab door and walked toward the gate to Merrell Barracks.

A handful of men walked toward the mess hall, their breath steamy in the cold winter air. Johnson had been called to his section early this morning, so Novotny was going to breakfast alone, not thinking about anything in particular. Ahead, he saw a familiar figure walking ahead of him.

"Hey, Turner," he shouted. "Wait up." Novotny jogged to catch up with his friend. "How're things at the motor pool?"

"Pretty good. Except Sergeant Anderson left."

"What happened?"

"He got some kind of hardship transfer back to the States. I'm gonna miss him. He was a really good guy."

The men walked into the mess hall, got in line, and each took a stainless-steel tray from a rack. There wasn't much variety to breakfast from one day to the next. But the food was filling and it actually tasted pretty good, except for the coffee.

Watching over the food service was Sergeant Percy, who seemed to go out of his way to make everyone feel at home.

"Mornin', good buddy," he said to Novotny in his gentle southern drawl.

"Good morning, Sergeant," Novotny replied, smiling.

Sergeant Percy called everyone "good buddy" and was always cheerful, whether he was supervising lunch or ladling out awful-tasting coffee from a mess truck on an alert.

Turner and Novotny found two seats near a window and sat down. "Have you been in town to look around?" Novotny asked.

"No." He added apologetically, "I don't speak German the way you and Johnson do. And I don't want to go to any of the bars where the GIs go and they speak English. I just stay around here."

Novotny took a forkful of scrambled eggs, followed that with a piece of bacon, and washed it down with a couple of big swallows of cold milk. "It's really an interesting city. Lots of history. Old buildings."

"I'll take a look around one of these days," Turner said.

"Johnson and Morris and I wandered around a few weekends ago. We ended up in some dive, listening to rock and roll. If you can believe that."

"Morris told me about it. That's where he met that girl he's seeing. Right?"

Novotny hadn't talked to Morris for a while, and he was surprised to hear the news. "He met a girl when we went out. But I didn't know he was seeing her."

"He says she's really nice."

Novotny spread some strawberry jam on a piece of toast and took a bite. "I just met her once. But she seems nice."

He wasn't sure just what her story was. He just hoped that Morris wasn't getting into something that would be a problem.

"You ought to get out a little, Turner. Meet some of those German girls yourself."

Turner shook his head. "I've never been very good with girls. It's just not somethin' that comes easy to me—bein' around girls."

"You mean you're not smooth? You don't have a good line?" Novotny exaggerated the way he said it, as if it were from some B movie.

"Yeah. You know what I mean." Turner took a sip of orange juice and shrugged.

"Look at it this way, Turner. There are millions of babies born every year. And they're born to all kinds of people who don't have a good line and don't know the first thing about being smooth."

Turner took another drink of his juice, then put the glass down and looked sad and lost.

"What's the matter, Turner?" Novotny asked, making certain he said the words as gently as possible.

"If I was with a woman, I wouldn't even know what to do. If I was with a woman, she'd probably just sit there and laugh." He took a bite of his toast and looked out the window as he slowly chewed it, then took yet another sip of his juice.

"Turner, I guarantee that if you were with a woman who was ready to . . . ah . . . you know, to do it with you, you'd know exactly what to do. Nature would take over and you'd be just fine." He took a sip of coffee and said, "Tell you what. I've got a deal for you."

"What kind of deal?"

"How about if you and Johnson and I go into town and walk around this Saturday. Drink some beer. Just mess around."

"Sure."

"And suppose we ended up where there were women who would be willing to do it with you. Would you be willing to give it a try?"

"You mean pick up some hooker?" Turner asked, obviously not excited about the idea.

"No, I'm talking about something a lot classier than that."

"I'm not sure."

"I'm not trying to push you into something. When we get there, if you're not comfortable about it, we'll just walk away from it. No problems. No questions. And we'll forget about it." Novotny lit a cigarette to have with his coffee. "What have you got to lose?"

"Nothin', I guess."

"OK, Johnson and I will pick you up about five o'clock on Saturday. Wear civvies. We'll go out and have dinner and then do the rest of it."

"How much is this going to cost?"

"Just bring a couple of bucks for dinner."

"I don't know what this is all about," Turner said, finishing off his juice. "But I trust you, Novo, so I'll just go along with it." He shrugged. "What the heck."

Johnson was stretched out on his bunk, having an after-dinner cigarette and reading *Stars and Stripes.*

"How'd your day go, Bob?" Novotny asked.

"OK," Johnson said without enthusiasm. "Novo, Listen to this." he paused paused and then read, "'Speaking to the General Assembly of the United Nations last year, Soviet Prime Minister Nikita S. Khruschev said the Warsaw Pact countries would bury the West.'"

Johnson looked at the next paragraph, and read, "'In a speech this week, Khruschev appeared ready to make good on last year's threat.'" Johnson paused again and then went on. "'At a meeting of officials from the Soviet Union, the Democratic Republic of Germany, and the other members of the Warsaw Pact, he said the countries of Eastern Europe can no longer tolerate the illegal occupation of West Berlin and the rest of West Germany by the United States,

England, and France.'"

"Terrific," Novotny said, shaking his head.

"It goes on, 'U.S. military officials reportedly view the statements with concern, but not alarm. According to a Pentagon spokesman, U.S. troops in Europe remain at a high state of readiness and are capable of countering any Soviet threat.'"

Johnson dropped the paper on his bunk. "There's only one thing for it, Novo."

"What's that?"

"We've got to go out on Saturday and get laid," he said, with a slight smile. "You know, Lili Marlene on the eve of battle and all that sort of thing."

"Actually, I wanted to talk to you about that," Novotny announced, sitting on his bunk and lighting up a cigarette.

"You're horny too?"

"Of course. But I wanted to talk to you about Turner."

"What about him?" Johnson asked.

"Well, you know he's not the most confident guy you've ever met."

"I'll buy that."

"He's really down. He's just having a really hard time."

"I don't know if there's much that you and I can go about that. That's the way he is," Johnson said, shrugging.

"Well, here's what I thought. You know that German vet I told you about that bought me the wine?"

"Yeah."

"He told me about a city-run brothel. It's clean. The women are supposed to be nice. And they have medical checks all the time."

"Yeah."

"Well, I thought you and I could take Turner over there on Saturday."

Johnson shook his head. "Look, we've got enough to worry about ourselves. Just tell him where it is and tell him to try it out."

"In the first place, he wouldn't do it. He hardly leaves the post for anything."

"And?"

"It's off limits."

"Oh, come on, Novo. You want us to go over, take Turner with us, and get into all sorts of trouble, just so Turner can get laid. Let's just buy him a copy of *Playboy*."

"Here's what I thought. You and I have the German civvies we bought here. I'll give Turner my trench coat to wear. It'll be big on him. But it'll work. And we'll all appear to be at least kind of foreign."

Johnson looked skeptical.

"You and I can speak German as we go in. Turner can just nod, or say '*ja*.' They'll think we're Danish or British with our accents."

"What does it cost?"

"Forty marks. Ten bucks."

"So you want me to go with you, so we can speak German so they'll think we're not GIs while Turner just breezes in with us."

"Yeah. But there's one other thing."

"Novo, I can hardly wait."

"Will you split it with me? That ninety dollars a month we get doesn't go very far, and I'm kind of short."

"I can't believe this."

"Look at it this way: he shouldn't have to pay for it the first time, should he?"

Johnson took his billfold out of his pocket and gave Novotny a five-dollar bill. "I'm not sure why I'm doing this, Novo."

"Bob, you'll never regret it." Novotny smiled and shook his friend's hand. "When it's over, you'll be glad you did it."

Johnson just shook his head, not believing what he had just done.

It was about seven o'clock in the evening and the overcast sky was dark. The air was cold, and piles of shoveled snow lined the streets. The three young men walked side by side, with Turner in the middle. There was almost a solemn air to the trio, as if they were on their way to an important ceremony. In a way, they were.

Novotny wore a bulky sweater, a wool cap, black wide-wale corduroy pants, and desert boots. He had a woolen scarf around his neck, with one end thrown over his shoulder in the style of RAF pilots.

Turner was bareheaded and wore the tan trench coat that Novotny had bought a couple of weeks ago. It had more buttons, epaulets, straps, and attachments than Novotny had ever seen on such a coat before. It reminded him of the coat that Humphrey Bogart had worn in *Casablanca*. Turner had buttoned the coat all the way up to the collar and looked pale and anxious.

Johnson was wearing a trench coat similar to Novotny's and a tweed cap, like those worn by men on the Scottish moors. Over his shoulder, he had slung a "schnitzel bag," a cloth sack used by Germans to carry their lunch or anything else they might need.

They had just finished a simple, pleasant dinner at a small restaurant they had found on their last visit to town. Novotny and Johnson had ordered beers and tried to get Turner to join them, but he wouldn't.

Following the directions Novotny had been given; they walked away from the center of town. Two blocks down the street, they made a left down what appeared to be a dead-end street. On the right, was a modern, three-story building, painted in pastel colors and looking like one of the many new apartments that had gone up where the original structures had been destroyed by bombs.

A short sidewalk led to what was obviously the main entrance. They waited until two other men approached the building, and then followed them in. The two Germans spoke briefly to a matronly woman seated at a desk and then walked through another set of double doors. On the wall behind her was a large sign saying, "Off Limits to All U.S. Military Personnel."

Johnson approached the desk first. "Good evening, madam," he said in his best formal German. "How goes it with you?"

"It goes with me very well, thank you," she said, carefully surveying him as she spoke. "And with you?"

"Also very well, thank you."

"You are not German," she said coolly. "Where are you from?"

"We are from England," Johnson replied, without hesitating.

"And what do you do?" she asked, never taking her eyes off of him.

"We are students," he said, gesturing to Turner and Novotny. Novotny nodded in confirmation.

"I hope you have a pleasant visit," she said, waving Johnson toward the next set of doors.

As Turner approached the desk, she held up her hand to stop him. "And you? You are also a student?"

Turner swallowed hard and looked down at his feet.

Novotny moved closer to Turner and put his arm around his shoulder. "He speaks no German," Novotny said, leaning toward the woman and almost whispering. "It is his first time to be with a woman. He is somewhat afraid to be here."

For the first time during the encounter, the woman smiled slightly. "I understand. Tell him we have only good girls here. Tell him he need not be afraid."

"I will tell him," Novotny said. "Thank you."

The interior of the building was simple. Each floor had pastel-colored walls and long halls lined with doors. There were five rooms on each side of the hallway; times three floors would be thirty rooms. That's a lot of women, he thought.

"Looks like a dorm at school," Johnson noted.

"What do you think of this place, Turner?" Novotny asked.

"It's not what I expected. It seems real clean. I thought it would be grubby or somethin'."

Men, most of them appearing to be in their thirties or forties, walked the halls, looking into rooms with open doors. Novotny, Johnson, and Turner saw an open door about halfway down the hall and stopped. The space was dimly lit and consisted of a sitting room with a daybed against one wall, a table, and a couple of chairs. To the left was a door that Novotny assumed led to a bathroom. A few framed landscape prints were on the walls.

Inside, a woman was standing in front of the window, smoking and looking out into the night. Novotny cleared his throat and the woman turned to see the three men standing in the doorway. She was an exceptionally pretty, slender young woman, with long reddish hair, wearing a black lace robe. My God, she's gorgeous, Novotny thought.

"Good evening," she said in German to none of them in particular. "Would one of you like to come into my room?" She took a long drag on her cigarette, tipping her head up and blowing the smoke toward the ceiling, then crushing it out in an ashtray.

"Do you wish to come in?" she asked, again to no one in particular.

There was a brief hesitation and Novotny answered, "No, thank you." The woman turned back to the window without saying anything in response.

"Good call, Novo," Johnson said as they walked down the hall, away from the open door. "She was really cute, but definitely not right."

Novotny felt a need to explain to Turner. "We have to find someone who's special for you. She was good looking, but she was too cold."

Turner said nothing, and just followed the other two men as they walked, looking for open doors. They stopped at four other rooms on the first and second floors, sometimes exchanging a few words with the women inside, sometimes just looking in and walking on.

Novotny could tell that Turner was getting more and more anxious about this whole thing, and realized that something would have to happen soon. On one hand, he didn't want to leave here without completing the process.

On the other hand, he was concerned about having them find the right person, given Turner's fragile psyche. To do this wrong could make things worse for Turner. As the minutes went on, Novotny began to think that maybe this had not been such a great idea after all.

At the end of the hall, they walked up the stairs to the third floor and stopped at the first open door. A dark-haired woman, about thirty, sat on the daybed reading a book.

"Good evening," Novotny said in German.

The woman looked up and smiled. "Good evening. Are all three of you here to see me?"

"No, just our friend," Johnson replied, tapping Turner on the shoulder.

"Does he also speak German?" she asked, putting a mark in the book and setting it on the table next to the bed.

Novotny shook his head. "No. He speaks only English."

She looked at Turner. "I do not speak English well. But a little," she said, holding her thumb and index finger an inch apart to demonstrate the point. "What is your name?"

Turner swallowed hard. "My name is Harold. Harold Turner."

"And you are an American soldier, Harold?"

Turner looked at Novotny and Johnson, as if to seek counsel. When neither said anything, he answered, "Yes, ma'am. I'm an American soldier."

She stood, pulled the belt tight on her maroon robe, and walked toward the door. She wasn't especially pretty. Not like the first one they'd seen. The redhead. But she sure wasn't ugly. She was just sort of plain in comparison to some of the women they'd seen. Although it was a little hard to tell, given the cut of her robe, Novotny decided she was probably pretty well built.

She stood next to Turner, but not so close as to be intimidating. "Harold, would you like to be with me for a while?"

Turner nodded.

Novotny said, in German, "Excuse me, miss. I must tell you something about my friend."

She looked at Novotny, smiled, and said in German, "I know you are soldiers, not students. And there is nothing you need to tell me about your friend." She took Turner gently by the arm and led him into the room. "But I must ask you to leave," she said to Novotny and Johnson. "Please return in thirty minutes."

They stood in the hall as she closed the door. Novotny looked at his watch and took the cigarette that Johnson offered.

"That was a good choice, Novo. Definitely a good pick. My guess is that you've done this before."

Novotny took a quick puff on the cigarette, shook his head, and laughed softly. "I've never done anything like this before in my life. And I've never been in a place like this before."

"You've never made it with a hooker?"

"No. It just never appealed to me. I can't imagine making love with someone you don't care about." They slowly walked toward the end of the hall.

They went down to the second floor and walked down the halls, looking into rooms and talking to some of the women. "This place is amazing," Novotny observed. "Run by the city. Clean. It seems a whole lot more civilized than seeing women standing in doorways, motioning to guys driving by in cars, like they do in Chicago."

"Wonder why we don't do is this way in the States."

"Who knows?" Novotny said, looking at his watch. "Guess we'd better get back there. I wonder how he did?"

Johnson chuckled. "He did fine. I'm not worried."

When they got to the door, it was still closed, so they leaned against the wall and waited.

"You really like Turner, don't you?" Johnson asked.

"He's a nice guy. He's miscast for the army. And he's a little strange. Not someone I'd probably ever know outside of the army. But I like him. And I guess I kind of worry about him."

The door opened and Turner was standing in the hall, looking back into the room. The woman stood in the doorway, her robe as tightly belted as it had been twenty minutes before.

"Goodbye, Harold," the woman said.

"Bye," Turner replied quietly.

Reaching into his trench coat, Novotny pulled out an envelope and handed it to the woman. In it were two German twenty-mark notes—ten dollars U.S.—and an American five-dollar bill. He didn't know what Amy Vanderbilt would say about tipping prostitutes. But she seemed particularly nice, and he had decided to include the extra money, whether it was proper or not.

"Many thanks," she said in German. "Perhaps you will come to see me one day?"

"Perhaps," Novotny replied politely.

Novotny watched her walk back to the daybed, sit down, and find her place in the book. He stood in the doorway, saying nothing.

"Will you stay for a while?" she asked Novotny. "Your friends will wait for you." She smiled and cocked her head with a mischievous look in her eyes.

"No," he finally answered. "No, thank you. We must go now."

"I understand," she said. "But I hope you will remember me. My name is Elke."

"I will remember you." As he said it, he knew he would.

The three men said nothing as they walked down the hall to the stairway and headed out the doors toward the madam's desk. As they approached her, she motioned to Novotny. "One moment, please,"

He stood in front of the desk, wondering if something was wrong. "Yes," he said.

"I ask that you do not tell your friends about this place and that you have been here," she said.

Novotny frowned, not sure he had completely understood.

"I do not want this place full of soldiers, whom I must then send away," she explained, sounding like a kindly aunt.

He smiled and nodded. "You knew when we came here?"

"It is quite easy to see. You are dressed as Europeans. But there is no question that you are Americans. American soldiers." She smiled and said, "The way you walk. The look on your face. It is very easy to see you are American soldiers. But I decided you would not make any trouble."

"Many thanks," he said, thinking about that day, months ago, when Sergeant Duff told him that he had been indelibly marked.

The three men walked out into the cold night. "Was there some problem?" Johnson asked.

"Not really. She just knew from the beginning that we were GIs."

They walked back toward the center of the city where they would be able to find a cab. Johnson and Turner buttoned up their coats. And Novotny hunched over and put his hands in his pockets to keep warm.

"OK, Turner. How was it?" Johnson asked.

"It was pretty good," he replied.

"Christ, Turner, you've got to tell us more than that," Johnson said in mock anger. "After all, we sponsored this trip."

"I really appreciate you guys doin' this," Turner said. "I just didn't last very long."

"When you pay for it, it doesn't matter," Johnson explained. "It's not like satisfying your wife. With a hooker, you're the customer."

"The big question is this," Novotny said, rubbing his hands together as they walked. "If you had a girlfriend or a wife or whatever, would you know what to do now?"

Turner walked a few steps before answering. "Yeah," he replied. "I'd know what to do." Then he added, in that soft voice of his, "If I ever had a wife or a girlfriend."

Sergeant Rogers scowled as he watched Novotny approach his desk. "Here's what I want you to do," he said. "Get your field gear together, draw your weapon, and requisition a jeep. Then get back here by fourteen hundred. Got that so far?"

"Yes, Sergeant," he replied coolly.

"You know, Novotny, I don't like your attitude. I don't like the tone of your voice. And basically, I don't like you. I'm telling you that so you know where I stand."

Novotny stood silently in front of the sergeant's desk.

"Now what is it I want you to do?

"Get my gear, my weapon, and a jeep, and be back here at fourteen hundred."

"That's very good, Novotny. And when you get back here, you'll pick up Captain Nelson from S-4. You'll take him to the Hof border operations camp, where you'll be doing some translating. You'll be out about two days."

"Is that all, Sergeant?"

"Novotny, if I had anything else to say to you, I'd say it. Now why don't you just get your ass in gear and do what I just told you to do?"

"Yes, Sergeant."

Novotny went to the motor pool, checked out the jeep, and picked up the captain.

Once out of Nurnberg, there were few towns. Just an occasional village that seemed to grow organically around a church spire.

Separating the villages were long stretches of well-manicured German forests. The forest floor was green where the sun could penetrate through and support the growth of grass. Acre after acre of pine trees appeared to have been pruned to free them of any dead, or even imperfect, branches. The Germans seemed good at getting rid of things that didn't fit the plan.

"Those forests are really amazing."

"They sure are," the captain replied, studying the trees.

"A German I met said the foresters who take care of the trees know each one as if it's part of his family."

"I'm not surprised."

Novotny studied the empty road ahead and thought about how good he felt. He was going to be away from Sergeant Rogers for a couple of days. He was driving through some beautiful scenery. And he was on his way to the border, the arbitrary line that separated West Germany from Czechoslovakia.

He would be within ten kilometers of Domazlice, where his grandmother was born. That would be strange. To be so close yet unable to go anywhere near the place. He wondered what the town looked like. Whether it would seem different from the German towns on this side of the line.

"Where did you learn German?" the captain asked.

"I was in language training at Meade before I came here." He hesitated and then added, "My family is Czech, and I speak Czech better than German."

"Here's what we'll be doing," the captain said. "When the war ended, and the Wehrmacht—the German Army—was disbanded, they set up a kind of paramilitary organization called the *Grenzshutz.*"

"Border protection," Novotny translated.

"That's right. They're not part of the regular German Army. But they use military vehicles and equipment. We patrol the border with them. They provide us with information, and they make the Germans who live along the border feel that their government is doing something to protect them."

"Sounds like a good arrangement."

"The meeting tomorrow is with Border Protection officers to work out some details about supplies and equipment that we're giving them. We'll be working with H Troop, which is on the border now."

Novotny smiled. "That's my old company. I took basic with them."

"Well, you'll have a chance to see some of your buddies."

An hour later, they drove through the gate of the border outpost, a cluster of single-storied wooden buildings, centered on a tall pole topped by an American flag. Novotny pulled the vehicle into an area where about a dozen other jeeps were parked.

Some of the jeeps were armed with .30-caliber machine guns, and others were equipped with radios. Typically, a patrol consisted of one of each kind, with an NCO and five enlisted men making up the team. Field gear was lashed to the hood of each jeep in compact packages. All of the vehicles were dusty, looking as though they'd just come back from a long run on dirt roads, which they had.

Novotny wasn't sure how the arrangement had been made, but somehow the Russians and the Allies had agreed that only jeeps were allowed along the border. No tanks or artillery. Just recon vehicles and cavalry scouts. It struck him as all very gentlemanly, given that they were, at the same time, prepared to blast each other off the face of the earth.

Novotny hadn't seen Stein since they had arrived in Germany, and he was looking forward to catching up with him.

"What's it like on the border?" Novotny asked Jesse Stein over dinner.

"We just go back and forth along the border, looking at Ivan, and sending reports in about what he's up to." Stein took a bite of the apple pie on his tray. "We do it all the time. Whether it's cold or hot. Rainy or dry. In snow. It doesn't matter, we watch Ivan. And he just goes back and forth on the other side, looking at us," he explained matter-of-factly. "Once in a while we get an incident of some kind. Occasionally someone tries to cross the border. But mainly, we're here. And they're there. And we hope it stays that way."

The meeting with the border police started about eight o'clock the next morning and lasted until about noon. As Captain Nelson had said, it was pretty routine stuff. But Novotny found it fascinating even so, translating information from German to English and then the other way.

At the end of the meeting, the officers walked to the courtyard, and Novotny translated good wishes between the two groups of men. Near the gate were two World War II American half-track scouting vehicles, marked with a Maltese cross. Standing nearby were a handful of German border policemen.

Novotny did a double-take when he saw them. The cut of their jackets was the same as the German Army had worn in World War II. But most striking to him were their helmets. The steel headgear was exactly like the ones he'd seen in the newsreels; slightly square, with a flared protector from the ears back.

Captain Nelson saluted the ranking German officer, who returned the gesture. Novotny saluted as well. Watching the jeeps pull out of the compound, the captain said, "Seems a little strange, doesn't it? These guys are our allies now."

"I guess it's the helmets," Novotny said. "That kind of startled me. When do you want to head back, sir?"

"Around oh six hundred tomorrow. Until then, just take it easy. Do whatever you want."

"Yes, sir," he said, walking toward the day room in the border outpost to see who he could find.

Jesse Stein was walking toward the row of jeeps, a carbine slung over his shoulder. "Hey, Novo," Stein shouted. "We're going on patrol. Want to go along?"

"Sure. I'm free until oh six hundred."

Stein took him over to Sergeant Morales, the squad leader, to see if it could be arranged.

"Is it all right if Novotny goes out with us, Sarge? It'd be a good way to let headquarters know we're doing our job out here. Right, Novo?"

The sergeant thought for a moment. "Ah . . . yeah, I guess it's all right. Do you have any ammo?"

Shaking his head, Novotny felt silly at being unprepared.

The sergeant walked to one of the jeeps, opened a pack, pulled out a clip of ammo, and gave it to Novotny. "You know how to use that thing, right?" the sergeant asked.

Novotny nodded and put the clip in his field jacket pocket.

"All right, men. Let's go," he said to the small group of cavalrymen who had gathered around the vehicles.

The sergeant's driver headed the jeep out of the compound, with the other jeep following closely behind. Buds were starting to form on the canopy of tree branches over them as they wound their way along the narrow dirt road. They passed an occasional farmhouse with neatly kept fields, and saw a farmer now and then, stopping his work to watch the vehicles pass.

"You're Czech, right, Novotny?" the sergeant asked.

Scrunched in the back of the jeep Novotny leaned forward to answer the question. "Yeah, my parents are Czech."

Sergeant Morales pointed to a spot on the side of the road, sheltered by a small but dense grove of trees. The driver pulled over and the second jeep stopped just a few feet behind it. The men gathered around the sergeant, waiting for orders.

"Lock and load," he said. Novotny and each member of the patrol set the safety latch on his rifle and inserted a clip of ammunition. They walked into the grove and knelt as they peered to the east.

They looked across an open expanse of tranquil fields. About half a mile away, Novotny estimated, was a wide, unplanted strip that wound its way from north to south like a dry riverbed. Large, white pyramids, set in perfect rows, marked the center of the serpentine strip. On the other side were more fields and beyond that was a forest.

Sergeant Morales studied the scene through his binoculars. "That's Czechoslovakia. Over there on the other side of the plowed strip," he said, pointing.

"My mother's from Domazlice. About ten kilometers from here."

"That's too bad. Goddamn Ruskies."

"What are those white things?" Novotny asked.

"Dragon's teeth," the sergeant explained. "Tank traps. The idea is to slow us down when we go over them, and expose the belly of the tank. Where the armor's light. Then hit us."

"So that's the iron curtain," he said, fascinated.

"That's it. The plowed strip is mined here." He handed Novotny his binoculars. "See that wire fence in the middle?"

Novotny focused the binoculars and could plainly see the fence. "Yeah."

"It's electrified. Now look off to the right. See that tower?"

"Yeah."

"They've got a clear field of fire up and down the border."

"Does anyone ever get across?"

"Not here. It's too flat. But some people make it where it's hilly."

The sergeant took back the glasses, scanned the border, and made some notes in a pad he kept in his pocket. "Let's go," he told the men.

Carefully they made their way back to the jeeps, cleared their weapons, and headed south down the quiet dirt road, traveling slowly so as not to kick up too much dust.

Gradually, the terrain changed and the flat farmland gave way to rolling hills. Sergeant Morales motioned to his driver, who again pulled the jeep off the road, to the base of a small knoll. As the men were gathering to crawl to the top, the unmistakable sound of a rifle shot broke the quiet of the spring day.

"Lock and load," the sergeant shouted. "Let's go! Let's go!"

Novotny took a clip out of his pocket, quickly aligned it in the slot at the base of his carbine, rammed it home with the palm of his hand, and pulled the bolt back, loading a round into the chamber. That done, he scrambled up the knoll, his heart pumping hard as he took a position on his belly at the top.

The plowed strip was closer than before. Maybe a quarter mile away. And unlike the other place, it was straddled with steep ravines and groves of trees rather than tilled soil. Still there was an open area that meandered into the forest, delineated at the center with a barbed-wire fence.

He was breathing hard, partly from exertion and partly from fear. He had no sooner gotten himself into position, his carbine pointed at the line and his finger loosely against the trigger, when he heard another shot, the crackling sound reverberating through the trees.

Looking to where the sound came from, he saw a man running across the plowed strip, like a football halfback evading unseen tacklers. A soldier, wearing the uniform of the Czech Army, was standing at the edge of the forest. Novotny could see three or four other soldiers running toward him from the woods.

Slinging his rifle over his shoulder, the Czech border guard cupped his hands to his mouth and seemed to be shouting something to the running man. The man stopped and turned back toward the soldier for a moment, and then began running again.

The soldier knelt and put his weapon to his shoulder. Novotny's breath was coming in short, shallow gasps. "Don't shoot," he whispered. "Please don't shoot."

Another report echoed through the valley, and still the man kept running. Once more there was the sound of a shot, surrealistically bouncing from one hill to another. This time the man fell, first to his knees, then facedown on the plowed dirt.

"Jesus," Novotny spat through his clenched teeth. Suddenly he heard another shot and felt the stock of his carbine hit his shoulder. He instantly realized that the sharp crack of a rifle shot had come from his own carbine.

He shook his head and dropped his face into the grass, realizing what had happened.

"What in the hell are you tryin' to do?" Sergeant Morales shouted. "Start a war? Get down to the jeeps," he said, furious. "Peterson. Keep an eye on what's happening."

Novotny slid down the embankment and stood by the jeeps. Sergeant Morales had calmed down by the time he walked over to the chagrined young soldier.

"Clear your weapon," the NCO ordered. Novotny took out the clip, put it in his pocket, and then pulled back the bolt to eject the round in the chamber. "Now, what happened?"

"When we heard the shots and you told us to lock and load, I loaded. But I didn't set the safety," he said, shaking his head. "When the guy was shot, I just must have flexed and accidentally squeezed the trigger. I don't remember doing it." He shook his head again. "It was really dumb, and I'm sorry."

"Well, we're not going to report it. We'll just let it pass as if it didn't happen. I'll tell the squad." The sergeant took out a pack cigarettes, lit one, and offered them to Novotny, who declined. "Who knows? Maybe it'll make those guys wait a little longer next time before they shoot."

"Maybe," Novotny said, obviously depressed by the whole episode.

Sergeant Morales patted him on the shoulder. "Don't be too hard on yourself. I understand," he said, nodding. "Either one of those guys could be a relative."

Novotny ran his hand over his face. "Yeah. Either one."

He tried to sleep and push yesterday out of his head. But he couldn't. He had never seen a man killed before. Consciously, intentionally killed.

He wondered what the border guard had said. The man had stopped and looked back. Maybe the guard tried to persuade him not to cross. Maybe the guard even pleaded with the man, telling him he had no choice but to shoot him if he continued to run. Maybe the guard is lying on his bunk right now, wishing he could push it all out of his head.

The guard was just doing his job. If anyone attempts to cross the border, the orders probably say, warn them and then shoot them. And, if you don't shoot them, then you will be court-martialed.

The fact that the man wasn't armed and had his back to the guard doesn't mean a thing. The fact that the man was trying to be free was irrelevant. The border guard's job was to stop him. And that's exactly what he did. Maybe he'll get a medal for it.

In fact, Novotny thought uncomfortably, I'm the incompetent in this episode. You have a man running across the border and certainly aware of the risks. You have a Czech border guard, doing his job. And you have me, concealed behind a ridge, forgetting to lock my weapon, twitching, and firing a round that could have started a war.

Suppose . . . Once again there was the seemingly inevitable speculation. And the images. Detailed and realistic images of what could have happened. Just suppose . . .

The Czech border guard heard the shot from the knoll across the border. As he'd been trained, he fell to the prone position, making himself a smaller target.

Four border guards took sheltered positions at the edge of the forest. One was carrying a machine gun. A second was obviously his loader.

The guard pointed to the knoll where Novotny and the patrol were positioned. Moments later, he heard the *papapapapapapapa* sound that machine guns make. Instinctively, Novotny scrunched lower against the crest of the knoll, checking to see if the machine-gun fire was hitting their position.

Sergeant Morales skidded down to the base of the knoll and ran to the radio jeep a hundred feet away. Grabbing the microphone, he said, calmly but intently, "Bird dog six, bird dog six, this is bird dog niner, over."

Novotny couldn't hear everything the sergeant said. But one message was clear. "Request permission to return fire. Repeat. Request permission to return fire."

The NCO scampered back to the knoll. "Return fire," he ordered.

Novotny consciously clicked the safety lever, allowing him to fire his carbine. Moving slightly to the right, to a clump of shrubs, he edged up to the top of the knoll.

"Jesus," he said, under his breath. There were now fifteen or twenty soldiers on the other side of the border. Some wore the uniform of the Czech border guards. But it looked as though others were wearing Russian uniforms.

His heart pounding, he watched Sergeant Morales rush back to the radio jeep. "We need reinforcements," the sergeant said. "Bird dog six. This is bird dog niner. Urgently need to be reinforced."

Novotny turned again to the border and took a deep breath, trying to absorb what he saw. There must have been a hundred soldiers. "Oh, God," was all he could say. Fearful, his heart continued to beat hard and his breath came in gasps.

The firing from the other side of the border was now an ongoing set of single pops from rifles and repeated sounds from machine guns. To his left, members of the patrol were returning fire. And Sergeant Morales was directing the driver of the machine-gun jeep to get into position to return fire.

Novotny looked down the sight of his carbine. He wiped the sweat from his brow and swallowed hard, his mouth sticky and dry. Shifting the barrel to the right, he took aim on a group of three border guards who had moved closer to his position. More likely to get a hit, he thought, given the carbine's limited range.

He squeezed off a round, then another. The three men looked toward the shrubs that concealed him. Taking careful aim, he fired a third round and saw one of the guards drop his rifle, put his hand to his chest, and fall to the ground.

The firing had taken his attention away from what was happening behind him. Another patrol had just arrived. Six men with another radio jeep and one equipped with a .30-caliber machine gun. They were still outnumbered. But the odds were getting better.

Novotny ran his tongue around his lips, trying to get his mouth to be less dry. Then, taking out his canteen, he took a gulp of water to wet his mouth, and a deep breath to try to settle himself down.

"Armor, armor," he heard one of the cavalrymen shout. Looking to the left, he saw a column of Russian T-54 tanks moving slowly along a dusty road to the border. Once again Sergeant Morales scrambled to the radio jeep.

"This is bird dog niner. T-54s taking position opposite us," he said in what Novotny considered a very unemotional tone, given the situation. "We need armor. Repeat. We need armor."

A third patrol arrived. There were now about twenty cavalrymen spaced out along the knoll. On the other side of the border were probably seventy-five Communist troops and about six T-54s.

Most of the troopers were to his left. But a group of four had taken up a position about a hundred feet to his right. Hearing a thump from one of the Russian tanks, Novotny slid down the knoll and hugged the ground. Seconds later there was a terrible whistling sound and an earth-shaking explosion as the 100-mm round hit in front of him.

He looked to his right and saw that the others were doing exactly what he had done: getting as close to the dirt as possible, and edging down the protected side of the knoll.

"Armor! We need armor!" Sergeant Morales shouted into the microphone, this time more urgently.

The clatter of tank treads caused him to turn and look back to his left. Coming down the road, sheltered by the knoll, where six M41 light tanks. Their 76-mm guns were no match for the T-54s. But at least they had something more than rifles and a couple of machine guns.

And then, unexpectedly, he heard the whine of jet engines and saw a formation of F-100 Super Sabers roar overhead. The reassurance of their arrival was instantly offset by an additional columns of tanks that Novotny saw moving toward them from the other side of the border.

Ivan was making his move. The balloon was going up because an idiot Pfc had been careless and fired a round. And the 2d Cav would do what it was assigned to do: slow the Russians down until NATO could organize a counterattack.

Novotny sat up, shook his head, and opened his eyes wide. What in the hell is your mind doing? he asked himself. He felt like an idiot for what he had just allowed his brain to do. Could it happen like that? Could a simple dumb mistake start a war?

No, there are too many safeguards. Too many checks and balances.

Maybe, he decided. But maybe not. Staring into the darkness of the room, he tried to push it all aside, hoping sleep would come soon. And in a matter of a minute or so, the images of the border were gone, replaced by Khrushchev saying, "We will bury you."

Shaking his head, all he could do was be amazed at the tricks one's mind could play.

It was just the right kind of task. Demanding enough to keep his mind occupied and away from the images of a few days ago. Standing on the ladder, he took the end of the crepe paper and turned it into a neat spiral. When it seemed sufficiently decorative, he taped the red, white, and blue streamers to the wall and made his way back down the floor.

He looked at his handiwork and nodded approvingly. Red, white, and blue for the United States, and red, black, and yellow for West Germany.

The hall reminded him of the recreation room of the Presbyterian church he had attended as a kid. At one end was a stage, with a scruffy upright piano. Folding chairs were neatly lined up along the walls. Tacked above them were travel posters showing San Francisco, Chicago, Munich, and Berlin.

A large banner hung over the stage. The top line said, "*Herzliches Willkommen für unsere amerikanischen Freunde!*" The line below, in English, reversed the greeting, saying, "A hearty welcome to our German friends." A little hokey maybe. But appropriate.

Novotny leaned against a wall and watched the final preparations. People moved quickly to sweep here, pick up things there. A large clock over the main entrance read 8:10 PM. Just below it, a young German girl was setting up a table that would serve as a ticket booth.

Novotny looked toward the stage and saw a young woman talking to a group of older German women, obviously chaperones. Oh, God, he said to himself. It was that WAC lieutenant. What was her name? Allen. That's it. Allen.

He figured he had two choices. Ignore her and assume that she wouldn't recognize him. Or go over to her and get it over with. Yeah. Might as well do it, he thought. The rest of the evening will be more relaxing if I get it over with.

As he walked toward her, he saw that she was wearing a different kind of uniform than the fatigues he'd first seen her in. She was wearing a white turtleneck sweater, a watch-plaid skirt, and a blue blazer. She heard him walking toward her and turned as he approached.

"Good evening, Lieutenant," he said, smiling.

She obviously didn't know who he was.

"I'm Pfc Novotny from the 2d Cavalry. I met you a couple of weeks ago. Brought over a report."

She nodded, recalling the embarrassing exchange. "Of course," she said. "I didn't recognize you out of uniform."

"There was a notice on the bulletin board at Merrell Barracks. It said they needed volunteers to help set up. So I came over." He pointed to the colored streamers. "That was my assignment."

"They look great. I'm on the German-American Relations Committee. I guess you'd say I'm the officer in charge of this . . . event."

She looked nervously around the room. "I just hope it turns out all right."

"Well," Novotny said, gesturing to a group of young German girls who had gathered along one wall, "over there are young, innocent *frauleins* wondering if they'll meet a GI tonight who will end up taking them to the promised land across the sea."

The lieutenant nodded and smiled.

"Over there," he said, pointing to a knot of young Americans, neatly dressed in civilian clothes, "you have a bunch of GIs figuring out ways to get to know these young frauleins without having to take them back to the States."

The lieutenant nodded, "I'm afraid you're right."

She looked at the bare bandstand and then at her watch. "I'm getting worried about the band," she said. "I hope they show up." She shrugged again and smiled at the young GI. "And if they do get here, I hope they can play something that people can dance to."

Novotny nodded in agreement. "Prussian marches are not what you'd call romantic tunes." He looked at the ticket table, which was now crowded with young men and women. "As long as the band shows up, looks like you've got a success here." She nodded and smiled. "See you later, ma'am."

"Thank you for helping," she said, walking nervously toward the empty bandstand.

"Glad to do it." As he spoke, he had an idea for something that could be fun and reduce the pressure she was under. Crazy, he thought. But what the heck.

Novotny headed slowly toward the refreshment table. Ordering an orange drink, he gave the woman behind the table a quarter for the drink and another quarter for her. He took a couple of sips of the sweet, yellow liquid and carefully put the bottle in the inside pocket of his tweed sport coat.

Walking past the ticket table, he stopped for a moment, allowing a German girl to stamp a green sailboat on his hand. Once outside, he looked to his left and saw the distinctive lamp of a neighborhood bar, advertising the featured local beer.

As he jogged down the street, he took the soda bottle out of his pocket and poured the contents into the gutter, then slipped the empty container into his jacket. Stopping outside the *gasthaus*, he caught his breath and then walked slowly into the smoky room.

"Good evening," he said in German to the owner, standing behind the bar. The man nodded in reply, courteously if coolly.

"I would like a glass of white wine, please," Novotny said.

The owner took a bottle of Mosel from behind the bar, pulled out the cork, and poured a glass. "One mark, twenty," he said, placing the glass on the bar.

"Thank you," Novotny said. About thirty cents, he calculated. Cheap, he thought, casually taking a couple of sips from the glass.

When the patrons were again talking, he slipped into the WC and locked the door. Reaching into his pocket, he rinsed the last drops of orange soda from the bottle. Then, as if he were transferring a priceless elixir from one crystal container to another, he poured the wine from the glass into the soda bottle. That done, he pressed the metal cap in place with his thumb and slipped it carefully into the inside pocket of his sport coat.

Walking straight to the bartender, he deliberately drank the last few drops of wine from the glass and set it on the bar. "Thank you, and good night," he said.

"Good night," the bartender replied, obviously curious about the brief visit to his establishment.

Novotny jogged back to the hall, flashed the green sailboat on his hand to the young woman at the table, and looked around the room. The band was playing reasonably danceable music, and a large, well-behaved crowd had gathered in the hall.

Lieutenant Allen was standing in a darkened corner of the room, intently looking at everything that was going on. As he walked toward her, he reached in his pocket and popped the metal cap off the bottle. She seemed surprised to see him.

"I thought you had left," she said.

"Nope. I just went for some refreshments." He handed her the bottle. "Here, Lieutenant. This is for you."

"Why, thank you," she said, pleasantly surprised. "I could go for a martini about now. But this'll do just fine." She held up the bottle. "I really appreciate this."

She took a sip. She looked quizzically at the bottle, then took another sip. Shaking her head, she said, "I don't believe this."

Novotny shrugged and smiled. "They were out of Gordon's."

She took another swallow, smiled, and said, "This is a real surprise. And I'm not sure how I'm supposed to take this."

"Take it any way you want, ma'am," he said.

The band began a popular German tune and she turned to watch them play. When she looked back a moment later, the young GI had walked away and was lost in the crowd.

Novotny found an open spot along the wall and leaned against it, looking the situation over. He had no particular plan for the evening. But if there were someone who looked as though she wanted to dance, he wouldn't walk away from the opportunity.

When the song ended, he listened to the awkward conversations of young men and women who were both strangers and culturally separated. GIs were trying to use the few German words they knew. And German girls were putting their accented classroom English to use.

In the mixture of voices and languages, he suddenly tuned in to a conversation between two people just to his left. For the first time in his life, he was hearing Czech being spoken by two real Czechs. Not that his parents weren't Czech. But these were Czechs in Europe, which somehow made them seem more Czech than Czechs in Chicago.

It sounded exactly as he had learned it. He looked to see who the speakers were and saw a young man and a young woman standing ten feet or so away from him. Slowly, as if he were approaching an animal he didn't want to frighten, he edged toward them.

"Pardon me," he said in Czech. "I have heard you speaking Czech." They seemed surprised to hear an American GI using their language.

"Where have you learned to speak Czech?" the young man asked cautiously.

"My family is from Czechoslovakia. From Prague and Pilsen. I am from Chicago."

"You speak Czech very well," the young woman said, nodding with approval.

They introduced themselves as Anna Placekova and Lada Hruzek. Anna had been in Germany just two months, after escaping across the border. Lada and his family had run away to Germany two years ago.

The three talked about ordinary things. The weather. What was it like to live in Chicago? The famous old town square in Prague.

"Is it true that Chicago has many gangsters?" Lada asked.

"I do not know," Novotny replied. "I have never seen one." He left it at that, deciding he didn't want to get into the complex issues of crime and machine politics just now.

"Perhaps you know my father's cousin," the young Czech said. "His name is Antonin Husak, and he lives in Chicago."

Novotny shook his head. "Perhaps my parents know him. But I do not." Moving the conversation to easier ground, he said, "I am stationed at Merrell Barracks."

Anna replied, "We live at the displaced persons camp called Valka Lager."

Talking about DPs was an obvious lead-in for questions he'd really like to ask. What was it like, living as a DP? Literally without a country? How did they get across the border . . . without getting shot? Was there any chance the Czechs would do what the Hungarians had tried two years ago? What was it like to live under a Communist government?

Maybe there would be a time to ask these questions. But not now.

Anna talked about a Czech restaurant in Nurnburg that she went to whenever it was possible. "They have the traditional Czech food," she said.

Lada interjected, "But it is somewhat expensive for us, so we cannot go there very often."

"Someday perhaps we can all go there," she said. "You would like it. I am certain of it."

As she spoke, Novotny studied her, trying not to seem as if he were staring. She must be about his age, he guessed. Probably twenty-two or twenty-three. He estimated that she was about five foot five, and she was slender, with brown eyes and brown hair. Her cheekbones were slightly pronounced, just like his mother's and grandmother's.

She spoke with a curious quality to her voice, as if her mind were here and somewhere else at the same time. Novotny wondered why. Who knows what she has gone through, he thought.

The band played "There's a Small Hotel" and Novotny decided this was as good an opportunity as any. "Would you like to dance?"

"Yes," she said tentatively.

He looked at Lada, and asked apologetically. "May I?"

"Yes," Lada answered quickly, understanding the reason for the comment. "We have only come to this dance together."

They walked to a fairly open area on the dance floor, and he put his right arm about her lean body. He took her hand and began leading her in time to the music. Nothing fancy, he reminded himself. Just nice, basic dancing.

"You dance well," she said, looking up at him.

"I have not danced for some time. You are a good partner."

He edged his arm just a little farther around her waist, and she responded by moving comfortably closer to him. The song ended and they stood on the floor still holding each other. Seconds later, the band began playing again. This time, it was "Blue Skies."

Novotny put his arm higher around her back and she edged even closer to him. Smiling, she said, "I like this."

She wasn't wearing perfume, but being close to her he relished the clean, natural scent of her hair. He could feel the back of her bra through her sweater and almost instantly reacted with a tinge of arousal. Oh, God, he thought, she's going to think I'm some kind of sex fiend, and that will be the end of that. He turned his body slightly to make sure she didn't know.

The good news, he decided, was that the mechanism still worked. It confirmed that the saltpeter or whatever it was that they supposedly put into their food had not destroyed the urge.

When the song was over, they walked back to their place along the wall. Lada was there with a cute German girl, and he seemed to be enjoying himself, so Novotny did not feel guilty about monopolizing Anna. They danced to most of the songs that were played, except the polkas and those with a heavy dose of *oom-pah-pah*.

When they weren't dancing, they talked. About Czech history. About the music of Antonin Dvorak. About things to do in Nurnberg. Not once did they talk about plowed strips threaded with electrified barbed wire and seeded with land mines.

It was about eleven thirty, and Novotny was already thinking about making curfew. The bandleader announced that next they would play "Stardust," the last song of the evening. Novotny took her hand as they walked onto the dance floor. A few bars into the score, he gently took her more closely into his arms.

"Is this how you dance in Chicago?"

"Not with everyone. Only with special people," he answered softly.

He forgot about the fact that they were in a club hall in Nurnberg, dancing to Hoagy Carmichael. He forgot about the fact that he was an American soldier, stationed thousands of miles from home. His mind was occupied by the Czech girl he held in his arms. A strangely distant, attractive young woman whom he had known for a couple of hours and might never see again in his life.

She looked up at him. "I like this, Joseph."

"I also like this," he said. "I like this very much." He wished the band would make the tune last for an hour or so, and that the midnight curfew would somehow go away. But the song ended. He leaned down and kissed her.

As they walked off the dance floor, she squeezed his hand. "Will I see you again?" she asked in the gentle voice that Novotny had come to like very much.

"Can we have dinner? Maybe Sunday?" he asked, hoping he wasn't coming across as too pushy. "I would like to visit that Czech restaurant."

She nodded. "That would be very nice." She stopped, her brow furrowed as she thought of meeting places. "We can meet at the railroad station? At the front entrance."

"How about two o'clock?" he suggested.

"Yes. Two o'clock."

The three young people walked to the door, where Novotny shook Anna and Lada's hands.

"Joseph, you must come to meet my parents at Valka Lager," Lada said as they left the hall.

"Yes, I will do that." He watched them leave the hall and turned to see the WAC officer surveying the room as it emptied.

"It was a very nice dance, Lieutenant," Novotny said, lighting a cigarette. "There was a good turnout. The music was fine. And everyone seemed to have a good time."

"You seemed to have enjoyed it," she said, smiling.

Novotny shrugged. "Well. She's a Czech DP. And that's what the dance was all about," he answered a little defensively. "So local people and GIs could meet one another."

"That's right. That's exactly what it was all about." She took a deep breath. "Well, thanks again for your help."

He nodded and headed out of the hall down the dark street toward Merrell. Filling his brain were all sorts of ideas placed there by what had happened on the dance floor tonight.

He tried not to smile. But he couldn't help it. He thought of how Anna had felt next to him. I don't believe this, he said to himself. I just don't believe this.

When they had arrived by train from Bremerhaven, Novotny was tired and hadn't paid much attention to Nurnberg's main railroad station. But today, he admired the classic architecture of the structure.

Anna wasn't due for twenty minutes, so he decided to look around. Inside the terminal he studied the tracks lined up in parallel rows, looking like Monet's painting of the station at Saint Lazare. All of these old European stations probably looked pretty much like this, he decided.

Its high ceilings were designed to let the smoke and fumes of the old steam engines rise. Exposed black steelwork supported the roof, like a giant Erector Set. And everywhere, there was gray concrete, bleak and dramatically accented with splashes of colorful, modern neon. Although the colors of the building were bleak, the steel and concrete were probably new. He couldn't imagine that Allied bombers would have avoided this as a target.

Trains pulled by modern diesel engines were arriving and leaving with their tearful partings and joyous greetings. He watched the conductors and baggage handlers. Their uniforms fascinated him, with their peaked, brimmed hats and the formal cut of their uniforms. With a little extra braid any one of them could have passed for a Nazi field marshal. The Germans love uniforms, he thought, recalling pictures of Goering in his incredible outfits.

The large clock in the main waiting room showed 13:50. Guess I'd better get out there, he told himself. He wondered if she would show up. He had been deliberately vague about the arrangement when he told Johnson, just in case. He didn't want to lose face, even with his friend, if she didn't make it.

He walked through the main waiting room to the street and saw her standing by a recently planted bed of spring flowers. She wore a black raincoat, a khaki skirt and blouse, and low-heeled shoes. She saw him walk out of the terminal, waved, and smiled.

"I am glad you are here," he said in Czech, shaking her hand.

"Did you think I would not come?"

"I was just not sure that everything would happen the way we had talked about it. And I did not know how to call you."

"Unfortunately, there is no telephone where I live." She smiled and took his hand. "But if I say I will be someplace, then I will be there. I am very glad we are doing this."

"I am also glad."

The sun was warm, and they spent a good part of the afternoon walking. From the castle above the city, they looked at Nurnberg spread out in front of them, with its church towers and ancient streets. Novotny was going to comment on the light and dark stones in so many of the structures, and how much of the city had been rebuilt since the bombings of a dozen years ago. But he decided not to bring it up.

She pointed to a horseshoe-shaped indentation on a stone set in the castle wall. "They say that one of the old heroes of Nurnberg was trapped here," she said, outlining the shape with her slender finger. "They were going to kill him. But he had his horse jump over there and ran away. His horse left this mark."

Novotny looked across the moat, which must have been fifty to sixty feet wide. "That would be a long jump. But I never disagree with such stories."

They walked past the bench where he had met his friend Dieter Holtz, down the cobblestone road leading to the streets below. The stones were uneven, making it difficult to walk. Mainly to help her, but partly to see what would happen, he took her hand. She didn't seem to mind.

At the bottom of the cobblestone road, he thought about suggesting that they stop at Fidelio, but decided against it. He had no idea what she thought about the Germans. To make it seem as though he was too friendly with them could blow this whole thing.

They meandered along the streets of downtown Nurnberg, past the beautiful structure that was supposed to be the spire of the *Frauenkirche*, the Church of our Lady, set on the old town square. Whoever ran Nurnberg in those days decided it was too beautiful to put on top of a church and had it set in the square where people could admire it close up. Another legend, he thought. But it sounds logical enough.

Walking by a small *gasthaus*, they heard music. Looking in, they saw an accordion player dressed in lederhosen.

"Do you want to stop here?" he asked.

She smiled the slight smile that he had come to like so much, and nodded.

They took a table in a corner and a buxom waitress, wearing a colorful Bavarian dirndl and showing at least three inches of cleavage, brought them each a stein of beer. Novotny shook his head and grinned.

"What are you thinking, Joseph?"

"I hope I can explain this to you," he said, taking a cigarette out of the package. He held the package up for her, but she shook her head. Lighting up and taking a puff, he thought about how to say it. "In our country, they have advertising about going into the army. They want to make it sound good to be a soldier."

"Yes," she said, wondering where this was going.

"They tell you that you will travel to interesting places. And in the advertisements, they show soldiers with beautiful young women." He shook his head and laughed at the fact that he was actually saying this.

She nodded.

"But no one really believes that such a thing will happen. Everyone believes . . ." The idea was getting more complicated than his Czech vocabulary could handle.

"Yes," she said, encouraging him to finish the thought.

"Many people believe such a situation is not really possible. They believe that it is just an advertisement."

"Really?" she asked.

"But many hope it will happen. So they go into the army." He tried not to grin, but couldn't help it. "And you see, here I am in this place far from home. And I am sitting with a beautiful young Czech woman. So . . ." He paused again looking for a way to say what he meant. "So, I am living the picture that the advertising shows."

Anna blushed, smiled, and took his hand. "I do not believe that I am a beautiful woman. But I understand the dream that you say." She squeezed his hand. "You see, it was also a dream for me."

The music, the beer, and the situation nurtured seeds of euphoria that were stashed away somewhere in his brain. There was nothing he could think of that he would trade for what he was experiencing at this moment. Not money. Not power. Not knowledge. Nothing.

He just sat there relishing every moment and marveling that it was actually happening. And in his mind, he wrote a letter to whoever wrote ads for the army.

"Dear whoever you are. I know your motive in writing those ads is to conjure up fantasies in the minds of vulnerable people like me so we'll join the army. I don't have any quarrel with what you've done, any more than I object to ads for soap or cigarettes. *Caveat emptor* and all that.

"But if you find yourself thinking that maybe it's all a lot of bull and that you're causing guys to do things they'll later regret, I'm writing to put your mind at ease. In at least one case, mine, I actually walked around an ancient city in Europe, holding hands with a very pretty young woman from Czechoslovakia, whom I never would have met if I hadn't signed up.

"So, even if you made it all up, what I've done today makes you honest. Sincerely, Pfc Joseph Novotny, United States Army."

In his mind's eye, he folded the letter, stamped it, and mailed it to the guy who was responsible for the ads used for recruitment.

"Would you like a Czech dinner?" she asked.

"Yes," he replied, nodding. "I would like that very much."

The restaurant, tucked away on a side street, was called Café Bohemia. It was small, seating thirty people at most, and had a tiny bar near the entrance.

A cheery woman, who could have been his favorite aunt, greeted them at the door. "Good evening, Anna," she said in Czech, smiling as she greeted the guests and wiping her hands on her apron.

"Good evening," Anna replied.

The woman looked at Novotny, unsure of how to greet him. "Good evening," he said in Czech. "I am a Czech-American," he added, to explain the situation.

"We are glad to have you here," the proprietress said, beaming. "Please sit down."

They ordered classic Czech dinners. Roast duck for him. Beef with sour-cream gravy for her. Both with ample helpings of Czech dumplings and the sweet kraut that his grandmother had made when he was a boy.

The owner treated them as if they were family. She checked their table when things were quiet, making sure they had extra dumplings and gravy to accompany their dinners.

"How long will you stay at Valka Lager?" Novotny asked Anna.

"Until my papers are checked." She added, "Which will be soon, I hope."

"Then you will stay in Germany?"

"No." Her answer was abrupt and had a hard edge to it.

"You do not like Germany?"

"No," she said icily. "I hate the Germans. I want to leave here as soon as it is possible."

Novotny was surprised at how strongly she had reacted to the question.

"You know of Lidice?" she asked.

"I know it was a village that the Germans destroyed after Czech partisans killed the Nazi governor. My grandfather told me about it."

"Yes," she said coldly. "The Germans killed all the men and boys in that village. And sent the women to concentration camps," she said, as if she were reciting a report in a history class. "In all, 173 men and boys were killed by the Nazis. One was my uncle."

She looked directly at Novotny, her eyes icy cold. "He was thirty-eight years old."

He shook his head, not knowing what to say, then took her hand and held it.

"Also killed was my brother, Vaclav. He was visiting my uncle. He was sixteen years old."

Not knowing how to express what he felt in Czech, he took a deep breath and squeezed her hand.

Then, as if the whole thing had somehow gone away, her voice changed and she was on to other things. "But that was sixteen years ago," she said, smiling. "And we are here today."

Novotny was still stunned by what she had told him.

"Joseph," she said, "let me ask you something. Why do you think you are here?"

He wasn't sure, what, if anything, she was getting at. "We're helping protect Europe from the Russians. That's the main reason." He would just as soon be talking about something else, but he was curious to see where this conversation would go.

"Do you think the Americans could stop the Russians? They are strong, you know."

He was growing a little impatient with her comments. "You sound as if you are on their side," he said, wishing he had been a little more tactful as soon as the words were out.

"If I was on their side, why would I run away? To live in a DP camp?" She looked at him directly in a way that made him a little uncomfortable. "I ask because I know the Russians. I have lived with them. Under their power. I worry that the small forces you have on the border will not be able to stop them."

He was angry now. "There are 5,000 men in our regiment. And there are two other regiments like ours on the border." He lit a cigarette, partly because he wanted one. But mainly because he wanted to think about what he was saying.

"We are very well trained. We could not stop the Russians. But we can slow them down until NATO can push them back."

"Joseph, I have lost family in the war. I ask you these questions because I hope you will not be killed." She shook her head sadly, seemingly on the verge of tears. "In war, it is young men like you who become . . . how do you say it . . . ah, food for the cannon."

"Cannon fodder," he said in English. He crushed out his cigarette, looked at the check, and put a stack of marks on the table. "Tell you what," he said, still in English. "Let's go someplace and make out for a while. I'm tired of all this war talk."

"Make out?" she asked.

"Yeah. Neck. Watch the submarine races. Do a little heavy petting. Mess around." He smiled, and then started laughing at the idiocy of what he had just said.

She laughed with him for the first time since they'd met, and said in Czech, "I do not know what you mean."

"Don't worry," he said. "Someday I will explain it to you."

They left the table, waved at the smiling proprietress, and walked out of the restaurant, hand in hand.

He opened the door to his room slowly. It was dark, and he went in quietly. "You awake, Bob?" he whispered.

"Yeah. I just climbed into the sack."

Novotny draped his clothes over the end of his bunk and crawled under the blanket. "I think I'm in love."

"Come on, Novo. In the finest traditions of the cavalry, you get them all excited. You make all sorts of promises. Then you give them a yellow scarf to remember you by, and you take off. But for God's sake, you don't fall in love."

"All I can say is that she's really incredible. Particularly after all she's gone through."

"Like what?"

"I'll tell you later. She's just had a lot of bad stuff happen to her. But she can still laugh." He chuckled to himself. "And she's a terrific kisser."

"You worry me, Novo. You really do," his friend said. "Look, sleep on it. Tomorrow the urge will go away."

Novotny didn't answer, because he knew that she was definitely a unique and special person. He closed his eyes and fantasized about what could happen in the months to come. In a matter of minutes, he was asleep.

Most of the guys hated guard duty. But Novotny didn't mind it all that much. It wasn't that he liked walking around a motor pool or ammo dump for hours through the night. But it took him away from everything. It put him in a situation where he had plenty of time to just think. He liked that.

The night was cool but not cold. There were almost no sounds except the crunch of his combat boots on the gravel as he walked along the rows of vehicles and then followed the prescribed route around the fenced perimeter of the vehicle park. Once in a while, he heard a dog bark in the distance as he passed the jeeps, APCs, tanks, and trucks.

Looking to see if anyone was coming down the access road, he sat on the running board of a truck and laid his carbine across his knees. In the subdued light of a nearby lamppost, he studied the oiled walnut stock and dull black metal of the barrel.

He wondered if this weapon had ever fired a shot in anger. It could have been used in Korea. That was only five years ago. Maybe even in World War II.

Then it dawned on him. The rifle had fired at least one shot in anger—even though it was accidental and stupid to have done so. It would be more accurate to say a shot fired in frustration. He shook his head. Poor guy. I wonder who he was.

He looked at the ammo clip, neatly positioned just under the chamber. In the clip was one round of ammunition, which seemed strange to him each time he was on guard duty. What could you do with one round if you really needed it? Fire it, so more people could come with more ammo? But what about you? With only one round. He shrugged at the unanswerable question in his brain, and decided it was time to walk again.

He thought about Anna. They'd seen each other just about every weekend for about two months. But he hadn't been able to see her for a couple of weeks. A church bell rang, its sound bright and clear in the night air, even though it came from far away. He looked at his watch. Oh five hundred. One more hour until he was relieved for the night.

As he walked, alert for anything that seemed out of place, it occurred to him how comfortable he was doing this. Not just walking around a motor pool in the middle of the night. But wearing a uniform. Getting up at five o'clock. Going out on alerts. Carrying a carbine over his shoulder.

The comfort seemed odd to him. Here I am at the edge of one political system, positioned near the edge of another political system that has as one of its goals the destruction of the system I'm part of, he thought. And I'm comfortable.

He stopped to look down a row of vehicles. Enemies of a few years ago, he thought, are friends. And friends are now enemies. One small spark and in a couple of hours we could be blowing each other up. We could end up destroying everything in a monstrous flash. And it all seems normal to me.

That certainly says something about the adaptability of man, he decided. And what about Anna. Imagine what she's been through, with her brother and her uncle killed by the Nazis. He wondered what else had happened to her.

Turning to retrace his steps to the other side of the motor pool, he thought again about Anna.

What was happening between them? Maybe he was in love with her. He wished he could define it. Maybe then he'd know if it really was happening. He wished there was a ten-point checklist that he could use to find out if he was in love.

All he knew was that she was very special and unlike anyone he had known before. But he assumed that part of the feeling had to do with her Czechness, and that was something he would have to sort out.

He reached the end of the motor pool and stopped to look out into the darkness beyond the fence. Sure it was happening in Europe. And yes, she was attractive. Yes, she was Czech. And she did seem to feel something as well, or so it appeared.

He shifted his carbine to his other shoulder and began walking again. There was definitely some kind of link, and it must be love. He was attracted to her, no doubt about that. But it wasn't just a physical thing.

"Be careful," his mother had cautioned. "Some of those women in Europe would use soldiers to get a ticket to America." He wondered if Chas was going to be in that spot. Or if Helga really cared for him.

He saw the lights of a vehicle coming up the dirt road to the motor pool. Taking a position in the shadows with a clear view of the gate, took his carbine off his shoulder. Two soldiers walked to the gate. One unlocked it, and they entered the vehicle storage area.

When they had walked a few yards into the motor pool, Novotny shouted, "Halt! Who goes there?"

The men stopped abruptly and turned toward the sound of his voice. "Sergeant Lewis," one of the men shouted back.

"Advance and be recognized," Novotny ordered.

The men walked into the glare of an overhead light. "For Christ's sake, Novotny. What are you trying to do?"

Novotny walked to the sergeant and the relief guard. "Just doing it by the book, Sergeant," he said, smiling.

The sergeant shook his head and laughed. "I wish I could put you on report for being a wiseass. But I can't." He added impatiently, "Brief Williams, and let's get back to the guardhouse."

"Nothing is happening," Novotny told the replacement guard, whom he barely knew. "Great time to just walk around and think." Novotny patted the guard on the shoulder.

"Have fun," he said, walking with the sergeant toward the jeep. Novotny was finished for the night, and glad of it. But a number of questions still needed to be answered.

The streetcar stopped with a series of clangs. Novotny stepped up into the trolley, handed the conductor a coin, and took a seat next to the window.

When he first saw German streetcars, their proportions seemed odd to him. They seemed too high and narrow. Too square. Germans didn't seem to share the American preoccupation with styling. After all, the Volkswagen looked very much as it did when Hitler had it designed in the '30s.

It wasn't that he didn't like German streetcars. Quite the opposite. He and Johnson found them to be a cheap and pleasant form of recreation. Sometimes, on Sunday, they would get on a streetcar and ride it to the end of the line, regardless of where that might be. They'd get out, walk around, look at the neighborhood, have a beer, and then head back to Merrell.

He also liked riding the streetcars because it was good language practice, hearing conversations about shopping, neighbors, local politics, or whatever, and then translating the words in his head.

He was in civilian clothes, but still obvious as an American. His short haircut and plain black, GI-issue shoes, gave him away to anyone who looked at him carefully. Usually, he rode the streetcar to the center of Nurnberg. But today, he was headed in the opposite direction, toward the outskirts of the city.

The conductor announced the street, and Novotny got off and looked around. There were a few run-down apartment buildings and not much else. Mainly the area was surrounded by a pine forest. Spotting an elderly gentleman walking down the street, he asked for directions to Valka Lager, the DP camp, and learned it was about six blocks away.

It was warm and sunny, and he felt good. For the past week, he'd been on assignment with the 2nd Battalion in Bamberg. He'd been told that he wouldn't be back until Tuesday, so he hadn't asked Anna if they could get together over the weekend. There wasn't any way to call and tell her he was coming. So he had decided to take a chance that she would be there. He was curious about the place, and liked having an excuse to see it.

About a block ahead of him was a concrete wall, painted dull tan and about ten feet high. It seemed to cover the entire block and had the bleakness that he associated with a prison. He looked for signs and didn't see any. But this was obviously the place.

There was only one entrance, an opening in the wall about twelve feet wide. He leaned against a pine tree just outside the compound and looked in. Row after row of long, one-story buildings were lined up inside the fence, separated by dirt streets. There were no trees. There was no grass. Just tan buildings that needed paint, separated by dirt streets and surrounded by a tan concrete wall.

Clusters of people stood at various locations in the compound, talking, smoking, or just standing and looking at nothing in particular. Anna had said that the first few weeks in the DP camp were the most difficult. The anxiety of leaving everything behind was aggravated by being detained here while the police did a background check to confirm their identity.

"It was cruel," she had said. "It was as if I had escaped from one prison only to go to another." She spoke bitterly about the whole process. "And what good is it? How can they tell if you are a criminal?"

Novotny had agreed sympathetically.

"But I now have some freedom," she had said. "I can now leave the camp so you and I can walk and have dinner." She had managed to get a job as a clerk in an office that handled DP affairs, so she had at least a little spending money. But she still had to wait for papers that would allow her to emigrate somewhere. She had made it clear she would not stay here.

Novotny watched the people in the camp, hoping they didn't notice him standing there, peering in. He wondered what would happen to them. Where would they end up? What would they do?

He crossed the street and walked through the gate. A guard, with a pistol on his hip and wearing a uniform that Novotny had never seen before, stopped him.

"You are looking for someone?" he asked in German.

"Yes. Anna Placekova."

"One moment, please," The guard walked into an office, and Novotny watched him leaf through a stack of papers on a desk. "She has left the camp. I do not know when she will return."

Novotny thought for a moment. "Do you know where I will find Lada Hruzek?"

"Is he in Valka Lager?" the guard asked.

"I am not certain. He is Czech."

"Oh, yes," the guard said. "I will show you where he lives." He pointed to a group of six long buildings about half a block away. "There," he said, pointing. "He lives in the second building."

"Thank you for your help." As Novotny turned to go, the guard gave him a casual salute and went back into the office.

Following the guard's directions, he walked to the building and knocked on the door. It opened slightly, and a man of about fifty-five peered out.

"Yes," he said in German.

"Excuse me," Novotny replied in Czech. "I am looking for Lada Hruzek."

"One moment, please," the man said cautiously. Seconds later, Lada was at the door.

"Do you remember me?"

"Of course, Joseph," he said, smiling broadly. "Come in. Come in."

Novotny stepped into the small unlit room and looked around. The apartment—if it could be called that—was divided into four areas. The space where they stood served as an entry and storage room. A galvanized steel sink was mounted on one wall, used for washing people, dishes, clothes, and whatever else needed cleaning.

To the left was the toilet. The door, which gave some privacy, was partly open, and Novotny could see that it was only slightly larger than the ones found on airplanes.

Across from the toilet was a small room with two cots. This was where Lada and his brother, Jan, slept. To the right was a room about eight feet by ten feet. During the day, it was the kitchen, dining room, and sitting room. At night, when the dining table was pushed against the wall and the couch was unfolded, it was a bedroom used by Lada's parents.

Lada introduced Novotny to his family: Pan Hruzek, the father; Pani Hruzekova, the mother; and Lada's brother, Jan. Novotny had always been curious about why feminine Slavic names had the "ova" suffix..

"Our home is quite small, as you can see," the father said apologetically. He took Novotny's hand and shook it warmly. "But we welcome you. Lada told us about you. And we hoped we would meet you one day."

"Thank you," Novotny said. "I am glad to be here."

"Would you like some coffee?" the mother asked.

"Yes, please."

Pan Hruzek herded Novotny and his sons toward the small table, moving furniture so everyone would have a place to sit. The four men settled themselves at the table while Pany Hruzekova heated coffee over a crude, two-burner gas stove.

They began by talking about the same things that Lada, Anna, and Novotny had used for conversation at the dance. Chicago. Prague. Nurnberg. The weather. Novotny's parents and grandparents. Czech history.

He listened to Pan Hruzek describe Hradcany castle in the hills above Prague, and it reminded him of the many times that his grandfather had verbally walked him through the ancient city.

Four people living in a space that size in Chicago would probably be declared unfit for so many residents. Still, these people seemed genuinely happy to be there.

He listened to Pan Hruzek vividly describing the country he had left, and he wondered whether or not it was safe to probe. To find out what it was like to run away from everything. To live as a displaced person, a DP, waiting for some country to put you on a list that would allow you to emigrate to another sort of life.

Pan Hruzek paused in his descriptions, and Novotny said, "If you do not mind my asking, how did you escape?"

The man shook his head. "No, we do not mind your asking. We will tell you—though it is not a special story. It is like others. But not many are successful."

Pani Hruzekova set cups of coffee on the table for the men, placing one next to the stove for herself as she stood, watching them talk. He began matter-of-factly, with occasional comments from his wife. The sons listened without speaking.

They had paid a guide to get them out, he explained. Their instructions were simple. They had an old car, and they were to take it to a small town in Western Bohemia, about ten kilometers from the border. To avoid suspicion, they were to take only what they could use on a weekend trip, nothing more.

"On the second day, we were to have an early dinner," Pan Hruzek recalled. "Five o'clock. Is that correct, Helena?"

Pani Hruzekova nodded her agreement.

"He said he would come to the dining room at the hotel, and we were to greet him as a friend. We were nervous as we waited."

"We were afraid he would not come," Pani Hruzekova added.

"Finally, he was there and we sat together, talking about small things." Pan Hruzek opened a drawer in the table and took out a package of Ernte 23 cigarettes. He held out the pack to Novotny. "Would you like one?"

"No. No, thank you," Novotny replied quickly, taking a package of Kents from his pocket. "Here, take one of mine."

Pan Hruzek took a cigarette and studied it for a moment before lighting it. Novotny took one for himself, lit both of them with his Zippo, and put the pack on the table.

He watched as Pan Hruzek took a long, deep drag on the cigarette, seeming to gather his thoughts. "We got into our car and drove to a small lake, a few kilometers from the border."

"Wouldn't someone have been . . . ah . . . interested . . . ah . . . in what you were doing?" Novotny asked. It wasn't exactly what he wanted to ask, but he didn't know the Czech word for *suspicious*, and he hoped the idea would be understood.

"No, it was common to visit the lakes in this area. And we tried to make it seem very normal." As Pan Hruzek answered the question, he again sucked smoke into his lungs and blew it toward the partially opened window. He sipped the blackish-brown coffee and was silent for a moment.

Novotny could see that these recollections were becoming more difficult as the man retrieved memories from his brain. Each spoken thought seemed to bring back other thoughts that were not said.

Novotny saw it as a chance to get a firsthand look into what the iron curtain was all about. Novotny had met other Czechs whom patrols had brought in from the border—people who had been successful in getting across. But there weren't many, and they were usually so frightened and disoriented that they had little to say.

"What did you do then?" he asked quietly.

"We walked around the lake and into the woods. It was getting dark then, and no one could see us." He took another puff on the cigarette and another sip of coffee. "When the guide told us, we turned and walked toward the border."

The two young Czech brothers watched the conversation. They saw the American soldier of Czech parents absorbing every word and every expression. They saw their father conjuring up images that had both excited and terrified them when they decided to go through with it.

"What happened when you got to the border?" Novotny asked.

"Our guide told us to wait in a thick part of the forest. He went ahead to watch for the border patrol. When they passed, he came back for us."

Novotny waited, concerned about causing the man to recall a time that was obviously difficult and emotional. But Pan Hruzek continued. "We came to a ravine and stumbled down in the dark. It was difficult to walk. But it was also too steep for watchtowers or the plowed field that is along much of the border."

The picture was clear in Novotny's mind. He had looked down steep ravines where there were no watchtowers.

He had also seen the plowed land and the open meadows that were minefields with tall observation towers, armed with machine guns.

He'd watched a man try to make it there, and fail.

"There was a small river running down the ravine," Pan Hruzek explained.

"From the forest, we could hear the water," Pani Hruzekova added.

"There was a dam. The top of it was covered with moss, and our feet slipped as we crossed it. We walked holding hands." He looked at the cup in front of him, and turned it slowly on its saucer. "If someone had fallen, we would have all gone into the water. Certainly some of us would have died."

His voice carried the heaviness of the thought. No one had fallen. But what if someone had? He was the father. He carried the weighted vote that came with the patriarchal democracy of the family. He had gotten them on the dam. And he could have kept them from it. If someone had slipped, it would have been his responsibility.

Abruptly, his voice changed. "Once we were on the other side," he said, smiling, "we were free."

"It was the most exciting moment of my life," Pani Hruzekova said, smiling at her husband.

"Did the guide stay with you?" Novotny asked.

"No," Pan Hruzek answered coolly. "He went back across the dam."

"He must be a brave man."

Pan Hruzek crushed the stump of the cigarette into an ashtray, which his wife immediately took and emptied. "I do not think *brave* is the right word," he said.

"Because you gave him money?"

"I gave him that. And the keys to our car. And to our apartment."

Pani Hruzekova replaced the ashtray on the table. "We could not bring anything. And we also could not give anything to our friends," she explained.

"Helena is correct. There was too much risk. If they found out that we had given something to a friend, they could be guilty with us." He shrugged. "And, I do not like to say it, but it would be possible that one of our friends— or even relatives—would report us to the police."

"Then perhaps *wealthy* is a better way to describe your guide," Novotny suggested.

"No," Pan Hruzek replied. "He is dead. He was caught on the third border crossing after us."

"But you and your wife and your sons were certainly brave," Novotny said.

Pan Hruzek looked at Novotny, cradling his chin in his hand. "Joseph, forgive me, but I must again disagree with you. We were not brave." He thought for a moment. "We were unhappy. We hated being under the thumb of the Communists. We had no future. No freedom. It was those feelings that caused us to leave. Not bravery."

Novotny drained the last few drops of the bitter coffee from his cup.

"You would like more?" Pani Hruzekova asked.

"Please." He watched the woman, plain and kind, fill his cup. Now he was looking out the window, at the scrawny tree in the area separating this from an adjacent building. "It must have been difficult. Leaving everything behind." He imagined what it would be like if his family had to leave their house, taking only what would seem appropriate for a weekend trip.

"Joseph, most of what we left behind means little today. Some furniture. Dishes. Clothes. Our ten-year-old Skoda that would never start in the winter."

"Even so," Pani Hruzekova interjected, "we were fortunate to have even an old car. Most people do not."

"But the important things we left behind can never be replaced," Pan Hruzek said. As he spoke, he stared at his cigarette, rolling it over and over against the rim of the ashtray, neatly removing all of the ashes from the end. "We left the church where Helena and I were married. And where Lada and Jan were christened. We left people we had known for thirty years and longer. People who we believed were our friends. But even at times we wondered about that."

Tears welled in his eyes. "We left the graves of our parents. And their parents. You see, Joseph, we left part of our soul back there in our country. And we will never be able to get it back."

Watching the man as he spoke, Novotny fought back tears himself. The momentum that his questions had started kept the thoughts and words coming from this gentle man who had risked so much.

"We walked away from our country, Joseph. We left with fear. With sadness that our democracy was crushed first by the Nazis and then by the Communists. We crossed the border full of anger for what we had allowed to happen to our country. We let the Russian bear into our house, and it destroyed us." Tears rolled down his cheeks, and he took a handkerchief from his pocket and wiped his eyes.

"Lada and Jan are young. They can start again. They can look ahead. But Helena and I are not young. We can only look back."

Taking a deep breath, a couple of sips from his cup, and a short puff on his cigarette, he smiled slightly. "But it was the right thing to do. I have no regrets. We are better off here than we were in our home country."

Novotny wished he could go back twenty minutes in time and start again, asking about kings, castles, the music of Dvorak, and art, and leaving questions about escape unasked. What a self-indulgent thing for him to do—to consciously lead this gentle and thoughtful man through a step-by-step exercise in sadness and painful recollection. Just so he could hear it. Just because it was something that he wanted to know.

"Pan Hruzek, I am sorry that I have asked so many questions. I should have been more considerate of your feelings," he said. "And for the feelings of your family."

"No, Joseph. There is no reason to apologize," Pan Hruzek said, shaking his head. The sound of his voice and the look in his eyes said that he understood why Novotny was asking. The young soldier simply wanted to know what they had experienced, and why they had done it. And that was reason enough to share his feelings.

There was one other question that Novotny wanted to ask, and this seemed like the right time to do it. "You have been here for two years," he began. "What will happen next? Where will you go?"

"We are on the list for America," Pan Hruzek said. "It is the best country, and we will wait as long as we must in order to go there."

Novotny sat silently, sipping his coffee. There was nothing more that could be said about the future.

Novotny looked at his watch. "I must go now. Thank you for your hospitality."

"We hope you will come again," Pan Hruzek said. "Next time we will not talk about politics."

Lada walked him to the streetcar stop, saying little. Disconnected thoughts rattled around in Novotny's brain. He moved the pieces around until they where shaped into something that could be asked. "Lada, do you think the Czechs will ever try to throw out the Communists?"

His answer was quick and blunt. "No."

Surprised at the finality of the answer, Novotny said, "I mean, the Czech people do not want that kind of government. Do they?"

"Definitely not. But there is no choice."

"I guess not," Novotny reluctantly conceded. The fact that he was not convinced was obvious in the tone of his voice.

"Let me tell you something, Joseph," Lada said as they reached the streetcar stop. "The only way this could happen would be with help from the West. From the United States."

Novotny thought about the idea. "What kind of help?" he asked.

"Supplies," Lada explained. "Guns. Ammunition. Medical supplies. Everything that is needed to fight." He added, "And soldiers."

Novotny thought about the Czech GI he and Johnson had played pool with. What was his name? Smetana. He assumed that one of the things the Special Forces would do was airdrop people like Smetana, along with equipment, to do just what Lada was saying.

"We could do that."

"Yes. You could. But you would not."

Novotny didn't like what he was hearing. He could feel himself getting defensive, and he decided not to respond.

"Joseph, two years ago we were listening to broadcasts on Radio Free Europe with some Hungarian DP friends." His voice took on a hard edge, like Anna's when she talked about Lidice. It wasn't the sound of anger. It was a harsh acceptance of something awful that had happened.

"We listened to the RFE announcer telling the Hungarians to fight. To stand up to the Russians. It was said that there would be help from the West." Lada paused and took a deep breath. "I myself have heard this on the radio."

Novotny sat quietly on the trolley bench, listening intently.

"So the Hungarians fought. But there was no help. The Hungarians had to fight Russian tanks with rocks and small bottles filled with gasoline."

Shaking his head slightly, Novotny took a deep breath, waiting for the rest of the story.

"We listened every night to Radio Budapest. In Valka Lager, we listened with Hungarian DPs. One night, we heard the man on the radio pleading for help. He said the situation was becoming hopeless."

Lada stopped for a moment, and when he resumed, his voice was so quiet that Novotny had to listen carefully to hear what he was saying.

"The man asked over and over for help. For weapons to stop the tanks. For medical supplies, because they had none. For all of the things needed to fight the Russians."

All Novotny could do was sit and listen.

"We listened to him for almost one hour. Then we heard gunshots. The station stopped broadcasting. And in two days, the revolt was over."

Novotny looked across the street at the pine forest, quiet, cool, and green. He tried to stop his brain from replaying the newsreels that he'd seen of Hungarians throwing rocks at Russian tanks. And of Hungarians lying dead on the littered streets.

"So you see, Joseph. This is why we will not revolt. Our people are unhappy. Our people are oppressed. And we are still proud. We are ashamed that we have allowed this to happen to our country. But we are not foolish."

"I understand," Novotny said, nodding.

"If it happens, it will have to happen from the government." He shook his head sadly. "And I can tell you, it will never happen in our lifetime."

A streetcar turned the corner, about two blocks away. Novotny watched it come slowly toward them, then come to a stop with a metallic, grinding noise. Novotny got up and shook Lada's hand.

"Joseph," he said, "the next time you come, we will only talk of happy things."

"Yes, only happy things."

The streetcar started to pull away. "Lada, I forgot," he shouted. "If you see Anna, tell her I will be away for one week." The young Czech nodded slightly and waved, but didn't return Novotny's smile.

Sitting down in the nearly deserted streetcar, he thought about the afternoon. He would come back here again. He was certain of that. He would tell his parents about these people. Maybe there was something they could do to help them get out of here and relocate to the States.

He had already mentioned Anna in a couple of his letters, just in passing, being careful not to make a big deal out of it. Maybe one day he would write them to say that he was bringing her back with him.

They weren't officially going together. They just did things together and made out a little. She did seem to like him, but they never talked about where this could go.

He would be gone for a week on leave. When he got back, he would sit down with her and see what the possibilities really were.

The bus was parked in front of the railroad station near the place where he had met Anna for their first real date. He wished he had been able to see her before going on leave. But it was hard to reach her. It had been about two weeks since they had last spoken.

He walked to the shiny maroon bus with its huge windows and showed his envelope to the driver. "You may take any seat you wish," the driver said in heavily accented but friendly English.

Novotny stowed his AWOL bag on the overhead rack and took a seat. Maybe he would be lucky and have the seat to himself. He scrunched around, settling into the contour of the soft gray velour. It seemed as though it would be comfortable, even for the long ride.

He studied the bus. It was different from the Greyhound he had ridden to Detroit. Essentially different. The way that a Mercedes or a Volkswagen is different from a Plymouth or an Oldsmobile.

Novotny glanced at his watch. Nine thirty. Right on time. The driver read off a list of names and got twenty acknowledgments in reply. All of them were in civvies, and Novotny guessed that fifteen were GIs or air force personnel. The others—three women and two men—were probably civilian employees of the military. They just didn't look like active-duty people.

All of them were taking advantage of one of the incredible deals that came along from time to time. This was six days on the French Riviera for ninety dollars. True, it was most of a month's pay. But it included hotel, meals, and transportation.

At first, he had hoped that someone from the 2d Cav would come with him. But Johnson couldn't get off. Morris spent every bit of free time—and all of his money—on Helga. And even though he liked Turner, he decided he wouldn't be the best company on a trip like this. So he decided to go on his own.

The driver closed the door, started the diesel engine, and eased away from the railroad station. Within a few minutes, they were at the outskirts of Nurnberg, heading west toward the French border.

Novotny tilted his seat back slightly and looked out the window. The villages and fields and forests of the German countryside passed by like a nonstop travelogue. He let his mind shift and imagined that he was sitting still and the panorama was actually moving from left to right in front of him while he stayed one in place. It was like the Cinerama movie he'd seen about the great sights of the world, like the Grand Canyon and Niagara Falls.

He thought about Anna and wished she could be going with him. He wondered if, at some point, they would go somewhere together. Maybe a weekend in Munich, or just heading off to some village and hiding out for a couple of days.

No, that isn't likely, he decided. She would have to pose as his wife in order to stay anywhere, unless they took separate rooms. And he couldn't picture her pretending to be anything. Certainly not the wife of a GI. What's more, he wasn't sure he could pull it off either, without getting very nervous about the whole thing.

It didn't matter. He was on his way to France. And when he got back, he'd see her and they would walk and talk as they often did on Sunday afternoon. He closed his eyes and thought about now lucky he was and how good he felt. The sense of well-being led easily and quickly to sleep as the bus made its way west.

He woke with a start, hearing the driver's voice. The bus had stopped and a man in uniform was standing in the aisle. He wore a round, visored hat that Novotny associated with General de Gaulle.

"Please have your identification ready for the officer," the driver said. Novotny fished his GI identification out of his billfold and held it for the officer to see as he walked up the aisle. The official didn't seem terribly concerned about any illegal passengers on the bus, and in a few minutes they were again on their way. He was in France.

He looked out the window, fascinated by how abruptly things had changed. The rigid order and structured cleanliness was gone. Everything seemed more random on the streets of the city they were driving through. It all seemed very foreign from what he had come to know in Germany.

Strange, he thought, how an arbitrary line on a map can change so many things. The way people speak. The way they live. The things that are important to them. It's really odd. We are so much the same. But we're so different; depending on which side of the line you happen to live on. Different to the point of killing each other.

Outside the town, the bus stopped at a small restaurant in a grove of trees at the side of the road. Novotny got off the bus and stretched in the warm afternoon sun.

Inside, it was everything a French restaurant should be, at least in the mind of a young soldier from the Midwest. There were checkered tablecloths. Plants in the windows. And a vase of fresh flowers at each table.

The proprietress was a cheery French woman, about thirty-five, who greeted them warmly even though it seemed that the driver was the only one who knew what she was saying.

A young girl in a black dress with a white apron brought steaming bowls of onion soup to everyone's place as soon as they were seated. This was followed with a plate of chicken cooked in wine sauce. *Coq au vin*, the waitress repeated carefully to each of the travelers as she placed the plate in front of them. Chicken cooked in wine, Novotny thought. Maybe he wouldn't have trouble with the language after all.

A plate of fresh steamed broccoli was served with the chicken, along with roasted potatoes and what Novotny decided was the best bread he had ever had in his life. Strangely, a green salad was served after the main dish. But it seemed to be done without apology, so he assumed that was the way it was supposed to be. All through the meal, the proprietress and her young assistant filled the guests' glasses with delicious red wine poured from simple pitchers.

When the salads had been eaten and the dishes cleared, each guest was given a small apple tart and a steaming cup of coffee. Novotny put the last forkful of pastry into his mouth and washed it down with a swallow of rich, black coffee. Touching his lips with his white linen napkin, he decided that this had been the best meal he had ever had in a restaurant, anywhere.

In Chicago, it would have cost a small fortune at one of the elegant places off Michigan Avenue. Here, it was routine. Or so it seemed. Just a regular meal for a busload of travelers.

He relished a cigarette with a second cup of coffee, and soon the driver was herding the passengers to the bus, the way kindergartners are shooed back to class after recess. When his charges were settled in their seats, the driver tapped his horn and the proprietress and her assistant appeared, waving as the bus pulled onto the empty two-lane highway.

The sun felt good, streaming in through the bus window and warming his face and shoulder. He closed his eyes and starting calling up images of Anna. Clear, vivid images. He imagined her slender figure and soft brown hair. Her deep brown eyes—like his mother's—that said so much. But they also revealed how much hadn't been said, and probably never would be.

He really wasn't sure how to describe the situation with Anna. It wasn't like dating someone in school and then settling into that comfortable thing called "going steady" or "getting pinned" or whatever.

This was different. They went out when schedules allowed. They would go for walks around Nurnberg and stop somewhere for dinner. And she seemed to like dancing closely at the Enlisted Men's Club or the Flying Dutchman in town. On a few occasions, they had found a quiet, private place where they could kiss and hug.

But he couldn't really say they were going steady, because he had never asked her to be the only person she dated. He just assumed, since she had never said no to him when he asked her out, and because she seemed to like being with him, that they were sort of going steady. He had no idea how it was done in Czechoslovakia.

He was a little anxious about bringing it up, concerned that the subject might chase her away. So he had decided he would just see how it went. He would keep asking her out. And then someday, when the time was right, he'd bring it up.

Maybe he'd start a new tradition, he thought, chuckling at the idea. It would happen on a Saturday afternoon. She'd be standing on the steps of 2d Cavalry headquarters. The regimental band would play "Garry Owen" or some other Cavalry song.

When they were finished, he'd walk up the steps in his best Class A's, his boots incredibly shined and a neat crease on his yellow scarf. He'd pin a regimental crest on her sweater, just above her left breast.

Then Johnson would bring a dozen yellow roses, which Novotny would give to her. He'd give her a kiss and the band would play "In her hair she wore a yellow ribbon." When they were finished, the colonel's OD staff car would pull up and take them to a really nice restaurant. They would have an incredible, candlelit dinner, serenaded by three violinists from the Seventh Army Symphony Orchestra.

Novotny chuckled again and said to himself, "You lead a very rich fantasy life."

It was dark when the bus reached the ridge of the mountains and began its descent to the coast. The Mediterranean was a black void just past where the lights of the land ended. When they reached the water, they turned right

240

and headed west along the shoreline.

Novotny moved to an empty seat on the other side of the bus so he could look into the blackness. The headlights of the bus made a beam of light that was wide enough that often he could see waves ahead of them.

He was looking at the Mediterranean. The actual, honest-to-God Mediterranean Sea. From here it looked pretty much like Lake Michigan. But the water was different. It had been made historic by people passing on it for centuries, even though it was quite likely that not one molecule of water in that sea had been there when the Phoenicians used it to carry cargo to the great cities on its shores. Or when the Greeks and the Romans had used it to move their troops from one conquest to another.

Amazing, he thought. I'm looking at the Mediterranean.

At about ten thirty they pulled up to the Hotel Mirabelle in the town of St. Maxime. By eleven o'clock, Novotny had checked into his room and was curled up in his bed. Amazing, he thought. I never imagined that I would one day fall asleep on the Riviera. About two minutes later he did.

Slowly he made the transition from sleep to being awake. It started with a gradual awareness of where he was. He was lying under a soft white comforter on a big, comfortable bed in a small French hotel instead of a utilitarian bunk with a scratchy wool OD blanket. Having registered that, he opened his eyes and took in the details of the room.

There was a simple dresser. Framed prints of French village landscapes were hung on the walls. The sun was filling the room with light through lace curtains.

He took a deep breath, relishing the oxygen filling his lungs. His instinct was to jump out of bed and enjoy the morning. But he consciously stretched out in bed without moving, just to prove it wasn't necessary to rush to a morning formation. Even though he had no plans to do so, he reassured himself that he could stay in this bed all day if he wanted.

Rolling over, he looked at his watch. Ten after eight. He'd gone to the kitchen after dinner last night and persuaded the cook to bag him a lunch. Even though it was against hotel policy, she had agreed to do it, as long he picked it up by nine thirty.

That gave him plenty of time to shower, shave, put on a sweater, and load his German schnitzel bag with a book and his camera. He stretched, thought about how he would rather be waking with Anna, and folded back the blanket.

The kitchen was empty, but on a counter he spotted a paper bag. Peering in, he saw that the cook had prepared him a feast. Half a loaf of French bread. A small, round, wax-covered cheese. A good-sized chunk of salami–like sausage. A neatly wrapped slice of pâté. And an apple.

He fished around in his schnitzel bag to make certain that the collapsible corkscrew was there and then stowed the lunch among his possessions for the day. Finding a small piece of paper, he wrote, "*Merci,* J. Novotny." Putting the note, along with some francs, on a saucer, he set a cup on it all to keep it in place.

The town of St. Maxime was just starting to show signs of life as he walked to the dock. Merchants were opening the fronts of their shops. Women were hanging laundry to dry in the warm Mediterranean sun. Children played in the narrow cobblestone streets.

The town was pretty much what he had expected: Quaint, old buildings. Houses and apartments, jammed together. And a sense that it had all been here for a very long time.

Even so, the area had surprised him in some ways. It was more arid than he expected, despite being on a great sea. The hillsides were scraggly and brown, and he saw olive trees for the first time, gnarled and seemingly struggling to stay alive.

A statue stood heroically in a small park. He looked at the inscription and realized there was no point in even trying to understand what it said, other than to note the name and the year. Raul LeBret. 1875. A very distinguished-looking man who must have done something special for this town or for France.

Across the street was a small shop that looked something like an Italian deli in Chicago. Walking in, he exchanged nods with the man behind the counter and began browsing the two narrow aisles.

Along the left wall were long rows of wine bottles. He studied the colorful labels, having no idea which to buy. Selecting a bottle only because he liked the elegant coat of arms on the label, he took it to the counter.

Pointing at the bottle, he shrugged. "I have no idea what I'm getting, or what it will cost," he said. The owner said something in French. Novotny shook his head, retrieved an assortment of franc notes from his pocket, and held them out to the shopkeeper.

The man smiled, took some of the money, and put it in a box under the counter.

Walking out, the wine safely in his bag, he did a quick calculation. It worked out to about thirty cents for a bottle of wine. That's hard to believe, he thought. Thirty cents.

The dock at St. Maxime was long, with large mooring cleats every fifty feet or so. A few people stood around waiting for the ferry that Novotny was told ran every half hour. The water was calm, and the sun was warm on his back.

Walking along the bare concrete pier, he looked back at St. Maxime, set along the coast and edging up the side of a hill. He noticed a brass plaque just ahead and walked over to check it out.

There was a French inscription, and below it, in English, it said, "On August 15, 1944, American, British and Free French troops landed here as part of the invasion of Southern France. This memorial commemorates that event."

My God, he thought, nearly aloud. I didn't even know there was a southern invasion. I thought it all happened at Normandy. He looked at the placid water of the bay, and imagined landing craft coming in waves toward this dock.

Had GIs been killed here, as they had been in Normandy? What units landed here? Where did they go? What did they do? Was this held by the Germans? It must have been. Someday, he would have to find out.

He looked at the plaque again. It seemed as though everywhere he went there was evidence of the war, whether brass plaques or bombed-out buildings. He stared at the dull metal. If Ivan comes across the Czech border, he wondered, will anyone put a plaque at that spot? If that happens, there may not be many people left to place plaques. Not with the kinds of weapons we have now.

Looking up, he saw a small ferry heading toward him. The skipper brought it precisely to the point where the handful of people stood, and the craft's lone crew member tied the boat to one of the cleats as the passengers hopped on board.

Minutes later, he was on his way across the bay, heading toward St. Tropez, the place that symbolized modern hedonism. It was here, if you could believe the articles, that Brigette Bardot and countless other French beauties spent time with their yacht-owning, rich boyfriends.

As the ferry crossed the bay, he decided he was glad he'd made the trip alone. Not for any particular reason. He just kind of liked doing this by himself.

As the boat approached the dock, Novotny stood at the rail, fascinated by the view. St. Maxime was quaint, but a little common. He had seen a lot of places that looked like St. Maxime. But St. Tropez was different. That was obvious, and he hadn't even set foot on the place.

Wooden fishing boats were tied to the pier, intermingled with glistening, white-hulled yachts. A row of closely packed three- and four-story buildings faced the wharf, their pastel yellows, ochres, and greens brilliant in the morning sun.

The street along the waterfront was lined with outdoor cafés, their tables shaded by large, colorful umbrellas. As the ferry made its approach the dock, Novotny pulled his camera from his bag and took a couple of quick shots. I want to remember this, he thought.

Novotny stepped on the dock and looked around. The town was quiet, partly because it was early in the day, but also because the real season wouldn't begin for a month or so. He walked to one of the cafés and took a seat at an outdoor table. Reaching into his bag, he retrieved the copy of *Walden* he had brought along.

A waiter came to his table, and again he felt the helplessness that came with not knowing the language. The man stood silently, waiting for the order. Novotny wasn't sure quite what to do, and felt himself flush with embarrassment. He noticed a man sitting a couple tables away, sipping what looked like a cup of coffee. Novotny pointed to the cup.

"*Café au lait?*" the waiter asked.

Novotny nodded. A couple of minutes later the waiter returned and placed a steaming cup of creamy liquid in front of him.

"*Café au lait*," the waiter said. Novotny nodded.

Carefully, he took a sip of the hot liquid. As far as he could tell, it was a rich cup of coffee with a lot of milk in it. *Café*, he said to himself, probably means "coffee," as well as "small restaurant." *Au* probably means "with," as in *coq au vin*—; chicken with wine. So *lait* must mean "milk" or "cream." Coffee with milk. Easy enough.

Café au lait. Three words. He decided to add up his total French vocabulary. *Oui. Non. S'il vous plait.* Those, plus the other things he knew how to order from a menu, and he was probably up to about twenty-five words.

He had thought about buying a French phrase book at the Merrell PX, but never got around to it. He would just have to make do. At three or four words a day, he would gradually build up a vocabulary, and in twenty or twenty-five years, he'd be able carry on a basic conversation.

He took another sip of the delicious coffee and lit a cigarette to go with it. What a great cup of coffee, he thought. And what an incredible place to be drinking it.

Beyond the boats tied up to the dock was the blue water he had just come across, and in the distance, St. Maxime. It was hard to imagine that about fourteen years ago, this beautiful bay must have been filled with military ships and landing craft.

It seemed too peaceful and beautiful to have been an invasion site. Invasions, if they must happen, should be at ugly, characterless locations. They should happen only on gray, overcast days, not clear, sunny mornings like this, when everything is so bright and cheerful.

Maybe it would be possible to add this to the Geneva Convention that dealt with the rights of prisoners. Pleasant days and pleasant places must be reserved for pleasant activity, the amendment would say. And by specifying that battles can take place only in grungy, run-down areas, you'd be doing those places a favor. That is, if they turned out better the second time around.

He thought about Nurnberg, with its great old churches and the massive wall around the old city. He pictured in his mind the photos he'd seen of the city as it had been leveled by Allied bombers.

He took off his glasses and rubbed his face with the palms of his hands. It was a technique that seemed to work when his mind went off on tangents that he was not ready to pursue. As it was also his habit to do, he lifted his wrist to look at his watch. Ten after ten. But what difference did it make? The last ferry wouldn't leave until ten o'clock tonight.

Even if he missed it, so what? He could sleep on the beach or walk around the bay to St. Maxime. He guessed it was only about four or five miles.

Then, taking a sip of his café au lait and a long drag on his cigarette, he pushed everything out of his mind and relished just being in this incredible setting.

It's hard to imagine, he thought. St. Tropez. What's missing, he noted, looking left and right, are the gorgeous women in bikinis.

The beach curved away from the town, forming a broad arc of bright sand against the blue of the calm sea. The sun was high, and it was warmer now. Still there were no people on the beach. Pretty uninhabited, he thought, for a place where Europe's wealthy and famous people passed their time.

As he walked away from the town, he saw two people heading toward him. Once they were close enough for him to identify, he saw that they were a fully clothed, middle-aged couple. Just my luck, he thought. Instead of Brigette Bardot, I get a couple of characters from *Mr. Hulot's Holiday*.

Nodding to them as they passed, he spotted an area sheltered from the sea breeze by a cluster of pines. Like an animal looking for a nesting place, he checked out the contour of the sand, the position of the trees, and the view of water and selected what seemed to be the optimal place to settle.

Pulling a towel from the schnitzel bag, he spread it neatly on the sand and took his lunch—including the bottle of wine and the corkscrew—out of the bag. Then, stripping to the bathing suit he wore under his clothes, he carefully folded each item and placed it in the sack where the lunch had been.

The lunch, packed by the cook at the hotel, was delicious, made even tastier by the accompaniment of the thirty-cent bottle of wine.

With lunch complete, he stowed everything in his bag and pulled out *Walden*. A perfect place to read this, he decided.

He had barely found his place in the book when he saw another person walking along the beach, heading toward town. He kept his head aimed toward the book, turning his eyes to watch the person approach without seeming obvious about it. Pretty sneaky, he told himself, the position of his eyes concealed by the dark lenses of his sunglasses.

His companion on the beach was a slender woman, about forty or forty-five, he guessed, but possibly a little older. It was hard to tell from a distance. She looked as though she were going to continue walking toward town, until she saw Novotny's sheltered cove. Angling toward him, she stopped about thirty feet away and spread a very large, blue-and-red beach towel on the sand.

Novotny turned his head more toward the book, and his eyes more toward her. To make the ruse more authentic, he turned a page of the book.

"*Bonjour,*" she said, smiling, using one of the handful of French words he knew.

"Bonjour," he replied. She didn't look like Brigette Bardot, but she had the same kind of smile. "Pouting" was the way the newspapers and movie magazines described it. He never understood why. The term really didn't seem to fit.

He angled his head toward the book and turned another page. But he positioned his eyes so he could check her out—without her noticing, he hoped. She was gorgeous. Her long brown hair was pulled back and tied with a yellow ribbon. Something a cavalryman had no doubt given her, he decided, smiling at the silliness of the thought.

The bright red polish on her finger- and toenails was flawless.

Her sunglasses were large, stylish, and obviously expensive, probably costing as much as he had paid for this whole trip. He also noted the gold bracelet on her slender wrist. Simple and elegant. That was probably worth a year's salary as a Pfc.

She kicked off her white leather sandals and set them next to the towel.

Novotny surreptitiously studied every move she made. His right arm had fallen asleep from the weight of his head, but he dared not reposition it. First things first, he told himself. He would worry about restoring circulation later.

With a graceful move of her thumb and index finger, she freed the buttons on her stylish white slacks and slid out of them as if shedding a layer of skin.

Novotny turned his eyes back to the book. But concentrating on this nineteenth-century man's view of the natural world was not where his mind wanted to be. He turned another page and slowly let his eyes angle to the left.

He realized that in his brief absence, she had undone the top button of her blouse. With incredible grace, she worked her way down to the second and then the third button from the top.

Only once before had Novotny felt this aroused. It had been when he, Al Kender, and Larry Wilson had gone to Minsky's burlesque theater on South State Street in Chicago. Just about everyone at the frat house had made the pilgrimage there at one time or another.

One of the strippers had driven them all to the brink of erotic insanity. She hadn't strutted around the stage and done the exaggerated bumps and grinds that most of the strippers had done. She had just stood there and slowly taken off her clothes, teasing the assortment of men who were sitting in the large, darkened theater.

Driving back to the campus, all three of them admitted that someday they would very much like to have a woman do that for them. Not in a theater with a bunch of horny guys. But privately. All alone. And, as they drove up the Outer Drive to Evanston, they also agreed that it was unlikely that it would ever happen.

But now, here it was. Happening twenty feet or so away from him. She could have spread her towel anywhere on the beach. But she had chosen the spot just a short distance from him.

Maybe she was a hooker. Get the guy aroused to the point where he can't say no. Then pop the question and quote the price.

No. She was far too classy to do that. Maybe everything they said about St. Tropez was true. And maybe there was nothing more to this than a woman taking off her slacks and blouse to get some sun.

Slowly, she worked her way down to the last button of her blouse. Then, after running her hands through her hair, she slowly raised her shoulders until they almost touched her ears, then relaxed, smiling at Novotny as she slipped off her blouse.

Novotny had laid his left leg over his right to keep his arousal to himself. He realized that he had now lost much of the feeling in his right wrist and hand, on which he was resting his head. I should probably move it, he thought. Get the circulation going again before something serious happens to it. No, he decided. This is more important. Besides, they can do wonders today with physical therapy.

She folded her blouse and laid it on top of her slacks as Novotny studied her tiny, red bikini. The top made it easy for him to determine the size of her breasts. Not large. But perfectly proportioned to her slender body and covered by two small triangles of cloth. A third triangle covered that part of her body where her marvelously sculpted legs converged.

Giving him yet another smile, she stretched out on her towel, lying on her perfectly flat stomach, her elbows on the towel and her chin propped up on her hands.

Novotny turned his body slightly and, as discreetly as possible, began rubbing his right wrist and hand, trying to get them to work again. His skin prickled as he encouraged the circulation to return. That done, he turned his attention back to *Walden*, not certain whether or not he admired the naturalist's woodland celibacy.

He had barely read two pages when the woman spoke to him, the sounds of her French speech striking him as particularly melodic.

She said, in her native tongue, "You seem very interested in your book. What are you reading?"

Novotny looked up and instantly felt a tinge of panic. First, he had no idea what she was saying. But more important, he had no idea how to respond to what he saw. She was still lying on her towel, propping her chin in her hands. But the red top of her bikini was lying limply on the terrycloth of her towel.

Her bare breasts hung provocatively in the shadow of her body.

Novotny's estimates of their size and shape had been accurate: smallish and magnificently formed. He reached into his bag and pulled out a pack of cigarettes. He definitely needed time. At least a few seconds to pull himself together. He offered the pack to her, but she declined.

Lighting his cigarette, he finally decided how best to handle this. In English, he admitted, "I hate to tell you this, but I have what would be called a very limited French vocabulary," he said somewhat sheepishly.

"I do not know what you are saying," she said in French, cocking her head to one side and frowning slightly.

Novotny thought about how to get the message across. He pointed to the fingers of his right hand, one at a time. "*Merci. Bon jour. Au revoir. Oui. S'il vous plait.*" He stopped to think for a minute and then touched his fingers again. "Oh, yeah. *Coq au vin. Café au lait.*" Smiling, he said, "I'm not sure how many that is. Maybe a couple dozen. Or less. But that's about it."

"American?" she asked.

"*Oui.*" He smiled at being able to use one of his 25 French words, and decided to try the other languages he knew. "Do you speak German?"

She shook her head and then waved her hand from side to side, as if to say that she wouldn't use the language even if she knew it.

"Do you speak Czech?" he asked, in Czech.

Again she shook her head. "I speak only French. And some Spanish and Italian."

Mimicking him, she pointed to each of her slender, beautifully formed fingers as she said in heavily accented English, "Hello. Goodbye. Coca-Cola. TV. Whiskey. Ah . . . Sank you." Shrugging, she said, "No English."

The conversation, if you could really call it that, had distracted him. But now, hoping his sunglasses concealed the direction he was looking, he stared at her breasts. Studying them, he noted that they were as tan as the rest of her beautiful body.

"You don't happen to have a French/English dictionary with you?" he asked, smiling and seriously wishing he could magically conjure up a French/English dictionary.

She shook her head again, affirming her inability to know what he had said. To Novotny, even that slight gesture was enormously provocative.

Realizing the situation was hopeless, he decided it might as well be fun. "Well," he said, "let me ask you this in English, which I know you don't understand. There wouldn't happen to be a college or university within a quarter mile or so with a foreign language department, would there?" He was feeling very silly now, and let himself chuckle.

She laughed, obviously not understanding him but sharing his humor. And joining him in the silliness of whatever he had said.

What a great opportunity, he thought. He could say anything he wanted and she wouldn't understand a word of it. Or so he assumed. "Well, all I can say is that you are an absolutely gorgeous woman, with probably the most beautiful breasts that may exist in the world, and when I look at you and talk to you, all I can think about is sex."

Without the benefit of a common language, he had said something that he would never imagine saying to a woman who understood him. Being able to say such things seemed very risqué—probably yet another French word—and strangely exciting.

"Sex," she said in English, while nodding and pointing to another one of her fingers. Looking at Novotny, she said in French, "I forgot. That is one more word that I know in your language. So how many is that? Nine?

Ten? I can't remember."

He watched her laugh, and asked, "Are you sure you don't know what I'm saying?"

She listened to him while he spoke and then tilted her head, as if she were trying to penetrate the linguistic barrier by force of will. "You are a very appealing young man," she said. "It is a pity that we are not able to speak with each other."

Now the situation was reversed. A moment ago, he was talking and she was wondering what the words meant. Now it was his turn.

"I would like to know about you," she said almost in a whisper. "You are young. Maybe a student. Possibly a soldier. Whatever brings you here, you smile with appealing innocence."

She stopped for a moment and then continued, "Your manner suggests that you have little experience with a woman, or so it seems to me. Is that so?"

She looked intently at him, hoping that somehow he would be able to understand and answer. But all he could do was look at the rich brown of her eyes and wonder what this was all about.

"If I could ask you to come with me, I would take you to my home," she said. "There are many things I believe I could teach you. There are many ways that I could please your young body and mind." She shook her head slightly and rubbed her cheeks with her hands.

"But I do not even know how to ask your name," she continued. "I could make some signs to you. Telling you that I want you to come with me. But you would probably think I was a woman of the street. So there is nothing I can do but look at you, wish the situation were different, and remember your face when I am alone."

Novotny shrugged, signifying that he hadn't understood what she had said. He wondered about the sadness in her voice, apparent even though he understood none of what she was saying. Maybe he reminded her of a husband or a lover who had been killed in the war.

Whatever this was about, it had come to a point where something had to happen. They had no common language. He couldn't just go back to reading his book. He had no choice but to leave.

He packed his things in his bag and stood a few feet from her. He had forgotten about her bare breasts, having been totally occupied by the conversation that he couldn't be part of. He saw her as a fascinating and beautiful woman, from whom he had been separated by an invisible, but impenetrable, wall.

"I sure wish I spoke French," he said, hoping that she had gotten some sense of what he meant. Slinging the bag over his shoulder, he waved and said, in French, "Au revoir."

She smiled and replied in English, "Goodbye."

Walking along the beach toward the town, he wanted to turn and look back, but resisted the urge. Shaking his head, he told himself that this was what happened in the movies. But not in real life.

Fighting the desire to look over his shoulder, he walked on toward town, relishing the fantasy in his subconscious.

It was only a few minutes before the pastel buildings of St. Tropez came into view. And for the first time since he had been on the beach, he thought of Anna. What if the fantasy had come true? Suppose the French woman

had motioned to him and they had walked together down the beach to
who knows where? Wouldn't that have been cheating, even though they had
never talked about going steady? How could he have gone back to Anna,
held her hand, and kissed her good night when he'd been with someone else
just a few days before?

But it didn't matter. It was all academic. All in his mind. All he was really
guilty of was checking out her gorgeous body and thinking prurient thoughts.
No crime there.

It was midafternoon when he got back to the wharf, and there was
noticeably more activity. More people in the cafés. More boats coming and
going from the waterfront. He thought about going back to the restaurant
where he had sat that morning, feeling a curious allegiance to the place. But
he decided to go to another café a few doors down and sit inside. He'd had
more than enough sun for one day.

The interior of the restaurant was plain and neat, with a long bar
running along the right wall. A dozen or so patrons—looking very much like
regulars—stood at the bar, talking, drinking wine, and watching the tourists.

Novotny found an open spot at the bar and leaned against it, watching a
waitress wiping glasses with a towel.

"For you?" she asked in French.

"Red wine," he said. But it was obvious English wasn't going to work; she
replied with a shake of her head. Did not understand. She raised her index
finger, signaling him to wait.

A moment later, a man walked from the far end of the bar and stood
next to him.

"You speak English?" the man asked.

"Yes. I do. You also speak English?"

"Yes. A little. Michelle asked me to help you."

Novotny caught Michelle's eye and smiled. "Merci," he said. She smiled in return.

"Will you have a glass of red wine?" the man asked, and moments later, the waitress placed two glasses of red wine on the bar.

Novotny held the glass toward the man. "Cheers," he said. "And thank you."

"Please. It was nothing," the man said, taking a sip from his glass. "You are a student? Or are you a soldier?"

"I am a soldier," he answered. He guessed the man to be in his sixties. He wore a black suit and a white dress shirt, its collar buttoned at the neck, but no tie.

"You have an excellent army," he said, speaking with authority.

"I think we do. Were you in the army?"

"I was somewhat old to be a soldier in the war. But I was in the Resistance. Do you know of it?"

"Yes. I believe the Resistance fighters were very brave."

"Yes," the man answered, nodding slightly.

As with Pan Hruzek, Novotny wanted to learn. To ask about what the man had done. To ask what it was like to fight the Germans. "Those must have been difficult times for you," he said.

"Yes, it was a difficult time." The man took a sip from his glass. "Very difficult."

"What did you do in the Resistance?" Novotny asked, trying not to sound too inquisitive, but realizing that was the way it had come out.

"My friend," the man said, looking down at his glass, "it is difficult to speak about these times. To talk about them brings back thoughts that I would rather lose in my brain. I am sorry to seem rude to you."

"No, please," Novotny said, flushed with embarrassment. "I was rude to ask. I apologize."

The two men stood looking out the open front of the restaurant at the boats coming and going in the harbor. The man motioned to the waitress, who brought two more glasses of red wine and took four coins from the money the man had left on the bar.

"Thank you," Novotny said.

The man took a blue pack of Gitanes French cigarettes from his pocket, carefully took one, and handed the package to Novotny. Choosing a wooden match from a glass holder on the bar, he lit both cigarettes.

"Thank you."

Lifting his glass, the Frenchman said, "To your army. It is the best army in the world."

His arms tingling in response to the man's comment, Novotny touched his glass to the Frenchman's and took a sip of the wine. "Thank you for saying that."

Novotny took a deep drag of the French cigarette. Its aroma was different from American cigarettes. And it was stronger, much stronger. Just as a cup of good French coffee was stronger and more aromatic than American coffee. Novotny said nothing, deciding that it was better just to let the conversation go wherever it was heading.

"I was in Paris when the Allied forces liberated the city." The man paused to collect his thoughts. "It was the most wonderful day of my life."

"I can understand how that would be."

"The Allied soldiers, thousands of them, marched on the Champs Élysées." The man took another sip of his wine, pulled cigarette smoke into his lungs, then exhaled, slowly and completely.

"I was only ten years old when the war ended," Novotny said. "But I had an uncle who fought in France. A photo of the soldiers marching was in all the newspapers. We looked, and were certain that we saw his picture."

The man took another sip of the wine in his glass, followed by another drag on the aromatic French cigarette. "I stood there," he recalled. "I watched them. And I had a strong impression about each of the armies."

Novotny said nothing, deciding to let the man say whatever was on his mind.

"The Free French Army was allowed to go first. We had lost to the Germans very quickly in 1940. But it was a matter of honor for our troops to be first in the parade."

His eyes seemed not to focus on anything, as if he were watching a picture of that event in his mind. "The French troops were leaving their ranks. To kiss the girls. To take bottles of wine and pass them among the marching soldiers."

He shook his head. "That is why we lost so easily to the Germans. Our soldiers were more interested in women and wine than they were in fighting for our country."

He pulled another long draft of smoke into his lungs. "When the British troops passed, you could see that they were good soldiers. Very disciplined. But there is a failing in the British Army. Do you know that?"

Novotny shook his head, not sure where this was going. He took a drink of the wine and waited for an explanation.

"There are officers. And there are soldiers. They are two very different classes of people. And if the officers—the leaders—are lost, their army can be beaten."

Novotny nodded, not sure that what the man said was true, but agreeing with the logic.

"But your army is different from any army in the world. I saw this when your troops marched by." Nodding at the truth in what he was about to say, he took another drink of his wine and another puff on his cigarette.

"You could see that if an officer fell, there were many soldiers who could lead the troops. You do not have a class separation in your army. A common soldier can become an officer. Is that not true?"

He didn't attempt to conceal the pride that he felt at the man's comment. "Yes, that is true."

The man crushed his cigarette into the ashtray. "And that, my young friend, is why you have the best army in the world. It is why I am glad that you, and your army, are here in Europe."

"Thank you for your thoughts," Novotny said. "And thank you for the wine."

The man drank the last drops of red wine, set down his glass, and stood in front of Novotny.

"It was my pleasure," he said, shaking Novotny's hand and waving to the waitress as he left.

Novotny stood for a moment, thinking about what he had just heard. Nodding and smiling at the waitress, he walked out onto the now sun-drenched dock, his forearms still tingling at what the man had said.

Part III

Always Ready

Technically, Novotny was still on leave Saturday, so he was able to sleep in after the long ride back to Nurnberg. Johnson had sacked out before he had arrived the night before and was gone by the time Novotny had gotten up.

He puttered around, showered, shaved, and put on civilian clothes, deciding to wait until Monday to get back into uniform. He had lunch, picked up a newspaper, and went to the Service Club to have a cup of coffee and read. It was nearly deserted when he got there.

The soldiers on pass had already left Merrell Barracks to chase frauleins and drink beer. The ones who were left had pulled details, spent their month's pay, or just decided to hang around the post library or shoot pool in the day room.

Novotny liked the Saturday ritual he had begun soon after arriving here. After getting off duty at noon, he would have lunch in the mess hall. After lunch, he would go to the PX and pick up a copy of the European edition of the *New York Herald-Tribune* from the woman who ran the newsstand. She always kept a copy for him, in case he was late getting off duty. In return, he would give her an occasional package of Kents.

Then he would go to the Service Club, take a seat on a couch near the window, and read the paper from cover to cover. It was one of the highlights of his week, giving him a sense that he had some idea of what was happening back in the States and in the rest of the world.

Having been away for a week, he was particularly engrossed in the paper when Johnson walked up to him.

"Novo."

"Hey, Bob," he said happily, folding up the paper. "I was going to come look for you in a little while. Got to tell you about the Riviera."

"I want to buy you a beer," Johnson said, frowning. "Let's go to the EM Club."

Novotny didn't like the way Johnson spoke or the way he looked. It wasn't like him to be this serious. "What's wrong?" he asked.

"I need to talk to you."

"Sure, let's go." He followed Johnson to the EM Club a short walk away. It too would be almost deserted now, and Novotny was glad. He was getting anxious to know whatever it was that was troubling his friend.

They said little, other than to order a beer, and when the two glasses were served, Johnson looked straight at Novotny. "I'm seeing Anna," he said.

"You're what?" he asked, visibly shocked.

"I'm seeing Anna," Johnson repeated. "Anna and I are going out. And I think it's starting to get serious."

He waited for Novotny to say something. But he just sat there looking at Johnson, trying to absorb the announcement.

"I wanted to tell you before someone else did." Johnson hoped that Novotny would say something in response. But he just sat there, now glaring at him. "It started the night that you were on guard duty and they had that party at Amerika Haus." He lit a cigarette and passed the pack to Novotny, who was now looking down at his glass of beer and paid no attention to the offering.

"I'm sorry, Novo. I'm really sorry this happened."

Novotny lifted the glass and studied the white foam, then took a long drink.

"Are you going to talk to her?" Johnson asked.

"She knows how to get hold of me," he answered curtly.

The two young men sat without saying anything, neither able to look at the other.

"I just don't know what else to say to you, Novo."

"You already said it," he replied quickly. His voice was hard edged and cold. "I just didn't know this was Screw-Your-Buddy Week." His chair scraped loudly on the floor as he brusquely pushed it back and stormed out of the club.

It had really been hard. After being so close, to have a big, ugly wall between them. What made it particularly bad was that they were bunkmates.

Novotny had made it a point to stay away from the room as much as he could, hanging out at the Service Club or the day room and then coming back just after lights out.

In the morning, he'd somehow gotten the alarm clock in his brain to wake him up about five o'clock, half an hour before reveille. That way he had shaved and showered before Johnson was awake, and dressed while Johnson was in the latrine.

Even so, it was awkward as hell, and sooner or later, he'd have to see about getting assigned to another room. Walking to the PX on Saturday afternoon to get his paper, he thought hard about it and wished it were different.

Deciding to go to the regimental headquarters building where it was quiet, he signed in, telling the duty NCO he had some extra work to do. Spreading the paper on a desk, he looked out the window. The sooner he got over this thing the better, he told himself. It had been great while it lasted. But that was it.

Thanks a lot, poster man, he said to himself, remembering the imaginary letter he'd written to the creator of the recruitment posters. I take back everything I told you, even if it was just in my head. I got set up and dumped. For my best friend. Thanks a lot. He smiled at the childish attack at the only scapegoat he could think of. Then he wondered why his target was the anonymous poster writer and not Johnson.

To hell with it, he decided, looking at the headlines in the paper.

On page three, his eyes focused on a story about a group of university students in Belgium who had organized an American film festival, using 16-mm copies of old classics: *Gone with the Wind* and the like.

He thought about it for a minute, took the military phone directory from the shelf behind him, found the number, and dialed.

"Sub-Area Finance. Lieutenant Allen," the woman's voice at the other end announced.

"Lieutenant, this is Pfc Novotny. Over at the 2d Cav."

"Well, hello," she replied, obviously not sure what to say next.

"I know this is a strange time to call. But I'm at my section office, and I had an idea for the German-American Relations Committee. I just thought I'd see if you were there. And if so, I'd pass it on to you."

"I'd like to hear about it," she said hesitantly. "But I'm just finishing up a report for Seventh Army." She paused and then added, "Actually, I'll be a Merrell Barracks later this afternoon. Will you be there?"

"Yeah," he said, then quickly corrected himself. "Yes, ma'am."

"Could we meet at the Service Club about five thirty?"

"Sure," Novotny said, nodding at the phone. "I'll see you there, Lieutenant."

It was about five fifteen when he arrived at the club and sat down in his favorite chair by the window. He was wearing civvies and had the neatly folded paper stashed in the jacket of his sport coat. He lit a cigarette and wondered what the lieutenant would think of his idea.

At exactly five thirty, he saw her walking toward the club. She wore a gray skirt and blue sweater and carried a tan raincoat over her arm. He stood as she entered the club and looked around for him.

"Hello, Lieutenant," he said, smiling slightly.

"Thanks for meeting me here," she replied, draping her coat over an empty chair. "I'm really interested in hearing your idea."

"It's no big thing," he said, spreading out the *Herald-Tribune*. "I have this ritual every Saturday, reading the paper," he explained, folding the paper into a more manageable size and pointing to the story. "Look at this. We could have that kind of film festival here."

She read the story and said, "We could do that. There must be some way to get copies of films like that. And we can borrow a projector from Troop Information." She nodded. "I think it's a great idea. I'll do some checking on Monday."

She stood and he rose with her. Putting her raincoat over her arm, she said, "Well, thanks again for your suggestion. I really appreciate the interest you have in the German–American program."

Novotny looked at his watch. "Lieutenant, I was going to head to the old town center and have some bratwurst. You want to come along?"

"Sure," she replied, hesitating. "Ah, why not?" She thought about it for a minute. "On one condition. That I treat."

"No. I'm sorry, Lieutenant. Can't do that."

"Well, then. Dutch treat?"

"That's a deal," he agreed, wondering what in the world had ever possessed him to suggest having dinner with a WAC lieutenant.

The delicate sausages were served on a pewter platter, set on a wooden base. A small dish of potato salad was positioned precisely in front of each platter. And an ample portion of freshly cut *schwartzbrot*, the wonderful dark brown bread that Novotny had come to relish, was placed on the table between them.

Novotny picked up his stein of beer. Lieutenant Allen did the same, gently touching the gray crockery of her stein to his.

"Cheers," she said, smiling.

"*Na zdravi.* To your health," he replied.

They were about halfway through the meal, having talked about the film festival idea and plans she had for other programs, when Novotny changed the subject. "This is sort of a personal question, Lieutenant. But why did you join the WACs?"

She thought for a moment. "Well, I suppose I was running away."

"From what? If you don't mind my asking."

"No." She took a sip of the cool, richly flavored beer. "I wanted to do something on my own. Instead of what other people wanted me to do."

He ate the last bite of his sausage, took a bite of bread, and washed it all down with a swallow of beer. Setting his knife and fork neatly on the plate, the European signal that he was finished, he reached into his jacket pocket and took out a pack of cigarettes.

Offering her one, he wasn't surprised that she declined. With a click, he opened his Zippo lighter and lit the cigarette. What a great lighter, he thought. What an incredibly simple and efficient machine.

All of this was to stall for time, to avoid saying anything and see what else she would say. He pulled smoke into his lungs, exhaled, and looked at her.

"My parents and friends had strong ideas about what I should do," she explained. "I just wanted to do something on my own."

"So you joined the army."

She nodded. "I joined the army."

"Do you like it?"

"Some parts I do. I studied accounting, and I like working in finance. And I like seeing Germany."

She paused and then added, "But, I'm really not cut out for the structure of it all."

Novotny took another sip of his beer.

"And the whole thing about officers and enlisted men . . . Well, I'm just not comfortable with it." She smiled, embarrassed. "You probably figured that out when you saluted me over at the Finance Center."

"That wasn't any big deal. I should have been paying more attention to the fact that you are an officer."

"What about you?" she asked. "Why did you join?"

"I didn't want to wait around to get drafted. So I signed up in March. Graduated in June. And went in about a month later."

"You still didn't tell me why."

"You got me," he said chuckling. "I have a habit of asking a lot of questions and then sidestepping them when they come back at me." He thought for a moment. "I guess I was running away too. Trying to avoid deciding what I really want to do with my life."

The conversation stopped while they absorbed this essential information.

"How are your German friends?" she asked. "The ones you were talking to at the dance."

"Oh, they're Czech. They're fine."

"Are you dating the girl you were dancing with?"

"No," he said, shaking his head. He took another drink from his stein, wondering why she was asking about Anna. "Well, I hope this film festival works out. I think it would be a good project for the program."

"I do too," she said, beaming. "I'm going to check it out on Monday."

He looked at her and asked, "Is it against regulations for you to be having dinner with an enlisted man?"

"If it was social, I assume there would be a problem," she replied, nodding. "But this is army business. We came to talk about your idea."

In a clumsy sort of way, he was trying to figure out what this was really all about. Johnson had always told him he was incompetent when it came to picking up signals.

Once he had told Johnson what a waitress had said to him in Baltimore on a weekend pass. He couldn't even remember what the waitress had said. But when he told Johnson, he couldn't believe it. "Of course it was a signal, Novo. You've got to pick up on these things," he had scolded him.

But Novotny wasn't sure what was happening. Maybe she was trying to tell him something. Maybe not. What's more, what difference did it make? She was an officer, and he was a Pfc.

He looked at his watch. "Well, Lieutenant, it's getting a little late. I'd better head back to the barracks."

She nodded in agreement. "I just have one thing to ask."

"Sure. Go ahead."

"If we get together to work on this film festival . . ." She hesitated. "Well, if we get together in civilian clothes, and there aren't any other servicemen around . . ." Again she hesitated. "Well, I'd like it if you just called me Judy, instead of Lieutenant."

"OK, that's a deal," he agreed. Now, that's a signal, he decided. A real, honest-to-God signal. No doubt about that.

"What do you want me to call you?"

"Well, my first name's Joseph. Joe. But most of the guys in my unit call me Novo. It's one of those army nicknames that sticks."

He thought about the signal and wondered what it meant. If it meant anything at all.

"I'm a little curious," he began. "Why did you want to know if I was dating the Czech girl?"

"At the dance, it looked as though there might be something happening."

That wasn't good enough. "Was that the only reason?" he asked, careful not to sound accusatory.

She'd been trapped, and her face showed it.

"Well, no." She reemptied her already empty stein. "I saw her at the bar over at the Army Hotel. She was with another GI. I just didn't want to see you get hurt."

Now, that was a signal. But he didn't know what it meant. He wished he could talk to Johnson about this.

"I shouldn't have said anything," she said.

He looked at his watch again. "I've got to get going."

"Want a ride?"

"No thanks. I'll grab a tram."

At her car, he took her hand and shook it. "Hope this film thing works."

"I'm sure it will," she said confidently.

"Well, good night, Judy."

"Good night, Novo."

He watched her drive away and then walked to the nearby tram stop. What a signal, he thought. Then shaking his head, he wondered what it meant.

"Hey, Turner," Novotny hollered to the slightly built GI walking ahead of him. "Wait up."

Turner smiled slightly and stood, waiting for his friend.

"How's it goin'?" Novotny asked as they resumed their walk toward the mess hall.

"Pretty good," Turner answered. "But Sergeant Murdock is bein' sent back to the States. Some family problem. I'm sorry to see him go. He's been really good to me."

Over breakfast, the two men talked about all the trivial things that made up the typical day of GIs on duty in Europe. Detail assignments. The weather.

On the way back, there were troopers ahead of them and behind them, each heading toward their quarters to get ready for the day's work. Walking about twenty-five feet ahead of them was a lone, burly soldier.

He turned to see who was behind him and stopped abruptly, standing in the middle of the sidewalk. "Turner," he said menacingly, "I don't want you walkin' behind me. You understand?"

Novotny and Turner were surprised by the unprovoked outburst, both wondering what it was all about. The source was a Spec 4 named Ward, who worked in the supply room. All Novotny knew about him was that he had been in for about eight years and seemed a little odd.

"What's wrong, Ward?" Novotny asked innocently.

"I said I don't want Turner walkin' behind me. Get it?"

Novotny was both puzzled and angered by the comment and the soldier's tone.

"What's the problem?" Novotny asked, now just a few feet from Ward.

"I'll tell you what the problem is," he said, pointing at Turner. "I saw guys like him in Korea. They'd come into a unit, and a couple of days later, he and four or five other guys would get it." He glared at Novotny. "I know his kind. And I don't want him anywhere around me. Understand?"

Novotny's confusion about the situation turned to anger. "He's got as much right to be on this sidewalk as you do."

The hulking GI grabbed Novotny by the collar of his field jacket. "Guess you don't understand. I don't want him, and I don't want you—his queer-lovin' buddy—anywhere around me." With that he gave Novotny a hard shove backward. Losing his balance, Novotny fell into a pile of leaves next to the sidewalk. Giving them both a glaring, hate-filled look, the soldier turned and walked toward the barracks.

Novotny got up, brushed the leaves off his butt, and straightened the cap on his head.

"You OK, Novo?" Turner asked.

"Yeah. What a jerk."

Turner said nothing as they approached the building where their quarters were, and Novotny imagined what was going on in his head.

"Forget him, Turner," Novotny said, smiling. "After all, this is a guy who's been in the army for eight years. And he's still a Spec 4 handing out bedding from the supply room."

Turner said nothing, and Novotny decided it was better just to let it pass. At least as far as Turner was concerned. But he had his own questions about what had happened. Why had he stood there and let this jerk say those things and then shove him down into a pile of leaves?

He knew how to avoid that. He also knew how to flip Ward—even though he was bigger and heavier—and put him on his back. Instead, he'd just stood there, letting this guy hold him by the collar and then push him into a pile of leaves, without doing a thing.

If I can't handle a simple thing like this, he asked himself, how the hell could I deal with a Russian coming at me with a bayonet? They taught me the techniques, he said to some other part of his brain. But could I do it?

Inside the barracks, when they got to Turner's quarters, Novotny patted him on the shoulder. "Just forget it," he said, wanting to sound casual. Walking to his own room, he wished he could do the same.

Silver Arrow is what the NATO maneuver was called. And, sitting in the back of the deuce-and-a-half with Johnson and the heavy safe filled with codes, and supposedly, German marks, Novotny decided it wasn't a bad name. It could have been a lot worse, he thought. Like Ivan Crusher or Commie Bloodlust.

Altogether there'd be tens of thousands of troops probably a dozen countries, running around Bavaria shooting blanks at each other. He watched the sand-colored dust swirl in their wake, some of it blowing back into the

OD canvas-covered area where they rode. Pulling out his handkerchief, he wiped the dust from the blue-black barrel of his carbine. "Treat your weapon like your best friend," Sergeant Duff had said. "Because if we get into a fight, that's exactly what it'll be."

Johnson too was looking out the back of the truck and wondering where they were. Moving slowly as part of a long convoy, it was hard to know how far they had traveled since leaving the barracks just before dawn.

It was still awkward for both of them, sharing a room and riding in the back of the same truck on alerts and maneuvers. Novotny had worked out his schedule so they rarely had a chance to talk. But sitting in the truck for hours, it was definitely uncomfortable.

Johnson pulled out a pack of cigarettes and offered one to him. Reluctantly, Novotny took it and leaned forward so Johnson could light it and then light his own.

Exhaling, Johnson said, "Can I explain what happened?"

"There's nothing to explain," Novotny replied coolly. "But if there's something you've got to say, go ahead."

"I walked her to the streetcar one night when you had guard duty. Then you were on leave in France and I went to a thing at Amerika Haus," he said, pausing for a reply. "Anna was there." He paused again in case Novotny wanted to talk. "It was late, and she asked me if I'd walk with her."

Novotny looked at the dust swirling behind the truck, listening but saying nothing.

"She was going to be back at Amerika Haus the next day, and asked if I could meet her," Johnson said. Taking a drag on the cigarette, he continued, "And I did."

Novotny still said nothing.

"I didn't think anything about it. It didn't seem out of line just to go there. We had coffee, and she said she felt you were interested in her only because she's Czech."

"That's not true," Novotny snapped angrily.

"Look, Novo, I'm just telling you what she said." Johnson took another deep drag on his cigarette. "She said she thought you wanted to take her back to the States like some kind of prize. To show to your friends. And your family. And she didn't want to do that."

He took a deep breath. "She said she likes you. But she didn't want you to think that she's . . . well . . . She doesn't want you to think that there's anything really there for you."

Johnson paused again, watched Novotny shake his head, and then went on. "I told her she needed to explain that to you. And she said that as soon as you got back from leave, she was going to tell you."

Novotny looked out the back of the truck, wondering where they were.

"We went out several times, and it looked like it was getting serious. She couldn't seem to make herself tell you. So I figured I'd better do it."

"So you didn't ask her out?"

"No. The first time I walked her to the streetcar with nothing in mind. But it started when she asked me to walk her to the streetcar the next time I saw her."

"And you didn't go out with her until she told you all that about me? That she didn't want anything to happen between us?"

"That's right, Novo." He shook his head. "I really wish it had happened differently."

Novotny took a final puff on the cigarette, squashed it out with the sole of his combat boot, and then field-stripped it, throwing the remaining tobacco out the back of the truck.

"I'm glad you told me that, Bob," Novotny said, nodding.

"I probably would've felt the same way. I know you really liked her. And that's why it's been so damned hard on me too. I just hated to see you so mad at me."

"Let's just say it's all done," Novotny said, smiling. He extended his hand to his friend.

As they shook hands, Johnson asked, "Can I pull my transfer request?"

"You were going to transfer?"

"Yeah. Better that than putting up with you," he answered, laughing. Novotny couldn't help but smile as well.

He was glad it was behind him. A prize, he thought. Maybe she was right. "Mom and Dad," he would have said proudly, "this is Anna. She's from Prague."

The convoy rumbled on, then stopped by the side of the road so the drivers could check their vehicles and anyone who needed to could walk into the forest and relieve themselves on a tree. Minutes later, they were moving slowly along the dirt road again.

Novotny took off his helmet, put his field pack on the wooden bench to use as a pillow, and stretched out.

Sleeping was hopeless as the deuce-and-a-half lurched along the rough road, the driver noisily working up and down the gears and the air inside the back of the truck dusty and dry.

It really was exciting, Novotny thought. No doubt about that. Here they were, part of a major army in a maneuver just short of combat, testing what they had learned and trained for. The 2d Cav was part of the Red Army. Other units made up the Blue Army, the theoretical adversary.

The two armies were made up of NATO soldiers from countries all over Western Europe. The purpose was to get ready for what they all hoped wouldn't happen: war with the Russians.

Part of the test was communications. We have soldiers from all these countries, Novotny thought. All these languages. That's one reason why I'm here. I'm a translator. He wished that he spoke German as well as he spoke Czech, though he was doing better with German now that he had a chance to use it regularly.

As he thought, it also occurred to him that, if there were a war, he'd probably be transferred to S-2, intelligence. He assumed he'd end up translating when patrols brought in Czech prisoners.

That would be strange, he decided, and more than a little uncomfortable. He thought about the day in basic that they'd gone through interrogation drill—the day he had really screwed up. We'd do it by the book, he assured himself. By the Geneva Convention.

"How long before we're there, Bob?" he asked.

"Should be there anytime," Johnson replied. "I'd have thought we'd be at our first position by now."

"I hate to confess this," Novotny said. "But I'm kind of excited. It's really amazing. All these troops in the field." He thought for a minute. "If we had plans to head east, this would sure be the time to do it."

"Yeah. But it won't happen. Just another NATO maneuver."

"Wonder what this costs the American taxpayer," Novotny mused.

"I don't know that figure. But I saw a planning report, and civilian damage alone is budgeted for twenty-four million dollars."

"For what?"

"Roads chopped up with tank treads, I suppose. Collapsed bridges. That kind of stuff," Johnson said. "We're going to be running all over the countryside. Lots of things for us to break."

He looked out the back of the truck, and said, "You won't believe this, Novo, but there's another part of the budget."

"What?"

"They've budgeted for ten civilian deaths."

"What?" Novotny asked, instantly sitting up on the bench. "Civilians? How?"

"Easy. Hans leaves his wife to clean up the kitchen and heads to the village gasthaus. Has four or five beers with his kraut buddies, then decides to go home. Steps out of the gasthaus, and bam, gets hit by a jeep out on night recon, speeding along with nothing on but blackout lights. One down. Nine to go."

"I wonder if his wife would understand that it was all worth it. Preserving democracy for her country and all that." He imagined the scene that Johnson had just described, realizing that it could very well happen. "No big deal. Just part of the cost of keeping Ivan on his side of the line."

They soon arrived at the bivouac site, and quickly started what would be several hours of hard work setting up the regimental command post. Tents were pitched, vehicles positioned, and radio links established. Even mundane tasks had to be done, such as digging slit trenches that would serve as latrines.

Novotny was just about finished setting up when Sergeant Rogers walked over to him. "Novotny, get a jeep and bring it to S-3 at twenty-one hundred," the sergeant ordered. "Got that straight?"

"Yes, Sergeant," Novotny replied. He'd signed up voluntarily and was willing to do whatever he had to do. But he sure didn't like doing it with Sergeant Rogers.

"Remember, blackout lights only, so be careful," the motor pool sergeant said, handing Novotny his trip ticket. The NCO held a flashlight while he filled in every detail, and then carefully put it into a field jacket pocket.

This ticket was going to be kept absolutely by the books. No reason to give Sergeant Rogers any reason to be on his back.

"Thanks," he said, starting the engine and feeling around the dashboard for the light switch. Finding it, he turned it one click. In that position, the instruments were lit by a dull, red glow. At the front of the vehicle were two sets of four white dots of light. And at the rear, two sets of four small red lights. The small lights didn't show you where you were going. But they helped you keep your distance from the vehicle in front of you.

Here he was, in the dark, carefully trying to find his way back to the 2d Cav's command post. Luckily, the clouds broke up and the moon provided enough light to stay on the road. At the S–3 tent, he turned off the engine and checked his watch in the glow of the instruments. He reached for the trip ticket and dutifully wrote "8:45 PM" on it.

Pushing aside the canvas jeep door, he stepped into the tent. Three men stood in the bright yellow glare of a kerosene lantern. Sergeant Rogers looked at his watch as Novotny stood squinting in the sudden light.

"Novotny, this is Air Force Lieutenant Tolson," the NCO said coolly.

"Hello, Lieutenant," Novotny said, nodding and noticing the wings sewn over the pocket of the officer's fatigues.

"Hello, Novotny."

Sergeant Rogers pointed to a Pfc standing in the corner. "Do you

9

know Orloff?"

Novotny nodded. "Hi, Jerry." Orloff was a radio operator whom he knew slightly. He had seemed like a decent guy, though he hadn't spent much time with him.

Although he wasn't particularly excited about spending the night with Sergeant Rogers, he was looking forward to the assignment.

The lieutenant was a forward air controller. Tomorrow morning at oh six hundred, a squadron of U.S. jet fighter/bombers would attack a hill where a German battalion was dug in. American infantry would then assault the hill, just after the jets pretended to bomb and strafe the location.

Orloff would contact the aircraft by radio. Then the lieutenant would direct the air strikes, talking directly to the pilots in the jets.

"The lieutenant will ride with Orloff in the radio van," the sergeant said with great authority. Novotny knew what was coming next. "You'll be my driver, Novotny. Any questions?"

The sergeant opened a metal box and pulled out a band of red cloth, like the ones that he, Orloff, and Novotny had tied to their arms. "You'll have to wear this, Lieutenant. We're part of the Red Army. The krauts are blue." He pulled a white band from the box and gave it to Novotny. "You're neutral on this one. They want the interpreters to be able to translate for both sides.

"We'll proceed now to a hill facing the one where the Germans are positioned. That way we'll be in place when the air strike is scheduled," Sergeant Rogers announced.

As they drove slowly along the dirt road, Novotny was glad that he'd folded back the canvas top of the jeep. He could look up and see the silhouette of the trees lining the road. And the cool night air and the scent of the pines felt good in his nostrils. The stars and the glow of the moon over his head contrasted with the blackness of the dense forest on each side of the road.

He looked in his rearview mirror every few minutes to make sure he could see the small dots of light from the van behind him.

After driving for close to an hour, Sergeant Rogers said, "Stop here." Novotny carefully slowed the jeep so Orloff could see what was happening. Turning off the engine, Novotny stood and stretched, glad to relax for a few minutes.

Orloff and the lieutenant came to the vehicle just as Sergeant Rogers finished spreading a map on the hood of the jeep. Shielding the lens of his flashlight so there was just a small circle of light, he pointed to a series of concentric contour lines.

"Here's where the krauts are," he announced. "And this is where we'll be."

Back on the road, they headed down a grade from which they could see the silvery ribbon formed by a small river. At the bottom of the incline, there was a fork in the road, barely visible in the darkness. "Go to the left," Sergeant Rogers ordered.

"Don't we want to go to the right, so we're on the east side of the river?" Novotny asked, knowing instantly what the sergeant's reaction would be.

"Novotny, I've been in this army for seventeen years. How long have you been in?"

"A year and a half."

"Well, for some reason you seem to think that you know more about soldiering than I do. And that's why you and I are never going to get along very well." He paused long enough for the message to sink in. "Now get this damn jeep moving down that road," he said, pointing to the left. "Is that clear?"

"Yes, Sergeant." Novotny put the jeep in gear and slowly headed to the left, checking often to make sure the van was behind him. He drove for about twenty minutes, saying nothing. Then, without notice, the sergeant ordered, "Stop here." Novotny carefully brought the vehicle to an abrupt stop.

When Orloff and the air force officer arrived at the jeep, Sergeant Rogers directed them to a position under a tree. As they gathered around the vehicles, Sergeant Rogers made another announcement. "Lieutenant, you and I'll sleep in the van. The men will sleep outside."

Novotny looked for a sheltered place to sleep and decided to curl up in the back of his jeep.

"See you in a few hours, Jerry." Novotny said.

He unzipped his sleeping bag. Taking off his combat boots, he shoved them to the bottom of the bag. That way, they'd be warm when he put them on in the morning. It was already chilly, and likely to be colder before the sun came up.

Folding his field jacket into a sort of pillow, he scrunched around, getting as comfortable as he could. Lying on his back, he admired the stars above him and in a few minutes was sound asleep.

He awoke with a start, feeling someone shaking his shoulder through the wool of his sleeping bag. For a couple of moments, he wasn't quite sure where he was.

But as he rolled over to see what was happening, he was suddenly wide awake, his heart pounding. About a foot from his face was the barrel of a rifle, aimed directly at him. In the dull, predawn light, he could see that the soldier holding the weapon was wearing the field uniform of the Bundewehr, the

West German Army.

The soldier motioned with his rifle, signaling Novotny to get out of his sleeping bag.

"Hands high," he ordered in German. The young soldier was obviously serious, and Novotny decided the prudent thing to do was follow the instruction. He unzipped his sleeping bag and stood in his combat fatigues and socks, his hands held over his head.

A second German soldier walked over, wearing the rank equivalent to an American sergeant and carrying a submachine gun.

The younger German pointed to Orloff's sleeping bag under a tree.

The sergeant put his finger to his lips in the universal sign of silence.

It's all a game, Novotny reminded himself. But it was close enough to being real that he felt the essence of fear, even though he was in no danger. It was like seeing a scary movie and sharing the manufactured anxiety of the actors on the screen. Only this time, he was one of the actors.

"I speak German," he told the sergeant. Again the German put his finger to his lips, and then walked to within a foot of Novotny.

"How many are you?" he whispered. "Why are you here?"

Automatically, he began the litany. "My name is Joseph Novotny. I am a private first class in the United States Army. My serial number is USA55625067."

Name, rank, and serial number. That's all he owed them. And that's all they'd get.

The German NCO scowled at him. "I am an underofficer of the Bundeswehr, and as your superior, I order you to answer my questions."

Novotny recited the basic facts and stood there, his hands still over his head, now beginning to shiver in the predawn cold. He remembered the time at the Sigma Nu house when Ed Benson had asked him if he had ever made it with Carol Mitchell, a pretty coed he'd dated for a while. He had not, but said, "I'm a very discreet person, Ed. You'll never know."

Ed had taken his arm and pushed it behind his back, firmly but not hard enough to really hurt. Mimicking the line from World War II movies, he had said, "We have ways to make you talk."

And the Nazis obviously did. There was plenty of evidence for that. They had very efficient ways to squeeze facts out of people. And ways to kill. The sergeant was about the right age. Maybe he'd shot men and boys at Lidice. Or maybe he'd herded women and children into boxcars to be shipped to places like Dachau.

"Put on your boots," the sergeant abruptly ordered, visibly annoyed at Novotny's lack of cooperation. Novotny fished out his combat boots from the bottom of the sleeping bag, laced them up, and then put on his field jacket. Seeing the white band on his sleeve, he thought, Jesus, I'm dumb. I completely forgot.

"As you can see, Sergeant," he said, pointing to the armband, "I am neutral. I am a translator."

The sergeant was now even more annoyed. Had this happened not many years ago, he had no doubt the sergeant would have had him taken into the woods and shot.

"You have wasted my time," the sergeant said, furious. Having heard the commotion, Orloff got out of his sleeping bag and was immediately grabbed by a couple of German soldiers. Pointing to the van, the sergeant told Novotny, "Get the men out of that truck."

Novotny opened the back of the van. Sergeant Rogers quickly sat up and growled, "What the hell's going on?"

"Some Bundeswehr soldiers are here to take you prisoner," Novotny replied, trying hard not to smile as he said it.

"I don't like your sense of humor, Novotny."

"I'm serious, Sergeant. You and the lieutenant better get out here. These Germans aren't in a real friendly mood."

The Bundeswehr sergeant shouted, "Tell those men to get out quickly."

"Damn," Sergeant Rogers muttered under his breath.

Minutes later, Sergeant Rogers, the air force lieutenant, and Orloff stood in front of the radio van, their hands over their heads.

"Looks like you got us on the wrong hill, Sergeant," the lieutenant said, obviously not happy about the situation.

"Tell them we will go to our command post," the Bundeswehr sergeant ordered. Novotny conveyed the message and watched as the group disappeared into the forest.

Packing up his gear, he spread the map on the hood of the jeep. He had been right. If they had taken the other fork in the road, they would have been on the opposite hill. Not the one that was supposed to be attacked by the air strike.

All of a sudden the quiet of the morning was shattered by the roar of jet engines as four F-100 Super Sabre jets flew over low in tight formation. They made several passes, obviously trying to make contact with the ground controller. Then they were gone.

For a few seconds, he smiled at how Sergeant Rogers had screwed up. But the self-satisfied grin quickly left his face. In a real war, it would have been different. Four men would have been real prisoners, for months. Maybe years. Or, worse yet, become casualties.

The troops on the ground, counting on air support, would have had to attack without it. And, because Sergeant Rogers had put them on the wrong hill, more of those guys would be killed or wounded.

But what was the point? Stay out of combat because every unit can have incompetents like Sergeant Rogers? No, because the choice isn't yours. It is the luck of the draw. All you could do is hope that you end up close to guys like Sergeant Duff. Guys who really know how to soldier.

Luck was the key. No doubt about it.

Right now he could be a clerk-typist with some admin unit at Fort Leonard Wood, filling out forms all day long. All he would have to worry about would be what kind of pizza to get on Saturday night.

No, he said to himself, shaking his head. Luck had worked his way. Even with Sergeant Rogers in the picture, he would much rather be here than pushing papers Stateside. No doubt about it.

Here, there's not much risk as long as Ivan stays on his side of the line. If our luck goes the other way, then a lot of us will die.

He settled into the seat of his jeep, started the engine, and thought for a minute or two about what to do next. His regiment was probably nowhere near where it had been when they'd started out last night.

He was neutral, which was good news. No need to worry about being captured or turned into a pretend casualty. As he thought, his growling stomach made the decision for him. It was simple. Get back onto a road and find a mess truck. Grab some chow and then figure out what to do next. Just take it one step at a time.

Heading back along the ruts in the dirt, he saw what looked to be the road they had been on last night. Turning left for no particular reason, he drove slowly, partly because he had no idea where he was going. But also because it was very pleasant morning and he decided to enjoy it, despite his growling stomach.

A couple of kilometers down the road, he saw a cluster of jeeps and trucks, hidden under the cover of pine trees. He backed into a wooded area that would prevent the jeep from being seen from the air. A hundred yards or so into the forest, he saw what appeared to be a mess truck, and headed straight for it.

"Just shut down breakfast," the cordial mess sergeant said, peering down from the mess truck. "But let me see what I can get for ya."

Novotny waited patiently as the sergeant talked to one of the cooks, then came back with a fried egg sandwiched between two pieces of bread.

"Thanks, Sarge," Novotny said, smiling and filling his canteen cup with hot, black coffee.

"You look like you could use a little chow," the sergeant said, grinning.

"Sure can. Thanks again."

He found a comfortable-looking tree not far from the mess truck and relaxed with his sandwich and coffee.

Not bad, he thought. Not bad at all. A gorgeous day. Some food in my belly. A chance to relax. Nope, not bad.

Two sergeants walked toward the mess truck, their rifles slung over their shoulders, talking intently. Novotny couldn't help overhearing them as they filled their canteen cups with coffee.

"Damn," one of them said, obviously frustrated. "Everyone said he spoke English."

The second NCO shook his head. "Now we've got a kraut officer there, pissed off because we didn't get a translator. Somebody should've known."

"Gonna cost someone a stripe," the first sergeant said. "Sure glad it won't be me."

Novotny quickly finished off the last of his coffee, put his canteen cup back in its place on his web belt, and got up.

"Excuse me," he said.

The two NCOs turned to see who was talking.

"You looking for a translator?"

"Yeah," one of the sergeants said, curious about the reason for the question.

"I speak German," Novotny said.

"You do?" the second NCO said, smiling. "Somebody's lookin' out for us," he said to his partner.

The NCOs took Novotny to a spot where a group of ten officers stood on a small, wooded hill overlooking a broad, open field. Three of the officers were Americans. The rest wore all manner of uniforms, most of which Novotny didn't recognize.

He was introduced to an American major, who rushed him over to a German Bundeswehr officer.

Novotny stood in front of the officer and saluted. "I am private first class Novotny, sir," he said. As he made the announcement, in his best formal German, he realized that the officer wore the insignia of the Bundewehr general.

The officer returned his salute. "Where have you learned to speak German?" he asked.

Novotny described his language training at Fort Meade.

The major and the two sergeants anxiously watched the initial exchanges, and when things seemed to be going well, they visibly relaxed.

Below them, a combined armor and infantry maneuver was just beginning. Tanks to their left moved in formation, leaving trails of blowing dust, then stopped. The turrets turned and white smoke puffed out of the cannons. Seconds later, they heard the distinctive sounds of the tanks' cannons firing. *Pfuuump. Pfuuump.*

The tanks on their right responded, maneuvering and firing, with infantrymen moving behind the armored vehicles.

The general asked about the units that were participating, the types of equipment that was being used, and the status of the mock combat. Novotny diligently repeated the questions in English, and then translated the major's reply back into German.

For the most part, it was pretty easy, dealing with words he knew. At the end, the major said, "The engagement is now finished."

The officers stood around talking and the general asked Novotny, "Your name. It is Czech. Is that not true?"

Yes, sir," Novotny replied. "My family is Czech."

The general nodded, then shook Novotny's hand. "Many thanks for your help."

I was glad to do it, sir General," he said, coming to attention and saluting. The general smartly returned the salute.

The major walked with Novotny back toward the mess truck to get a cup of coffee.

"You came along just in time, Novotny," he said, smiling. "General Ritter was starting to get a little testy about needing a translator."

Novotny stopped walking, unable to believe what he had just heard. "General Ritter? General Helmut Ritter?" he asked.

"Yeah. You've heard of him?" the major asked. "He's at NATO." The major looked at Novotny's face. "Something wrong?"

"No, sir. It's nothing, sir," he replied, still not able to believe it. General Helmut Ritter.

"Thanks again, Novotny. I'll see that your CO knows about what you did this morning."

"Thank you, sir," Novotny said, saluting.

Sitting in his jeep, a string of sounds and pictures were re-created in his brain. Pictures of bodies stacked high at places like Dachau and Buchenwald. The sounds of Radio Prague saying things like, "This man, Ritter, a butcher of the Czechs, is now a high-ranking general in NATO." He had pretty much written it off as propaganda when he had heard it. Now he'd actually met him.

The very man that Radio Prague was talking about had made a comment about his name being Czech, then shaken his hand and thanked him. What was he thinking—the general—when he did that?

Novotny shook his head. This is something that will take a while to sort out, he decided. He started the jeep, not knowing where he was going. But it was definitely time to get moving.

He headed north, toward where he thought the 2d Cav was likely to be. All he could do was shake his head, thinking about whom he had just met. And what he had just done. General Ritter. The real guy himself. He even shook his hand. And saluted him. What a small, scary world—if the Radio Prague report was true.

Every kilometer or so he would come onto a roadblock, and each time the drill was the same. He would point to his white armband and get waved through, moving on as if he really knew where he was going.

Rounding a bend, he saw several vehicles blocking the dirt road and a group of soldiers standing around. Pulling off to the side, he got out to see what was happening.

About a dozen soldiers, carrying rifles and wearing helmets, stood in a loose circle around a GI lying on the road. His helmet was a couple of feet away from his head. His arms and legs were in awkward, abnormal angles. And his green fatigue jacket was marked with oily, wet blotches that looked black until they seeped red onto the ground. Near him was his M1 rifle, the end of the barrel in the tan dirt, the stock covered with dust.

Novotny turned to a colored soldier standing next to him. "What happened?"

The GI stared at the body and answered almost inaudibly without turning to see who was asking. "Got hit by that truck," he said, pointing to a deuce-and-a-half pulled over under a grove of trees. Sitting on the running board was a soldier, apparently the driver, with his shoulders slumped and his head down.

"Truck came from over there," the soldier continued, motioning up the road that Novotny had just driven on. "Guess they didn't neither one see each other."

"Too bad," Novotny said, and then thought about what an inane comment he had just made. "Did you know him?"

The colored soldier sniffed, and continued to stare at the body in front of him. "He was my buddy." He sniffed again and Novotny saw tears running down his brown cheeks.

"I'm sorry," Novotny said. "I'm really sorry."

"I better get going," the saddened soldier said. "See you."

"See you," Novotny replied, thinking about the comment and how unlikely it was that he would ever see him again.

He looked at the dead soldier's gray face, thinking about how the accident could have happened anywhere. Anyone could have been hit by a vehicle while crossing a street. But as he looked at the corpse, its mouth awkwardly open and eyes closed, he shook his head.

No, he told himself. It wasn't the same at all. This kid wasn't just another traffic statistic, the kind the National Safety Council reported on the news after the Memorial Day weekend.

This was a dead soldier, wearing a combat uniform and carrying a weapon. He was a casualty, not an accident victim, Novotny said to himself angrily. He was as much a casualty as if he'd been hit by a round from an AK-47 or a blast of shrapnel from a Russian grenade.

As he stared at the dead soldier's face, he counted and realized that this was only the third corpse he'd ever seen in his life. The first two were his grandparents, who, four years apart, had gone into the hospital and died. The last time he saw them, they were calm and peaceful, dressed in their best clothes, hands carefully folded on their chest and their faces framed by the satin that lined the coffin. Not like this, all askew in the mud that was created by the soldier's own blood.

An SFC broke through the ring of curious, young soldiers. "OK, men. Let's give 'em room." Novotny turned and saw an OD ambulance, its red cross bright against a white square, slowly moving toward them. It stopped with a lurch, and two medics hopped out and jogged toward the NCO.

"All you need's a bag," the NCO said calmly. One of the medics stopped and walked quickly back to the vehicle. The other knelt next to the limp body, holding its arm and feeling for a pulse. He tried several different places and then gently laid the arm back on the ground.

His partner had brought a dark plastic bag, just like the ones Novotny and Johnson loaded onto the ambulance when they went out on alerts. Laying the rubberized fabric on the ground next to the dead soldier, the medic unzipped it and spread it open.

Part of him wanted to walk away. He'd seen enough of this, Novotny said to himself. But for some strange reason, another part of him wanted to stay. To watch this to the end. Maybe it was some morbid fascination with death, which he hadn't seen much of in the twenty-three years of his life.

Maybe he was just glad it wasn't him, or someone he knew. Just a friend of a colored soldier from an infantry division whom he would most likely never see again. Maybe he subconsciously felt that it would be disrespectful to the dead soldier to leave before he had been properly taken care of.

In the end, he had no idea why he stood there. But he did, watching intently as they slid the body into the bag, zipped it up, and carried the limp cargo to the ambulance.

He imagined the process repeated dozens or even hundreds of times in combat. "It ain't much fun," the medic had said to Johnson and Novotny when he had talked about filling bags like that in Korea while they loaded the boxes of body bags into the ambulance.

The ambulance slowly drove off, taking the body to wherever they take guys who get killed on NATO maneuvers. Then he would be sent home to whatever town he had come from.

"It was a traffic accident," someone would probably explain to the mourners at the funeral.

Like hell it was, Novotny told the relative appearing in his mind's eye. He was a casualty. There's a big difference, so don't forget it, he admonished the imaginary family member.

How many GIs would be like this one? Run over. Or blown up by a misfired artillery round. Killed when a chute didn't open in an airborne drop. There were all sorts of ways to get killed while soldiering, without having someone shoot you.

Novotny realized how tense his body was. I'm mad, he thought. Mad about what I've just seen. Then another part of his brain corrected him. You're not tense because you're mad. You're tense because you're scared. You're afraid someone will set this whole thing off. And instead of it being a war game, it'll be real. You're afraid that if that happens, you'll end up on your face in the dirt like that guy. Your arms and legs bent at strange angles. And your skull cracked, just the way his was.

You're chicken, he told himself. You're afraid to die.

"The excitement's over, men," the sergeant announced. "Get on with your duties."

The circle of soldiers broke up as men walked away slowly in ones and twos. Novotny stood there looking at the reddish mud in front of him, and then started to walk toward his jeep. Everyone seemed to have forgotten about the truck driver, still sitting on the running board of his vehicle remorsefully looking at the ground.

"It wasn't your fault," Novotny said softly.

The driver looked up. "Thanks," he said.

He had to ask around, but finally found the 2d ACR headquarters about four miles from where he had started the night before. Johnson had moved

Novo's gear with his and pitched the tent. After checking in with S-3, he spent most of the afternoon translating a string of messages from a number of Bundeswehr units. His next assignment was to go out with a patrol in case they needed someone who spoke German. It was an all-nighter, and he was told to get a couple of hours sleep.

After dozing for a while, he ate supper served from the mess truck, then walked over to S-2 to check in. It was nearly seven and getting dark. The duty officer was Lieutenant Gordon, whom he'd gotten to know pretty well and whom Johnson—who was off duty—liked.

"Pfc Novotny reporting, sir," he said, saluting. "I'm scheduled to go out on a patrol tonight."

A few minutes later, Sergeant Morales came in and reported to the lieutenant. "Hey, Novotny," the NCO said, shaking his hand. "You ridin' with us tonight?"

"Yup," he replied, hoping the sergeant had forgotten about the border incident.

The patrol was made up of three jeeps. One had a .30-caliber machine gun mounted on a tall pole-like base. The second was equipped with several radios. And the third was just plain, like the one Novotny had spent so many hours in since last night. Counting Novotny and the sergeant, there were eight men in the patrol.

The sergeant rode in the lead jeep, with the machine gun, and the other two followed closely, winding their way down a dirt road at about ten miles per hour. All the vehicles were completely blacked out, without even their tiny driving lights showing in the dark.

After about twenty minutes, they saw the lights of a small village ahead, probably two kilometers down the road. As they got closer, they saw an illuminated beer sign next to the door of an old stone building, identifying the local gasthaus.

The lead jeep turned into a muddy area next to the building and parked so it was heading out toward the road. The other two vehicles duplicated the maneuver.

The men stood at the entrance, waiting for the sergeant to give them instructions. "McDermott and Torben, you stay with the vehicles. Let us know if anything happens."

"Right, Sarge," McDermott replied.

The sergeant opened the door and went in first, with Novotny right behind him, squinting at the bright light. The others followed, forming a loose line along the wall. The gasthaus looked like every other local village pub in West Germany. There were six wooden tables spaced neatly around the room. One, larger and set off from the others, was the *stammtisch*, reserved for special guests and friends of the proprietor.

The four people sitting at the stammtisch looked anxiously at the GIs. One of the men, wearing black trousers and a white dress shirt, got up from the table and approached Novotny, probably because he was the only one not carrying a weapon. The men sitting at the table—dressed in the plain garb of German peasants and with the ruddy complexion that came from hard work outdoors and many nights of beer drinking—watched to see what was going to happen.

"Tell him we want eight bottles of beer, eight rolls, some cheese, and some sausage," the sergeant instructed Novotny. "And be sure he knows we're going to pay for it."

Novotny nodded. "Good evening, sir" he said in his best German to start the conversation.

Obviously anxious, the proprietor asked, "Is there something I can do for you?"

"Yes," Novotny answered, reciting the sergeant's grocery list. "We will, of course, pay you for these things," he made a careful point of adding.

The proprietor looked at the three Germans watching the encounter, then turned and looked at the GIs. All had the grubby look of soldiers that had been in the field for days.

"I am very sorry," the proprietor began, shaking his head. "I cannot sell you these things. It is forbidden by the U.S. Army Military Police."

Novotny relayed the message to Sergeant Morales. Without saying a word, the sergeant slipped his carbine off his shoulder and threw the bolt back with his thumb. With a metallic clank, a round of blank .30-caliber ammunition was rammed into the breech.

He turned and looked at the men lined up along the wall. Almost in unison, they also unslung their weapons, pulled back the bolts, and held the blank-loaded weapons casually in front of them.

"Novotny," the sergeant said, "please tell the owner that we want eight beers, eight rolls, some cheese, and some sausage." He added, "And be sure he knows that we're going to pay him for it."

Looking directly at the owner, Novotny said, "The sergeant says that he would like eight bottles of beer, eight rolls, some cheese, and some sausage. We will, of course, pay for this food," he added.

The proprietor looked at Novotny, then at Sergeant Morales and the rest of the soldiers. Realizing he had no choice, he said, "Ask the sergeant what kind of cheese he would like."

When the newly acquired rations were carefully stowed in Sergeant Morales's jeep, the three vehicles slowly made their way along a dirt road, using only the faint light of the stars to help them see where they were going.

Sergeant Morales was sitting on the hood of his jeep. Its windshield had been folded down onto the hood, and the NCO whispered directions to the driver. The other two vehicles followed closely behind.

It was good, Novotny decided, being out here in an open jeep, heading out on yet another adventure. Real enough to be exciting. But not so real as to be life threatening. Except, he corrected himself, for a guy like the soldier who had been hit by a truck coming around a blind corner.

About fifteen minutes later, the sergeant stopped the small convoy in the middle of the rough and rutty road. Over a midnight supper, he reviewed the plan with his men. The Blue Army was believed to have a concentration of infantry on a hillside, about a kilometer from where they were. The troops were part of a French battalion, and they were supposed to be pretty well dug in.

The patrol's assignment was to confirm where they were and to get an idea of their strength. It was a classic cavalry reconnaissance patrol. Just what the 2d ACR was trained to do.

They drove about halfway to where the troops were supposed to be, then parked the jeeps and walked. Novotny wasn't sure how the sergeant knew where they were going. He had watched the NCO checking the map from time to time. But it seemed as though he was working as much on instinct as anything else. And, unlike Sergeant Rogers, Novotny had a strong sense that the sergeant knew exactly where they were supposed to be.

The patrol came to a small valley and were told to take positions along a ridge facing the dark forest in front of them. Novotny's heart started pounding with excitement, even though he had no weapon and was supposed to be neutral.

"Let's go," the sergeant whispered. Novotny got up, and in a half crouch, for no particular reason, since it was dark, followed the patrol leader and the rest of the men.

A few minutes later the men were again instructed to take positions, this time on a small knoll. Novotny lay on the ground next to the sergeant.

The patrol leader whispered, "My guess is that the main body is over there." He pointed to a ridge that stood out black against the starry sky.

"Right," Novotny said softly.

"You don't have a weapon. But have you got a lighter?"

"Yeah," Novotny replied, feeling around in his fatigue pocket to be sure the Zippo was where it was supposed to be.

"No need for a translator here," the sergeant said. "Go over and give McDermott a hand."

"Right," Novotny answered, not sure what he was supposed to do. He edged toward a figure on the ground a few yards away.

"When Sarge tells us, flick on your lighter," McDermott said softly. "Cover it with your hand on the side so they won't see it."

"Got it," Novotny replied.

"Now," the sergeant said, whispering but loud enough for the patrol to hear. Novotny immediately spun the wheel of the lighter with his thumb and shielded the flame with his hand.

McDermott held the wick of what looked like an OD cherry bomb firecracker into the flame, waited until it sputtered, and then threw it toward the hill. A moment later, it exploded, sending sharp echoes up and down the valley. Others went off, one after another, to their left and right. As soon as McDermott lit one and threw it, he would put another one to the flame and repeat the process.

Smaller explosions in quick succession were intermingled with the sound of the cherry bombs, sounding like small-arms fire.

It took about a minute for the hillside to respond. Then, all of a sudden, there were the sounds of what seemed to be hundreds of weapons firing at them. In the dark, it was easy to tell where the shots came from, tracking the report and flash of each weapon to its source.

"OK, hold it," the sergeant said, listening and making notations on his map illuminated by a small flashlight, but mostly covered by his hand. The firing on the other side of the valley continued, then gradually quieted down. Finally there were just a few random shots, and then it was quiet.

"Let's get outta here," the sergeant said. "These guys know we snookered 'em. They aren't going to like that much."

Novotny closed the cap on his lighter, slid it into his pocket, and followed the patrol as it moved quickly to the jeeps, guarded by the two soldiers the sergeant had left behind.

Cranking up the vehicles, they moved as fast as they could in the dark, heading back in the direction from which they had come. A couple of miles down the road, the sergeant stopped the vehicles and issued a round of beers and food to his men.

"Good job," he said as he made additional notes on his map.

Flipping aside the wire retainer that held the porcelain stopper in place at the top of the bottle, Novotny took a sip of the delicious German beer and watched the sergeant translate what they had learned into intelligence information. That done, he called in a report to S-2 via radio. The information would make its way up the chain of command, and be used by some general—maybe General Ritter—to decide what to do about the French infantry dug into the hillside.

He watched the sergeant and admired the skill with which he practiced his craft. His abilities were just like those of anyone who does his job well. The only difference was that in combat, how well he did his job could either cost or save lives.

The sergeant folded the map and put it in his pocket. "As soldiers, the French are pretty useless," he said to Novotny. "You couldn't pull that off so easy against a good battalion of GI infantry."

No one responded to the comment.

"If the balloon goes up," he continued, "I hope those frogs are up in Belgium or somewhere. Sure as hell don't want them around here."

Novotny remembered what the Frenchman had told him in St. Tropez. Sergeant Morales was exactly the kind of soldier the Resistance fighter had talked about. "That's why you have the best army in the world," the Frenchman had said.

Nodding slightly, Novotny agreed.

The vehicles were lined up as neatly as possible in a meadow surrounded by forests. It was five thirty in the afternoon. Although he was neutral when he went on a translating assignment, the rest of the time Novotny was Pfc in the Red Army. Red as opposed to Blue.

He looked at the assemblage of trucks, jeeps, ambulances, tanks, and armored personnel carriers, and felt like a shepherd guarding his mechanical flock. All the vehicles were covered with dust and mud. No time or reason to keep them clean out here. Once in a while another vehicle would come in and join the pack. And the crews that left them had the same dusty, weary look.

Like them, he was bone tired from too little sleep. And his brain was getting tired of playing war and trying to figure out what it all meant. He thought about being back at Merrell Barracks. Taking a long shower. Sleeping in his own bunk. Eating real meals at the mess hall. They'd been out for only six days, and he wondered how guys had managed to do this for weeks or months in the war, and in Korea.

Across the meadow, the 2d ACR had set up its headquarters in a pine forest. Tents were tucked away under trees, and APCs with tentlike additions to create more working space were positioned seemingly at random in the forest. Pup tents, where the men lived while the unit was here, were everywhere, concealed under trees and shrubs.

The 2d Cav was going to move out tomorrow about oh five hundred and be part of an assault force taking on a major Blue Army position. If infiltrators got to his vehicles and put dummy explosives on them, an umpire would take them out of action, and the Cav wouldn't be able to get where it was supposed to be. And that could affect the outcome of the battle.

In real war, of course, if he screwed up, it would almost certainly mean that guys would be killed, or wounded, or—like Sergeant Rogers, Jerry Orloff, and the air force lieutenant—captured. He was determined to do this right.

The meadow was traversed by a pair of ruts that had been formed by truck tires and tank treads. The vehicles were backed up close to the pine forest, which, like so many forests Novotny had seen, was perfect. Not a branch seemed out of place, something he had been curious about ever since arriving in Germany and seeing them for the first time. Who takes care of them? he wondered.

As he walked between his OD-painted charges and the forest, he thought about what Sergeant Duff had taught them about overpowering a guard. Find a spot where you can get some cover. Like the young pines with branches that were growing pretty close to the ground, he thought as he surveyed the forest. If you're lucky, the guard will have his weapon over his shoulder, instead of at the ready. Even a dying man can squeeze off a round if his rifle is at the ready.

Come up from behind, and put your hand over his mouth, pulling his head back so he can't yell. Then shove your bayonet between his ribs, making sure you get his heart. It's got to be done quietly and quickly, the sergeant had said.

Neither Novotny nor any of his buddies had ever asked, but they had no doubt that he had done it exactly as he had taught them. The description was definitely spoken in the language of a practitioner, not a theoretician.

Sergeant Duff had also taught them how to stay alive as guards. Carry your weapon at the ready at all times, except in wide-open areas. Unhook the strap on your helmet. It's supposed to come undone if someone pulls it back, trying to choke you. But half the time, it doesn't work.

Stop and listen for any kind of sound. A twig breaking. A nervous cough from a guy who isn't particularly excited about having to kill you. The flapping and squawking of frightened birds leaving the security of their trees. The metallic sound of a bayonet being unsheathed. All of them are warnings that someone is out there.

He listened, heard nothing, and walked to the end of the motor park. About a hundred yards away, he saw Turner guarding a supply dump. Holding up his thumb in the style of an RAF pilot, he smiled and nodded at Turner, who waved back.

Some guys looked normal in fatigues, a helmet and combat boots, with a rifle over their shoulder. And some didn't. Turner was one of those. The gear just didn't seem to be right on him. But it wouldn't be too long before Turner could go home, get rid of the uniform, and work in a gas station or do whatever he was going to do next in his life.

Pay attention, he reminded himself. Do your job. For God's sake don't let some Blue Army infiltrator put dummy charges on your vehicles. The 2d Cav has to move out of here early. He pointed his rifle casually toward the forest and did what Sergeant Duff had taught him. He listened. Very carefully, he listened.

Novotny liked the sound of the engine as the driver moved up and down through the gears. Everything seemed perfectly in order. The OD safe was in its place at the front of the truck. His pack, filled with socks and underwear that reeked of old sweat, was neatly stowed under the wooden bench. His carbine was on the bench next to him. Johnson sat quietly opposite him, watching the landscape pass by.

After eight days in the field, the pretend war was over and they were heading back to Merrell. Johnson had checked their last position and estimated that they were about forty miles southeast of Nurnberg—probably a couple of hours away.

Bouncing along in the back of this truck, and with the NATO exercise done, he felt very much like a soldier. More so than he had ever felt before. They had come as close to real combat as he had ever been before, and he now had a pretty good idea what it was all about. Only guys weren't getting killed. Except for the soldier who had been hit by a truck. And, no doubt, others like him.

They passed through a small village, made up of simple stone buildings with orange tile roofs, black with age. The road was narrow and paved with cobblestones laid in careful patterns.

Only a few people were visible, standing in doorways and wearing the colorless clothes of twentieth-century peasants. Novotny smiled and waved at a toothless old woman wearing a black shawl and a long brown skirt. She looked at him coolly, without returning the greeting. This probably reminds her of convoys in '45, he decided. Can't really blame her.

As they passed through the village, he saw the small church that was so common in these postcard-like hamlets. Probably hundreds of years old. One corner of it had been seriously damaged, leaving chunks of ancient masonry scattered on the cobblestone street. A tank cutting it too close, Novotny speculated. Maybe that's why the woman didn't smile back.

He thought about how well organized the maneuver had been. Two very large armies, running around the German countryside fighting each other. There were umpires all over the place, watching units battle it out with blanks and then declaring who was dead, who was alive, and who had won.

He had done the same thing when he was seven or eight years old. The handful of kids in the neighborhood would get together, divide up, and fight each other. Holding pretend rifles or pistols, they would make "t" sounds with their teeth close together. As it turned out, the sound wasn't much like the real thing, but it didn't matter.

He'd make the sound and point his finger at Art Keller. "You're dead."

"I am not," he would protest.

"You are so. I got you when you came around that tree."

"OK," Art would concede. "I'm dead this time. But next time you're gonna be dead."

There wasn't much more to it than that. No one wanted to be the Japs or the Nazis, so it was just "us and them." Much like the Red Army and the Blue Army, politically anonymous. And since there was no definition of who were the good guys and who were the bad, it didn't matter much who won.

That wasn't to say that they were oblivious to the war. It was part of their lives. A fighter pilot came to visit their school and encouraged them to buy War Stamps and save scrap metal. He was handsome in his uniform, and they were impressed by all the medals displayed over his pocket.

Once a month, if you took an old pot or pan to the theater on Saturday morning, you'd get into a movie free. It made them feel good to get in without paying while helping the war effort.

As for Novotny, he would wake up every day and think about his father, away in the navy, and his uncles in the armed forces, scattered around the world in Europe and places like Guam and Tinian, which he had never heard of before.

When his father was drafted, Novotny, his mother, and his little brother had moved to a small town in Michigan to be near his grandparents. His bother was so young that he really didn't understand what the war was all about. For Novotny. the war seemed even closer there than it had been in Chicago. At the local fruit exchange, German prisoners of war, with POW stenciled on their blue work shirts, loaded bushels of locally grown apples and pears.

They looked pretty much like anyone else living there. Most of them were young, smiling, and sweating as they moved produce on and off trucks. It was hard to imagine that these were the same people he saw in the newsreels, helmeted and dressed in Nazi uniforms. The soldiers who killed civilians, even kids like him and his friends.

Just about every family had someone in the service. You could tell how many by the small banner most people displayed in their windows: white with a red border and gold fringe and decorated with stars. His grandparents were very proud of theirs with its three blue stars—one for his father and the other two for his uncles, one in China and the other in France.

Mrs. Draper, a widow on his paper route, had the most stars of anyone he knew. Five. The banner was right next to her front door, and he couldn't miss it each time he threw the paper onto her front porch.

One day he noticed that the banner was missing. When it reappeared, three of the stars were blue, but the two at the top were gold. The next day, as he was folding his papers getting ready for delivery, he saw the story on the front page. Bill, her oldest son, had been killed in the army in Europe. And Ernie, the second youngest, had gone down with his ship in the Pacific.

Even though he hadn't known them, he was sad every time he saw the gold stars as he threw the papers onto the porch. And he was never able to look Mrs. Draper in the eye again when he collected on Saturdays.

He looked out the back of the truck and wondered how much longer it would take to get back to Merrell. Johnson stretched and smiled at his friend. "Almost there."

"I was just thinking that this was pretty realistic," Novotny observed. "The only problem . . ." Novotny paused to gather his thoughts. "It's close at times. But it's still not real."

"What are you getting at, Novo?"

He looked out the back of the truck, figuring out how to answer the question. "When we go out on alerts, and when we do things like this exercise, I still wonder what I would do if it was for real."

"Just forget it. You'd do fine."

"No, I'm serious. I wonder if I could kill a guy," he said. "I wonder if I'd chicken out." He thought for a couple of minutes, and then added, "It's as if we're on a football team. We practice hard. But we never play a real game. We never find out if we can win."

"I know how to deal with this," Johnson said. "We'll have a short war."

"How short?"

"I don't know. Maybe even a few minutes."

"Nah, that won't work," Novotny said, shaking his head. "It has to be long enough to take casualties. Otherwise we might as well just keep doing what we're doing."

"Right," Johnson agreed. "But it can't be long enough for someone to decide to use the atomic stuff."

"How about twenty minutes?" Novotny suggested.

Johnson nodded. "That's just about right. We get set on the border, blast away for twenty minutes, and then just settle down where we began. Long enough to get shot at and prove you're not chicken. And there'll be enough casualties to make the fear real. How's that?"

"A twenty-minute war," Novotny said, nodding. "It's a great idea. We all find out what we're made of. And a bunch of guys can get medals."

Novotny looked at the road behind them.. "And then we just go back to patrolling our side of the border, and they patrol theirs. Until next year, when we do it again."

"I'll suggest it to the commanding general next time I see him,"

Johnson said, laughing.

They had left the dirt road and were on the autobahn now, moving along at about forty miles an hour. Couldn't be much longer. Novotny stretched, closed his eyes, and chuckled to himself. A twenty-minute war. What a great idea.

Novotny walked into the Flying Dutchman bar and looked around the noisy, smoky room. He spotted Helga sitting at a corner table as she declined a GI's offer to dance. *Hans Altman und Seine Kometen*—Hans Altman and His Comets—was now the regular band, blaring out the Top 10 tunes of eighteen months ago. He edged his way through the dancers and headed toward her table. She smiled as he got close and asked in German, "How goes it with you?"

"It goes very well, thank you. And with you?"

"Also good. Will you sit?"

"Thank you," Novotny replied. He liked speaking German with her, partly because it was good practice. But mainly because she had agreed to correct his errors in the language's complex grammar.

"Where is Jazz? And Bob?" she asked, a hint of concern in her voice.

"They will be here soon. They had some work to do at the barracks."

Novotny waved over a waitress and ordered two beers.

"How was the maneuver?" she asked.

"It was good. We learned a lot." He offered her a cigarette, which she declined.

"You know that Jazz has spoken about staying in the army?" she asked.

"Yes. We have talked about it."

"May I ask you something, Novo?" she asked tentatively.

"Of course."

"What would it be like for a German woman to be married to a Negro in America?"

Novotny took a drag from his cigarette.

"It would not be good," she said, answering her own question.

"In some places it would be impossible," he said.

"Yes, I know that."

"In other areas, I believe it would be difficult, but not impossible. But there are places, in the large cities, where it would be possible." He wished his German vocabulary were better so he could have made the point more clearly. But she got the message.

She took a sip from her stein. "Jazz has told me this. I was afraid that he believed I wanted to use him only as a way to get to America."

She took another sip from her stein. "I have little education. My family is poor in a small village. But I want to be with Jazz. I believe he is a good man."

"Yes. He is a good man, Helga."

There were so many things that he wanted to say to her. But they would be only his opinions, and he didn't want them to be the basis of any decisions she made. It wouldn't be easy. No doubt about that. But she seemed very aware of the situation. That was about all he could hope for.

Johnson and Morris were at the door, and she smiled and waved to them. They sat down and more beer was ordered over the noise of the German rock-and-roll band playing "Blue Suede Shoes."

They made a kind of strange foursome, Novotny thought. Two white guys in tweed sport coats, button-down shirts, and loafers, looking as though they were at some fraternity event. A colored high-school dropout from a tough St. Louis neighborhood. And a plain, though pleasant-looking, German girl who had come to the big city from some little village and had a job as a clerk in an office.

As they talked, shouting over the din of the band, two young Americans walked toward the table. It was obvious that they were military. And it was equally obvious that they were drunk. One, tall and lanky, stood in front of Helga.

"Wanna dance?"

She shook her head. "No, thank you," she said in English.

"Come on," he said cockily. "No sense sittin' around with these clowns."

"Yeah, dance with my buddy," the shorter of the two said. "He's a good dancer."

Johnson looked up at the two young men. "She just doesn't want to dance," he said softly but assertively. "That's all."

"I wasn't talkin' to you, yo-yo," the tall American said, his voice slurred. "I was talkin' to her."

Novotny leaned over to Helga and whispered in her ear, "Come with me." He picked up her purse from the table and led her quickly to the front door.

"I don't like this, Novo."

"Do not be worried. It is just better for you to go."

Outside, he opened the door of a cab and closed it behind her as she got into the backseat. Handing the driver a five-mark bill, he poked his head into the cab. "There will be no problem."

As the cab pulled away, she turned and waved at him through the rear window. He rushed inside and pushed his way through the crowd back to the table. The two Americans were still standing there, being ignored by Johnson and Morris, who sat calmly drinking their beer.

"What'd ya do with the kraut whore?" the taller one asked.

Novotny sat down and picked up his stein to take a drink.

"I said, what'd ya do with the kraut whore?" the man demanded, loud enough to be heard at nearby tables even over the sound of the music, and causing people to stare.

Taking a slow sip from his stein and then putting it down on the table, Novotny answered, "Well, first off, she's not a whore. And second, what I did with her isn't any of your business."

The lanky American shook his head. "Know somethin'? You look too smart to have a whore for a girlfriend."

"She ain't his girl," Morris blurted, his fists clenched on the table. "She's mine."

"Oh, God," the antagonist said, shaking his head. "A whore and a nigger lover too." He looked at Novotny. "You did me a favor. I wouldn't touch her now for nothin'."

"Why don't you guys just take off?" Johnson asked.

"You tellin' us to leave?" the shorter one asked arrogantly.

"The girl's gone. So why don't you guys just take off?" Johnson's voice was controlled, but loud enough to be heard.

The tall American rolled up his sleeve. On his right forearm, the emblem of the airborne forces had been tattooed. "You know what that means?" he asked Johnson.

"It's a tattoo. So what?"

"It means we're airborne, and you're not gonna tell us to go anywhere. What kind of candy-ass unit you with?"

Morris glared at the figure standing over him. "We're in the 2d Cav." His voice was hard-edged with anger. "We wouldn't even use airborne to clean our latrines."

"You got a big mouth, nigger," he said, slapping Morris across the cheek.

Morris pushed aside the chair where Helga had been sitting, stood quickly, and rammed his fist into the paratrooper's gut, forcing him to take a couple of steps back to regain his balance. But Morris's blow hadn't done any particular harm, and the drunken soldier gave Morris a sharp punch to the face.

Morris staggered and ended up with his back on the table, his feet still planted firmly on the floor. Johnson and Novotny started to stand up to prevent any further punches from being thrown. But as they got up, Morris looked to his right and saw Johnson's half-empty beer stein just a couple of inches from his hand.

Wrapping his fingers around the handle, he quickly straightened up his body. His arm swung in a smooth arc as his back left the table. The paratrooper had his fists in place, ready to hit Morris again. Seeing the circle formed by Morris's swiftly moving arm, he tried to get his hands up over his head. But he was too late. The movement of Morris's arm stopped abruptly as the stein crashed onto the paratrooper's forehead.

He crumpled to the floor, surrounded by shards of the beer mug. His head was wet with beer, and he sat, staring off into space, unaware of the blood running down his forehead, his cheeks, and his nose.

Morris stood in a semi-crouch facing the smaller paratrooper, holding the handle and the jagged remainder of the stein. The blood coming from his lip and nose was difficult to see against his dark-brown skin. But where it dripped onto his light-blue shirt, it made a reddish-purple pattern of dots and streaks.

"Drop it, Morris," Novotny said. "Let's get out of here."

Johnson had already started making an opening in the crowd of servicemen and Germans who had gathered around the table. "Excuse us, please," he said in German, without a trace of urgency in his voice. "We have to take this man to the hospital."

Novotny pushed Morris between himself and Johnson, and the three made their way to the front door.

"Where's Helga?" Morris asked.

"I sent her home in a cab. She's OK."

They heard a siren from a few blocks away and walked briskly across the street. A short block away, they stepped inside a darkened doorway. They could tell the sirened vehicles were stopping at the Flying Dutchmen. Careful to stay in shadows, they kept moving for another three or four blocks until they were in a residential neighborhood.

Novotny stopped Morris under a streetlight. "Let's see what he did to you."

Wiping the blood away with his handkerchief, he took Morris's lower lip in his fingers and folded it back.

"Easy, Novo. That hurts," Morris complained.

"Take a look, Bob," he asked his friend. "I'm not a doctor, but it doesn't look too bad."

"Cut lip and a bloody nose," Johnson said. "Take the medics only a couple of minutes to patch you up when we get back to Merrell."

Novotny patted Morris on the shoulder. "You're quite a street fighter, Chas."

"He just made me mad. That's all."

The three men started walking back to the commercial neighborhood where they could catch a cab.

"But the way you handled yourself, it looked as though you must've had at least a little practice," Johnson said.

"Just training here in the Cav," Morris said, shaking his head. "Before that, I never hit nobody. Never."

Novotny neatly folded the *Herald-Tribune* and gently placed it in the wastebasket next to his chair. He stood and stretched, enjoying the awareness of his body. That done, he settled back into the brown vinyl chair and lit a cigarette. A great Saturday afternoon ritual, he thought.

Suddenly, the door to the Service Club burst open and Morris came rushing toward him.

"I was hopin' I'd find you here, Novo," he said breathlessly.

"What's wrong?" he asked, putting out the cigarette.

"It's Johnson."

He felt his body tense. "What happened? Is he OK?"

"I don' know," Morris replied, shaking his head. "He's at the EM Club." Wiping his wet brow with the back of his hand, he explained, "I asked him what was wrong. But he wouldn't tell me anything."

"Thanks, Chas," Novotny said, already on his way out the door. It took only about five minutes for him to jog to the EM Club. Racing up the stairs, two at a time, he looked around the virtually empty club. Johnson was sitting at a table with his back to the wall. When they'd had breakfast that morning, he'd seemed fine. There hadn't been a trace of anything being wrong.

Johnson looked up as Novotny approached the table. "Hello, Novo." He spoke slowly and didn't seem surprised at his arrival.

"Thought I'd come over and have a beer," Novotny said, sitting down and lighting a cigarette, wanting to be careful what he said until he understood what was going on.

Johnson smiled and shook his head. "That's bull, Novo."

"You're right," he replied, nodding. "Morris told me you were here. What's happening?"

Johnson took a sip from his glass. "Well, I'm glad you came. Because it has to do with you." He drained his glass and waved the waitress over to the table. "Ballantine on the rocks, please," he said, his speech noticeably slurred. "And a beer for my friend.

"Well, Novo, you're probably wondering why I'm sitting here getting shit-faced. Right?"

Johnson's mouth was turned up in the silly kind of grin that alcohol seems to produce. But his eyes were alarmingly sad.

"What happened? Want to talk about it?"

"Sure," Johnson said, taking a sip from the fresh glass the waitress had just set on the table. "You ought to know. If it weren't for you, it wouldn't have happened." He slurred, "But I'm not mad at you. Don't want you to misunderstand."

Novotny took a sip of his beer. What in the world was going on? He wished Johnson would get to the point.

"It's about Anna," Johnson said, sadly shaking his head, the drunken smile gone.

"Is she OK?"

"I guess so." He took another sip of scotch. "A guy from the Counter Intelligence Corps came to S-2 this morning to see me."

"About Anna?" he asked, obviously surprised.

"Yeah," Johnson said, laughing. "She's a damn spy."

"Come on," Novotny said, assuming it was some kind of joke.

"I'm serious, Novo. She's a spy." He shook his head and then took another sip from the glass. "Can you believe that? Spying for the damn Russians. And you know what the CIC wants me to do?"

"What?" he asked.

"Want me to keep going out with her. Feed her false information, and tell them what she's doing."

"Are you going to do it?"

"Hell, no," he said, shaking his head. "I love her. At least this morning I did." He shook his head again. "Even if I wanted to, I couldn't pull it off. I'm no actor." He drained his glass and held it up for the waitress to see.

"Did you tell her anything?" Novotny asked.

Johnson scratched his head. "I've been tryin' to remember that all morning. I don't think so. Nothing classified." His speech was now so slurred that Novotny was having trouble understanding him. "But I thought about something you said."

"What's that?"

"You told me how much she worried about you, when you were going with her. About how she talked about cannon fodder. Remember?"

"Yeah."

"That was just part of her game. She said the same kind of stuff to me. Just to keep us worried."

The waitress brought another scotch and a glass of beer for Novo.

"How do you know it's true?"

"The guy from CIC showed me some of the reports she filed. Don't know how they get that stuff. But I knew it was real when I saw your name."

"My name?"

"Want to hear something funny?" Johnson didn't wait for an answer. "She dumped you because I was more useful. Guys in S-2 make better sources than a translator, for God's sake." Johnson laughed out loud. "That's what the CIC guy told me. But no offense, Novo."

Novotny shook his head. "No offense. What are you going to do now?"

Johnson swirled the ice around in his glass of scotch. "First thing I'm going to do is get bombed. Which," he added, "I may already have done."

"Right," Novotny agreed.

"Then I'm going to the room and sleep it off. So be a little quiet. OK?"

"Don't worry."

"Then tomorrow, I'll hang 'round the barracks wallowing in self-pity because I feel so rotten."

"Right."

"And on Monday, I'll still have a headache, and my stomach will still be a little jittery."

"And?"

"Tuesday, I'll feel fine. And she'll be out of my mind."

Novotny took a drink of beer and stroked his chin. "Obviously it's the classic American cleansing ritual that's been practiced by everyone except the Puritans." He nodded. "Unwanted spirits and thoughts are purged from the body through the use of alcohol."

Johnson laughed. "You're funny, Novo. Yeah, it's a tribal ritual."

Novotny took a sip of his beer and said, "On Tuesday, when your headache is gone, you can start looking for a replacement."

Johnson shook his head. "I just can't believe it. She's a damn spy."

Anna was never seen or heard from again. Not at Amerika Haus. Not at Merrell. Not at regimental events. Not even at the Czech restaurant. She simply disappeared.

She was so memorable that once in a while, someone in the unit would ask Johnson or Novotny, "Do you ever talk to Anna? Or see her?"

"No," would be the reply. "I'm not sure where she is."

"Where are we going?" she asked.

"To one of my favorite places in Nurnberg," he said, smiling. "And if we're lucky, you'll meet one of the nicest guys in the city. The German vet I told you about."

They walked a few blocks until they were directly under the old Nurnberg castle, and there on a narrow side street was the small wine bar called Fidelio.

It was only a little after four, and the charming, comfortable place was empty. As they entered, the proprietor appeared from a back room and said, "Good day, Joseph. How goes it with you?"

"It goes well, thank you. And with you?"

The proprietor shrugged and said, "Not so good."

"Judy, this is Gerd, the owner of Fidelio, the finest wine bar in Nurnberg."

"Hello," she said.

"I am happy you have come to this place. I hope you will enjoy it," Gerd said in heavily accented English.

"I know I will," she said.

"Come, Joseph," he said, pointing to the Stammtisch. "Sit, please." He gestured at a seat for Judy, which she courteously accepted.

"Can you sit with us for a few minutes, Gerd?"

"Only for a moment," he said. Sitting next to Novotny, he said in German, "Joseph, I have bad news for you."

Novotny waited for what was to come but had a pretty good idea of what it would be.

"Last week, Dieter died."

Novotny took a deep breath, and Judy watched his face, wondering what was wrong.

"His body had been bad since the war. He knew he would not live long."

Swallowing hard, Novotny said, "I am very sad to hear this news. He was a good man." Realizing that Judy had been left out of the conversation, he said, "The soldier . . . the veteran I told you about . . . Dieter . . . died last week."

"I'm so sorry, Novo," Judy said, putting her arm on his shoulder.

"He liked Joseph very much," the proprietor said.

Novotny stared ahead without speaking.

"Joseph?" Gerd said.

"Yes."

"Dieter left a gift for you, when he knew he was not going to last long."

"I do not understand."

"One moment, please."

The proprietor left the table and hurried to the back room, returning moments later with a tall green bottle of wine on a silver tray with three glasses and a corkscrew.

Novotny tried hard, but couldn't stop the tears from forming at the corners of his eyes.

"This wine comes from the town of Bauendorf in the Mosel district," he explained to Judy. "The vineyard is next to a church, so they call it Bauendorfer Kirchen, the church wine of Bauendorf."

He picked up the bottle. "It was Dieter and Gerd's favorite wine. They went to the town in 1940, on kind of a quick vacation just before they went into the army. Dieter left this here for me . . . for us."

He looked at the bottle. "What was the name of the hotel where you stayed? Where you first had this wine?"

"It was . . ." Gerd paused for a moment. "I always have to think about it." He pursed his lips, and then remembered, "It was the Hotel Golden Eagle. In Bauendorf."

"Gerd, what was the . . ." Novotny paused, trying to come up with the right word. "What was the greeting that Dieter made when we drank this wine together for the first time?"

"He said, to the comradeship of ordinary soldiers, in whatever army they serve."

All three touched glasses and took a sip of the luscious wine. Now tears streamed down Gerd's cheeks.

"Thank you, Joseph. I must now go," he said, drying his eyes. "We will soon have guests."

Novotny nodded as the proprietor walked to the back of the wine bar and organized rows of sparkling glasses.

"That was really nice of your friend to do," Judy said, lifting her wineglass and taking a sip. "I think this is the most delicious wine I've ever had."

As they sipped on the wine, Gerd brought them a plate of cheese, pâté, and bread. "Do you like jazz?" Novotny asked out of the blue.

"What do you have in mind?"

He looked at her mischievously. "Trust me."

They took their time finishing the bottle of wine, relishing each sip. When the last drops were gone, Gerd took away the empty bottle and the glasses, and then returned to the table.

"I hope you will visit here again," he said to Judy in accented English.

"I will come back," she answered.

"Thank you, Gerd," Novotny said, shaking his hand.

It was a special moment. On many counts. A special, unforgettable moment, he thought as they left the comfortable wine bar and went out onto the street. He was glad Judy had been there to be part of it.

It was dusk and the streets were getting dark. Judy put her hands in the pockets of her jacket, and, crossing a street, he put his hand in the crook of her elbow. Harmless enough, he thought. Less symbolic than taking her hand. But contact nonetheless.

"Novo, are you really sure you know where we're going?" she said. It was true that the neighborhood hardly seemed like the kind of area to listen to music.

"Lieutenant," he replied, speaking in the affected manner of an actor in a bad movie, "you're looking at a highly trained member of the 2d Armored Cavalry. Knowing where we are is as natural to us as breathing."

The neighborhood took on an increasingly eerie character as they passed the shells of bombed-out apartment buildings, surreal in the darkness. A bare lightbulb marked a stone archway in one of the dark ruins.

Painted over the arch, in faded white, were the letters LSR. Seeing her noticing them, he explained, "It stands for 'air raid shelter.'"

They stopped and looked down a long, dimly lit stairway.

"Are we going down there?" she asked, a tinge of anxiety in her voice.

He didn't answer. Instead he held her arm tighter and began walking down the stairs. About the equivalent of a flight and a half, the stairs turned left, then left again. Judy realized this was a sort of test and decided not to say anything. The stone was a dirty brown, and there was a musty odor, smelling the way you would expect a medieval dungeon to smell. She matched him step for step, the sound of their shoes echoing in the semi-darkness. Halfway down the flight, she took her hand out of her pocket and intertwined her fingers with his.

The stairway ended at a heavy wooden door. "You still game?" he asked.

"Sure," she replied, somewhat less than confidently.

He knocked on the door, and a small peephole was opened.

"Yes," a voice said in German. "Who is there?"

"Novo," he responded. "Let us in, Sheriff."

"One moment, please," the voice behind the peephole said.

There was the sound of a metal lock being undone, and then the heavy door opened slowly. The room looked like a catacomb, with vaulted ceilings breaking the space up into smaller areas. It was dimly lit, with tables scattered at random in the cubicles. Young German couples occupied most of the tables. A few of the young men were obviously American, and probably soldiers.

Novo shook hands with the keeper of the gate. "This is Judy."

"Welcome to the Cave," the man said in English. She nodded and smiled in reply.

Looking at the vacant tables, they took one not far from the battered piano on a small, slightly elevated stage.

Once they were settled in their chairs and had ordered beers, she asked, "Do you come here often?"

"Whenever I can." He pointed to the curved ceilings. "We're about three stories below the street. Pretty good shelter from what was going on there," he noted, gesturing upward.

He was about to say something else when a lanky Negro with a trimmed beard walked to the table and put his arm around Novotny's shoulder.

"What's happening, Novo?" he asked, taking a seat next to Novotny.

"Hey, James. I had to bring my friend down here so she could see what was going on. This is Judy."

He nodded, saying, "Glad to meet you."

"James is without question the finest jazz piano player in Nurnberg," Novotny said, grinning. "Maybe in all of Germany, and possibly all of Europe."

"You're just saying that because you want me to play something," James said, chuckling. "What do you want to hear, Novo?"

"'Small Hotel.'"

"Got it. See you cats later."

The group consisted of James on piano, plus a bass, drums, and two saxophones, a tenor and an alto. James was the only colored member of the group, the only American, and, it was soon apparent, far and away the best musician.

The setting and the music fascinated Judy. Standards that she enjoyed. Having her intent on what was happening in front of them gave Novotny a chance to carefully check her out without being too obvious about it.

She was intelligent, no doubt about that. And pretty. And game. After all, she had come down here with him. He liked being with her. But he wasn't sure where this was going to go.

The one thing that was sure about it was that this was all real. He had thought the same thing about Anna, and that had proved to be something quite different from what he had believed it to be. But there was no doubt about this.

James said something to the drummer, casually pointed at Judy and Novo, and began playing the gentle rhythms of "Small Hotel." When they finished the tune, Novotny led the applause, which was enthusiastic and obviously pleasing to the musicians. The sound of the clapping gradually died, and the musicians set aside their instruments, getting ready for the next break.

Judy picked up her purse, and as she got up, Novotny stood with her.

"I'll be right back," she said.

James came to the table, and as he sat down, Novotny motioned to a waitress and signaled for three glasses of beer.

"I like your friend, Novo. What's she doin' over here?"

"You won't believe this," he said, shaking his head. "She's a WAC lieutenant."

"No shit?" he said, lifting the stein that had just been placed in front of him and taking a drink. "You gonna make it with her?"

Novotny drank from his stein and just grinned.

"That'd be wild. A private and . . ."

Novotny interrupted. "I'm a Pfc."

"That's wild." He looked at Novotny. "Well? You planning on doing it?"

Novotny shrugged. "We'll see."

"That's the trouble with you smart white guys, Novo. You do it all with your head." He ruffled Novotny's hair. "Thanks for the beer. Now I got to play some more." He walked toward the piano, and then turned and said, "I like your friend, Novo."

At about eleven o'clock, Novotny pointed to his watch. Judy nodded. Damn curfew, he thought. A GI raped and killed a German girl a couple of years ago, and they treat us all as if we're delinquents, he thought.

Shaking hands with the Sheriff, he and Judy said goodbye as the heavy wooden door was opened.

Walking up the dank stone steps, he wondered what it had been like to be down there, hearing the sounds of hundreds of bombers, then the crashing explosions of bombs. They had sat down there in the dark, hoping the building wouldn't collapse as apartments and shops were destroyed above them. Listening to the sounds of destruction then.

Now you heard the gentle sounds of jazz.

Back up on the street, they walked back toward the center of the city where Judy's car was parked. Fifty feet or so from her blue Opel, Novotny stepped into a dark doorway and gently pulled her with him.

Taking her face in his hands, and sensing no resistance, he gently kissed her. She put her arms around his waist. Four or five kisses later, they were holding each other tightly.

He again took her face in his hands. "I've got to get going."

"I know," she said, giving him a kiss on the cheek. "This reminds me of living in a dorm at college, worried about being locked out and standing by the front door until the very last minute."

"You know what happens if I miss curfew?"

"You get court-martialed or something," she replied.

"No, I turn into an M-48 tank," he said, chuckling.

He gave her one more, very gentle kiss and then opened the door to her car.

"Good night, Judy," he said as she got in.

"I liked Fidelio. And I liked the Cave," she said, smiling. Then her face became serious. "And I'm really sorry that your friend died."

"So am I," he replied, closing the door and waving as he walked to the corner where a taxi was parked, waiting for a fare.

One of the reasons he liked Grace Kelly was because she had so much class, he decided as he watched the young actress walk across the screen toward Jimmy Stewart. The movie was *Rear Window*, and Stewart played a photographer with a broken leg, who happens to see a crime committed. A really good movie, he thought.

Grace Kelly was perfect in everything she did. Unaffected. Just right. He smiled as he thought about Cindy Hanson, a friend at Northwestern, talking about the actress soon after she had become well known. "I think she's great," Cindy had said, "because she's given people like me—women with small boobs—respectability."

Cindy was right. Grace Kelly had an elegant appeal that, unlike Dagmar, Jayne Mansfield, Sophia Loren, and a long list of others, had nothing to do with her bra size.

Actually there were a fair number of similarities between Grace Kelly and Judy. He imagined that the actress probably dressed like Judy when she wasn't on a movie set. Classic tweeds, sweaters, and blazers. There were also physical resemblances. For example, their lips. Finely formed, not lush and wildly sensuous.

They had the same kind of smile. And they had the same way of speaking. Softly, without forcing their thoughts on anyone. Funny, he thought, the same things applied to Anna. Well, at least there's some consistency.

The screen went black and the lights came up. Novotny stood, stretching. Even though he'd missed part of the plot by letting his mind wander, he had enjoyed it, even if it had been around for a while. Ninety minutes of Grace

Kelly for thirty-five cents. Not a bad deal.

It was nearly nine o'clock, which meant that Johnson would be off his shift in a few minutes. Maybe he'd be interested in a beer before they hit the sack. He sat in the dark on the steps of the headquarters building, smoking and conjuring up images of Grace Kelly. The door behind him opened and Johnson came out, surprised to see his roommate.

"I just fell in love with Grace Kelly again," Novotny said, expecting a wise response from Johnson. Instead, Johnson's voice was somber.

"Hey, Novo,"

"What's wrong?"

"Trouble on the border," he said glumly.

"Want a beer?"

"Sure," Johnson replied. "I could use one."

"What's going on?" Novotny asked as they walked toward the EM Club. He knew it was serious. Johnson was hardly an alarmist.

A couple of hours ago, a patrol called in, reporting five T-54s on the border, Johnson explained. The Russians and NATO had agreed not to put armor or artillery on the border, allowing only patrols to be on the line. The T-54 was a Russian tank generally comparable to the M-48. It was hard to get any straight answers, but some guys thought the T-54 was a better tank. One thing was certain: they had a lot more of their tanks than we had of ours.

And they carried external fuel tanks on the rear deck. It was a simple idea. They used the external tanks to get to battle, and then they dumped them and used their internal, armored tanks, which were full. The M-48s had only internal tanks, which cut their operating time. A tank without fuel is a sitting duck. An "iron coffin" as the infantry liked to call them.

"That was just the first report," Johnson added ominously. "That last count we had, there were eighty T-54s on the border."

"What do you think it means?"

"I don't know. But it's serious, that's for sure." They'd walked as far as their barracks, and he added, "Think I'll skip the beer."

"Yeah," Novotny agreed.

Novotny slept fitfully, partly out of anxiety and partly because of the sound of engines as tanks, trucks, jeeps, and APCs were being positioned to move out.

The recorded sounds of reveille blasted through the barracks, and Novotny begrudgingly opened his eyes from the first real sleep he'd had all night. Suddenly remembering what had happed, he jumped out of his bunk. Johnson was already up and quickly putting on his fatigues.

Dressing hurriedly, they walked briskly toward the parade ground for morning formation, this morning led by the CO instead of the first sergeant, who usually handled it.

The men formed into ranks and stood at ease.

"I'll tell you everything I know, men," the CO said. "T-54s have taken positions on the border. Our patrols are continuing to monitor the situation carefully." He paused to gather his thoughts.

"A complaint has been filed with the Russians, telling them to pull back. We don't know what they've got in mind." He paused again. "All passes and leaves have been canceled until further notice." He paused and looked at the company spread out in front of him. "In the meantime, go about your regular duties. We'll let you know if we hear anything more."

In the mess hall, groups of young soldiers carried on quiet, tense conversations. Some dove into their breakfast, whereas others picked at the contents of the stainless-steel trays. They talked about the Russian tanks. And about how their own would likely fare against the Russian armor.

Some, including Johnson and Novotny, talked about the "brinkmanship" policy of Secretary of State John Foster Dulles, and of Khruschev's declaration that the Russians would "bury" the West. There was obvious concern and anxiety. But everyone seemed ready for a fight, if it was about to happen.

It struck Novotny as more like a football team getting ready for a big game than a force of young men who, if things got out of hand, could find themselves as players in the beginning of another world war.

After breakfast, Johnson and Novotny went back to their room without saying much. There was little left to say about the situation. And everything else seemed less important at the moment. Novotny fished around in the bottom of his laundry bag and pulled out a small contraband bottle of Asbach-Uralt brandy. Neatly wrapping the small bottle in a pair of fatigue trousers, he carefully tucked it into his field pack.

As instructed, everyone went to their normal duty assignment, but in most areas little real work was being done. It was difficult to concentrate on anything other than the wish that whatever was going to happen, would.

At the motor pool, it was quite another story. Turner and the others who worked there hastily checked every vehicle, making certain they were ready to roll. In the motor office, Warrant Officer Burns signed form after form and gave instructions to his men.

The supply room was equally busy as the men inspected shelter halves, rations, tools, and large squad tents. Medics in the infirmary also checked their supplies of bandages, pain-killing injections, disinfectant, drugs, splints, and, unobtrusive in their ordinary-looking boxes, body bags.

In the basement of the old SS barracks, Sergeant Vincent and his armorers were stacking metal boxes of .30- and .50-caliber ammunition near the entrance, so they could be loaded quickly into the trucks. And, for the first time since they had arrived in Germany, wooden crates of hand grenades were moved to the front of the arms room and distributed among several vehicles.

Novotny was given a series of messages to translate that had come in from the German Border Police. Nothing special. Just routine operational reports that didn't shed much light on what was happening. The things he had wanted to know about would go directly to S-2, where Johnson would no doubt see them. But the phones were shut down to all but essential calls. So he would just have to wait and catch up with Johnson later.

It was just after eleven o'clock when the normal buzz of work came to an abrupt and jarring halt as the intense sound of the alarm echoed loudly through the post. Novotny pulled a half-finished translation from his typewriter, laid it neatly on his desk, and bolted for the door. Grabbing his carbine and field pack he ran to the deuce-and-a-half that was his assigned ride.

Men were jogging everywhere. Not in a panic, but in an orderly and well-rehearsed rush. It seemed just like a normal alert, except everyone was a little more serious and moving a little faster than usual.

Just twenty minutes later, Novotny was sitting in the back of the truck, wondering if Johnson was going to make it. Hearing the sound of boot steps hurrying toward the vehicle, he slid close to the tailgate just in time to see Johnson running toward him. Novotny took Johnson's rifle and field pack and laid them on the seat opposite him as Johnson climbed over the tailgate.

"Thanks, Novo."

"Wouldn't want you to miss the ride."

"You're all heart."

Johnson had barely gotten into the truck when it began to move. MPs blocked the traffic on Allersbergerstrasse as the long convoy pulled out and headed east.

"What's the scoop, Bob?"

"It's pretty simple. The Russians have about eighty tanks on the border. We've given them until the end of the day to pull back. If they don't, we've said we'll take, quote, appropriate countermeasures, unquote."

Novotny took a deep breath, and as the convoy pulled out onto Allersbergerstrasse, he saw a line of dependents—as wives and children were called—gathered by the Merrell gate, waving as the long line of vehicles slowly passed by.

"Look at that," Novotny said to Johnson. "They're waving goodbye to their husbands who may not come back, if the balloon is about to go up."

"They're amazing," Johnson said, shaking his head. "Their cars are never less than half full of gas. And their trunks are always stocked with water, clothes, and blankets." He waved at a cluster of dependents. "If this is it, they'll be ordered to head west to who knows where while their husbands are in a convoy on the autobahn going east to the Czech border to fight the Russians."

Novotny shook his head. "Those are truly brave women."

The convoy droned on, skipping the usual ten-minute breaks every hour. Just over two hours out, they left the paved road, pulled into a wooded area, and stopped. Radio operators hastily rigged antennas and began sending and receiving a steady stream of messages.

Tents were being set up and vehicles positioned. Positions were established, armed with machine guns and mortars. And a few guys were assigned to dig the long slit trenches out of sight in the trees to serve as a latrine while they were here.

Someone shouted that there was food at the mess truck, and with tents up and equipment functioning, there was nothing to do for the time being, Novotny and Johnson walked over and were handed a cardboard box of C-rations. Finding a couple of comfortable-looking trees, they took off their helmets, carefully laid their weapons on the ground, and ate the cold meat patties in gravy and crackers that made up the meal's main course.

Washing his meal down with a swallow of water from his canteen, Novotny looked at his watch. "I wonder if anything has happened in the Kremlin."

Johnson shook his head. "I doubt it. But it seems to me that Khruschev is just playing games. What point is there in starting a war?"

"That's why we're here. To make him think twice." Novotny unwrapped the small chocolate bar that had been included in his ration pack, saving the powdered lemon drink for later. "You know it's really strange."

"What's strange?"

"On one hand it's so real. And it seems so possible. We're here, ready to go, waiting to make contact, hold the line as long as we can, and then fall back while NATO gets a counterattack organized."

"And everyone knows that that would mean," Johnson interjected cynically. "I mean in terms of casualties."

"Sure," Novotny added. "Someone at Seventh Army has it all figured out. How many men we'd lose. And how many the 11th Cav and the 14th Cav would lose."

"It's all in the plan."

"But at the same time, it doesn't make any sense at all. Two land armies chewing each other up. Then we start trading atomic warheads. And that's it.

How can anyone win? It's dumb."

They sat around for more than an hour, ready to do whatever they would be called on to do.

They saw Sergeant McLaren from S-3 walking toward them. Before they could say anything, he ordered, "Police up the area, then mount up, men. We're heading out."

He said it so calmly that it could mean only one thing. But Novotny had to hear it to be sure.

"Which way, Sarge?"

"Back to Merrell."

Vehicles were positioned, and the convoy slowly rolled west. Novotny began rummaging around in his field pack.

"Lose something, Novo?"

"Here it is." He pulled the small flask of brandy from his pack, twisted the metal top off, and took a swallow. "Here," he said, offering the flask to his friend.

Johnson held up the flask and said, "To the Russians and NATO who were both smart enough to avoid being blown off the planet today."

"Hear, hear," Novotny said, holding his canteen in the air.

For the next hour, they talked about trivia, or so it seemed, compared with their conversations of earlier in the day. Interspersed with their dialog were sips from the small brandy flask.

They talked about the leave they wanted to take to Berlin. And what a jerk Sergeant Rogers was.

Johnson looked at the small amount of liquid left.

"Here. That's yours," he said to Novotny. "It's an ancient custom. The guy who brings the flask gets to take the last of it."

Tipping the flask, Novotny relished the last few drops of brandy.

"So, what's going to happen with you and the lieutenant?" Johnson asked, feeling relaxed.

"Hard to say," Novotny replied, not really sure how to answer the question.

"Come on. It's serious. Written all over your face." Johnson smiled. "You're smart not to play poker. No secrets from you. Just have to look at you."

Novotny said nothing, just smiled.

"OK, I'll let that one go. Here's another question for you." He looked intently at Novotny's face. "Are you glad we're goin' back? Or do you, deep down, wish just a little that we were heading east?"

Novotny thought for a minute. "If we were about to have our twenty-minute war, I'd want to go east," he answered, thinking about how he had replied to the question. "I still want that test. I still want to know what I would do."

He took a deep breath. "But since twenty-minute wars don't happen, I'm glad we're going back to Merrell."

Johnson nodded in agreement. "I'd say that's pretty much the way I feel."

Having resolved this very important question, at least for the moment, they sat looking out the back of the truck, feeling very warm and mellow. An hour or so later, the truck slowed and turned into the vehicle gate at Merrell Barracks. A group of dependents watched and waved as the convoy entered the fenced-in motor operations area.

Novotny saw a boy, probably five years old, holding on to the chain-link fence with both hands, looking for someone, probably his dad. How do you tell a five-year-old what this is all about? And what do you tell that five-year-old if the convoy keeps rolling east, and his father comes back in a rubberized plastic bag?

TDY. Temporary Duty. Almost always, it was a windfall. A day, a week, or longer assigned somewhere other than your regular duty station. If you were an athlete, it might be three months of football on the regimental team; instead of being a scout, a rifleman or radio operator. "Win, lose, or tie, it's all TDY," the jocks would say, grinning at their good luck.

For Novotny, TDY had been a week near Munich on a field training exercise with the Bundeswehr, the German Army. His German improved by having to rely on it every day. Plus, he had a jeep, which gave him an unusual amount of freedom while on duty.

The exercise done, all he had to do was fill up with gas and head back to Nurnberg, about a hundred miles to the north. Easing onto the Munich-Nurnberg autobahn, he settled into an easy 50 mph pace, carefully noting the BMWs and Mercedes passing him at twice that speed.

He had driven about half an hour on the superhighway when an exit sign startled him out of the relaxed state that had been generated by the easy drive and pastoral Bavarian scenery. Blue with white letters, it was like hundreds of others that he had seen before. It said, simply, "Dachau 4 km."

How many Dachaus could there be in Germany? he wondered. With a strange sense of foreboding, he slowed the jeep and left the autobahn. Minutes later, he was in the center of town. It was like all the rest of the towns and smaller cities in Bavaria. Much of it consisted of old buildings with red-tile roofs.

Others were in the new, boxy, practical style of post–World War II architecture. Either replacements for ones we bombed, he thought, or symbols of West Germany's new prosperity. But one thing was certain, Dachau hadn't been hit as hard as Nurnberg or Stuttgart or many of the other places he had seen.

Two women were walking along an uncrowded street. Novotny pulled over and leaned across the empty seat next to him. "Pardon me," he said in German. "I wish some information."

The women, both stout and rosy cheeked, smiled, apparently pleased that an American GI would speak to them in their language. "How can we help you?" one asked pleasantly.

"Where is the place of the concentration camp?"

The women's smiles were gone in an instant. The second woman pointed down the street. "In that direction." That said, they both turned abruptly and walked away.

"Thank you," Novotny said courteously as they left. There's no doubt that this is the place, he thought, heading in the direction the woman had pointed. About ten blocks down the street, he saw a small sign. It said, in German, "Concentration Camp, Historical Site and Memorial."

An arrow pointed to the right, and Novotny made the turn. A few blocks away another sign pointed to a large, gravel, nearly empty parking lot. He pulled into a spot and turned off the engine.

He couldn't place the time exactly, but it must have been 1944 or early 1945 when he had first seen the pictures. Bodies strewn around like cast-off trash. The figures didn't appear to be real people, their bones clearly defined under layers of skin.

But the thing that had haunted him most—that had been the source of so many nightmares—was the eyes of these dying and dead human debris. There were nights, he recalled more clearly than he wanted to, when the images were so vivid in his mind's eye that he actually prayed that he would go to sleep to make them go away.

And now he was here. At one of the places where this had happened. Where the pictures were taken. Why am I doing this? he asked himself. Without an answer, he climbed out of his jeep and began walking down a gravel, tree-lined path. It is quite likely, he thought, that GIs very much like him had walked down this path not all that many years ago, weapons at the ready, wondering what was ahead of them.

The trees opened into a large barren compound, wide and long. There were a few wooden buildings still standing. But mostly the area was made up of building foundations, separated by wooden curbs and narrow gravel roads. Row after row of them. Too many barracks to count.

He pictured what the buildings had looked like in the photos. Inside, rows of wooden racks served as beds, but they looked more like shelves. Wooden shelves holding an inventory of discarded human beings, waiting to die or be killed.

Walking down a gravel path, he headed toward a guard tower. Looks like it was designed by the same guy who did the ones on the Czech side of the border, he thought. Ugly and efficient. He touched the rusting metal bracing of the tower. It was the first tactile evidence that this was real, not just a well-designed museum diorama.

To the left of the guard tower was a long barbed-wire fence. White ceramic insulators at each post indicated that it had been electrified, which involuntarily conjured up another image from the archive of his brain.

He saw a gaunt-faced man with his hands on the wire, dressed in the baggy, striped uniform of these places. The unshaven face in the image was looking over his shoulder, his deep-set eyes open, even though he was dead. The odds of getting out over the fence were probably zero, but the man apparently had tried it anyway. Maybe it was intentional. Maybe he figured that being killed by a charge of electricity or an SS guard's bullet was better than dying minute by minute for however long it would take. Whatever his plan, the sunken eyes seemed to say, I've finally gotten out of this hell.

Novotny blinked and the wires were bare again. He walked around the perimeter of the camp and turned down a path that led to a quiet grove of trees. The idea of greenery seemed contradictory after seeing the gray gravel and row after row of concrete foundations. Looking around he saw that there were only two other people in the entire place, walking slowly on the other side of the barren camp site. How strange to have so few human beings in this place where thousands had once suffered and died.

At the end of the path, surrounded by trees, was an ordinary-looking brick building, as big as a good-sized house. The door at the front was open, and he walked into a large room. Everything within sight was one of three colors. Dusty brick red. The nondescript brown of rusting steel. And concrete gray.

Along one wall was a row of metal doors, set in arched brick structures. He physically tensed as he realized what he was looking at. The ovens. The places where the remains of what had been living people were converted into a more readily disposed-of form of matter, ash.

He stared at the rusting ovens and the bleakness of the room. Then, surprising even himself, he turned and kicked the rusting door frame with the toe of his combat boot, shouted, "How in the hell could this happen?" and walked quickly out of the room.

Walking briskly toward his jeep, he was glad the sun was shining. Seeing the sun made it easy to associate with life. And that's what he needed now. Strong associations with life to push out the intense and vivid thoughts of death. Not the death of an old person who finally decides to pack it in with a last quiet breath. Not even the abrupt death of a young GI who inadvertently stepped in front of a deuce-and-a-half.

No, it was about callous, intentional, painful death for people who had no control over why they were selected for the brutal process. That was what he needed to push out of his brain. The senselessness of it, and the fact that he couldn't understand how it could happen. How could they let it happen? The people who sat next to him in a streetcar, or sold him a beer, or worked in factories, or drove him and his buddies in taxis from the Flying Dutchman back to the barracks.

Maybe the same people he saw in Nurnberg every day. How could they do it without losing their minds? Someone had to say, "Kill them." And others then did it. With a bullet, a dose of poison gas coming out of a fake showerhead, a rifle butt, a bayonet, or just standing by, day after day, making certain that they had so little to eat that their skin slowly tightened around their bones until there was nothing left to support life.

And then someone had to take what was left of them to that room with the ovens, by the hundreds. No, he corrected himself, by the thousands.

Back at the camp entrance he looked back at the rows of foundations and the brick building tucked away in the trees, its chimneys still visible through the branches. In a way, it was like other places he had seen. Like Arlington. Like Gettysburg. "Hallowed ground," President Lincoln had written on a small piece of paper before addressing the people there.

Most memorials he had seen had the aura of heroism. Patriotism. Fighting for what's right. This had a very different feeling. It was about abused power. Pointless suffering. And that made it different.

Back in his jeep he looked across the parking lot and saw that on the other side was a cluster of homes and apartment buildings. Not the clean geometric architecture that followed the war. They were old buildings that were certainly there in 1944 and 1945. The people in those buildings must have known what was happening there.

Starting the engine, he backed out of the parking place and headed toward the street. As he approached the sidewalk, he saw two men, probably in their fifties, walking together.

The men turned as Novotny hit the brakes and skidded to a stop on the gravel. Jumping out of the vehicle, he walked quickly to them. "How was this possible?" he asked in German, angrily pointing toward the camp site.

They looked at him curiously, wondering what the confrontation was all about.

"Tell me. I want to understand," he asked insistently, but knowing there was no answer. "How could this happen?"

Saying nothing, the two men paid no attention to him or his questions and continued walking. He stood there for a moment, watching them walk away, then got into the jeep, put it in gear, and gunned it, the spinning wheels spewing gravel as he raced out of the parking lot.

Novotny made his way back through Dachau on his way to the autobahn. Back on the superhighway, he soon spotted a sign that said, "U.S. Army, Sub-Area Headquarters" with an arrow pointing to an exit. Chuckling, he slowed and left the autobahn.

It was about four o'clock when he got to the old German barracks occupied by the army. Walking into the headquarters building, he spotted an

NCO sitting at a desk.

"Is there a phone I can use to call Nurnberg?" he asked.

The sergeant pointed to the black phone on his desk. "Go ahead," he replied. "Just don't be long."

Novotny dialed the three digits that got the tape-recorded, German-accented, female voice saying, "Furth. Dial your number," over and over again. Pretty good system we have, he thought. Some of the recorded voices were more appealing than others, and the word got around. "Hey, Novo," a buddy would say. "Try Frankfurt. Great voice." And, of course, he would. Imagining all the while the lovely Aryan maiden sitting in front of a mike reciting the message.

His call went through quickly, and when an enlisted man answered the phone, he asked, "Lieutenant Allen, please." A moment later she was on the phone.

"This is Pfc Novotny," he said. "I'm on my way back to Nurnberg from Munich. I just wanted to let you know that I have the information about the German-American Relations program."

There was silence on the other end of the line. Then she said, obviously puzzled, "I'm not sure what you're talking about."

"I know you've got that program to submit to Stuttgart, and if you need the information, I can drop it off when I get back."

"Oooooh," she said, her voice giving away the fact that she was obviously smiling at the situation. "That would be great. Sure, drop it off."

"OK, Lieutenant. I should be back about eighteen hundred and I'll get it to you."

Carefully putting the phone back on its cradle, he said, "Thanks, Sergeant."

"Don't mention it," the NCO replied, looking up and nodding.

Back on the autobahn, he smiled and decided that this was an insane thing to do. But what could happen? he asked himself It was just about six o'clock when he got to the WAC bachelor officers' quarters, found the listing for "Lt. J. Allen," and pushed the button.

Moments later she came to let him in. "At first, I couldn't figure out what you were talking about," she said, leading him down the hall to her open door. "But then I got the idea. You're pretty clever, Novo."

The building looked a little like a college dormitory, with a long hall and one door after another. Her apartment, if that's what it could be called, was made up of two rooms. A combination dining, living, sleeping, and cooking room. And a bathroom. Not much to write home about. But it had privacy, and that was more than he could say for EM housing.

"Sit down," she said, pointing to a couch that unfolded into a bed. "You must be exhausted." She went to the kitchen counter and turned a corkscrew into a bottle of French red wine. As she started to pour the wine, he shook his head. "Sorry, Lieutenant, I'm still on duty." Setting aside the glasses, she poured two glasses of Coke, and joined him on the couch.

"I really did put together some ideas about how we can do more things with the Germans," he said, reaching into his fatigue jacket and handing her a piece of paper.

She set it on the table. "I'm sure there're lots of good ideas there. I'll go over them tomorrow. To your ingenuity," she said, gently touching her glass to his.

"All I have for dinner is steak and a salad," she said. The comment came across as an apology.

"Sounds great," he said, taking another sip of the bubbling soft drink. "Is it legal for me to be here?"

"Not really," she replied. "Especially since you're . . ." She paused, trying to think of how to say it best.

"Since I'm an EM," he said, finishing the sentence for her.

"Well, yes," she said. "But I don't think there's any problem." She smiled and added, "Particularly since I'm not going to suggest that you spend the night here."

She cooked a simple supper, and they ate on a coffee table in front of the couch. He told her about his week with the Bundeswehr. He wanted to tell her about the stop in Dachau, but decided against it. What he would have said had no place in this conversation. Maybe some other time. Almost certainly, some other time.

The food, the long drive, and a week in the field had made him very tired. He didn't feel much like talking about anything, and she didn't seem to need conversation. He unlaced his combat boots, kicked them off, and lay down on the couch, his head on her lap. From this angle, looking up at her chin, she actually did look a little like Grace Kelly, with the same fine features.

She ran her hand gently down his face, starting at his forehead. As it passed his eyes, he closed them. He felt her lean down and kiss him, then run her hand through his hair, matted from a week without shampoo. It was a magical touch. Relaxing, soothing. Pushing nightmare images of death out of his consciousness and replacing them with a state of euphoria. He started breathing slowly and deeply, feeling tired, but very, very good. Maybe as good as he had ever felt in his life.

He gradually became aware of one kiss after another. On his forehead. His throat. His eyes. His lips. For a moment, he couldn't figure out where he was. Then the surroundings made sense again.

"It's eight o'clock, Novo," she whispered. "You'd probably better get going."

He stretched, then lifted his head and kissed her. "I'd rather stay here."

"I'd rather you stayed here too," she said, smiling.

He got up, put on his combat boots, and laced them tightly. Then, putting on his field jacket, he took her head in his hands. "Thanks for dinner."

She opened the door and looked both ways to be sure no WAC officers were in the hallway.

He took her hand in his. "There are a whole lot things I'd like to talk to you about." Chuckling, he added, "Ma'am."

"Then let's set aside some time to talk," she agreed. "You're already getting pretty short. It won't be too long before you head back to the States."

"Yeah," he said, nodding. "Thanks again for dinner." Then taking her in his arms, he gave her a big hug and a kiss and quietly headed down the hall.

It was Sunday morning, and Novotny was lying on his bunk, reading a copy of *Der Spiegel*, a German magazine similar to *Time* or *Newsweek*. His pocket dictionary was close by, and he referred to it regularly, learning new words with each story.

He had been paid for the month and had about eighty dollars in his pocket. He was determined to spend as little as possible and stash next month's pay as well in preparation for the trip he and Johnson were taking to Berlin.

He had had a long talk with Judy on the phone that morning, and that made him feel good—particularly since they were going to have dinner on Wednesday at a nearby and really inexpensive place they'd found in the city center.

He dredged up the image of her when they first met. The awkward saluting thing. If it hadn't been for that German-American dance, years from now he probably would just recall her as a WAC officer, preoccupied with military courtesy.

He wished Johnson were here. He liked the fact that they could talk about anything. Which they did, hour after hour. But he was on duty in the War Room and wouldn't be back for a couple of hours. Things were still a little tense after the Russian tanks had lined up on the border, and they were manning the S-2 Intelligence Section with more people than usual. And more scouts were added to the border patrols, watching everything that Ivan did on the other side of the line.

He looked back at the magazine and was about to find his place when there was a knock at the door.

"Come on in" he said.

"The door opened. "Hey Turner. Have a seat," he said, sitting up and pointing to Johnson's bunk.

Turner sat on the bunk and they talked about the Russian tanks.

Novotny said, "Johnson told me that it was pretty close. The good news was that everyone backed down. Otherwise it would have been really bad."

"That's for sure," Turner said, nodding. "Well, guess I'll get goin' now," he said quietly as he got up off the bunk. "I've got some stuff to do. I was just down at this end of the barracks. Thought I'd stop by."

"Anytime, Turner. Just poke your head in."

Turner opened the door, then turned, faced Novotny, and said, "Thanks, Novo." He hesitated for a moment. "Thanks for all the stuff you've done for me. I really appreciate it."

"It's nothing," Novotny said, laughing off the comment. "See you later," he said as the door closed.

Stretching out on the bunk, he picked up the magazine and began reading a story about Soviet military planning. His reading was interrupted by a word he didn't know. *Einfall.*

He reached for his pocket dictionary, and it took him only a minute to find it. *Einfall.* Incursion. Closing the dictionary, he was pleased to have added another word to his vocabulary. Incursion. But he then realized that soon it wouldn't matter. He, and the other soldiers who had spent most of the past two years here, would soon be going home.

For Novotny and Johnson, it was a cheap and easy way to spend a Sunday evening. Dinner at the mess hall. Tonight it was fried chicken, which was one of Novotny's favorite army meals, and, of course, free.

Then a thirty-cent movie. And now a thirty-five-cent stein of beer at the EM Club. That was an evening's entertainment without depleting their cash in anticipation of the Berlin trip.

The movie had been *The Pride and the Passion*, the story of a huge cannon, with lots of big battle scenes and the voluptuous Sophia Loren.

"Novo, you've got to admit that she is the most gorgeous woman in the world," Johnson announced as they walked toward the EM Club.

"Sure, she's got great jugs," Novotny agreed. "Particularly falling out of those costumes. And luscious lips. And great, sultry eyes. I'll give you that." He stopped to light a cigarette, taking a long, deep drag and tipping his head up to blow out the smoke. "But she's really nothing compared with Grace Kelly."

"I can't believe you said that," Johnson responded with exaggerated disbelief.

"Grace Kelly is twenty pounds underweight. She has an adolescent figure. And she always looks like she just got out of the shower. There's no comparison."

"You have a right to your opinion, regardless of how far off base it may be," Novotny said. "So go ahead and take Sophia Loren. She's yours. And I'll take Grace Kelly."

Having said that, he thought of the similarities between Grace Kelly and Judy, then smiled at the fact that he was making the comparisons. But he really liked being with her. They were certainly dating, though carefully, given the fact that Novotny was a Pfc and she wore silver bars. And although they hadn't really talked about it, it would seem that there was at least the possibility that something could happen when they both got back to the States. For him, that would happen later this year. She had another full year to serve in Germany.

For no particular reason, they had taken the long way around the parade ground to get to the EM Club. Three or four other GIs had decided to do the same thing. On their right was the motor pool, its rows of trucks, jeeps, tanks, APCs, and ambulances silent in the night. Most were in shadows, but a few were brightly lit by bare bulbs set in round, downward-pointing reflectors on poles above the vehicles.

The trucks all had white stars painted on their doors, something Novotny had never been able to understand. Paint the vehicle camouflage OD, and then put a big white star on the door, a perfect target for anyone who wanted to knock it out.

"Still thinking about Grace Kelly," Johnson asked.

"Yeah. I'm definitely in love. No doubt about it," he answered.

A sharp sound startled them, and they stopped to look into the motor pool where the noise had originated.

"What was that?" Johnson asked, pressing against the fence, squinting to try to see into the darkness.

"It was a rifle shot," Novotny said, running to the fence.

"Where are you going?" Johnson shouted.

"The guard might be hurt," Novotny said, grabbing onto the chain-link fence and starting to climb. "Somebody call the MPs," he shouted.

It was hard to get the toes of his loafers into the diamond-shaped wire mesh of the fence. First, the openings were too small for his toe to get a good foothold. And, because of the angle of the wire, he had to turn his feet at an angle to get any grip at all.

Breathing in sharp gasps, he slowly made his way up to the top of the eight-foot-high fence. Once at the top, he had to deal with the real hazard of the climb, the three strands of barbed wire. Now panting, his breath coming in quick, deep gulps, he carefully grabbed onto the wire and gingerly straddled the barrier, careful to avoid the razor-sharp barbs.

He paused to listen, and heard nothing but the voices below him.

Putting his left foot into one of the chain-link diamonds, he edged his right leg over the barbed wire. Almost there, he said to himself, his heart pounding and his breath coming in quicker gasps. Easy. Just get my other leg over on this side. Careful.

He was just inches away from clearing the sharply barbed barrier when he felt his left toe slip out of its precarious foothold and his right arm drag over the barbed wire as he fell. Suddenly he was in a pile at the base of the fence. It wasn't the way he wanted to arrive. But at least he was inside the motor pool.

Standing up he dusted himself off and felt a sharp pain surge through his body from his right ankle. The pain was so intense that he had to hold on to the fence for support. "Damn," he said under his breath.

Taking a tentative step, he determined he could move as long as he kept the weight on his left foot and just hobbled on the right one. Even so, every step sent pain through his body.

"Hey, guard," he shouted as loudly as he could. "Where are you, guard?"

There was no sign of anyone in the motor pool. Just the ghostly rows of vehicles, mostly just shapes in the dark.

"Hey, guard, where are you?" he shouted. He stopped for a moment under a light to let his right ankle rest. He walked slowly and painfully down row after row of vehicles, shouting but getting no answer. Finally, he saw a figure sitting on the ground, his back against a two-and-a-half-ton truck.

Angry at the fact that the guard hadn't responded to his calls, he shouted, "What's going on? How come you didn't answer me?" He slowly limped toward the guard. "You all right?"

The guard sat there in the dark, looking ahead and saying nothing, though Novotny thought he saw him shake his head slowly in response. He looked down the row to see if there was anyone else around. Maybe even an intruder on the ground, shot by the guard.

As he limped closer to the guard, he said, "We called the MPs. They'll be along any minute." His eyes were now getting used to this particularly dark part of the motor pool. He gasped as he saw that the white star on the truck's door was splashed with red.

Rushing to the truck, he realized the guard was propped up in a sitting position by the barrel of the M1 stuck in his mouth. The butt of the rifle was set in a hole neatly dug in the gravel of the motor pool. His helmet had tilted down over his eyes, covering much of his face.

"Oh, God," Novotny murmured as he realized what he was seeing. He looked at the guard's nametag. "No. Oh, God," he moaned as tears filled his eyes. "No, no, no." Sobbing, he sat down next to the dead guard.

"Why did you do it, Turner? Why?" he asked, tears running down his cheeks. "We're practically finished here. It wouldn't be long before you'd be going home." Sobbing, he put his hand on his friend's knee. "Why? Damn it, Turner," he said, weeping and sniffing. "Why?"

Sitting there, he gradually became aware of the throbbing pain in his right ankle, and a different kind of pain coming from his right arm. He also started to realize that he was very tired. Not just sleepy. But a strange kind of all-encompassing fatigue. The sobs were just shallow gasps for air now, and he felt he was gradually getting himself back together again. Except for feeling so tired. Why am I feeling like this? he asked himself. That was the last thought he had before he fell sideways and facedown onto the gravel.

The group of men ran toward the scene. "Get some light on here," Sergeant Duff ordered. And in an instant, the lights of a jeep illuminated the area. The NCO reached to Turner's throat and felt for a pulse. Finding none, he gently lifted Turner's body and laid it on the gravel. "Cover that man's face," Sergeant Duff said, and one of the men put a blue sweater over Turner's face and shoulder.

Kneeling next to Novotny, Sergeant Duff looked for a pulse at several places on his wrist. Then, anxiously, he pressed his fingers on the side of the unconscious soldier's neck.

"Damn," he said under his breath as he saw that the right sleeve of his sport coat was soaked with blood. Slipping off the coat, Duff pulled out a pocketknife and cut off the sleeve of Novotny's shirt. His arm was drenched with blood. But even so, a deep, three-inch-long incision across the inside of his elbow was clearly visible.

Blood oozed from the wound in weak, slowly spaced pulses. Sergeant Duff pointed to one of the men. "Give me your shirt," he ordered. Surprised, the young man just stood there, not moving. "Soldier, I said give me your shirt," the sergeant said angrily. "Or do you just want to stand there and watch this man bleed to death?"

"I'm sorry," the young man replied, embarrassed and hastily removing his shirt. Using his pocketknife, the sergeant sliced a long, narrow piece out of the shirt. Wrapping it around Novotny's upper arm, he knotted it, inserted his ballpoint pen into the knot, and turned it until it was tight, stopping the flow of blood.

Not more than five minutes later, Novotny was placed in the back of an ambulance by two medics, with Turner's body next to him. Moments later the vehicle was out of sight, and the small crowd began to leave the motor pool.

Anxiously, Johnson asked Sergeant Duff, "Is he going to be all right?"

"He lost a lot of blood. But my guess is that he'll be OK." The sergeant wiped the pocketknife with his handkerchief and carefully put it away. "What happened?"

Johnson explained everything up to the time when Novotny climbed the fence.

"When you heard the shot, did he know Turner was on guard duty?"

"No, we didn't know," Johnson replied.

"Some people would say Novotny wasn't real smart, climbing that fence," the NCO said. He paused as if there was something else that he wanted to say. If so, he changed his mind. "Let's go to the infirmary and see how he's doing."

After a brief stay in the hospital, Novotny had been back on light duty for the past couple of weeks. He felt fine now, except that his ankle was still a little tender. It was Sunday afternoon and they were in the old town area, having a cup of rich, steaming coffee and a succulent pastry.

Novotny looked across the plaza and said, "Climbing that fence was a pretty dumb thing to do."

"You just did what you thought was right at the moment," she replied, touching his hand. "Don't be so hard on yourself." She squeezed his fingers. "And stop blaming yourself about Turner. You and Bob did everything you could to help him. You know that."

He took a bite of the delicious chocolate pastry and washed it down with a swallow of coffee. "Pretty good stuff," he noted, smiling.

"I think it's great that you and Bob are taking a leave to Berlin next month," she said. "It'll be good for you to get away. And you might as well use it up before you rotate."

Novotny nodded in agreement. He really was looking forward to the trip. Even though things were still tense there.

"You'll really be short when you get back," she said, a hint of sadness in her voice. "How many weeks after that?"

"Let's see. We should be on our way back to the States about six weeks after we get back," he said, counting on his fingers. "Yeah. Six weeks."

"I'll have another year," she said quietly. Taking a deep breath, she added, "I'm going to miss you."

"Let's not talk about that now," he said, smiling. "Let's figure out what we can do between now and then. Something special."

She took a sip from her cup and said tentatively, "Well, there's one possibility that I've been thinking about."

"What's that?" he asked, curious about what she had in mind.

"No," she said, shaking her head. "It's probably not a very good idea."

"Come on," he said insistently. "You brought it up. Now you have to say it."

Realizing she was trapped, she blushed and looked down at her coffee cup. "I hope you won't take this the wrong way."

He was going to press her further, but decided to just wait it out.

"OK," she said, taking a sip of her coffee. "Why don't we take a weekend and go to that town on the Mosel River?"

"Bauerdorf?"

"I can't remember," she answered, frowning. "The place where the wine is made. The wine that your friend bought for us."

"Bauerdorf. That's it," he confirmed, nodding and grinning broadly. "That would be great." He added excitedly, "We could do it a couple of weeks before I head out of here. I could just take an overnight pass."

He smiled as he thought about the idea. Maybe they could even stay at the same hotel that Dieter and Gerd had talked about. He nodded and said, "We could get a bottle of Bauerdorf Kirchen wine and drink it right there," he said, the excitement very apparent in his voice. "Right where they make it. Maybe we could even visit the vineyards."

"Sounds wonderful," she said, beaming.

That night, stretched out on his bunk, with Johnson sound asleep on the other side of the room, he wrote another letter in his brain. "To the guy who writes the recruiting posters. You set me up when I first got here. With a great Czech girl, creating a terrific fantasy for me. Except she was a spy, which blew the whole thing. Not just for me, but for my buddy, Johnson.

"So then I wrote and said you were really a fraud, and that I took back all the good things I'd said to you."

He nodded at the appropriateness of the text so far. "But now I'm into something really serious because of you. So I'm writing again to thank you for convincing me that I should sign up and be a soldier, which got me here in the first place."

He again nodded in approval. "But, there's a problem. It's illegal. So for God's sake, don't write a poster that says something like, join the army, travel to interesting places, meet a terrific WAC officer, and fall in love. That could pose some real problems for a lot of people because Pfcs aren't supposed to date officers. And certainly are not supposed to fall in love with them."

Now the question was how to end this letter.

He thought for a minute. "So all I'm saying to you is that you're off the hook. The Czech girl turned into a really bad situation. But the thing with the WAC officer seems to be working out great. So, thanks. Just don't tell anyone. Signed, Pfc Joseph Novotny. 2d Armored Cavalry Regiment. Nurnberg, Germany."

He was still smiling when his eyes closed and he fell soundly asleep.

The train moved slowly through the countryside. There wasn't much to see in the darkness, other than an occasional village along the side of the tracks. Novotny peered into the night and thought about how strange it was to be traveling down this narrow corridor through the land of the enemy,

East Germany. This link that served as a lifeline for West Berlin, an island surrounded by the communists.

In '48, the Russians had shut this connection off, which would have been simple enough to do. The idea was to keep food, fuel, medical supplies, and everything else the West Berliners—and the U.S., French, and English troops stationed there—needed to function.

A plain old siege that the Russians kept in place for about a year, assuming it would cause the Westerners to cave in and leave Berlin.

But it hadn't worked out that way. The Western countries had set up an airlift and flew everything in until the Russians finally called the thing off. Now he and Johnson were on that tenuous connection, moving slowly across East Germany for Berlin.

"Wonder where we are," Novotny said, shielding his eyes from the light in an effort to see something that would give them a clue.

"About halfway there, I'd guess," Johnson said, moving to the window so he could take a look too.

The train slowed to a crawl as they came to what appeared to be the outskirts of a town, and then stopped. Novotny slid the window down, and the two young men leaned on it, taking in the fresh night air and looking into the blackness. The train lurched and slowly moved forward a hundred yards or so, then stopped again.

"Look," Novotny said, pointing to the right. Not more than twenty-five feet from them, standing in the dark, was a Russian soldier. His rifle was slung over his shoulder, its bayonet pointing to the sky.

They looked at him, not saying a word, as if they were watching an animal in the forest, not wanting to frighten it.

"He's obviously there for two reasons," Johnson whispered. "So we won't get off. And so some East German with an idea of heading to Berlin won't get on."

"Good evening, comrade soldier," Novotny said in Czech. The soldier turned quickly and looked at them. Then he came to attention, looking straight ahead.

"You think he understood you?"

"All I said was good evening. There's a lot of similarity to the Slavic languages. He probably has at least an idea of what I said."

"Ask him if he wants cigarettes."

"Do you smoke? Would you like some cigarettes?" Novotny asked.

The Russian soldier stood at attention, saying nothing and given no indication that he had heard or understood what had been asked.

"That's the enemy, Novo."

Novotny nodded. "Yeah. Looks pretty much like any one of our guys."

The train began to move slowly. Novotny reached into his pocket and pulled out a package of Kents, dropping them on the gravel near the soldier's feet as they passed.

"This is a gift from two American soldiers to you," he said in Czech. The train picked up speed and went around a curve, making it impossible for them to know whether he picked up the gift.

The next morning they attended the obligatory briefing about being in Berlin.

"As you know, you are in one of the most sensitive areas of the world, militarily and politically," the lieutenant told the men who had arrived late the night before. "This is particularly true because of the statements that have been made by Nikita Khruschev threatening to kick us out of here."

The officer continued, "Consider yourselves as guests of the people of

West Berlin, and behave accordingly. Any violations of military or civil law will be handled severely."

He paused and looked around the room, as if to make certain that the message had been understood. "If you are interested in seeing East Berlin, there is only one way to do so. That's by special bus tour, Monday through Friday. The vehicle will leave here at thirteen hundred and return at fifteen hundred. Class A uniforms are required."

Again the officer paused to let the message sink in. "Take your international travel documents with you at all times. Along with your army ID card. Any questions?"

There being none, the lieutenant dismissed the young soldiers. Chairs scraped on the concrete floor as the men rose and left the room.

"Want to take the bus tour?" Johnson asked.

"Let's check out West Berlin first," Novotny suggested. "We can do the bus thing later."

"What's the matter? Not interested in being in a bus with a bunch of GIs in Class A's?"

"Something like that," Novotny said, smiling.

Sitting at an outdoor café on the *Kurfurstendam*, drinking coffee, they agreed that this was without a doubt the most active and bustling street they'd seen in all of Germany.

It was midafternoon, and well-dressed women were coming out of fashionable shops with packages under their arms. Men in suits and carrying briefcases walked purposefully, obviously on their way somewhere to do something important. And the street was clogged with the latest models from Mercedes, Opel, Taunus, DKW, Auto Union, BMW, and Volkswagen, honking and slowly making their way down the boulevard.

The street was lined with trim, modern, glass-fronted buildings, monuments to the post-war prosperity in this island of a city. Adorning the rooftops were huge neon ads for all sorts of products. Cars. Cigarettes. Perfume. Brandy. Television sets and radios.

But a couple of blocks from where they sat, starkly contrasting with the street's contemporary architecture, was St. Michael's Church. Or at least what was left of it. The shell of the stone structure was blackened by fire, the beautiful lines abruptly broken with probably half of the building gone. Rather than dispose of the relic, the West Berliners had decided to leave the ruin up, in the midst of all the excitement, prosperity, and beauty, as a reminder of the war.

"What a gorgeous woman," Novotny said, with no warning.

"Where?" Johnson asked, thinking he may have missed a particularly special passerby.

"Nefertiti," he said. "Absolutely gorgeous."

They'd gone to the Dahlem Museum in the morning, and there she was. All alone in a small, bare room that had been painted all black. The ancient Egyptian queen's bust was encased in a climate-controlled glass case with spotlights shining down from the ceiling, accenting the exotic features of this stunningly beautiful woman.

"No argument on that," Johnson agreed. "What about Inge?"

Novotny thought for a moment. "She wasn't bad. Actually she was quite pretty. But a little old for us."

It had been a curious meeting. They'd heard about a place called Club Dore that a GI at Merrell had told them they had to see. So, about nine o'clock the night before, they had given it a try.

On all counts, it was a very classy place, with an orchestra playing music from the '40s, and velvet and velour everywhere. Tuxedoed waiters moved from table to table, delivering food and drinks with a slightly pompous air.

Just as they'd been told, it was pretty amazing. The tables were set on several levels, which gave people a good view of who was where. Most were occupied by either one or two women, ranging in age, they estimated, from about thirty-five to fifty-five.

There were only a handful of men in the entire place. But the thing that made it really curious was that each table was equipped with the kind of device used in department stores to pay for purchases and make change. The system of pneumatic tubes carried a small metal canister from one place to another.

On the table was a map of the club, showing the number of each table. Next to that, a notepad and pencil had been neatly placed, with instructions written in five languages. "They've even got translators somewhere down there, in case you don't have a common language," Novotny had marveled as he read the instructions.

As soon as two beers had been ordered—to the disdain of the waiter, who was prepared for a much larger purchase—Novotny had written a message in German. "Greetings from Table 48."

"What're you doing?" Johnson had asked.

"Trust me," he had said, grinning.

Putting the message in the metal canister, he had opened up the end of the tube and put it in. With a slight *whoooosh* the message was gone.

"Be discreet, but turn around," Novotny had said to his friend.

Sitting next to them, just a few feet from Johnson's back, was a particularly attractive and well-dressed woman, wearing an elegant dark blue dress and pearls around her neck. Novotny had guessed that she was in her mid- to late forties.

Johnson had said softly, "You didn't."

Novotny nodded, and moments later the canister arrived with the same kind of whooshing sound that had caused it to begin its journey. The woman had picked it up, opened it, and read the message. Then looking at the map on her table, she had turned to see the two young men smiling innocently at her.

"Good evening," she had said, lifting her glass of wine. "Thank you for the greeting. But you could have just told me. I am Inge."

"We wanted to try out the equipment," Novotny had said, now slightly embarrassed. She had complimented them on their knowledge of German, and they talked about Berlin and how much it was growing.

Then, without warning, she had said, "I feel that I must explain this place to you, so you will not have the wrong idea."

Curious about what she was going to say, they had listened intently to be sure they understood every word.

"Women such as me come here because there are so few men our age in Berlin," she said. "We come here with the hope that we will meet some nice man." She smiled and added, "Like you. But somewhat older."

"We understand," Johnson had said.

To make certain that the point had been made, she had said, gesturing to the tables around them, "We are not what you might think. Women of the street."

Novotny had quickly responded, "We did not think that for even one moment."

"We should've stayed there with Inge," Johnson said now, watching the people pass by. "She was really pretty. Classy. And I know she lusted for my Adonis-like body."

"The thought crossed my mind," Novotny admitted. "But there was only one problem. We've got thirty-five bucks between us for the rest of this trip. And we could have gone through the whole amount in about twenty minutes in that place."

"OK," Johnson acknowledged. "Time for some culture." Pulling out the map they'd bought earlier in the day, he searched for a landmark and then pointed to it. "There it is. *Brandenburger Tor.* The Brandenburg Gate."

"And?"

"We've got to go see it," Johnson said assertively. "I did an art history paper on it."

"And you want to share it with me?"

"Right."

A couple of hundred yards from the structure's classic arches, they found a bench and sat down to take in its beautiful lines. At the top was a dramatic statue of four horses and a chariot. "The *Quadriga*," Johnson explained. "Destroyed during the war. But they found the molds and recast it."

As Novotny's eyes studied the historic landmark, he noticed a sign about twenty feet from them, written in English, German, French, and Russian. "Caution," it said. "You are now leaving the British Sector and entering the Russian Sector."

Engrossed in what he saw, Novotny failed to see a hunched-over man of about sixty approach them.

"Is this place taken?" the man asked in German, pointing to the empty space on the bench.

"No, please," Novotny replied.

The man wore plain and well-worn work clothes, and carried a shoe box, tied with string, under his arm. On his feet were what appeared to be brand-new, very utilitarian shoes.

"You live in Berlin?" Novotny asked.

The man looked at the young men suspiciously.

"We are Americans," Johnson explained. "We are only trying to learn about your city."

"Yes," the man responded cautiously. "I live in East Berlin."

The conversation went well from that point on. The man was pleased to have a chance to chat with what appeared to be a couple of innocent, young Americans. And for Johnson and Novotny, it was an opportunity to learn about the mysterious city—or part of a city—just a short distance from them.

Novotny was careful about what he asked, but gradually the questions dealt with what it was like to live on the other side. When the time seemed right, he posed an important question. "If you can come across the border from East Berlin, why do you not stay here, in West Berlin?"

The man smiled sadly. "There are many reasons. My family is there. It is where I have always lived. I have no money. I could not live here. And I am too old."

Having said all that, the man got up and bowed slightly to the two men on the bench. "Until I see you again."

"Until I see you again," Novotny and Johnson said, almost in unison.

The man walked toward the gate, and Novotny hollered, "Sir, you forgot your box."

The man turned, shook his head, and continued walking in the direction of the gate. As he got close, he blended in with a group of about fifteen people, who walked together toward the gate's right-hand arch.

When the man was out of sight, Johnson undid the string and opened the box. In it was a pair of old shoes, worn so badly that it was hard to imagine anyone wearing them.

"That's odd," he said, dropping the box and its contents into a trash receptacle a few feet from the bench.

"Tell me again. What's the name of the statue on the gate?" Novotny asked.

"The *Quadriga*."

"The *Quadriga*," Novotny repeated, looking intently at the sculpture. For a long list of reasons, it was an important landmark, and he wanted to commit both the image and its name to memory.

Johnson and Novotny walked to the same bench where they had sat the day before. Looking at the Brandenburg Gate, Novotny said, "We've got two choices." Leaning back, his hands behind his head, he announced, "A, we do it. And B, we don't do it."

"One of the things I really like about you, Novo," Johnson said, chuckling, "is the way you're able to put things into such clear and relevant perspective."

"So? What is it?" As Novotny asked the question, he adjusted one of the many straps on the European-style trench coat he'd bought at a store in Nurnberg. The short-billed cap had been bought at the same place. And the boots came from the PX at Merrell but were made in England.

Everything that showed was made someplace other than America. And his outfit, coupled with the Eastern-European look of his face, gave him a reasonably European appearance. He had even left his horn-rimmed glasses back at the transient barracks, choosing to wear his nondescript GI ones instead. And replacing the Kents that he usually carried, he had a couple of packs of German–made Ernte 23s.

Johnson had a similar trench coat and a black beret. The two young men looked as though they'd come out of the pages of the same catalog. Nondescript. Nothing flashy. Certainly not stylish.

"Well." Novotny swallowed hard, and pressed again for an answer.

"There's only one thing for it," Johnson said, nodding. "We've got to do it."

They sat quietly looking toward the gate and the sign that announced the beginning of the Russian sector. A few people were walking slowly toward the arches from several different directions.

"This is a good time," Novotny said in German, with a touch of urgency in his voice. "We go."

The men walked toward the place where they had seen people rendezvous the day before, timing their arrival with that of seven or eight others. The group, which grew to an even dozen, walked cautiously and silently on the sidewalk leading to the gate. Johnson and Novotny maneuvered their way into the center of the group, so they were surrounded as they got close to the architectural treasure above them.

Looking toward the arch, Novotny's heart started racing as he saw two East German border police on one side and a third on the other, all with submachine guns slung over their shoulders. The group slowly passed into the shadow of the arch and was nearly on the other side, when one of the guards said, "Stop."

Now Novotny's heart was really pounding. Even though he wanted to look at Johnson, to his right, like the others, he kept his eyes straight ahead.

"You," the guard said in German. Novotny swallowed hard and turned his head slightly. The guard was pointing to a man, about forty, who was at the front of the group. The border officer gestured for him to come to where the two guards were standing. The man did as he was told, obviously not happy about what was happening.

"You others," the guard said coolly. "You may go."

Novotny decided not to talk to Johnson until they were well past the gate. Finally, he edged over to him. "It could have been a really short visit," he said.

Johnson said softly, "Or a really long one."

They were walking down a street that had been one of the great boulevards of Europe until the war. *Unter den Linden.* Under the linden trees. But the median that been planted with beautiful trees and flowers was now a bare strip of untended dirt, scattered bricks, and shattered concrete. There was not a tree in sight. They'd all been chopped down, Novotny had read, during the awful winter of 1944–45 by citizens who burned the wood to keep from freezing to death.

The ornate buildings that lined the street had once been a series of architectural treasures. That was easy to see. Now they were burned-out shells, dilapidated structures, or piles of rubble.

Even the streetlights showed their former elegance. Though the metal was twisted and there wasn't a piece of glass in any of them, they too showed their beauty, the way you can see in a ninety-year-old woman what she had been when she was young.

Ironically, next to the broken streetlights were what appeared to be newly installed and freshly painted poles topped by loudspeakers. Information—or more likely propaganda—was obviously more important than lights on this formerly great street.

The group that had crossed under the gate together began dissipating as soon as they were on the main street, strangely devoid of any cars. None of them spoke. As they walked, one would disappear silently down a side street to the right. Another would go to the left. And before they had walked many blocks, Johnson and Novotny were nearly alone.

As they walked, Novotny had a strange sense of uneasiness. "Stop here for a sec," he said. "I'm going to light a cigarette." He reached into his pocket and turned slightly as he lit it with a wooden match. About fifty yards behind them was a young woman, probably in her early twenties, pudgy, plain, and wearing a gray skirt, blouse, and uniform jacket.

She had stopped at the same time they had, and stood, embarrassed, because there was no apparent reason for her to be standing there on the sidewalk.

Novotny turned and they started walking. "We're being followed."

"You serious?"

"I'm afraid so," Novotny said, thinking about what would be the best thing to do. Ahead of them, across the street, was a museum with a large poster announcing an exhibit about "The Red Army Liberation of Berlin."

"Let's go in there," Novotny suggested. Once inside, they walked quickly to the second floor, glancing at maps that showed the last days of the Third Reich. Bold red arrows pointing from the East to Berlin identified the movement of Russian troops. Pencil-thin blue arrows moved in the other direction, labeled with unit names. The displays talked about the heroism of the Red Army, making only a slight mention of the massive Allied force that had chewed up the German Army from Normandy to the heart of Germany.

Carefully peering down to the main floor, where groups of uniformed schoolchildren were gathered, they saw the young woman in gray, looking intently into the exhibit rooms.

Walking to the back of the building, they found another staircase, less ornate than the one in front. Staying alert for the woman in gray, or for that matter, anyone, they went down to the first level, then continued anxiously down one more level where they found what appeared to be a back entrance to the museum.

"It looks like a pretty normal kind of door," Johnson said. "Let's try it." Slowly opening it, they found that it worked fine. No alarm went off, and it put them outside and at the back of the building.

They instinctively started back toward Unter den Linden. But Novotny suggested, "Let's go left instead."

"Good idea," Johnson agreed, and they walked briskly in the other direction, being careful not to look like fugitives.

A couple of blocks away, they came upon a small cluster of trees, the only ones they'd seen since crossing under the gate. A rusted bench was set back among the trees, and the two young men, breathing hard, sat down.

"What do you think?" Novotny asked.

"I think she decided to get some points from her local commissar by tailing us. Because we didn't look like East Berliners." Johnson thought for a few seconds. "I think if the border police had wanted us, we would've been pulled over with that other guy."

"Sounds reasonable," Novotny agreed. "That means we've got two choices."

"I know," Johnson said. "A or B. I'll take B."

"You sure?"

"Yeah."

"We keep going to see what's over here," he said, pointing down a side street.

"What was A?" Johnson asked.

"Go back to the museum," Novotny said, smiling. "Find the woman in the gray outfit. Turn ourselves in, telling her that we're American soldiers who snuck across the border and are here illegally." He chuckled. "Oh, yeah, and we tell her we both have security clearances."

"Guess I made the right choice," Johnson said, looking back toward the museum to see if there was any sign of the young woman. There wasn't. In fact, there were no people anywhere. Not a single person, in any direction. The streets were absolutely empty.

Hidden by the small group of trees in a setting otherwise devoid of any greenery, they kept an eye on the museum building, half expecting the woman in gray to suddenly appear, leading a couple of *Volks Polizei* to them. But after fifteen minutes of waiting, they decided it was safe to move on.

The neighborhood they were in was completely residential, the streets lined with three-, four-, and five-story apartment buildings. The buildings were all brick, darkened by the years and the battle that had consumed this once glorious city.

There were no signs of life in any of them, and probably half showed the scars of battle. Broken walls. An absence of glass in the windows. And like the ones they'd seen in Nurnberg, some with their fronts or sides or backs ripped off, exposing the rooms within.

In the next block, the buildings were in even worse shape. Every structure had been badly damaged. In some cases, as much as half of the building was gone. The remainder of these structures was a collection of fractured walls and random piles of brick and wood.

"This is really strange," Johnson said. "There's nobody here. Not a soul."

Novotny agreed, but added, "I've got a feeling there are people in there. Watching us. Probably wondering who in the world would be walking around this neighborhood."

The next block was even worse, with not a single building standing intact. Just irregular piles of brick, broken stonework, and partial walls. But it was the block after that that caused them to stop in disbelief. There was no sign of any functional structures. Just piles of rubble and broken walls. The thing that caused them to swallow hard and shake their heads was that blocks just like it went on and on. Ahead of them. To their left. And to their right. As far as they could see.

"My God," Novotny said, half under his breath. "I wonder if it was B-17s or Russian artillery."

"Probably a little of both," Johnson speculated, his voice barely audible.

They stood, looking at the terrible landscape ahead of them, each silently wondering what had happened to the people who had lived here. Did they get out? Were they still buried under the rubble? How many Russian and German soldiers had died right here? At this very place?

"Seen enough?" Johnson asked quietly.

"Yeah. Let's go back that way," Novotny agreed, pointing to a street ahead of them.

Walking along the broken concrete of the sidewalks, they made their way back toward Unter den Linden, carefully watching for any sign of the young woman in gray. They came upon the Marx-Engels Bridge and stood at midspan, watching the river's brown-gray water flow under them.

To their right, they heard the sound of loud engines on the empty street. They stepped into the shelter provided by what was left of a small courtyard. The sound was made by two Russian soldiers on motorcycles roaring toward them. Once again Novotny's heart started pounding as he and Johnson stood in the shadows, shielded from view.

They watched as the motorcycles raced by, the soldiers' rifles slung diagonally across their backs.

"Close," Johnson observed nervously.

Near the bridge was a huge, open plaza. There was room enough for thousands of East Berliners to rally in support of the Communist government. The perimeter was ringed with the loudspeakers they had seen earlier. And on one side of the square, behind rows and rows of bleachers, was a giant, full-color portrait of Lenin. It was probably sixty or seventy feet high, and accenting the bearded image were the flags of East Germany and the Soviet Union. Next to the flags was the slogan "Germany will fight all fascism."

"Pretty subtle," Johnson said.

Novotny shook his head.

Looking ahead, they saw what appeared to be a collection of new high-rise structures and decided to check it out. The street was six lanes wide, three in each direction. At one intersection, they stood looking at what appeared to be office buildings – ten stories or so high—with retail shops on the street level.

There was not a car to be seen on the broad street and not a single person on the sidewalk. Traffic signals were in place at each corner, but the lights were not working. And with good reason. There was no traffic to control.

The shops were mostly shut down and empty. Only one had merchandise on display in the window: four cans of beef heart, their labels faded from the sun. No one was in the store. No customers. And it looked as if no one was inside to sell anything, even the faded cans of beef heart, if a customer had come along.

"I figured out the story on that shoe box," Novotny announced as they walked slowly down the deserted boulevard.

"What?" Johnson replied, puzzled.

"On the bench yesterday. The shoe box," he said. "The guy we talked to has a relative in West Berlin, and he meets the relative who buys him a new pair of shoes. Then the guy we met wears them back across the border."

"Why would he do that?" Johnson asked.

"Because he can't buy them here, since there aren't any stores," Novotny added. "And he's not allowed to bring new ones across legally. In a box. So he dumps the old ones, and wears the new ones. And no one pays any attention. Or they just look the other way."

"You ought to be in S-2," Johnson said, grinning. "We could use that analytical mind of yours in intelligence."

They weren't exactly sure where they were, but they had a pretty good idea that they were headed in the right direction. Soon the buildings began to look familiar, with the military museum on the right. On the broken sidewalk in front of the museum was a metal stand containing what looked like a poster.

Stopping to study it, they saw that it depicted two cartoon characters. One was a Gypsy fortuneteller, with playing cards spread out on the table in front of her. Standing on the other side of the table was a buck-toothed, dumb-looking soldier with a U.S. emblem on his uniform cap.

"You are going to travel across the Atlantic, back to your country," the first line of the caption read.

"Does it say it in the cards?" the dim-witted soldier asked.

"No, it says it in Comrade Khrushchev's letter to your government."

"Pretty clever," Novotny noted. For months, the papers had carried stories about the Russian government's demands. And here was the same message in a cartoon poster.

"Except we're staying," Johnson said.

They walked slowly along the treeless boulevard. Before long they saw the distinctive shape of the Brandenburg Gate ahead of them.

"Should we head back?" Novotny asked.

"I think we've pretty much seen it," Johnson replied.

Slowing as they approached the gate, they saw people converging, one or two at a time, ahead of them. Joining the group of about twenty, they looked down at the ground and walked slowly, being careful to position themselves in the middle of the group.

The East German border guards watched the group approach, carefully scrutinizing each person. Novotny again felt his heart pounding. Just as when they had crossed in the other direction that morning, one of the East German guards shouted, "Stop. You. Come here."

This time the target was someone behind him, and Novotny made sure not to turn around to see who it was.

"You others may go."

It was about 100 meters from the gate to the sign that marked the British sector. When they crossed the Russian sector line, Johnson stopped and turned around. Novotny paused, then also turned to admire the four horses and the chariot that adorned the top of the Brandenburg Gate. On the street in front of them was another small group of people, gathering to cross under the shadow of the arches.

"No wonder Khrushchev wants us out of here," Johnson said. "Imagine being able to come over here from East Berlin and compare it with the other side."

"They're going to have to shut it down," Novotny said. "They can't let people cross like that. For shoes. Lunch with a relative. Or just to breathe free air. This can't last."

They turned and walked back toward the Kurfurstendam, having decided it was time for a beer, trading the bleakness of East Berlin for the traffic and bustle of this political island.

Novotny was, for the first time since they'd walked under the gate, ready to relax. He took a deep breath, glad to be on this side of the line. But also glad to have seen—firsthand—what the other side was like.

The waitress brought them two steins of local beer, and they held the glasses up to toast.

Johnson said, "To the riskiest and most irresponsible thing I have ever done."

"I'll drink to that," Novotny said, touching his glass to Johnson's.

Novotny had selected an intersection on Allersbergerstrasse that was a discreet distance from Merrell so as not to be seen. He stood on the corner, his schnitzel bag over his shoulder, watching the traffic moving toward him.

It had been a busy few weeks since he and Johnson had gotten back from Berlin. The 2d Cav patrols were keeping an eye on the border, which had been quiet since the tank episode. He had translated lots of articles from the local papers. And sent information about the unit's activities to the Seventh Army public information office.

A tornado had hit a small village not far from Nurnberg, and the regiment had sent its combat engineers to help clean up the damage. Novotny had been assigned to go along and translate. The engineers had done a great job with chain saws and heavy equipment, and the locals seemed to appreciate the help.

During the past week, the regiment's band had played for a community event sponsored by the Nurnberg Police Department. Novotny had been assigned to be there and talk about the regiment's assignment on the border to Nurnbergers who came by. A few said they appreciated the fact that the United States was protecting the border. And a handful made rude comments, which Novotny shrugged off.

Judy's blue Opel turned a corner and stopped, a few minutes early.

"Hi," he said, throwing his bag in the backseat and leaning over to kiss her cheek.

"Hi," she said, smiling. "This is like something from a spy movie."

They followed the "Autobahn" signs and soon were on one of Hitler's superhighways. Novotny had offered to drive, but she declined, which he didn't mind. He liked the way she drove, confidently working her way through the gears, her hands easily on the wheel.

Novotny pulled a map from the inside pocket of his tweed sport coat, and began announcing the exits they would come to next. With a brief stop for lunch, they made good time, with little traffic and no speed limit to slow them.

The scenery was beautiful. Rolling hills, quaint villages in the distance, and an occasional river. They didn't say much. They just enjoyed the pleasant ride and the passing landscape. And, without saying it, they liked the fact that they were together.

Exiting the autobahn, Novotny navigated and they were soon on a narrow, winding road that paralleled the Mosel River, the steep slopes of the valley covered with vineyards.

"Isn't it amazing," he said, "that vineyards can grow there."

About twenty minutes later, they saw the sign announcing that they were in Bauerdorf.

"This is exciting," Judy said, beaming. "I'm glad we're doing this."

"Me too," he agreed, gently squeezing her shoulder.

A cobblestone street ran through the center of town. Unlike the shops in East Berlin, the store windows were full of everything. Clothing. Groceries. Leather goods. Clocks. Even jewelry. But nearly all of the stores were closed, following the practice of shutting down at noon on Saturday and reopening Monday morning.

A lovely old fountain stood in the town square, and on the other side of the plaza an ornate sign said, "Hotel Goldener Adler." The Golden Eagle Hotel.

"There it is," Novotny said, pointing. Judy pulled the car into a parking spot right at the front door.

Turning off the engine, she announced, "We're here."

Novotny made no move to get out of the car or reach for his bag.

"You all right?" she asked.

"Well," he said nervously. "There's one thing we have decide before we go in."

"What's that?"

He had never been in a situation like this before. In fact, he had consciously avoided the subject. But now it had to be addressed.

"Well, the question is . . ." He paused.

"Yessssss," she said, smiling. "The question is . . ."

"One room or two?" he blurted.

"Novo, you're so sweet," she said, taking his hand in hers. She leaned over and whispered in his ear, "You decide."

He took a deep breath. "One."

"That's the choice I would have made too," she said quietly, as if she didn't want anyone else to know.

With his right hand, he turned over the class ring he wore on his left ring finger. Having the stone hidden on the palm side, the ring looked like a simple gold band.

Taking her left hand in his, he did the same thing with the birthstone ring she wore.

The proprietor greeted them as they approached the desk. Using his best, formal German, Novotny inquired about the availability of a room.

"One room?" the proprietor asked.

"Yes, please," Novotny replied as nonchalantly as possible.

"And you are married?" the proprietor asked.

"Yes, of course," Novotny replied, casually placing his left hand on the counter.

"Very good," the proprietor said, noting the gold band on Novotny's finger. "You have room number eight. It is a very nice room."

"Thank you," Novotny said, nodding slightly.

It was a nice room, just as the proprietor had said. Small, but spotlessly clean. And on the bed was a thick, white-covered down comforter that seemed to weigh nothing at all.

Novotny put his arms around Judy and held her. "I'm glad you suggested this," he said.

"I was getting worried that you weren't going to bring it up. So I decided I'd better do it before you got on that ship to go back to the States," she said, kissing him gently.

"Want to go for a walk and check out the town?" he suggested.

"That sounds great," she replied, smiling approvingly.

The main street of Bauerdorf was about ten blocks long, and they walked the length of it, admiring the architecture and peering into the windows of the closed shops. It was an ideal afternoon. Warm. Sunny. Comfortable.

At the western end of the street, one building stood by itself, set against a vine-covered hillside. "Weinstube Bauerdorf" the sign over the door announced. The Bauerdorf wine bar. As they walked up the steps, they noticed a trellised arbor along the far side of the building.

"Let's sit there," Judy proposed.

A charming young waitress came to take their order. When Novotny asked, in German, if they served Bauerdorf Kirche wine, she replied enthusiastically, "Oh, yes. It is our specialty."

Returning in a matter of minutes, she placed two bowl-shaped glasses on the table. "I hope you enjoy this wine," she said, seemingly pleased that it had been ordered.

Judy lifted her glass. "To a really special weekend."

"I'll drink to that," Novotny said, touching his glass to hers.

The wine seemed even more delicious here than it was at Fidelio, no doubt because of the setting, the company, the event, and the fact that it actually came from this place.

He looked up at the grapevines above them, crisscrossed on the overhead wooden trellis. In front of them was the Mosel River, its brownish water slowly making its way east to the Rhein. He took another sip of the wine, relishing the cool, fruity sensations it created.

"I wonder if Dieter and Gerd sat here, looking at this view," he said. "Getting ready to go into the army."

Holding the glass up to the light of the late afternoon sun, he admired the clarity of the wine and its slight tinge of green-gold color. He felt a sense of absolute joy at being here. At the same time, he experienced intense sadness because he would not be able to describe the experience to the man who had introduced him to this place and this wine.

Holding his glass in front of him, he said to himself, To the comradeship of ordinary soldiers, and especially the brave ones.

The cuckoo clock on the wall of the hotel restaurant struck nine just as Novotny was taking the last bite of the delicate apple strudel in front of him. Washing it down with a sip of rich, black coffee, he looked at Judy, smiled contentedly, and shook his head.

"Delicious," he said.

"It was a wonderful dinner," Judy agreed.

Their waitress cleared the dishes. "Would you like anything else?"

"No, thank you. It was wonderful," Novotny answered. Lifting his wineglass, he drained the last few drops. Delicious, he thought.

Back in their room, Novotny stretched out under the soft feather cover, wearing only his white, GI-issue boxer shorts, with the first letter of his last name and the last four digits of his serial number stenciled on the elastic band. He could hear Judy in the tiny bathroom brushing her teeth and doing whatever else women did when they got ready for bed. He had never been in a situation like this before, so it was hard to know what to expect.

She came out wearing a white cotton nightgown and looking beautiful. Sitting on the edge of the bed, she smiled and said, "Hello."

"Hi," Novotny replied, a little uncomfortably. "Fancy meeting you here."

She stretched out under the comforter next to him, relishing the softness of the comforter and the pillow that was so delicate it seemed to luxuriantly envelop her whole head.

"You look great," he said, propping his head up on his arm and admiring her finely featured face.

"Thank you," she replied. "So do you."

"Sure," he said, laughing, and pulling on the elastic waistband of his shorts. "These are particularly . . . ah . . . let's say, appealing."

He leaned over and gently kissed her forehead. Then her cheeks. And finally her lips. The soft, affectionate kisses—like the ones his mother had given him—gradually gave way to more intense contact of their lips. He put his arms around her, rolled her on top of him, and kissed her even more intently.

She moaned slightly and put her leg between his, returning his kisses with equally intense explorations of her own. Her arms were around his shoulders, holding him as tightly as he held her.

"Mmm," she murmured as their bodies seemed to merge into one.

Then, without warning, she rolled over onto her back.

"What's wrong?" he asked, concerned that he had done something to anger her.

"Oh, Novo," she said almost plaintively, shaking her head. "I'm sorry," she said apologetically. "It's just that . . ." She paused, obviously trying to figure out how to say what was on her mind. "Well, if we wanted to have a baby in nine months, this would be exactly the right time to do what we're doing."

Novotny looked up at the ceiling.

She sat up and looked at his intent, frowning face.

"Someday it'll be simple," he said, obviously frustrated. "Take a pill and forget about calendars or mechanical devices."

She laid her head on his chest. "Novo, that wasn't the reason I suggested coming here." Her eyes filled with tears. "I just wanted to be with you before you go back. Just so we could have some time together." She sobbed, "I won't see you for at least a year."

He put his hand on the back of her neck and gently rubbed the smooth whiteness of her skin.

"I don't even know where I'll be a year from now," he said.

"Wherever you are, I'll come there as soon as I get back."

"Really?" he asked.

Nodding, she said, "Of course I will. You know that."

"I know," he said, running his fingers through her hair. "And the year will go by quickly."

"Will you write to me?" she asked. "Let me know where you are? What you're doing?"

"On one condition," he replied, finally smiling again.

"What?"

"That you answer every letter."

She laughed. "That's easy. Of course I will. And more."

Stretching out next to him under the comforter, she took a long deep breath. Leaning over her, he kissed her just as he had done when she first climbed into bed. Gently. On the forehead, the cheeks, and the lips. She took another deep breath, kissed him, and turned over on her side, facing away from him.

He edged closely against her back, so that every part of their bodies touched. Like two spoons in a kitchen drawer.

"Good night, Novo," she whispered.

"Night, Judy," he said, relishing the feeling of her body against his and listening as her breathing became slower and quieter.

A couple of minutes later, he could tell that she was sound asleep. He thought about what it felt like to love someone. There were, of course, his parents and his brother. He loved them. And he had loved his grandparents. There were girls he'd dated in high school and in college. Girls he really liked. But he wasn't sure you could call it love.

And there was Anna. But he really had thought of her as a prize rather than as someone he loved. And since she was a fake, he had pushed aside any feelings that he had felt for her.

But, he told himself, this feels very much like love. In fact there's no doubt about it. This is love, he told himself. Real love. He had no idea where it would go. He had no idea where he would end up when he got back. Or what he would be doing. But because he was in love, it didn't matter.

All he knew was that, whatever happened, he would always love this person who was sleeping so soundly next to him. There was no doubt about it.

Having finally worked all that out, he closed his eyes and fell asleep.

He was glad the sergeant of the guard had given him the ammo dump to guard instead of the motor pool. For him, the rows of vehicles, standing silently in the blackness of the night, were still haunted. But in three weeks it wouldn't matter. He would be on a troopship heading home.

The gravel path around the perimeter of the ammunition storage area crunched under each step of his combat boots. It was really ironic, he thought. He had one round in his weapon, and in these storage buildings and underground bunkers were thousands of rounds ranging from .30-caliber ammo to 90-mm shells for the M-48s.

If anyone set this place off while he was here, walking his post, he would be lucky if they even found a boot with his name written on the inside.

But it was a glorious night, and that took away the thoughts of weapons and ammo and war. There was no moon, but the sky was filled with stars. He stopped to fill his lungs with the cool, cleansing air. A church bell began to ring, the sound crystal clear. He listened as the bells went through their ritual, ending with a deliberate set of three bongs telling the time.

Another hour and he would be relieved. There would be time for a cigarette, and a couple hours of sleep before cleaning up and getting back to his section.

It seemed strange to think that he would be leaving all this in such a short time. No more guard duty. No more morning formation. No uniforms. No freezing in the cold German winter.

When he had kids—if he had kids—what would he tell them about this two-year piece of his life?

He had translated a bunch of newspaper articles, and worked on programs for displaced persons. He had spent a lot of time on alerts and maneuvers and training while American scouts patrolled the border, every day, year-round, keeping a sharp eye on Ivan.

He had met a couple of women he had gone out with. He had fallen in love once, sort of. And he had fallen in love a second time, for sure. In a minuscule way, he had helped save the free world from Khrushchev and his threats about burying us. And—oh, yeah—one day he had just about started World War III with this guy right here, he said, affectionately patting his carbine.

He got thirty days' leave, and he could see and do quite a lot in that time. In exchange, he was on duty—or on call—most of the rest of the time. On maneuvers, we would be in the field for days or weeks at a time, often wearing the same fatigues, so he learned what grubby really means.

During the time he was there, the border between West Germany and Czechoslovakia didn't move even a fraction of a meter to the west. And Ivan didn't take over Berlin or any other city in Europe. So, at least for 1957, 1958, and 1959, we held our own in the cold war.

That was pretty much it. No big deal.

Maybe the fact that Novotny and his fellow 2d Cav troopers were here caused the Russians to decide not to order those eighty tanks—and whatever else they had there that night—to cross the line.

He had met an NCO from Seventh Army headquarters who told him that there was a series of alert triggers. When the seventh level was reached, we would take offensive action, according to this sergeant. He said we had gotten up to level five during the tank incident.

Two more notches up the ladder, according to the sergeant, and we would have been issued live ammo and kept going to the border instead of heading toward it and stopping.

There was also a guy he had met one night at the bar in the U.S. Army Hotel in Nurnberg. Except for the bartender, they had been the only two people in the place. Novotny had stopped by one Saturday evening for a quiet, reflective martini, but the guy seemed to need to talk.

He said he was a lieutenant in the air force. And over the course of a couple of drinks, which the officer didn't need, he told Novotny that he flew an RB-47, a recon version of the B-47 bomber.

"Where're you based?" Novotny had asked after telling him that he was in the 2d Armored Cavalry.

"Different places," the lieutenant had replied vaguely.

Curious, Novotny had asked questions. Nothing too direct. Just enough to keep the conversation going. Finally, one of the questions got the officer talking.

"We're called ferrets," the pilot had said, his eyes bleary and his voice slurred. "We penetrate Communist airspace, take pictures, and do radio and radar intercepts," he said almost casually, emptying his scotch on the rocks and pointing to the bartender for another.

"Don't they try to stop you?" Novotny had asked, finding this hard to believe.

"Hell, yes," he had said. "And sometimes they do." He had taken a sip from his fresh drink, and said, "Unfortunately, they're getting better at it."

"But we never hear about it," Novotny had said, indirectly asking yet another question.

"We lost one a couple of weeks ago," the officer said sadly. "Near Murmansk."

"I read about it in *Stars and Stripes*," Novotny said, nodding. "An equipment failure, it said." The lieutenant laughed cynically. "Equipment failure. It was an equipment failure all right. Hit a 47 with machine-gun fire, and you'll have an equipment failure. That's for damn sure."

"I didn't know we were doing that," Novotny said. But, as he made the comment, he remembered a flight crew that a 2d Cav patrol had picked up on the border the previous year, just after they were released by the Russians. "Navigational error" was what the report had said when they were forced down by a couple of MiGs. The Swedish Red Cross had arranged to have them freed and the 2d Cav patrol had been on our side of a bridge when the happy air force guys had come across. They were lucky. They were alive.

Studying the scotch in his glass, the pilot said, almost in a whisper, "The co-pilot was my best buddy in flight school."

"I'm sorry to hear that," Novotny said.

"We sure as hell don't talk about it," the pilot had said, seeming to have a need to explain. "And the Russians don't want anyone to know we're able to do it." He chuckled. "It's embarrassing as hell for them. Us flying over their territory. Taking pictures."

Bringing his thoughts back to the job at hand, Novotny stopped next to a large tree and pushed the thought of American planes flying over Communist territory out of his mind. He listened carefully to the sounds of the night, alert to anything unusual. But it was all very quiet, so he kept walking, making his way slowly around the perimeter of the ammo dump.

He stopped walking and leaned against a concrete bunker for a moment and thought about that conversation with the pilot.

The lieutenant had paid his tab, left a big tip, and gotten up gingerly from his stool. Standing unsteadily, he had put his hand on Novotny's shoulder. Speaking slowly and indistinctly, he had said, smiling, "Everything I just told you was BS. But it makes a hell of a good story, doesn't it?"

"Yeah. It makes a good story," Novotny agreed. "Want some help getting to your room?"

"No. But thanks anyway," he had said as he staggered toward the elevator. Novotny had sat there for a few minutes, finishing the martini on the bar in front of him and thinking about what he had just heard.

Focusing again on the predawn darkness, Novotny grasped the sling of his carbine. He started walking, stopping every so often to listen as Sergeant Duff had taught them to do.

It was beautifully quiet, except for the crunching sound his combat boots made on the gravel path.

So that's what he would tell his kids, Novotny decided. In a very small way, he had helped save the Western world from the Communist peril. But, he would tell them to ask again when they got a little older. He would have it figured out by then, and would be able to give them a better answer.

Novotny sat against a large tree, his carbine across his legs and his steel helmet on the ground in front of him. The alert alarm had sounded at about five o'clock, and he and Johnson had spent the next two hours in the back of the deuce-and-a-half that had been their assigned transportation since they arrived in Germany.

The alarm had sounded later than usual, and many figured this was their last alert. But they went through the alert-response drill with normal quickness, though there was no sense of urgency to the process this morning. Once at their destination in a forest, the men began their routines. Radio operators sent and received messages. Medics set up an aid station. Cooks began preparation of lunch. Perimeter machine-gun positions were strategically established. And scouts continued their recon patrols.

Johnson was busy briefing the GI who would take over his duties in the intelligence section when the rotation back to the States began.

For Novotny, there was very little to do. Somewhat bored, he asked the duty NCO if he could take a walk in the forest.

"Sure," the sergeant said. "We'll be heading back about fourteen hundred."

Novotny slung his carbine over his shoulder and walked along a rugged dirt road with no particular destination in mind. He marveled at how neatly kept the trees all were, with virtually no dead branches. And he studied the nearly pristine forest floor, wondering how it was possible to keep it clear of natural forest debris.

The forest darkened as he walked through an area with older, taller trees creating a dense canopy of branches. The dirt road ended and he was now walking in the forest itself, noting landmarks in order to find his way back.

He had walked about a quarter of a mile when he noticed a strange anomaly in the forest ahead of him. An area about half the size of a football field was devoid of any mature trees. All that was growing there were weeds, short saplings, and wild grass.

As he approached the area, he saw it had been delineated with a wire fence. He also saw that there were about twelve mounds side by side, probably three feet high, ten feet wide, and thirty feet long.

That's really odd, he thought. I wonder if someone tried to grow something here.

Walking around the perimeter, he saw an enamel sign written in German and secured to the fence with wires. Reading the sign, he gasped in shock. It said "Danger. No Trespassing. Mass Graves."

Under the long mounds there could be hundreds of bodies. Maybe more. Bombing casualties? We're too far from any city, he thought. And if this was a battle site, dead soldiers were likely to be re-buried. Virtually every German cemetery, large and small, had military graves. Graves are often simply marked as *"Unbekannter Deutscher Soldat"*— "Unknown German Soldier."

No, he decided. The use of mass graves would be for dead who did not merit a proper burial. For whom a mass grave was good enough. The obvious candidates for such treatment were Jews. Concentration camps were scattered all over Nazi Germany during the war. Not just the large, famous ones such as Dachau. But small ones where Jews were taken en route to the large ones.

And, to expedite the extermination process, many Jews and other undesirables were killed outright, rather than starved or worked to death. Maybe that was who was in the mass graves.

Looking at his watch, he realized that it was time to head back to the command post, and make the last trip to Nurnberg in the back of a deuce-

and-a-half. As he walked back to the CP, he continued to wonder who was in those graves. He would be on his way back to the States soon. The mounds would just be an unsolved mystery. A reminder of the brutal nature of war.

Novotny and Johnson loaded the truck, and the convoy was soon on its way back to Merrell.

Looking at the forest, then the developed areas along the autobahn, Novotny tried to sort out the pieces once again. Let's see, he thought. The Czechs—possibly relatives of mine—and the Russians are our enemies, though we were allies in the war. But the Czechs—and the Poles and the East Germans and the Hungarians and others—hate being under the thumb of the Russians. So our enemies are potentially our allies.

And our former enemies—the Germans, who did things like efficiently operate Dachau and other such places, and who buried people in mass graves like the one just over there, and who killed a lot of our guys—are our allies.

How do you make sense of that? he asked himself. He thought for a couple of minutes, and then answered his question. You don't make sense of it. You simply accept the reality of it, and do your job, day by day.

Johnson turned and looked at Novotny. "Are you ready to go back to the States?" he asked.

Novotny nodded. "Yeah," he answered. "I'm ready."

Nearly all of the thousand or so troops on board the USNS *Upshur* were on deck, excitedly waiting for their journey home to begin. After stowing their gear in the troop compartment below, Johnson, Novotny, and Morris found a spot with a clear view of the dock. "Oh," Johnson said. "Jesse called to tell us that he extended and is staying on for a while."

Leaning against the rail, looking sharp in their Class A khakis, they couldn't wait to get under way. The sounds of marches wafted up from an army band seated on the dock. Not bad duty, Novotny thought, if you are a saxophone or trumpet player. Every couple of weeks, you play a few appropriate songs for the next ship out. Never have to freeze in the snow. Never have to eat cold rations from a can. Never have to go without sleep. Not bad.

Ten days from now, according to one of the ship's crew members, they would tie up at the Brooklyn Army Terminal. After a few days of processing, they would be civilians again. Their tour in the active army would be over, though they still had two years of active reserve duty ahead of them. One weekend drill a month, and two weeks at summer camp.

Squinting in the sunlight, Morris said, "You know what really bugs me?"

"Tell us, Chas," Johnson said, teasing his friend with exaggerated interest.

"We're coming away with nothing. No medal for being here. Not any overseas service stripes. Nothing."

"Are you going to sign up to come back?"

He nodded to confirm what Johnson had just asked. "Maybe get married," he said.

"If you re-up," Johnson said, "I'll bet you a good lunch that you'll get a chest full of medals."

"Why is that?"

"Because there'll be a war," Johnson explained. "Maybe here. Maybe again in Korea. Maybe Indochina, where the French got booted out. Somewhere. So you'll get lots of medals. I'll put a good lunch on it."

Morris smiled. "Deal," he said, taking Johnson's hand to formalize the agreement.

Every few minutes they looked down on the dock to see if the ship was moving.

"Well, we did our job," Johnson said. "and we sampled some of the best beer in the world."

"We ate some great food," Novotny interjected.

"I got to meet you guys," Morris said, grinning.

"Definitely a major event," Johnson replied. "What's another one, Novo?"

"Let's see." He thought for a moment and then put his hand on Johnson's shoulder. "You met Anna," he said.

"That was an event, all right," Johnson said, shaking his head and laughing.

"Before that, I met Anna," Novotny said. "Which was also an event." He paused for a moment. "And I met Judy."

"We went on a bunch of alerts," Morris added. "And NATO maneuvers."

Johnson nodded in agreement. "Novo and I saw Berlin." He added, "And we all saw a fair amount of Germany."

"Yeah," Morris said, chuckling. "Mostly from a jeep, the back end of a deuce-and-a-half, or inside an APC."

Novotny pulled out a pack of cigarettes. His offer to his friends was declined, so he lit up alone, remembering what he'd thought about while on guard duty. "And, in a small way, we really did help protect the free world from Communism," he said.

"Definitely that," Johnson agreed. "That should be first on the list."

Novotny suddenly had a thought. Looking at Johnson, he said, "About the only thing we didn't do was have our twenty-minute war."

Morris looked puzzled, and Novotny decided it was too complicated to explain right now. Maybe later.

"That's not true, Novo," Johnson said, correcting him.

"What do you mean?" Novotny asked, taking a deep drag on the cigarette.

"Novo, most of the time, you're a reasonably smart guy," Johnson said. "But sometimes you're dumb as hell."

Novotny shrugged. "I don't get it."

"You had yours. At the motor pool. With Turner," he said seriously. "That was your twenty-minute war."

Saying nothing, Novotny tried to think the comment through.

"You had your war that night, Novo," Johnson explained, looking his friend in the eye. "You did fine. You put yourself at risk. Face it. You were brave. So you don't have to worry about the twenty-minute war. You're done with that."

Novotny swallowed hard, thinking about what Johnson had just said and about what had happened in the darkness of the motor pool.

"The rest of us still have it to do," Johnson said. "But you're home free."

Novotny tried to figure out how to respond. But his thoughts were interrupted by a long, loud, resonant blast on the ship's horn. The three soldiers turned and leaned on the rail to watch what was happening below.

Members of the ship's crew were freeing the heavy ropes that held the ship to the dock. Untethered, the vessel was now ready to begin the journey across the Atlantic, its decks covered with GIs eagerly waiting for the first sign of movement.

Novotny stood there, overwhelmed by the thoughts going through his mind and the emotions he felt. There was no way to isolate them and think about them logically or in any sort of order. They simply took over. A rush of interconnected thoughts and images. Turner. Judy. Sergeant Duff. The CO. Dieter. Soldiers' Field. Joy. Sadness. Pride. Fear. Excitement. They all blended into one complicated and completely involving emotion.

As the vessel began moving slowly and silently away from the dock, the bandmaster raised his hands. Moments later, the sound of music rose up, filling the summer air.

"*Auf wiedersehen,*" Novotny sang in his mind. "Auf wiedersehen." Until I see you again.

He turned and faced in the direction the ship was moving. Partly to take a look toward the North Sea ahead of them. But mainly so his friends wouldn't see the tears forming in his eyes. A few months, Turner. That's all that was left. Just a few months. Hardly any time at all.

Breinigsville, PA USA
16 March 2011
257772BV00003B/54/P